DAMAGE
CONTROL

the VALIANT KNOX series

JESS ANASTASI

Entangled Publishing, LLC
2614 South Timberline Road
Suite 109
Fort Collins, CO 80525
Visit our website at www.entangledpublishing.com.

Select Otherworld is an imprint of Entangled Publishing, LLC.

Edited by Robin Haseltine
Cover design by Louisa Maggio
Cover art from iStock

Manufactured in the United States of America

First Edition October 2015

For Mario
All the Small Things

Chapter One

The blaring drone of the battle alarm echoed through the gym, drowning out the raucous conversation of soldiers blowing off steam while they worked out.

Leigh returned the bench press to its frame and sat up, whipping his towel from where he'd draped it over his knee, and then swiping the cloth over the sweat running down his face. He wasn't on duty until oh nine hundred, when a transport of new recruits were due to arrive. But as the CAFF—Captain of the Fighter Force—a call to arms put him on edge like binging on half a dozen double-shot coffees.

He'd worked hard to train his fighter pilots to be the most elite squadron out of all the UEF battleships. He liked to say it was for their benefit, that they'd be more likely to survive out there in the black when they engaged the enemy. But it was just as important for him to know he'd done everything to ensure his pilots made it safely back on deck every day.

"*Attention, all available fighter pilots, report to launch deck immediately. Condition code bravo-one, I repeat, condition code bravo-one,*" the ship-wide PA system chimed.

Oh, shit. Leigh shot to his feet and sprinted to the locker room, into the chaos of every single other fighter pilot in the gym grabbing their crap and hauling ass to the launch deck. Bravo-one was a critical code, second only to alpha-one, when the ship itself was under attack.

He ran a fresh towel over himself and threw off the sweat-drenched tank top. Grabbing up his flight jacket and shirt, he followed the wave of personnel headed for the alpha level launch deck.

As he stepped out of the transit, his XO, Lieutenant Teresa Brenner, was waiting for him, his helmet and flight gloves in hand.

"What have we got, Bren?" He tugged on the gloves and took his helmet from her as they jogged toward the shiny row of V-29 fighter jets.

"The CSS are closing in on the troop transport crossing from the *Farr Zero.* The shuttle isn't going to get here before the enemy intercept. We've got maybe two minutes before our new recruits get blown out of the galaxy."

"Frigging underhanded bastards." He split off from Bren, who went to her own jet, while he scaled the side of his in a few short steps. In a matter of moments, he'd sealed the cockpit and skimmed toward the launch bay, where fighter ships were already streaming out into space like a swarm leaving the nest.

The CSS—Christ's Sunday Soldiers religious fanatics

who'd taken over the Brannon system—had split off from the United Earth Coalition, intent on turning the entire galaxy back into the dark ages of fearing God and shunning all "manifestations of evil," which they took to be any type of technology.

Funnily enough, that didn't stop the a-holes from matching them ship for ship and weapon for weapon in the war that had started nearly twenty years ago.

The runway in front of him cleared and he hit the juice, shooting his V-29 multi-atmospheric fighter jet into the black void beyond the battleship. His electromagnetic radar screen flickered to life, marking the positions of all the ships in the game. He set a course for the slow-moving transport, the other jets falling into formation behind him like they'd practiced a million times.

Goddamn. No way they'd make the transport before the CSS did. It'd be close, but the enemy was going to arrive a split second before them. Enough time to blow the transport out of the sky.

He switched his comms to encompass all the fighter jets on his tail. "Get ready to go in hot, people. The enemy will be engaged by the time we meet them."

The pilots all confirmed they were weapons-ready. Leigh shifted in his seat, forcing his shoulders down and taking a deep breath, centering himself for the battle to come. It would be chaos; it always was. Weapon's fire and other jets moving so fast, the mind barely had time to register one before moving on to the next. But, before the storm, he always took a moment of calm to blank his thoughts of everything except his focus on the mission objective: protect the transport and get it onto the *Valiant Knox* in one piece.

A yellow-white flash flared in the distance. The enemy had opened fire on the unarmed transport.

He came up on the scene in another moment, sending a stream of weapon's fire across the top of the shuttle, toward the half a dozen ragtag CSS ships closing in. A trail of smoky debris streaked out from the left side of the shuttle, which appeared to have trouble maintaining a level trajectory.

Hopefully the transport had only taken superficial damage. The CSS had bombed the main UEF outpost on Ilari a few weeks back. They needed every single one of the recruits on board that shuttle to fill out the decimated ranks.

He swore under his breath and looped in to engage one of the enemy ships, forcing them to break off.

"Bren, take the lead. Harper, Seb, and Lawler, with me. I want an all-points protective formation around that transport."

Leigh cut his ship out of the fight and took a long sweep around the enemy ships. Bren took his place at the head of the main squadron, covering him and the three guys who'd fallen in behind him.

He came in over top of the transport, slowing his speed to a near crawl to match pace. Harper and Lawler settled in on either side of the ship, while Seb got underneath.

"*Farr Zero* transporter, this is Captain Leigh Alphin escorting you in to landing. Your ship appears to be damaged; do you have a report?"

Radio silence and static met his hail. *Hell*. The damage must have taken out the comm system. Either that or the pilots were compromised. He repeated the call, but got nothing. Cursing under his breath, he shut down the comm and turned his concentration to keeping an eye out for any enemy ships.

Fortunately, Bren and the main squadron had cut the CSS off from pursuit.

With the shuttle puttering along, the trip back to the *Knox* crawled by while he worked up a double sweat under his helmet. A few stray streaks of weapon's fire came too close for comfort, but they got the transport into the landing bay without any more damage.

He put his ship down, hardly waiting for the engines to go offline before he pushed his way out of the hatch and slid down the side of the jet. He yanked his helmet off and dropped it to the deck, then jerked off his gloves and pulled the tabs open at the neck of his flight jacket for some cool air. Sweat dampened his shirt, making it stick to his chest. Lawler and Seb hurried over to join him, expressions similarly grim.

The shuttle was still maneuvering into place as he and the guys crossed the bay. A couple of deck maintenance personnel had the fire-dousing hoses out, spraying down the left side of the transport with gray foam.

He snagged the attention of some nearby soldiers as he headed for the damaged ship. "Report to the medico responders and prepare for wounded."

Lawler and Seb hung back while Leigh climbed the short wing to where the maintenance chief had started working to get the hatch open. When the section gave way and lifted, a cloud of thick smoke puffed out.

Not a good sign.

He went to take a step, pulling his shirt up over his mouth and nose, but someone grabbed his arm. He glanced back to see Lawler holding onto him, a grim expression on his face.

"You can't go in yet, not until they get the fire under control."

"I'm not going to stand here and watch these people burn." He shook off Lawler's grip as a couple of passengers stumbled out of the hatchway, coughing and gasping. Lawler caught one who almost fell off the edge of the wing, then slung the guy's arm over his shoulder and helped him down to the deck.

A shout came from the opposite side of the ship. The chief maintenance officer held his comm up to his ear. After a second, he lowered the device again, his face set in tense lines.

"Evac the deck. The fire's taking hold and the transport's engine hasn't fully shut down. The pilots aren't responding. The flight control team is going to seal the deck and vent the atmosphere to prevent an explosion."

A shock of disbelief tightened Leigh's shoulders and upper arms. "And what does the flight control team think is going to happen to all the passengers inside the shuttle when the entire launch bay vents?"

The chief maintenance officer glanced away from the transport, as if he didn't want to know. With steadily thickening black smoke in the air, people were scrambling to evac.

Were they really going to write off a whole shuttle-load worth of their own people?

"If this transport blows, Captain Alphin, it'll take the entire upper port side of the *Knox* with it. We'd be crippled and lose a lot more than a hundred or so personnel. Yang cleared the call."

The officer shook his head, expression grim as he hurried

to the edge of the wing and jumped down.

"Wait!" When the other man paused and looked back up at him, Leigh crouched down on the edge of the wing. "If someone shuts down the engine, will that save the need to vent?"

"The scans show the fire's blocked access to the cockpit. And while we're standing here yacking, it's getting closer to the engine. Not to order you, sir, but we need to haul ass off this deck."

The rest of the launch bay had cleared.

Leigh yanked at the zipper on his flight jacket, pulling it all the way back up to his chin. The material was flame resistant to a point to give pilots a better survival chance at ejecting if their jets caught fire.

"What are you doing?" the chief maintenance officer demanded.

"I'm going to shut down the transport engine. Give me three minutes. If the shuttle isn't offline by then, vent the deck."

"Sir! Captain Alphin! You can't!" the other man called as Leigh strode toward the hatch where black smoke poured out, backlit by the orange flicker of flames.

At the hatchway, he tabbed a three-minute countdown into his watch and leaned into the doorway, groping for the emergency panel. Once he found it, he wrenched it out. The oxygen masks were missing.

Cursing, he reached into the neckline of his jacket and yanked up his T-shirt, which wasn't going to help much — he'd be lucky to make it to the cockpit. But he had to try.

The *Knox* had to come first, but he was going to do everything in his power to save as many people as possible.

With one last breath of clean air, he plunged into the darkness, mentally mapping the short route to the cockpit. Interior emergency lights flickered intermittently.

He stumbled over a prone form and nearly went down. Stepping carefully over the still figure, he resisted the urge to check for a pulse. With his three minutes ticking away, he didn't have time to make sure every person he came across was still alive.

Heat pulsed against him in waves, making him feel like he was cooking inside his flight suit. Sweat ran down his face and neck. He coughed, his lungs protesting the fumes, the burning chemicals stripping his throat raw and stealing all the moisture from his mouth.

The front of the ship glowed and flickered with dancing flares of orange, deepening to red and blue. Entry to the cockpit looked impossible.

Goddamn it. How the hell was he going to get through that to shut down the engines? He dropped from a crouch all the way to his knees, cutting down an aisle away from the cockpit hatchway. Sweat stung his eyes and he blinked, wiping the back of his hand across his face. He checked his watch. Hell, he'd already used half of his three minutes.

Dizziness started messing with his sense of equilibrium, and he grabbed an armrest to keep himself steady. If he couldn't get into that cockpit in the next minute, he and the rest of the people on this shuttle would suffocate.

He forced himself to shuffle forward, thoughts becoming murky as though the smoke had gotten inside his brain and started clouding his mind. He grasped onto a single thought.

He had to save these people, had to save himself.

His knee knocked something and he dropped to his

hands. It was too big for an oxygen tank. Eyes streaming from the smoke and sting of sweat, he brought the cylinder closer to his face to focus on the writing. He couldn't make anything out except a symbol. It was a discarded, likely empty, tank of dousing foam for small fires.

When he depressed the lever, a jet of gray foam shot out. A spike of hope cut through the thickening murkiness of his mind, and he glanced up at the cockpit. There'd be nowhere near enough foam to clear the doorway. Instead, he held his breath, turned the nozzle, and sprayed the foam over as much of his body as he could.

Only forty seconds left.

This probably wasn't going to work. No doubt the only thing he'd achieve would be killing himself ten seconds before this bay got vented.

Nonetheless, he forced himself up, heart pounding a hard, uneven rhythm as he dragged back into the center aisle. Bracing, he took one second to tell himself he was crazy, then launched forward, running for the closed hatchway where flames licked over the surface.

With his flight jacket pulled over his hand, he slapped at the emergency manual override. But the hatch only cracked a bit and stopped. He wedged his arms in and braced against the doorway, yelling out in furious pain as the heat of the metal singed through his jacket.

But he ignored the burn and pushed, widening the gap until he could squeeze through. Inside the cockpit, the smoke wasn't as thick and the air had a weird tang to it. He lurched over to the control panel, forcing his eyes to focus, and hit the emergency engine shut down. The few remaining lights in the cockpit went dark.

Thank God.

He slapped a hand over the comm.

"This is Captain Alphin." His voice came out hoarse, and talking sent him into a short coughing fit. But he swallowed down the spasms in his throat by sheer force of will. "Engines shut down. Get the maintenance crew back on deck and put this fire out. *Now*."

He didn't wait for confirmation, since the dizziness yanked even harder at him. Bringing a heavy, aching arm up, he grabbed onto the lever for the cockpit's emergency hatch, popped it free, and gasped as clean air hit his face. He slumped to the floor, chest heaving as he sucked in oxygen. His stomach churned, the fumes making him feel sick.

After a long moment, he forced himself back to his feet, bracing a hand on the pilot's chair as he checked the two unconscious men behind the controls. They both had a pulse, but they'd obviously been overcome by the noxious vapors.

Now that he'd opened the emergency hatch, the medics would be able to get the two men out, but there were still people who needed help.

He looked back toward the gap in the open hatchway he'd squeezed through. Nothing but a constant trickle of black smoke underlaid by a hellish orange glow. His guts tightened, but he braced against the surge of apprehension and forced himself to step back into the inferno.

Mia Wolfe sucked in a long gasp of sweet, artificial oxygen, then held her breath and lowered the mask onto the face of her friend Penny, who'd been sitting beside her during the flight.

Eyes streaming from the stinging smoke, Mia couldn't see past the small space where she crouched between a row of seats and a bulkhead. The ship had jolted a few moments ago.

Please, let us be landing. But the hatch hadn't opened, and no one seemed to be trying to escape.

She held the mask against Penny's face as long as she could stand holding her breath and then had to shove it against her own mouth to gasp in another breath. Two this time. Dizziness started blurring the edges of her mind. But for every gulp of air she took, Penny breathed the toxic smoke without even realizing. She'd been knocked unconscious in the initial impact. And when Mia had taken cover, she'd dragged Penny to the safety of the corner with her, as far from the steadily spreading flames as they could get.

Somewhere off to her right, a shaft of bright light cut through the gloom and flickering orange lights. A waft of cool, fresh air brushed across her face, making her exhale in relief. Yet by the time she went to inhale again, the smoke seemed to have thickened. She coughed, slapping the mask back on her face. *Sorry, Penny.* Another three breaths and she held on again.

Several people rose nearby, stumbling toward the hazy light. Her legs tensed beneath her, wanting to flee the suffocating sensation in her chest. But no way would she leave Penny. And since her limbs felt like rubber, she wouldn't be able to drag her friend out. She steeled herself, heart spasming. No matter that the swaying dizziness got worse every second and blackness ate away the edges of her vision. She had to stay. Make sure Penny got enough oxygen.

She hunkered down closer to her friend so she didn't have to reach as far to share the oxygen mask. Seconds and minutes dragged by, but no help came.

Had she imagined the hatch opening? Maybe the smoke made her hallucinate. She wanted to check, but her limbs felt oddly heavy and clumsy, like they belonged to someone else. Logic told her the fumes were probably starting to affect her, sending a sharp lance of head-clearing panic through her. She pushed the near overwhelming dread back down. Someone would come.

She just had to stay awake and make sure Penny got enough clean air until then.

Voices echoed, sharpening her attention. Calm, authoritarian words ordered people out of the shuttle and set others to help with the rescue. She brought her head up, relief spilling through her like in a cool surge.

"Over here." Her voice came out so hoarse the words were barely audible. She took another breath from the oxygen mask and then forced her uncooperative limbs to get herself upright, though only made it as far as her knees. As she shuffled to the end of the seating row, a tall figure passed by. She reached out and snatched at the sleeve.

More smoke cleared and she got a glimpse of a tall, dark-haired man wearing a fighter pilot's jacket, his face obscured by the gray T-shirt he had over his mouth and nose. He wrapped an arm around her and pulled her up to her feet, but she resisted, pointing behind her.

"Come on. I'll get you out of here." His deep voice had a roughened quality to it, as though he'd been breathing the fumes for too long as well.

"No. My friend. She's injured." Her words rasped out at

a near whisper.

He shook his head and then ducked down until their faces were less than an inch apart. "Repeat the last, recruit."

She swallowed, the order helping to ground her. "There's a wounded recruit down here."

He straightened and let her go, squeezing by her to crouch down next to Penny. He tilted his head, murmuring into the comm attached to his jacket. A moment later, another soldier appeared. She stooped down to pick up the discarded oxygen mask while the two men lifted Penny out of the corner.

She moved back as the second soldier took Penny's weight by himself. Relief flooded her in a dizzying rush, compounding her unsteadiness. The blackness she'd been fighting swamped her. She stumbled, coming up against a solid body. The pilot swore, his arms wrapping around her.

Safe. She was safe.

"Let's get you out of here." His words sounded like they were coming from a lot farther away than the few inches separating them.

With someone else to hold her up, she gave into the vortex sucking her downward.

Chapter Two

L eigh swore, catching the slight weight of the recruit as she went down. He pried the oxygen mask out of her hand and grabbed a clean breath of air. Once his lungs didn't ache as much, he swung her up into his arms and headed for the shaft of light from the open hatchway.

At the emergency exit, he avoided a couple of masked medicos heading into the shuttle. He cleared the short wing and carried the recruit over to where a deck triage had been set up.

His entire body hurt as he lowered the girl onto a gurney. Bren appeared at his side and handed him a small, disposable oxygen breather and a bottle of water. "Couldn't follow orders, huh?"

He glared at her over the breather and then got attacked by a fit of coughing as clean air hit his throat.

Sub-Doctor Archie Moore stopped by them and bent over the recruit laid out on the cot. After a cursory check of the girl, Ace turned to him. Leigh gulped some of the water, trying to stem the coughing.

"Couldn't even get a mask on for your suicide attempt, Alpha? Man, you have a serious hero complex."

"Screw you, Ace." Forcing the words out only made him cough more.

"Get your ass on that gurney before you fall down, Captain." Ace fished a vial of yellow liquid out of his coat pocket and measured out a small quantity into a plastic dispenser.

"I'm fine," he forced out. Except a simple shift in his weight from one foot to the other sent him stumbling into the edge of the girl's gurney.

Bren swore, catching his shoulder and helping him upright. "Clearly you're not fine."

"There are people worse off than me."

The look Bren sent him in return would have sent a lesser man running. Knowing he'd be hard-pressed to win an argument with his XO when she had that hard gleam in her eyes, he gave up resisting and let her lead him over to the next gurney.

"Here, this'll fix your throat up. And breathe more oxygen or I'll go over your head to bench you." Ace handed over the medicine and slipped the vial away again, then turned back to the recruit Leigh had pulled out of the ship.

Sitting on the edge of the gurney, he knocked back the medicine and followed it with a mouthful of water, studying the unconscious girl. She had shining gold hair worked into two slick braids. Although ash and soot streaked her face, her skin looked smooth, with a smattering of freckles covering her nose, while her pink lips were full, the bottom one a little plumper. A strand of her hair had fallen across her cheek, and the urge to reach out and smooth it back jolted his clearly smoke-damaged brain with the absolute inappropriateness of even having the thought.

"What's her condition?" he asked Ace, who straightened once he finished checking her over.

"Unconscious from smoke inhalation. I'll get her on a breather to repair her lungs and airways. She should be fine in a few hours."

He nodded and shifted closer to the cot, reaching across the space between the gurneys and into the collar of her uniform to pull out her tags. *Mia Wolfe.*

She'd stayed behind at peril to her own safety to help another recruit. No matter what kind of training most soldiers had, teaching selfless bravery like that could be next to impossible. Yet it had come naturally to Recruit Wolfe.

"Your turn," Ace said matter-of-factly, stepping closer to him. Leigh dropped the recruit's tags.

He cooperated while his buddy checked him over, particularly his forearms where he'd braced them against the hot metal of the hatchway to get into the cockpit.

"You're damn lucky, Alpha. Your jacket protected you for the most part, so the burns are superficial. With some nano gel and a compression bandage, they'll be healed in a matter of hours. And your throat might feel raw, but you weren't breathing the fumes long enough to do any real damage."

"What about his head?" Bren asked.

Ace ran a gaze over his face. "Did you hit your head?"

"No." He shot an impatient glance at Bren. "My head is fine."

Her eyebrows lowered, her expression practically

fuming. "Clearly not. Otherwise he wouldn't have run into a burning ship when the flight control team had already decided to vent the deck."

He crossed his arms and then winced when he abraded his tender forearms. "I had to try something, Bren. Did you really want everyone in that shuttle to die?"

For the first time, some of the anger in her expression gave way to the fear she'd obviously been trying to hide. "No, I didn't. But I also didn't want to watch my CO get himself killed trying something so idiotic. Usually Seb is the one taking moronic risks."

"I was quite capable of making stupid choices long before Seb came along."

"Maybe when you were a hotheaded rookie. You're the CAFF, Alpha, in case you've forgotten. You're supposed to know when to make the hard calls to protect the *Knox* and everyone on board."

She was right, goddamn it. And Commander Yang was going to take him to task over this. "I'm sorry, Bren. I just couldn't let those people die."

She pressed her lips together for a moment, her next inhale catching slightly.

"I know you couldn't. But damn it to hell, I would have had to become CAFF if you'd been killed, and no offense, that's the last thing I want."

He reached out and caught her hand, giving her fingers a quick squeeze. His XO had built a tough-chick exterior around herself, but the few people she let in, she cared deeply for. He hated that he'd scared her, but he hadn't seen any other choice besides getting to that cockpit, even if he'd ended up sacrificing his own life.

Bren didn't say anything else as he shrugged out of his ruined jacket. The three of them were silent as Ace applied the nano gel and the pressure bandages to his arms.

Lawler approached, coughing and eyes red-rimmed from smoke. Ace offered him the same medicine and breather.

"Reports are starting to come in on the wounded," Lawler said once he'd stopped coughing.

"Any casualties?" The medicine had soothed his throat, thank God. At least he could talk and breathe now without feeling as if he might choke at any second.

"Only six, so far. With any luck, we won't lose any more."

Leigh stood, clenching his muscles against a head-aching shot of dizziness.

"Get me a clean shirt, we'll need to brief Commander Yang and reschedule the meet-and-greet for twenty-four hours from now," he said, directing the order at his XO.

"I'll see to it," Bren confirmed.

"Make sure the recruits who aren't seriously injured are recovered enough by then, Ace."

Ace nodded. "I'll pass the order onto the doctor heading up triage."

"Come on, Bren, we'd better get to the ready room and start postmission debriefing. Lawler, I need you and Seb to oversee things up here until this mess is cleaned up."

Lawler sent him a sharp nod and headed across the deck to where Seb stood directing the recruits who'd been evaced out of the transport, but weren't seriously wounded.

Leigh shot one more look at the recruit. Her eyelids fluttered and then opened. Velvet-brown eyes caught his and held. His heart pounded, once, twice. A rush of sparking sensation jolted him, like a livewire shocking his system.

Commander Yang's voice came through on his comm. *"Captain Alphin, drop whatever you're doing and report to ready room oh one on squadron level."*

"On my way, sir," he replied into the comm. He thanked Bren as she returned with a new shirt for him. She spun on her heel, clasping her hands behind her back as she headed across the chaos of the deck. He sliced one more look at the recruit, still staring at him with those rich brown eyes, and then he turned to follow his XO, shrugging into the clean shirt as he walked.

"Yang is going to be up in arms about this latest attack," he said as he fell into step beside Bren. "As if blowing up our main base of operations on Ilari and putting a double agent on our ship wasn't enough, now they suddenly have enough balls to fly right in between the *Knox* and the *Farr Zero* to intercept an unarmed transport."

"The better question is, was this a random attack, or did they know exactly what they were targeting? If we'd lost that entire shuttle of troops, it would have been months before we could ship in any more to make up the numbers, and in that time, who knows what the CSS forces could have done? Probably overrun our undermanned base for a start."

Yeah, the implications of that was the stuff of nightmares and left a ripple of cold uneasiness echoing through him.

In recent months, the CSS had switched up their tactics, actually gone on the offensive and changed the way the war was being fought on Ilari. Those in charge of the United Earth Force were still scrambling to catch up with this turn in events, and it didn't help that many of the casualties from the base explosion a few weeks ago had included a number of higher-ranking officers.

He and Bren arrived at the ready room to find Commander Yang and Colonel Cameron McAllister waiting for them, along with a guy called Stanton, one of the senior Command Intelligence agents onboard the *Knox*.

"Sir," he greeted as he fell into parade stance, Bren next to him.

"Captain Alphin, clearly you and I need to have a conversation about following protocol." Yang's expression was set into severe, grim lines. "But it'll have to wait. We have reason to believe that the CSS knew exactly what they were targeting when they opened fire on the transport."

Leigh clenched his jaw, clamping down on the urge to swear. Not many people had known the exact time or trajectory the transporter had been due to come in on. "How could they get their hands on that type of information?"

"That's what we intend to find out." Yang motioned to the Command Intelligence agent. "After the explosion on Ilari, Stanton put together a specialized team of intelligence agents to find out if there were any other moles in our ranks and if so, how deep the infiltration goes. It seems the CSS have dug deep claws into every facet of our organization. Including here, on the *Knox*. We could have as many as a dozen moles on board."

That little piece of intelligence made the rippling cold under his skin intensify, spearing right into his guts like sharp icicles. "How are we going to combat something like that?"

Fire fights in a jet he could do, while battle strategy and commanding men were ingrained into his very cells. But this shadowy espionage stuff? He had no clue, and although he didn't scare easily, the thought that people he knew, people he worked and socialized with on a daily basis, might actually be CSS double agents planning his demise, along with the pilots he commanded, scared the bejesus out of him.

"It's not going to be easy." Cam crossed his arms, expression drawn and pensive. Out of them all, he'd lost the most men to this new front the CSS had engaged them on. "This battle won't be waged on the front lines or the cities down on the ground. It's going to be here, in our homes. Psychologically, that's a whole different ball game."

"And if the CSS find out we're on to them," Stanton continued, "then they'll enact whatever endgame this whole thing is leading up to. Which is why the fewer people who know about this, the better."

Stanton shot Yang an annoyed look, which Yang pointedly ignored. Had Stanton considered Leigh one of the people who didn't need to know, and Yang had overruled him?

"Alpha, there's one more thing." Yang's voice had lowered with a foreboding tone that made his insides churn. But what could possibly be worse than the things they'd already told him?

"Yes, sir?"

"We have reason to believe that someone in the fighter-pilot squadron is one of those dozen moles. That's why I felt you needed to hear all of this."

Every muscle in his body clenched as the shock of those words crashed through him. One of his own men was CSS? Impossible. They'd all worked their asses off to get into his FP squadron—

But that would be the point—put a mole in a close-knit team like his and God only knew what kind of damage the bastard could do.

"Are you sure?"

Yang shook his head. "No, we're not. But if there's even the slightest possibility that it is, I knew you would want to be informed. I'm sorry, Alpha. I know what every single one of those pilots mean to you."

He sent Yang a stiff nod of respect. "Thank you, sir."

"Now, I believe you've got some new recruits to train?"

"Yes, we need to reschedule the meet-and-greet to tomorrow, since the incident with the shuttle has thrown us off track. If you'll excuse us, sir?"

Yang dismissed them and they nodded, before he returned the gesture. Once they were out in the passageway, Leigh blew out a long breath, muttering a couple of curses.

"I can think of a few other words I'd like to add to that," Bren said, her features now showing her sense of betrayal.

"You heard Yang. They're not even sure the intel is solid. This could just be the CSS attempting to undermined us, make us see shadows where there are none."

She shot him a sideways glance, heavy with disbelief. "You don't really think that, do you?"

He scrubbed a hand over his short hair. "No, I'm too smart to be so naive."

"What are we supposed to do about this, Alpha? I can't believe that one of our own—"

"Is a traitor? I don't want to believe it either. And right now, we can't do anything. You heard Stanton. They don't want the CSS to know we're on to them. If we start acting like we've got something to hide—"

"Then it might tip off the traitor." Bren's expression became troubled. "But sitting back and not doing anything just seems wrong."

"I know. But we can keep our eyes and ears alert and

keep the lines of communication between us open. If any-thing seems even the tiniest bit weird or suspicious to you, let me know, and I'll do the same."

Bren nodded as they reached the transit-porter—which acted as both an elevator and conveyor, able to go between levels or from one end of the ship to the other.

"I'm going to head down to med level and see where things are at with getting the recruits cleared medically. Go find Seb and Lawler to reschedule the meet-and-greet. I'll see you all back on deck."

Bren murmured an agreement, then turned on her heel to go track down Sub-Lieutenant Sebastian Rayne. Seb ranked third in the FP squadron and also had the reputation of being the team's cowboy. He probably would have been dead years ago, except the sub-lieutenant was the best damn pilot Leigh had seen in all the years he'd been with the UEF. While he might technically follow orders, the guy knew how to balance the line like a trapeze artist, and if something was both dangerous and insane, then the guy was there with bells on.

Sub-Officer Nolan Lawler on the other hand, was the exact opposite to Seb, yet somehow the two had become best buddies. He hardly ever saw one without the other. Lawler was the guy who followed the rules right down the line, but in the four years he'd been on the team, he'd become the go-to guy whenever he needed someone dependable, someone with their head screwed on straight and a willingness to do what was needed, no matter the task.

Leigh walked through the quarantine doors that sepa-rated the med facilities from the rest of the ship, passing a steady stream of recruits leaving. Looked like the medico staff were quickly clearing out those who didn't need to stay in the medbay. The rescheduled meet-and-greet should be able to go ahead.

Which was the *only* reason he'd come down here—to make sure they could get back on schedule. Not to check up on that dark-eyed girl he'd pulled out of the damaged transport... Recruit Wolfe. *Mia.*

He crossed his arms as he came to the large, wide-open ER designed to treat people en masse after a battle. Right now, it was less than a quarter full. As he passed each hover trolley, he glanced at the patients in the beds. Luckily, none of them seemed to have serious injuries. Most were using the breathers designed to repair damage from smoke inhalation.

He spotted Ace standing next to a bed in the opposite row, so he cut across to catch his buddy. "Hey, how are things looking?" he asked as he came to a stop.

The recruit who'd been sitting on the bed thanked Ace, paused to salute him uncertainly, and then went on his way. Ace kept his head bent over his datapad, filling in some information.

"Most of the passengers have been cleared, and we should get through this lot in the next twenty minutes. Some will need to stay in, though. One broken arm, a couple with burns, and a few who suffered more serious internal damage from the toxic smoke."

Leigh nodded, pressing a finger against his mouth as he glanced around the ER. He wasn't going to ask about anyone in particular.

"Oh, and I was supposed to tell you something if I saw you." Ace moved from the side of the empty cot, heading for the next occupied one. "Go to TC-seven-niner. Someone wants to see you."

He glanced along the row of trolleys, looking for triage cubicle seventy-nine, but unable to get a clear view from here. He slapped Ace on the shoulder.

"Thanks. Catch you tonight after messdeck. Give you a chance to win back some of last week's pay."

Ace made an annoyed face at him, but didn't reply as he turned to talk with the next patient.

Leigh made his way through the ER. A few of the beds were screened off with curtains, while others stood open. Some of the recruits regarded him with wide eyes and others averted their gazes. They might not have met him, but of course, they knew who he was by reputation alone. *Damn the UEF wanting their poster boys.*

Not too long out of pre military training after he'd earned his wings, he'd gone and gained himself a reputation. Getting promoted quickly through the ranks had only fueled the fire. When he'd been contacted a few years back and told he'd be used as an example of the UEF's finest, it hadn't been a request. It had been a courtesy call before they started plastering his face all over the known worlds.

So yeah, the recruits knew who he was before they got here. And he'd come across more than a few with serious cases of hero worship over the years. The idolizing made him feel like a fraud. He was just a guy doing a job—far from hero material.

He came up on TC-seven-niner, slowing his steps. The curtains were pulled closed and he hesitated as he reached up to grab the seam. There was no medico staff close enough to ask about the occupant, so he ducked around the curtain, flicking it closed behind him.

He'd taken two steps toward the gurney when dark chocolate eyes met his and he froze. *Mia.* For a moment she just stared at him, and his heart did that weird thumping thing again. But then she moved, pushing herself more upright against the pillows.

"Hi." One corner of her lips lifted into a friendly, but shy smile. "I was hoping I'd get to see you before…well, training hasn't officially started yet and—"

"Is there something you wanted?" His reaction to her caused a trickle of agitation to run through him, the reason his question was clipped. *Why?* She was just another recruit. Yeah, he'd pulled her out of that damaged shuttle, but so what? He didn't get what it was about her that sent his normally controlled senses into hyperdrive.

She tucked a loose strand of golden hair behind her ear. "I wanted to thank you for saving my friend Penny. She wouldn't have lasted much longer in there and obviously I couldn't do anything more for her."

His feet took him three slow steps closer, until he came to the very edge of the gurney to look down on her. "And what about yourself?"

She ducked her head, and the strand of hair she'd brushed away fell forward again. "Yes, I wanted to say thanks for that, too. I only wish I could have done more to help. There were so many injured people. And I'm sorry I passed out—"

He clamped his teeth against a grin, and just like that, the unease he'd been feeling drained away. She looked up at him, an expression of antagonism tightening her lovely features.

"You're sorry for passing out, like that's something you could have controlled? Well, that's a new one." He moved to lean a hip against the edge of her bed. "Look, I'm not one for giving out a lot of praise, but you did good back there at expense to your own well-being. That's more than anyone can ask of you, and isn't a skill they teach when you attend pre mil training. You earned my respect, and that's not something easily done."

Hell, he hadn't meant to say so much. Maybe the news of a possible traitor in his squad had done a number on his mind. Yet even as he said the words, he realized they were more than true. He *did* respect her.

He probably shouldn't have been so forward with her. Except what did it matter? By laws of statistics, she'd more than likely been assigned a ground posting. After today, he wouldn't see her again. So he let his guard down for one second, let someone know they'd done good for a change, instead of being the unfeeling, hard-ass CAFF.

She pressed her lips together, not seeming the least mollified by his speech. He studied her stubborn expression. Though he hated admitting it, even to himself, the girl was damned gorgeous. *And probably a good fifteen years younger than you, pervert.*

He cleared his throat and forced the thoughts away as he straightened. "I'll give you some advice."

One of her eyebrows lifted and he nearly wanted to grin, but worked to keep his expression stoic. He could all but hear her thinking, *Oh yeah?*

"Some days you'll love your job, think you've landed exactly where you were meant to be. Other days, a lot of days, you're going to hate it. But if you hold on to whatever it was that made you put the life of your friend before your own, you'll go a long way. And sometimes you'll be able to look back and be satisfied that you did what you could."

Her head tilted, and her lips parted slightly on a soft breath. "Is that how you feel?"

He stared at her for a long moment, and something unfurled within him. He'd been responsible for saving a lot of people, and some of them had thanked him. But he'd never met anyone he'd felt instantly comfortable with. Yet with her sitting there, looking like she actually cared, things seemed a whole lot simpler.

Just for a split second, he wished he could get to know her better. And with no age gap between them that left him feeling like he'd be taking advantage of her.

He nodded. "That's how I feel. Of course, some days I feel like the damned reaper, sending good men to their deaths. Never can tell when a simple mission is going to go to hell."

"The responsibility must really weigh on you."

He laughed, though the sound was grim. "You have no idea."

The alarm reminder in his watch went off, vibrating against his wrist. He tapped it silent and then looked back up at Mia. If she took a ground posting, would she become a casualty one day soon? The thought made his insides clench. Or maybe he'd be the one heading into the black sooner rather than later.

The depressing notion was, of course, the only reason he let his guard down long enough to wrap his fingers around hers. He gave her hand a small squeeze, knowing he'd crossed a big fat line and not giving a damn about it. Since they'd never see each other again, he just wanted to steal one slice of the forbidden for himself, touch her even though he shouldn't.

"Captain Alphin—"

"Leigh. Only don't ever tell anyone I said so."

A small smile tugged at her lips. "Leigh, there's something you need to know—"

His watch vibrated again and he swore at the damned precise contraption. He didn't have any time left to linger here.

"Tell me next time we see each other." Which would likely be never.

She took a breath, no doubt to tell him whatever she had on her mind, but he rubbed his thumb lightly across her palm then stepped away.

"Good-bye, Mia. Look after yourself."

He turned and left the cubicle without looking back at her. If he did, if he saw anything in her dark gaze, he'd end up doing something totally idiotic. Like following up on her posting and then not-so-accidentally arranging to see her. The last thing he needed in his life was a complication like Mia Wolfe.

Chapter Three

L eigh cut a look over his shoulder at Bren, Seb, and Lawler standing at attention behind him, ready and alert, as they should be.

He returned his concentration to the unorderly jumble of new soldiers spilling onto the launch deck and scrambling to find their belongings. The maintenance crew had tidied up from the battle chaos of the day before and retrieved luggage from the damaged transporter, leaving a huge pile of bags and other items in the middle of the hangar.

Usually the arrival of new troops didn't go down like this. If not for the attack, the transport would have arrived at delta level where all civilian or nonbattle craft docked and departed. Delta level acted more like a terminal, complete with luggage processing and baggage carousels.

He swallowed an impatient sigh at the pandemonium. The few seasoned officers among them were easily recognizable in the orderly way they found their crap and then went on with their business. Leigh pressed his lips together as a couple of recruits got into an argument over an unmarked rucksack. *Morons.* First rule of military travel? Always tag your goddamn bag.

Fresh out of the academy, the recruits would all be twenty-one, maybe a few twenty-two, no real battle experience to speak of. Most of the kids would be heading down to Ilari to make up much needed troop numbers on the ground. The onworld, or ground forces, fought the hard battles in trenches and on front lines, holding the territories the UEF had managed to occupy since the war started.

However, a small number of soldiers that had been selected by a computerized psyche-eval would be assigned to him. The ones whose profile said they had the grit, determination, smarts, and awareness of their own mortality to become class-A fighter pilots.

Half of them would wash out. Ninety-five percent of them would hate his guts.

He glanced back at Bren and returned the flashing grin she sent him. A small rush of anticipation had him clenching his hands tighter together where he had them settled in the small of his back. Okay, so maybe they got some fun out of breaking down the recruits and finding out what they were made of. But the ones who were left, the ones they built back up again, joined one of the most elite fighter-pilot units out of all the battleships in the UEF.

An announcement echoed in a repeating loop over speakers throughout the hangar, directing people to their destination. Gradually, recruits moved off toward the shuttles being prepped to go onworld, while a handful that had astronomical IQs were led off to be trained up for Command

Intelligence postings. CI was a whole other ball game.

One by one, the latest batch of potential fighter pilots lined up in front of where he stood with the other instructors.

He sensed Bren leaning closer to him. "Is it just me, or do these recruits get sloppier every year? I mean, where the hell is UEF Command pulling these kids from?"

With a skeptical eye, Leigh ran his gaze down the line of fifty or so recruits. Uniforms worn incorrectly. Hair not to UEF standard. Personal items and fashion accessories worn in a blatant disregard of uniform regulations. His head started aching behind his temples. Hell yeah, they were a sorry bunch this year.

"I think you're right. These slags would have to be the worst we've seen yet. Even more inferior than the class of thirty-three."

Bren swore. "And we only got four damned pilots out of that lot. Less than ten percent success rate."

"Want to lay down some money on how many we'll get out of this class?" Seb interjected. Typical. The guy would gamble on a fruit fly if it was doing something interesting.

"No thanks. It'll just make me depressed." He pushed his shoulders back and stepped forward. "At attention, recruits."

Only half of the lined-up soldiers paid him any notice. And the ones who did listen? Their salutes and parade-stance could have been performed better by four-year-olds. What the heck did they teach them at pre military training these days?

"I said at attention recruits! Do not make me repeat myself a third time or you will see the brig before you see any other part of this ship."

The kids shut up and made a half-assed effort at a formation. *Right.* Time to get down to business.

Leigh strode to the end of the line to get a closer look at each potential pilot. The first guy had a hat slouched over one ear. Leigh ripped it off and threw it toward the trash bag Seb was holding. The recruit burst out with an angry, "Hey!" but one hard glare shut the guy up quick smart.

He shot a scowl down the line of wide-eyed soldiers. "Almost all of you are in violation of uniform regs. I am going to start rectifying this immediately. If any of you have an issue with this, feel free to take it up with Commander Yang."

Silence met his announcement. None of these green recruits would want to face up to Yang, not with his reputation of being a fearless hard-ass.

Leigh moved on along the line, removing items in breach of uniform and directing some to tuck their shirts in or fix their shoelaces.

"Didn't your mammas teach you how to dress before you left home?" he yelled in front of one recruit in particular who had his shirt half unfastened, his undershirt inside out, belt loose, laces untied, and wrinkled pants that obviously hadn't ever been pressed. "What is your name, recruit?"

"Steve Robinson."

"Recruit Robinson, when you address me, you will start and end with 'sir' and nothing else. Do you understand me?"

The kid frowned, the mutinous spark in his eye suggesting he didn't appreciate getting singled out. "Yes, sir."

Leigh leaned in closer. "Wrong, recruit. Do you understand me?"

"Sir, yes, sir." The sulking answer didn't come out at

much more than a mutter.

Leigh glanced back at Bren, who had a terrier-like glint in her gaze. Looked like they'd found washout number one. Bren would ride this insubordinate jerk until he broke or turned into a better soldier. The latter not being all that likely.

Leigh moved onto the next recruit, amazed to find one in order. The next couple weren't too bad, but when he came to the fourth person after that, his breath ripped out of his body.

Oh, shit.

He swallowed, groping for his equilibrium and forcing himself not to react with anything but impersonal detachment.

"Recruit Wolfe, who authorized you to leave the medbay?"

She'd been staring straight ahead, not acknowledging he'd stopped in front of her. But at his mention of her name, she glanced up. And when their gazes met, a whole lot of complicated mess came crashing down on him.

Now that she was upright, he got a decent look at her. She was a good head shorter than he and most of the other recruits in line. She looked like a sixteen-year-old. Though she'd retied her hair into a smooth knot and cleaned her face, a smudge of soot marred her neck, just below her ear, streaking down to the collar of her uniform. His fingers twitched, the impulse to reach up and wipe the stain away from her otherwise-perfect skin shocking the hell out of him.

She's your subordinate, you moron. Goddamn, he needed to go out and get laid. Because lusting after a recruit, even for a split second, was wrong in more ways than he could count. He shouldn't have let himself touch her, let any sort of familiarity develop between them… If only he'd known. Was that what she'd been trying to tell him, that she'd been assigned to his damn training program?

He had to go into extreme damage control, *right now*. Destroy whatever small connection they'd forged in the medbay. Make her hate him like all the other recruits. His chest contracted around his organs. That was all he needed, to have a coronary from the stress of the crap he'd walked himself into.

He took a step back from her. "I asked you a question, Recruit Wolfe."

She swallowed, and he wondered if her throat was still raw. His own felt stripped dry and he'd only been breathing that smoke for a few moments.

"Sir, Sub-Doctor Moore released me. I feel fine, sir." Her gaze flicked away to focus somewhere over his shoulder.

"And what orders did the sub-doctor release you with, Wolfe?"

Her lips pressed into a thin line, and for a moment, he thought she wasn't going to answer.

"Sir, to rest for at least twenty-four hours and use the breather every two of that, sir."

He'd suspected as much. "Do you call this resting, Wolfe? And how long ago did you last use the breather?"

"Sir, I used the breather one hour and twenty-five minutes ago, sir."

And she so conveniently didn't answer his question about resting. He checked over her uniform, finding her neat except for the glint of a gold chain under her tags.

"We don't need any heroes in our ranks, Wolfe. We need dependable pilots. Take that gold chain off. You're dismissed until tomorrow. Follow the doctor's instructions, or you'll find yourself demoted to the front lines on Ilari before evening messdeck."

After what he'd done, he'd take any excuse he could get to see her wash out before the mistake he'd made turned into a full-blown catastrophe. However, he couldn't conscionably sabotage her on purpose and still call himself a decent CO. Still, he could sure as hell hope she didn't get through the first day or two.

Her expression tensed, but she saluted him and turned, picking up her rucksack and disappearing across the deck. Leigh shook his head. That one had complication written all over her, the likes of which he didn't want to know about.

He turned his attention to the next recruit in line to finish tidying up his sorry bunch of wannabe fighter pilots. Once he had the recruits looking closer to respectable, he stepped back into formation next to the other instructors and gave a run down of how things would play out. His crew took turns introducing themselves and then each recruit got handed a map of the *Valiant Knox*.

The *Knox* was one of the UEF's bigger battleships, with a few thousand military and civilian staff living and working on board at any given time. The ship even had a commerce level that acted as a trade center when the ship wasn't stationed in a war zone. For now, the level simply provided entertainment and places to socialize—like bars and restaurants—for the crew. There were several levels of crew housing apartments, a couple of dedicated levels such as the command center and the fighter-pilot-squadron level, and any number of other amenities and storage. The *Knox* was like a huge space-bound city or military base, with everything necessary to cope with long deployments.

But there would be no guided tour for these young soldiers. They learned the layout fast on their own or it was just one more way they could wash out. After all, if they couldn't navigate a battleship, how the heck did they think they'd be able to fly a fighter jet through space?

The recruits were dismissed and he caught more than a few looks of relief. He shook his head. They thought introduction-parade day one was hard? Wait until training commenced.

Leigh turned to Bren, Seb, and Lawler, who'd started discussing their initial impressions, none of which were glowing.

Across the hangar deck, where the recruits milled waiting for the Ilari shuttle, he caught a flash of shining gold hair. *Couldn't be*. Not after his specific instructions for her to get lost. Yet the glimpse of hair turned into a full profile as the crowd shifted. Yep. Recruit Wolfe, chatting away to another recruit like they were in a damned mother's club meeting. How had the psyche-eval come up with the brilliant notion that this five-foot-nothing chick would make a damned fighter pilot? Must have been a glitch in the system.

"What is it?" Bren asked.

He glanced at his XO; obviously some of his pissed-off had shown on his face.

"Nothing. I'll catch up with you later."

If Recruit Wolfe didn't want to rest, then he'd give her something to do. Keeping an eye on her, he crossed the deck, ready to teach her a lesson in how to follow orders.

Mia waved good-bye to Penny, who had pulled ground duty. Mia had promised earlier in the day to see her off. Who knew how long it would be before they got to see each other again? She was going to miss her friend, who embodied everything she'd always wanted to be. Penny was easygoing, confident in her body, and had the kind of personality that attracted people like bees to a pretty, shiny flower, reminding her not to be so uptight, and relax every now and then.

As her friend headed toward the Ilari-bound shuttle, she gave one last jaunty wave, then disappeared into the crowd. Mia sighed, her shoulders drooping and body aching in a way she just knew would make training tomorrow that much harder. Stupid of her to drag herself to the meet-and-greet parade, and Captain Leigh Alphin had called her on it in front of everyone.

Great way to start basic training, loser.

And just how had she ended up in training to be a freaking fighter pilot anyway? Sure, jets and ships fascinated her, but she'd wanted a Command Intelligence posting, or if her dreams were coming true, an aeronautical engineering position. Of course, such things were rare, most recruits ended up as grunt. She supposed she should thank herself lucky she hadn't been posted on the front lines.

Fighter pilot hadn't been at the top of her list when considering positions in the UEF. It hadn't even been *on* her list. In fact, she wouldn't have even put it on a backup list if she'd been so inclined to make one. But no one turned down the opportunity to join the UEF's elite air squadron, especially when their name got assigned to the *Valiant Knox* under Captain Alphin.

So many times she'd almost asked to be retested, but the computers were never wrong. And if she'd flat-out refused the opening, for the rest of her career, everywhere she went she'd be *that recruit* who'd turned down the chance to serve and learn with a living legend of the UEF. So here she was. And she'd do better than her best, because that was what she always did.

At oh six hundred tomorrow morning it would begin and she'd see just how far her body, mind, and attitude could get her. *Please God, don't let me wash out on the first day.* She pressed a hand against her forehead, a fine sheen of sweat dampening her hairline.

"God, what the hell am I doing here?" she muttered at the floor.

"They usually tell you that before you leave pre mil training."

Her head shot up, and she swallowed a gasp when she saw Captain Alphin standing there.

"Hope you didn't sleep through *that* class, Wolfe, or it'll be like floating through space when your aft-thrusters have been blown to hell."

She snapped to attention a little awkwardly, her breath catching in her throat.

Captain Alphin regarded her with a steady, cool stare, his expression unreadable. In the field they called him Alpha, the nickname he'd earned as a recruit. There'd been a class on him back at pre military school as one of the UEF's best fighter pilots currently deployed.

Well, she could say firsthand the man lived up to expectations. His cool, gunmetal-blue gaze shot all the way down her spine into her toes. Just like when she'd first laid eyes on him at the deck triage, the back of her throat dried up as she took in the masculine angles of his face and the military, short-cut perfection of his coffee-black hair. With a quick breath, she turned her attention to her boots, her pulse skittering enough to make her jumpy.

When he'd come to see her in the ER medbay, he'd been like a different man. She got the feeling he didn't let people see that side of himself very often. And it had taken until nearly the end of the conversation for her to realize he had no idea she'd been assigned to him.

The way he'd spoken to her, the depth of emotion in those gray-blue eyes...the feel of his large, rough hand gripping her fingers... She shivered, unable to help her sensory response. She'd already admired the man, because who didn't? Except by the time he'd left her room, she'd started having very un-soldier-like feelings for him. *God*, could she be any stupider?

As if training wouldn't be hard enough, getting starry-eyed over the CAFF would just add an extra layer of uncomfortable to the torment of the coming weeks. Okay, so he was freaking sexy as all hell. She'd have to be dead not to notice. And the side of him she'd seen this morning had opened up a crack in her heart.

There'd been rumors that every year at least one female cadet went crushing hard for him. And the story went that he never paid any of them the least bit of attention. If anything, they became more invisible to him.

Please don't let me be the idiot who gets the hots for the CO...aka God.

She'd already started things off badly enough without becoming a soppy-spined female over his handsome face.

And tall, muscled body. *And in that uniform.* She swallowed and cleared her throat, forcing her mind to go blank.

"Everything all right there, recruit?" Captain Alphin had moved to stand next to her while she'd been having her inner crisis and she hadn't even noticed. She tipped her chin up and set her gaze straight ahead, putting him in her peripheral vision.

"Sir, everything is fine, sir."

The few remaining recruits dispersed, leaving her standing alone with Captain Alphin.

Her legs had started trembling, muscles aching through every inch of her body. That rest Sub-Doctor Moore had recommended sounded better and better. But she couldn't walk off on the CAFF without being dismissed or committing career suicide.

"Sir, was there something you wanted, sir?"

"I seem to remember ordering you to follow the doctor's instructions, did I not, Wolfe?"

She locked her knees against her weakening muscles. "Sir, yes, sir."

Captain Alphin moved to stand directly in front of her again, but she didn't let herself focus on his face. She'd never seen that particular shade of gray-blue eyes before. One glance at him and she'd lose the small amount of nerve she was clinging on to.

"And did doctor's orders include gossiping in the launch bay, Recruit?"

She shook her head, not trusting her voice.

"Well, since you're so determined not to rest, come with me."

He waved his hand to indicate she should precede him,

even though she had no idea where they were going. Well, there was only one main corridor leading from the launch bay.

She caught a few interested glances cast her way as the CAFF marched her through the ship. Everyone greeted Captain Alphin with deference, even the few superior officers they passed. Every now and then, he would murmur a direction to her and by the time they'd gone down several levels, she'd started feeling like a prisoner being paraded about before heading for the executioner's chair.

The captain led her through the gym on squadron level, mostly deserted at this time of day, and continued into the locker room. Privacy on board a ship like this wasn't exactly ideal. A few soldiers, both male and female, were in various states of undress in the locker room and no one seemed too concerned about it. Her cheeks heated, and she kept her gaze averted. One more thing she would need to get used to.

At the opposite end of the locker room, down past the showers, was a small laundry room. It was divided down the middle with a fat yellow line, one side for dirty, the other side for clean. The dirty side had an overflowing, wheeled container of soiled towels sitting next to a chute that went into the ship's automated washing system. The clean side had another chute where the washed and dried items got spat out into another container.

Captain Alphin stopped and pointed at the dirty side. "Feed the towels in one at a time or the chute will get jammed. And let me tell you, the maintenance crew does not like crawling in there to fix it. In a few minutes the towels will come out on that side, and then they need to be folded and put away."

He turned to look at her.

Laundry duty?

She'd pulled stinking laundry duty her second day here because she hadn't followed the doctor's orders? Technically she hadn't even started training yet. She clenched her teeth over the tightness in her throat, because more than anything, she wished she had followed that advice instead of keeping her promise to see Penny off.

Except she got the feeling this might be more about what had happened between Captain Alphin and her in the ER. She'd seen his weak side and now he would do everything in his power to shove her away, make her fail, because they'd crossed a line. A very small infraction, but it had happened. If the truth came out, it would be bad for both of them. So she would suck it up and take whatever he threw at her.

"Sir, yes, sir." She moved past him to the overflowing container and picked up a damp towel off the top. Really, she didn't want to think about where it had been before it got here.

She fed it into the chute, waited a beat, and then followed it with another. Captain Alphin crossed his arms and watched her. She felt the weight of his stern regard all the way down to her toes. In a few moments, clean towels puffed out into the container on the other side. She went over and started folding, her back aching as she bent down to grab the cloths from the deep bottom of the container.

Captain Alphin nodded. "Very good, recruit. Carry on."

He spun on his heel and strode out of the laundry room, leaving her alone with the slight *vrooming* sound of the chute. And just how long was she supposed to keep this up for? Until the container of dirty towels was empty? She glanced at the towering pile. How long would *that* take?

A female soldier ducked in and tossed a couple more on the heap, shooting her a sympathetic look. With a sigh, Mia got to feeding the chute, blanking her mind of everything but getting through the task one sopping towel at a time.

Chapter Four

Leigh stepped out of the transit on alpha flight deck, glancing around to see the maintenance crew getting things back into order after the previous day's chaos, while a few medicos packed up the last of the deck triage.

He spotted his intended target standing next to an armed personnel carrier, facing off with Lawler.

"Cam, were you really going to leave without saying good-bye?" He clapped the colonel on the back as he stopped next to him, but his buddy shot him an annoyed glare.

"Yes, I was trying to leave before you made it up here, but Lawler wouldn't get out of my way."

"Just following orders, sir." Lawler shot Cam a bland smile, then gave a salute that had a definite edge of sarcasm to it.

"I already told Yang, I don't need an escort to the ground. I got here by myself just fine yesterday."

Leigh clasped his hands behind his back and shrugged one shoulder. "Like the sub-officer said, we're just following orders."

"When it suits you," Cam muttered in resignation.

He grinned and sent Lawler a nod, who stepped aside from blocking the hatchway to the personnel carrier.

"Don't consider us an escort, just pretend like we happen to be running a routine patrol on your exact trajectory. Either way, Lawler and I will be on your tail."

"Still a stubborn hard-ass, Alpha?" Cam stepped through the hatchway and shot him an unimpressed look, though it didn't have all that much heat to it. They'd known each other for too many years to really take offense at any small disagreements, especially since Cam knew full well that no one in the Brannon System had the balls to defy orders given by Commander Yang.

As the hatchway snapped closed on Cam's form retreating to the shuttle's controls, Leigh shared a quick grin with Lawler.

"Seems almost getting blown up should have given Cam a new perspective on life, not made him surlier." Lawler stooped down to scoop up his flight helmet where it'd been on the deck next to his boots.

Though the comment had been said flippantly, it sobered Leigh's light mood like flipping a switch. "Yeah, well I suppose if nearly all the other officers you'd worked with for the past ten or twelve years were killed in that blast, your life perspective would be pretty grim, too."

The amusement faded from Lawler's expression and he clenched his jaw. "Well, I guess we better make sure the damned CSS don't try for any more intercepts. And if they do, then so help them God."

Lawler turned on his heel and stalked over to his jet, pulled his helmet on, and then scaled the side.

Leigh went over to his own V-29, where his flight jacket and helmet had been left for him. In a matter of moments, he'd settled himself inside and taken up position on Cam's six, while Lawler took point as they left the launch deck.

They took a wide slingshot around the *Valiant Knox* and settled into a direct trajectory to the secondary Ilari base, which had become the focal point of ground operations since the primary base had been bombed a few weeks ago. The second battleship that had joined the front last week, *Farr Zero,* was only just visible on the horizon between Ilari's atmosphere and one of its three moons.

Since the attack the day before, all scheduled transport between the two battleships and the ground had been delayed while a permanent escort system could be arranged with the FP squadron. It was going to stretch their resources and put more strain on his already overworked pilots, but he knew not a single one of them would complain about it.

"Coming up on the edge of the safe zone in ten." Lawler's announcement through the radio brought him out of his thoughts, and he switched his sensors over to long range. "In four, three, two, one. And we're out."

"You picking anything up, Lawler?" His own scans weren't showing much, but some of the CSS ships were so old, they were occasionally missed by UEF sensors.

"Four coming up off the ground. Could be a coincidence, not sure if they're headed our way or not."

Leigh waited for his jet's computer to extrapolate a likely trajectory for the four ships appearing on his radar.

The readings scrolled across his screen, and he swore and tabbed his weapons live. "They'll be on us as soon as we break higher atmosphere."

"Yeah, I see it. Weapons are hot."

"Cam, leave us to engage. Keep your shields up and make it into the range of the secondary base's targeting system."

"Copy that. If I'd wanted to shoot stuff from inside a ship, I wouldn't have taken a ground posting."

Leigh grinned as his ship hit the resistance of Ilari's upper environment, his jet shuddering slightly as gravity and atmosphere changed. The engines made slight adjustments to keep him stable and at high speed.

By the time he broke through the burn, Lawler had already engaged the enemy.

One of the older CSS clunky, armed shuttles took a hit and spiraled out of control, leaving a corkscrew of black smoke as it plummeted toward the landmass below.

Leigh swung his jet out from behind Cam and swooped in close above the personnel carrier, destroying a blast of weapon's fire that would have put a serious dent in Cam's hull. The smoke hadn't cleared, but he followed it up with a second round of fire, relying on his jet's targeting system to lock onto the enemy ship.

A third enemy ship slipped around to his portside. An alarm beeped, warning him of a targeting lock on his position. He banked aggressively and cut back, putting him in a half loop. The streak of energy fire exploded out of the smoke and clipped his left wing, flipping him into a full spin.

"Alpha, are you hit?"

Leigh couldn't answer as he fought the controls in the

opposite direction to his jet's barrel roll. Sweat dripped down the side of his face, his heart galloping against the inside of his ribs. His upper arms and chest burned from the exertion.

He pulled the jet up and got it stable in time to see a second enemy ship exploded, with the last two breaking off from pursuit. He forced a slow inhale as he glanced out at his damaged wing.

The jet shook forcefully from the hit, trying to buck his control. He gauged the remaining distance to the secondary base, considered ejecting for half a second. They were only minutes away, so he'd take the risk on sticking it out.

Landing was going to be a bitch.

"Any damage to report?" He asked into his comm, glancing out to see Lawler's jet and Cam's personnel carrier both appeared to be in one piece.

"We're all good. But your wing looks like Swiss cheese," Lawler replied.

"Yeah, the maintenance crew is going to be really impressed. That was some nice shooting, Lawler, I owe you one."

"Thanks, Alpha, and I'd love to take full credit, but Cam shot down that second bastard."

He gave a short laugh as the relief of getting through another battle mixed with the downhill side of his adrenaline high. "For someone who didn't want to shoot at things from inside a ship, you've got killer aim, Colonel."

"Or a whole lotta dumb luck," Lawler interjected.

"I never said I couldn't, just that I didn't want to." The deadpan tone of Cam's voice came through loud and clear on the radio.

"Well if you ever get sick of being on the ground, I might

be able to find a place for you in FP squadron."

"Thanks, but no deal, Alpha. I like my boots planted firmly in the dirt."

They were coming up to the secondary base, and ground control contacted them, interrupting the conversation. Leigh confirmed he'd taken damage, and they directed him to a specialized landing pad, while Lawler and Cam split off to the general launch bay.

Tightening his already hard grip on the controls, he slowed his decent, fighting the jet's pull to portside, not quite able to lock into a level trajectory as he maneuvered over the emergency landing pad.

Clenching his jaw, he tipped the jet into the precise angle and lowered the thrusters, bringing himself down by gradual degrees. The closer he got to the ground, the more his jet shook, fighting to buck out of the slanted descent. By the time the landing clamps bumped into contact with the pads, his shoulders had seized up. He took a moment to drop his head against the back of the seat, forcing some of the tension out of his tight muscles.

Again, the CSS were on them, despite encoded launch times and trajectories. *Damn.* More and more, it pointed to a traitor in the FP ranks. He needed to get back to the *Knox* as soon as possible and talk with Bren.

When most of the aches had subsided, he hopped out of the jet, tugging his helmet off and wiping his forearm across his sweat dampened face. He paused to fill out the appropriate logs, then made his way from the emergency landing pad to find Lawler. If his sub-officer was feeling generous, they could both squash into Lawler's jet for the flight back, otherwise he was going to be stuck on the ground for who knew how many hours until the transports resumed. Of course, if he'd been feeling particularly mean, he could simply commandeer Lawler's jet and leave the sub-officer to cool his heels on the dirt for a few hours. He grinned as he walked through the base, imagining the look on Lawler's face if he decided to leave the guy on the ground.

Being the CAFF wasn't all bad.

Leigh shoved a spoonful of rice into his mouth and tried to pretend he wasn't looking for a certain golden-haired recruit. What the hell. Might as well give up the game and admit that, yes, he'd spent half the day since Lawler and he had gotten back to the *Valiant Knox* hoping to catch a glimpse of her when he wasn't preparing for tomorrow's class to start. But only so he could avoid her. Or work on totally alienating her.

He'd been sure he'd see her at midshift messdeck. All of the newbies tended to congregate in one area until they got to know the rest of the ship's crew a little better. But he hadn't seen any sign of her and had to assume she'd learned her lesson after folding towels and gone to rest.

Except now the evening crowd had started thinning, and he still hadn't seen her. Okay, so she might have been resting, but she needed to make sure she ate something as well. The unforgiving training regime would start tomorrow and fasting the night before wouldn't do her any good.

And why was that his concern? The faster she washed out, the quicker she became someone else's responsibility. Except he *did* care. And he sure didn't want to examine why that might be.

A couple of female recruits passed by his table, and like a damn mutt, his ears perked up at one of the newbies mentioning *Mia*, followed by *folding towels*. So they'd heard about it already, huh? Well, it would serve as a good lesson to them all. Follow orders, or pay the consequences. And he'd gone easy on her, because folding towels was one of the painless, nondisgusting duties.

He picked up his tray and trailed the recruits to where finished trays of food were discarded. Snatches of their conversation came to him and he paused, waiting for the pair to get on with dumping their leftover food. Except they'd gotten into some sort of disagreement.

"We should take something down to her. She hasn't had lunch or anything," the one with strawberry-blond hair said.

"They'll let her eat when they want her to eat," the dark-haired woman replied. "She's the one who didn't follow orders, and personally I don't want to go attracting the wrong kind of attention from the CAFF like she has already. You think that's going to make the next few weeks any easier for her?"

The words went on repeat in his head. Something about them—

Damn it to hell. Was Mia—*Recruit Wolfe* still down in the godforsaken laundry folding towels? He'd told one of the other recruits—Benton?—to go and tell her she was relieved of laundry duty not even an hour after getting back from escorting Cam to the ground.

He brushed by the two women, who both went wide-eyed and scurried off when they saw him. He slammed his tray down on the pile and then stalked out of the messdeck, across to the common room. He found Benton playing cards with a couple of other recruits.

"Benton!" His pissed-off CAFF tone echoed across the large room, plunging it into silence.

The kid jumped about meter and then fell off his chair. At any other time, he might have found the guy's scramble to get upright hilarious. Right now, with the way he was fuming, the stupid-ass fumbling just kicked his temper up a few more notches.

"Benton, did I or did I not order you to follow up on Recruit Wolfe?"

For a moment Benton stared at him blankly, but then he blanched, the color literally draining from his face.

"Sir, you did, sir. But Lieutenant Brenner asked me to do something else on my way there and I—" Benton gulped, snapping his mouth closed.

He leaned closer. "You what, recruit?"

"Sir, I forgot, sir."

Leigh stared at him. *Forgot?* "You mean to tell me you can't follow more than one order at a time, Benton?"

The kid swallowed again, keeping his lips compressed.

"Report to Lieutenant Brenner immediately. She'll be able to help you with that memory problem."

The guy needed to be reprimanded, but for the life of him, Leigh couldn't think of anything except hauling ass down to the gym and saving Mia—Recruit Wolfe—from the pile of dirty towels. Had she really been folding them all day? Surely she would have eventually asked someone if she'd done enough. Except he already knew the answer to that.

Benton sent him a sloppy salute and lowered his head,

then left the common room. Leigh cast a hard-ass glare over the recruits sitting nearby and they all suddenly made themselves look busy.

As he turned to head for the gym, Seb shot him a grin and a covert thumbs-up, while Lawler sent him a wise-guy half salute. Leigh shook his head as he passed, and the two guys shared a laugh before returning to the beer and poker game in front of them.

Leigh went down to the gym where the lights were low, the space empty. Occasionally he came down here at this time of night to run on the treadmill when no one else was around and tabbed up an image of an open road stretching in front of him on the vid screens instead of four ship walls.

Before he got to the laundry, he could hear the periodic puffing noise of the towels coming out of the clean chute. He stepped in, his gaze finding Mia—*goddamn it* Recruit Wolfe—leaning against the wall on the dirty side, feeding dirty towels into the yawning mouth of the wash system.

Stay on the ship long enough and a soldier got to learn pretty quickly that the container of dirty towels *never* emptied. Sure, a person could come close, but then a new influx of soldiers in the gym would stack it right back up again.

But now, the clean container was the fuller of the two, though it looked like she'd given up on folding a fair while ago.

"Stand down, recruit."

She didn't react, so he walked farther into the room. "You've done more than enough, Recruit Wolfe. Time to pack it in."

When she still didn't respond to him, he walked over and touched her shoulder. She dropped the towel she'd been holding and spun to face him.

Her dark eyes were glazed with exhaustion and she leaned back against the wall behind her, as though she couldn't even hold herself upright.

"Sorry, sir, I didn't manage to get through all the towels—" She listed to the side and he caught her before she crashed into the container.

Hell, he should have come down here himself and made sure she'd been released from duty. But he hadn't had a reason to suspect damn Benton wouldn't see his order through.

"Okay, let's get some food into you." He tugged her arm and led her into the locker room, where he urged her to sit on one of the benches. In the wall by the door was a vending machine full of protein bars and energy drinks. He ordered a couple of each, since dinner at messdeck would be over by now. He could have taken her down to commerce since there were places serving food twenty-four-seven on that level, but she looked too washed out for that.

By the time he brought the snacks over, she seemed a bit sharper, her dark gaze staring up at him warily. Her looking at him like he was the devil incarnate made his chest ache, even though it was exactly what he'd set out to achieve. Usually he enjoyed putting the fear of god into the newbies, but doing so to Recruit Wolfe sat uncomfortably on his shoulders for some reason.

"I'm not about to inflict another punishment on you, so quit looking at me like that." He ripped the packaging off one of the protein bars and handed it over to her.

She tilted her head down as she started eating, the soft light catching deep gold highlights in her hair, which had mostly unraveled from the knot she'd had it tied into. Wisps fell around her face and neck, making her look too damn touchable.

He tightened his hold on the energy drink. *Need to get laid, not lust inappropriately after new recruits.* Yet the thought of hitting the mattress with another woman didn't do anything for him. Annoyed at himself, he pushed all sex-related thoughts from his mind and started running training drills through his head.

Mia finished the protein bar, and he handed her the energy drink.

"Thanks," she murmured, her voice a little on the husky side.

"I'm sorry."

Her head snapped up, dark gaze clashing with his. He wasn't sure who was more surprised at the words. He sure as hell couldn't remember the last time he'd apologized to a recruit for anything. And this really didn't run with his plan of alienating her.

"You weren't meant to be down here this long. The messenger who was supposed to relieve you of duty never made it. I shot him."

Her eyes widened and a grin tightened his mouth, but he swallowed over the urge.

"That was a joke. But thanks to Lieutenant Brenner, he'll be wishing he'd been lucky enough to pull laundry duty."

"Oh." She took a small sip of the energy drink, her gaze slipping off to the side.

"About what happened yesterday in the medbay..." Jesus, did he really want to have this conversation? But avoiding it wouldn't help anything. He needed to know they understood each other. "I was inappropriate. You're aware we have to pretend like nothing happened, right?"

"I know. I should have said something before things went that far. It's not your fault. You didn't know I had been assigned to you."

Frustration pulsed through him. "Well it's damned well not your fault either. I shouldn't have acted so improperly, no matter who you are."

She speared him with a direct gaze. "It's not improper to want to talk to someone every now and then, to let out stuff that's been bottled up for too long."

His chest tightened and he clenched his fists. Why did she have to be so understanding?

She sighed and half turned away from him. "I'm sorry. I shouldn't have said that. It doesn't help anything. Sure, let's get on with pretending it never happened."

He locked his jaw against replying. Because deep down, he didn't *want* to pretend like it had never happened. However, circumstance dictated they do exactly that before he found himself in deeper trouble… If he wasn't already.

The last thing he wanted to do was hurt her, and he had a lot to answer for here. But personal feelings didn't count when it came to duty, and duty always came first.

Chapter Five

Sitting so close to Captain Alphin was unsettling in too many ways for her tired mind to catalog. He was an intimidating man; there was no doubt about it. Even though he'd been nothing but friendly with her since he'd come to relieve her of laundry duty, there was a hardness to his gaze that was common to many seasoned soldiers who'd seen death in all its terrible forms.

But the cool stare seemed in direct contrast to the glimpses of heartfelt honesty she'd seen from him in the medbay yesterday, and just now when he'd apologized for another recruit's mistake. She didn't want to feel any of these things for him, didn't want to wonder what else might lie under that tough, hard attitude. And she definitely wished that the feel of his large, warm, slightly roughened thumb sliding over the inside of her palm hadn't imprinted on her memory like a bright flash illuminating an otherwise-dull room.

It had been the briefest of touches, hardly lasting more

than a split second and probably not even done on purpose. But the sensation had rippled up her arm and lodged into her chest, her mind conjuring up the breathless feeling at the stupidest random times since. Thinking about that wasn't helping things right now, but neither was his knight-in-shining-armor routine, rescuing her from the evil laundry containers and then feeding her when she hadn't eaten anything all day.

Still, he hadn't said anything in response to her agreement they pretend like that conversation between them in the medbay had never happened. His hands clasped between his knees and he stared off across the gym, his features tense.

The aloof expression should have warned her away, but instead it widened that crack in her defenses she'd been trying to ignore. It shouldn't matter to her if he was lonely or what kind of life he lived outside of his role as her CO. But for some idiotic reason she did care—or maybe curious was a better word. Whatever it was, she was invested way too much, considering their respective positions.

Ever since the shuttle had been attacked on route from the *Farr Zero*, she felt like she'd been in a tailspin, unable to find her breath or gain perspective. She needed some time and distance. Maybe this whole thing with Captain Alphin didn't mean anything. Maybe it was some kind of deferred gratitude for the fact that he'd been the one to pull her out of the damaged transport. With a good night's sleep in a bed that wasn't a hospital gurney, she'd probably regain her common sense and then be totally mortified that for even half a second, she'd thought she'd started to like him a little too much.

Pushing to her feet, she grabbed on to the sanity of that

resolve, stepping back to put some distance between them—physical and mental.

"Thanks for the drink and the energy bar. I really should be getting back to the dorm."

He stood with a fluid movement, clasping his hands behind his back as he straightened.

"Let me escort you." Said in a tone that expected no argument. Yet the need to get away from him was swiftly building within her.

"That's not necessary." She took another step back, even though she couldn't leave until he'd dismissed her or at least given an indication that she was free to go.

One side of his lips quirked upward for a brief second in an expression that was more cynical than amused. "As one of the recruits assigned to my training program, consider that it is necessary."

Well, darn, she couldn't argue with that, not unless she wanted to risk getting booted from said training program before it officially started.

Despite the weird, unsettled sensations creeping under her skin, she nodded and turned, grip twisting around the energy drink as she headed out of the gym with Captain Alphin on her heels.

The silence stretched between them as they waited for the transit-porter. And of course the transit was empty when the doors opened. They stepped inside and Captain Alphin put in the destination of the recruit dorms. She focused her attention on the display that showed the transit as a red dot moving through a map of the ship, too aware of the man standing silent and impassive next to her.

The doors opened to several recruits waiting to board

the transit, and she ducked her head as she stepped out, unable to decide if she was relieved that they were no longer alone or embarrassed that some of her fellow recruits had seen her escorted around the ship by their CO.

Quickening her steps, she headed along the corridor, concentrating on finding her assigned dorm. When she reached the hatchway, she turned. Captain Alphin had lagged several steps behind her, obviously not in as much of a hurry as she was. The few recruits who'd been loitering in the passageway disappeared in wake of Captain Alphin, leaving them alone yet again.

"Sir, thank you for the escort, sir." She clasped her hands in a formal stance, hoping her *get lost* hadn't been too obvious.

He stopped in front of her, glancing at the hatchway to her dorm room before his gaze settled on her.

"Trying to get rid of me, Wolfe?" he murmured in a low tone.

Her heart bumped against the inside of her chest. "Sir, no, sir."

He leaned in a little closer. "You know, I think I'm starting to get a good picture of you. You're smart, maybe smarter than most recruits who come through here. Smart enough to know when to follow the rules to the letter and smart enough to know when you can get away with screwing the rules."

Though a sane person might have taken his assessment of her character as a warning—an assessment that was probably spot-on, despite the fact they'd only met less than twenty four hours ago—for some reason his words made her feel too warm.

She cleared her still-raw throat and tilted her chin up a

little. "I have no idea what you're talking about, sir."

"Plausible deniability?"

She didn't answer, but she did hold his intense gaze for a long moment, making her pulse rate kick up.

His expression relaxed a little into what could have passed for contemplation. "However long you last in this training program, I have a feeling it's not going to be boring while you're around."

Now *that* she didn't think he meant as a compliment at all, which only served to spark her temper. "Sir, I'll do my utmost to be as dull as dishwater, sir."

She clenched her teeth after the words slipped out. *Damn it.* Apparently she'd lost her common sense *and* her self-control since leaving the *Farr Zero* yesterday.

Luckily, Captain Alphin didn't seem pissed off. In fact, she could have sworn she caught a spark of amusement in his gaze before he glanced away from her. However, by the time he looked back, any hint of what he'd thought of her ill-considered words had gone.

He shifted a step closer until she had to tip her head up slightly to keep her gaze fixed on his face. His hand landed on her shoulder, and then he urged her into a pivot to face the door.

"Get some rest. You're going to need it." His low voice trickled over her like warm syrup and sent a tremble tripping down her spine.

She froze, cursing herself because he had to have felt that, since he was holding on to her shoulder. For a second he stilled and she caught her breath, waiting for him to release her so she could flee to her bunk and hide under her covers.

"Leigh—" She didn't know why his name slipped out on

a whisper, that one word filled with far more than she should have revealed to him. But apparently it was enough to break the spell.

"*Christ*." He let her go abruptly, leaving her off-balance.

Before she'd regained her equilibrium, he'd turned away and stalked off down the passageway, leaving her with nothing but cold shivers tracking under her skin.

Whatever his intentions in escorting her up here, she had a feeling that hadn't been it. And instead of resolving the little infraction between them, somehow they'd gone and made it worse.

She covered her heated face with her hands for a long moment. Disaster didn't begin to cover it. She had to get over this little burgeoning infatuation and start acting like the recruit she'd trained to be. She had plans for a career, and getting involved in an inappropriate relationship with a superior officer definitely didn't factor into that.

Jesus Christ. What had he been thinking?

Leigh sat up, damp sheets pooling in his lap, sweat cooling on his body and breath too hard to catch. He glanced at the clock in the wall beside his bunk. *Oh four hundred.* Shoving a hand through his hair, he swung his legs off the bed and set his feet on the cold floor.

After he'd fled the recruit dorms last night, he'd locked himself in his apartment, too wound up and pissed off to be fit for company. He'd thrown himself into a cold shower, loathing himself every second. How could he have succumbed to such a moment of weakness that could put a short, humiliating end to the career he'd put his whole thirty-six years into? Never once in all the time he'd been training potential new pilots had he been attracted to a single one of them, not even the slightest bit. His position as their commanding officer had made it easier to view them impersonally.

Maybe the stress of knowing he possibly had a mole under his command had screwed with his head, and Mia presented as a convenient distraction.

Except that wasn't fair on her, and made him seem like a shallow jerk. Okay, perhaps some of it came down to a weird sense of disconnection he'd developed ever since Yang told him one of the people he trusted with his life had betrayed him. Maybe he just wanted to feel connected to something or someone—

And maybe all this self-psycho-analysis crap was giving him a headache. He dragged a hand down his face, pressure building behind his temples.

Going to bed and laying in the dark had only intensified the problems. For one, that forbidden moment when he'd touched Mia's shoulder had gone on live-action replay in his head over and over. He couldn't stop it, as though his mind had imprinted the scene on his very soul. The feel of her soft, lithe body next to his. The sound of her breath catching. The exact curve of her lower lip. The light almond scent of her skin. The way she'd whispered his name, laced with darkly sensual things that were forbidden between them.

What would have happened if she hadn't murmured his name and jolted him from the spiraling path of his thoughts?

He'd half expected Commander Yang to come pounding on his door, dragging him up to the command center to bring him up on charges of misconduct, among other things. Yet the night had crept by and eventually he'd fallen into a fitful sleep, plagued by his own stupidity.

But even more unsettling? The conflicted feelings warring within him. How would he face Recruit Wolfe today and pretend like nothing had happened? Somehow he had to drag himself out of the dishonorable place he found himself and put things to right.

After shoving the sheets off, he then stooped to grab a pair of sweats and worn T-shirt, before yanking on some socks and shoving his feet into his trainers. An hour on the treadmill to wear down his body and clear his mind was what he needed to regain some of his sanity and get through the day.

He headed out into the hallway and down to the transit. As he reached out to the control screen, the doors opened, revealing Commander Yang.

For a second his heart went into a free fall, until he remembered that Yang had recently moved into Dr. Sacha Dalton's apartment on this level.

He clasped his hands behind his back and sent Yang a nod as he stepped out of the transit. "Sir."

"Alpha." Yang returned the nod, though a little less sharply. The commander looked tired, his usually neat hair sticking out and tie pulled loose, while his rumpled jacket was slung over his arm. "Late night or early morning?"

"Early start. Wanted to get some time in at the gym before classes start with the recruits. You?"

Yang ran a hand over his hair and sent him an exasperated look. "Late night, but I'm sure you can tell."

He sent Yang a quick half smile. "Of course not, sir."

"Well, I'll leave you to it. I'm hoping to catch a few hours sleep before the next crisis."

Yang started to walk by him, but Leigh turned. "If you don't mind me asking, sir, is everything okay?"

The commander paused, then looked back at him, a range of grim emotions passing through his expression before becoming carefully neutral. "You mean apart from the fact we have a number of unknown traitors in our midst and no idea what the CSS are planning?"

The betrayal he'd tried to avoid feeling about the possible mole in his squadron returned, lighting up to burn in his chest. If he felt this way at the prospect of facing a single traitor in his ranks, he couldn't imagine what Yang must be feeling, all on top of the PTSD he was recovering from after his time as a POW.

Yang gave a short sigh and stepped back toward him. "There's a lieutenant due to come over from the *Farr Zero* later today. To put it simply, his one task is to review the validity of my command."

A deluge of aggravation surged through him. *UEF and their bureaucratic BS*. More than half the brass who made decisions for them hadn't ever fought on the front lines. They were all about money, figures, and statistics, not about the actual lives of the people on the ground.

"So they gave you back command, but *now* they want to make sure you're fit for duty?"

"I knew there were conditions when I agreed to take back my post." Yang glanced over his shoulder, down the hall toward the apartment he shared with Sacha. "I just didn't tell Sacha about it. She needs to concentrate on herself and the baby, not worrying about whether or not the UEF are going to pull my posting any day now."

The irritation smoldered into anger on Yang's behalf. "They can't, sir. No one knows or cares about the *Knox* as much as you do. Commander Emmanuel did his best this past year and a half, but things didn't run the same without you. If they put someone else in charge of this battleship again, we might as well fly off in surrender right now."

Yang sent him the ghost of a smile. "Thanks for the vote of confidence."

"I'm not blowing smoke, Yang, I'm telling it like it is."

Yang reached out and clasped his shoulder for a moment. "When the lieutenant shows up, I'll be sure to send him your way so you can tell him that."

"Go ahead. Have him talk to every single person on board this ship. The only thing he's going to find is dedicated support for you."

"If it were a matter of the crew's opinion, it'd be much simpler. But I get the feeling it's going to be more about how my PTSD has manifested and whether or not it's impacting my ability to command."

Leigh crossed his arms, feeling cold at the idea of Yang under such scrutiny. There probably wasn't a solider on this ship who didn't have some small symptom of PTSD; even he struggled with nightmares occasionally. They'd all seen action, and this war had been dragging on for too many years. It made him wonder if this review wasn't about something other than Yang's ability to command.

"If there's anything I can do—" The words rang hollow, because they both knew he had no part in this situation.

Yang smiled briefly anyway. "I'll let you know. Thanks, Alpha."

The commander turned and strode away, his bearing tall, straight, and still radiating authority, despite the slight limp from an injury sustained while he'd been a POW.

Leigh sighed and stepped onto the transit. If he'd wanted a distraction from thoughts of Recruit Wolfe, he'd definitely found one. Whatever the UEF were thinking in this review of Yang's position, he got the feeling it didn't bode well for the rest of the *Valiant Knox's* crew.

Chapter Six

Oh four hundred. *More like oh God, kill me now.*

Mia stifled the third yawn in as many minutes as she dragged her sleep-deprived body out of her bunk and crept out of the dorm. At the UEF academy, she'd often gotten up around oh six hundred to exercise before classes at eight. Or get some extra study time in. She'd never had to get up and be at a class *by* oh six hundred before. *So not a morning person.* It always took her at least two hours to wake up properly, so if she wanted to be functioning on all levels by the time her first class started, oh four hundred was her new alarm time.

She grabbed a change of clothes and headed for the transit-porter, planning to hit the lap pools in the gym. There were only two of the small hydro pools on FP level, and she'd heard getting into one could be hard at peak times, because swimming was a good way to keep up muscle mass and lung capacity, especially for people who spent so much time in space. Hopefully because it was early there wouldn't be anyone else in the pools, and she could swim out her self-recriminations in peace. She'd already spent half the night agonizing over the fact that she'd imagined kissing her CO.

Shock had washed through her on the heels of a deep-seated need to feel his mouth closing over hers. Would he be reserved and keep his passions frustratingly locked-down, or would he burn so hot underneath that reserved facade that he'd singe her and leave her nothing but smoke and ashes?

Dear God, just how dumb could she be?

There was no scenario in which anything good could come of this attraction that had ambushed her. But, there were many, *many* ways in which it could destroy both their lives.

Captain Alphin had a pristine reputation, no hint of scandal in his personal life whatsoever. Stuff like that never stayed secret very long, especially on a ship like the *Valiant Knox*, where everyone knew everyone and privacy wasn't exactly an easy thing to come by. That right there was the number-one reason why she absolutely *could not* let anything happen between them. Someone would inevitably find out—which brought her right back around to all the ways in which this reckless little infatuation could destroy her life.

At some point in the small hours of the morning, she'd reasoned that her tired mind had been seeing things that just weren't there. Maybe Captain Alphin hadn't even realized the intimate manner in which he'd touched her shoulder. Maybe his low curse had been more about the fact that she'd slipped up and used his given name. Possibly when she saw him today, he was going to ride her harder than any other student simply because they'd become a little too familiar with each other.

The door to the transit-porter swooshed open in front of her. As if her thoughts alone had summoned him, Leigh stood toward the back of the transit, dressed down in a light gray pair of sweats and a faded navy T-shirt that stretched a little too nicely over his muscled chest, while his short hair was sticking out all over the place in a sexy, just-got-out-of-bed kind of way. Her next breath got caught in her lungs as her chest tightened, her heart feeling like it was being squeezed.

He looked up and straightened when he saw her, a flash of what could have been alarm crossing his features. Yeah, she was feeling pretty panicked herself. Maybe she'd just wait for the next transit to come by. She stepped back, but as the doors started sliding shut again, Leigh came forward and slapped a hand against the edge so the transit stayed open.

"We need to talk. Again." His expression had settled into determined lines, though he glanced up and down the deserted passageway before nodding in a way that indicated she should join him.

She swallowed down the unsettling mix of apprehension and anticipation being around him created. With a short breath, she stepped past him into the transit and then neither of them said anything as the doors slid shut.

"Where are you headed?" Leigh asked without looking directly at her.

"Gym. The lap pools, actually." She glanced at the display listing destinations to see that the gym had already been selected. Was that where he was going as well?

For a long second they both stood there, not looking at each other, while a growing awareness of them shut in here alone, and the hours she'd spent thinking about him, grew within her.

Finally, Leigh scrubbed a hand over his hair, then turned to look directly at her. As soon as his blue eyes met hers, it was like a flash of lighting streaking from the tips of her hair all the way to her toes. No other man had ever been able to do that to her with a single look. Was this some weird forbidden-authority-figure thing, or was it simply Leigh that made her feel that way?

"I feel like I should say sorry about last night, except honestly, we both know nothing untoward happened between us. However, I'm sure you're aware that for a moment there, things got a little hazy in terms of appropriate interactions. I apologize if I made you feel uncomfortable, and you can rest assured, it will never happen again."

Wow. She'd heard Leigh was an honorable, straight-forward, if somewhat hard soldier, but the fact that he was standing here, not trying to make excuses for what had happened surprised and impressed her. And she *really* didn't need to be any more impressed than she already was.

"I'm not sorry either." Yep, she had just said that, even though she probably shouldn't have. But Leigh being so straight with her made it easy to face facts, and if he was going to give her the bald truth, then she would return the favor in kind. "I was just as responsible. I could have stepped away, I could have not slipped with your name. The next few weeks in the training program are going to be hard, and I need to give my all to that, not be distracted by—"

Leigh's expression suddenly lost some of its tension and a grin transformed his features into somewhere around the level of mind-melting. Her damned heart skipped a beat, but she leveled a glare on him. "What's so funny?"

He shook his head, shifting a little nearer. "I'm not laughing. At you anyway. I am finding it funny that my manly pride wants to know if I'm being dressed down, when I'd planned on doing all the lecturing."

Oh, so now he had a sense of humor? She hardened her fluttering emotions against him and deepened her frown. "Since technically nothing happened, no one is lecturing anyone. We're just mutually agreeing to stay away from each other. Or, failing that, we'll strive to maintain a platonic, if not distant relationship."

"Mia, you are clearly too practical for your own good."

"There is no such thing as being too practical. And after this, we're not going to talk about it again, either."

The doors to the transit opened, and Leigh shot her a smile that bordered on intimate, making her heart skip.

"Good-bye, Recruit Wolfe."

He backed out of the transit, then headed toward the gym. She walked out at a more sedate pace, feeling far better now that they'd reached an agreement about how things should stand. Next time she saw him, he would just be Captain Alphin and she would be doing everything in her power to pretend like he was simply a commanding officer she didn't know one single thing about.

The messdeck echoed with dull chatter as Mia looked over the breakfast offerings and decided she couldn't eat anything other than the meager fare she'd already picked up: black coffee and a few pathetic slices of cold toast. Despite spending an hour in the lap pool, her lack of sleep was still making her feel unsettled, without much appetite. However, after she found a table and sat down, she forced herself to eat, because with training starting today, she'd need what little energy the toast provided.

And most of that energy would be expended mentally, trying to put Captain Alphin firmly in the past and forget she knew anything about him. At least she now knew he was on the same page, which should make it that much easier to get on with things.

Someone sat down across from her, and she glanced up to see one of the other female recruits, Kayla Dawson, picking up her fork as the rest of the seats quickly filled around her.

Mia shook her head slightly and forced her mind on the here and now—away from things she'd vowed to move on from—as the recruits around the table started up a conversation about what they might expect in the coming days.

"Captain Alphin needs to get that stick out of his ass." Steve Robinson sat a few seats down from her, a huge plate of bacon, eggs, sausages, hash browns, and other food piled in front of him. "Who does he think he is? Just coz he's the Captain of the Fighter Force."

"He's your CO dumbass," Kayla put in. "So unless you want to spend FP training wiping the floor with your face, you better kick the attitude, *Dogmeat*."

A few of the other recruits laughed at the nickname given to FP trainees who got picked on by the instructors, while Steve glared at Kayla. Mia examined her toast. She needed a bit of Kayla's spunk. Out of all the recruits, Kayla was one of the few sure to get through the next few weeks and make it look stupidly easy.

Steve grinned and elbowed the guy sitting next to him.

"Looks like Kayla will be the dumb bimbo who gets all hot and bothered over the CAFF this year." Steve guffawed at his own remark. A few of the guys near him threw in some lewd comments, but Kayla half turned away from him in her seat, sending him an obvious snub as she calmly sipped at her coffee.

Mia rearranged the bread she'd ripped up and slouched in her seat, a guilty blush creeping up her neck. The position of Dumb Bimbo Getting All Hot and Bothered Over the CAFF might have already been filled. God help her if someone like Steve Robinson found out. He would make her life a living hell if he got even a hint that she'd gone mushy for their CO.

She busied herself shoving another bit of her unappetizing breakfast in her mouth while the ribald banter between the guys continued. After chewing the half mouthful and gulping down some coffee, she pushed the plate away and stood.

"Are you heading to class already?" Kayla asked.

"Uh, yeah. Thought I might as well find a decent seat and start reading through the material we'll be covering today." She'd always liked getting to class before everyone else, choosing her seat and sitting back to watch the other students and teachers trickle in.

Kayla stood, then sculled the dregs of her coffee.

"Sounds like a great idea. I'll come with you." She slammed the mug down, which cut off a lewd story Steve had been telling. The two of them glared at each other and then Kayla moved around the table to walk next to her as they headed out of the messdeck.

"Mia, right? I'm Kayla," she said, holding out her hand.

Mia shook it as they exited into the corridor. "Yeah, I've seen you around campus at Ophelei UEF Academy. I was glad to see a familiar face at the first line up when we got off the *Farr Zero* shuttle yesterday."

Kayla glanced over her shoulder, then leaned closer to her. "I heard Steve and his buddies came from the Ackerly Academy, you know that all-boys school only the rich and potential elite soldiers make it into? That's why he's such a jerk. The soldiers who come out of that place are always jerks, think they're God's gift to mankind just coz their families are cashed-up and got them into some special school."

Mia grimaced. Well, that explained a lot. Everyone knew the reputation of Ackerly. Most people called the graduates Ackerly Assholes. Not to their faces, of course, that'd just be asking to get punched. Or court-martialed, since a good portion of the UEF's senior officers were Ackerly alumni.

"Remind me to stay off Steve's radar," she muttered more to herself, but Kayla nodded an agreement.

"He's a typical jerk. Pulling your strings to get a reaction. If you just ignore them, they get bored and move onto someone else."

God, she hoped she could calmly ignore Steve if the guy decided on her for his next target.

They reached the designated ready room where they'd be spending a good chunk of time learning the theory behind the fighter jets before they got any ideas about flight-time.

Mia went through the hatchway ahead of Kayla, but stopped short just inside the door. Kayla brushed by her shoulder and continued past, walking over to drop into a seat in the second row from the front.

Toward the back of the room, Captain Alphin stood chatting to one of the other instructors. He glanced over at her, but in the space of a breath had returned to his conversation, all but looking right through her.

She blew out a long sigh of relief and continued over to sit next to Kayla. What had she expected? Long, lingering looks? A flinch? Some kind of manly blush? Stupid, but she had been thinking that somehow, when she saw him again today, there would be some kind of silent admission of the agreement between them.

Except this was much better. Treating her as if she didn't exist was exactly what she needed to put them both back into their respective places, where they didn't socialize, didn't know each other outside of the platonic teacher-student roles, and certainly didn't ever, *ever* get up close and personal.

She picked up the datapad that had been left on the desk she'd chosen and tapped the screen to life, forcing her distracted thoughts to focus on the day's reading. The room filled up, recruits chatting excitedly as they took their seats. Would they be so enthusiastic in another twenty-four hours once they realized the odds stacked against them and the hard work they'd have to slog through in order to come out on the other side?

The following weeks would be a test of mental and physical endurance, putting their minds and bodies through a number of rigorous challenges. Every year, successful recruits numbered about a quarter of those who started out, if even that. Truthfully, she didn't like her chances of making it to the end. She knew her own strengths and weakness.

But she was determined to push herself as far as she could before becoming a washout.

Captain Alphin and the other instructor, Sub-Lieutenant Sebastian Rayne, walked to the front of the class. Rayne stuck his fingers in his mouth and let out an ear-splitting whistle, cutting off the noise with eardrum-bursting efficiency.

Captain Alphin took a few steps forward, stopping just in front of the lectern, and clasped his hands behind his back.

"I really hate having to use Sub-Lieutenant Rayne to get your attention, recruits. Having my eardrums perforated puts me in a foul mood, so I'm not going to say this twice. When any instructor is standing at the front of this room, there will be silence. If I have to get Rayne in here to use his superpowers, I will be pissed off, and you will pay the price."

Captain Alphin nodded at Rayne, who saluted and then retreated toward the back of the room.

"What a pompous hard-ass," someone muttered behind her, followed by a ripple of snickers from a few other recruits.

Mia turned her head far enough to see Steve had sat right behind her. *Great.* Just what she needed today—commentary from the a-hole contingent of the group. Steve saw her looking and flashed her a suave grin. Maybe some women would find that smarmy, rich-boy charisma attractive, but the prospect of him trying to charm her made a shudder trip down her back.

"Is there something going on over there I need to be made aware of?"

She turned her attention back to the front and found Captain Alphin glaring in her direction. Well, not exactly her direction, he seemed to be doing a really great job at looking through her still. No, that scowl seemed more directed at

Steve behind her.

No one answered, though a few of the recruits who'd laughed shifted in their seats, until the CAFF turned his attention to bringing the screen at the front of the room online.

"So, apparently you're all here to become fighter pilots. And the first thing a pilot needs to know is their ship or jet, and I mean from the inside out." Captain Alphin typed on the remote datapad, bringing up a couple of diagrams on the large screen. "On the datapads in front of you, you'll find schematics for the currently deployed V-29 multi-atmospheric fighter jet, as well as basic launch protocols every pilot must adhere to before each flight."

Captain Alphin set the datapad down on the lectern and then faced the room again. "We're going to head up to port level alpha, where, if you didn't already know, the fighter jets are housed in bays alpha-one to delta-eight. You'll get the chance to sit in a fighter jet and see the inside of a machine for yourself. After that, you'll have two weeks to memorize these diagrams and protocols, as provided on the datapads. There will be a final exam before your maiden flight. If you don't pass the theory, you will not be continuing any farther with the program, which most definitely includes flying any jets."

A ripple of exclamations and quiet groans resonated about the room as Sub-Lieutenant Rayne and Captain Alphin led the way out of the ready room, recruits falling in behind them.

"Since the test in a few weeks is all about brains and not brawn, it'll take out Steve and his crew, if they don't fail at something else before that," Kayla murmured from where she walked next to Mia.

"We can only hope."

Something tickled the back of her neck and she flinched into a half duck, before turning. Steve stood not a step behind her, conceited grin firmly in place.

"Were you ladies talking about yours truly?"

Kayla scowled. "Yeah, we were trying to decide how long we'd have to put up with seeing your annoying face before you washed out."

Despite Kayla's insult, Steve's grin didn't budge.

Mia crossed her arms. When it came to guys like Steve, ignoring them was always the smartest way of dealing. But even though she'd given him her best cold shoulder, he closed the distance to stride beside her. She trained her gaze in the middle of Captain Alphin's back as an icy, uneasy feeling washed through her.

"And how did you make it into the fighter-pilot program, sweetheart? It's cute, really, that you think you can cut it."

An angry flush rose up her neck, but she clamped her lips together against saying anything in retaliation. Steve was a classic bully, and no matter what she said in return, she'd somehow come out on the losing end.

As the group reached the transit-porter and squeezed on, Leigh spun, his sharp gaze landing on her, almost as if he'd felt the weight of her constant stare. His attention shifted to Steve beside her for a split second, then focused on her.

Something hot sparked in his eyes, his gaze lingering just a little longer than it should, before he turned away from her. A storm of tingling warmth rushed her, stealing her breath for a long second.

Common sense returned like a cold shower. Her plan

of staying detached around him was going to work *so well* if she had a mini-meltdown every time he met her eyes.

"So, what do you think?" Steve asked from right beside her.

Somehow, while she'd been in a mental free fall over Leigh's heart-stopping gaze, Steve had moved into her personal space and had apparently been talking to her.

"I'm sorry?" She took a big step away from him. Well, as far as she could get, considering the crowd jammed into the transit.

"Tonight, after messdeck, you and me, and a bottle of prohibited vodka…?"

She almost threw up, right onto Steve's incorrectly laced boots. "Is that supposed to be romantic or something?"

"No, that's meant to be two people getting together to blow off some steam in the best way possible. Naked."

Gag. Lucky she'd been too tired to eat much of her breakfast.

"Sorry, Steve, but I'll be studying after messdeck tonight."

Steve shrugged. "Another night, then."

Before she could correct his assumption that she would *ever* want to go anywhere alone with him and a bottle of prohibited vodka—let alone get naked—he'd moved off to stand with the other Ackerly a-holes.

Kayla eyed Steve as she might a rabid animal. "I get the feeling he's one of those guys who thinks when a girl says no, she really means yes, or maybe just needs a bit of extra convincing."

Chapter Seven

Leigh strolled around the far end of the fighter jet, nodding at Lawler, who was waiting for another recruit to finish their allocated five minutes in the cockpit to study the controls firsthand.

While many of the recruits took the morning's activity seriously, learning as much as they could, others still seemed to think this was some sort of high school field trip where they could goof around and slack off. Well, if those recruits hadn't found an attitude adjustment by the end of the day, he'd be more than happy to provide them with one.

He stopped and glared at one of the morons in question. Steve Robinson would not make it through this program, of that Leigh had no doubt. He saw the guy's type every year—overconfident, self-serving imbeciles who thought the world owed them and they didn't need to lift a finger to find success. Robinson was one of those guys seasoned soldiers knew to stay the heck away from because he was likely to get himself, if not someone else, killed.

Right now, said moron loitered a few steps away from Mia and another female recruit. He didn't like the way old Steve had been hanging around her all day, but clearly it was none of his business.

Maybe if he and Mia had met under different circumstances, he could have started something with her. She might be beautiful, smart, intriguing, and a million other things, but too many people relied on him to lose his sanity and choose a woman over that.

"Robinson being a d-bag again?" Seb stopped beside him, folding his arms over a datapad and holding it against his chest. "We've got to make sure we wash that guy out in the next session. You know he asked me before how a guy gets *special items and privileges* around here? Like, what, we might be running some kind cryztal-lab or bootlegging operation out of echo-ten bay?"

"Idiot," Leigh muttered, shaking his head. He cut his gaze away from said idiot. Instead, he glanced at Seb. "Where are we up to?"

Seb lowered the datapad and touched the screen, bringing up an alphabetical list of the recruits. "Almost done. Next recruit in the jet will be Wolfe, Mia."

"I'll take this one." The words fell out of his mouth before he'd thought about it, and he immediately wanted to take them back again. Goddamn it, what the hell had happened to his careful self-control? He wasn't impulsive. Yet the last three days had seen him slip off the straight and narrow several times.

Seb nodded and got distracted by some recruits who were messing around too close to a bench fitted with many very expensive, state-of-the-art tools. As the sub-lieutenant went to herd the rowdy children back with the rest of the class, Leigh strode closer to the nose of the jet, where Lawler oversaw the recruits who hadn't taken their turn…plus a few hangers like Robinson, who apparently had nothing better to do than pester the others.

"Recruit Wolfe."

Mia straightened to attention, stepping forward. "Sir, yes, sir?"

For some reason, her very correct response smashed right into the memory of her whispering his name last night, and he faltered a step before stopping.

"You're up next, Wolfe." He cleared his throat, since his voice had come out husky, and definitely a decibel lower.

Mia's gaze caught his in a way that seemed too knowing. Could she see how her mere presence agitated him? Worse, could *other people* see the way she stirred him?

He trailed a step behind her, over to the side of the fighter jet, and waited while she climbed up the side and lowered herself into the cockpit. Once she was in, he scaled to the top and then looked down, forcing himself to focus on the familiar controls and not the gleam of Mia's golden hair or the slender line of her neck.

With a few short directions, he showed her each instrument and then went through the prelaunch protocols. Every so often she would ask a question or interject an observation, which told him not only was she damned gorgeous, but he'd also been right when he'd guessed that she had a decent brain in that head of hers.

When he'd told her everything she needed to know, he descended the side of the craft and waited at the bottom, leaning back against the side. Like all the other recruits, she had five minutes to go over what she'd just been shown. Efficiently, when her time was up, she came out without him needing to remind her.

As she reached the last drop off the side of the jet, Leigh automatically stepped up and held a hand out for her, clasping her forearm to help her down. He'd done it a million times before—often with Bren, sometimes with Seb, Lawler, or other pilots. And occasionally he'd been the recipient of a hand-down himself after a particularly long or stressful battle. His fighter pilots were a close-knit bunch, and they looked out for one another.

But somehow, as Mia dropped down next to him and he hung on for longer than he needed to, the supportive gesture became weighted with a whole lot of other stuff going on under the surface.

"Thank you, sir." Mia's hand tightened where she held his arm, rebooting his brain that had apparently stalled at some point.

He dropped her arm and backed up a few steps. "Dismissed, Recruit."

Mia nodded and stepped around him, walking over to join the same woman he'd seen her with earlier.

Leigh gave himself a mental shake. *Are you ten kinds of moron, or what, Alphin?*

Did he *want* someone to realize he had an inappropriate interest in one of his recruits? Standing there, all but drooling on her was not exactly being subtle. He was at least fifteen years her senior, and her damned CO to boot. If that wasn't enough to ice-over his desires, he didn't know what was.

Leigh walked over to where Seb was lining up the last

two recruits.

"I'll take the group down to the physical training room for the next session."

Seb nodded. "See you down there in a few."

Leigh made an announcement over the general chatter and within a few moments, Lawler and he had the recruits headed down several levels so they could start the day's physical tests. He and the other instructors needed to see what they were dealing with in terms of fitness levels before the recruits could move on to any kind of endurance challenges.

The rings he made these recruits jump through to earn their wings might seem extreme, but if a pilot became separated from their squadron, he wanted to be sure that person could last in the vast, mind-altering emptiness of space, or pulse-pounding fear of being behind enemy lines until help arrived.

Bren was waiting for them down in the PT room, and once there, they got the recruits split up into separate groups; some would do a cardio test, some a strength test, while others would be tested in basic hand-to-hand combat, with each group rotating so the recruits had a turn at all activities.

Leigh tried not to notice that Mia had been assigned to Bren for hand-to-hand combat, along with Steve-Frigging-Robinson. Seb had been right; they needed to wash that guy out of the program. Even now he was big-mouthing about his fight prowess back at Ackerly. The moron was really starting to get on his nerves. The basic moves learned at pre mil were only the tip of the iceberg when it came to serious combat. If Steve was too full of his own self-importance to realize that, he'd simply wash himself out faster.

He set the two other groups going on their tests, and then paced back and forth across the open space between the workout machines and the mats, where Bren had matched the recruits against one another. He didn't want to be interested in Mia's progress, but it seemed the rational parts of his mind had abandoned him. Eventually, as each contest wound down and the numbers of recruits left standing dwindled, he gave up on pretending he wasn't watching. A crowd of other recruits who'd already bombed out of their own tests had gathered around the mats to cheer on their favorites, so Leigh took himself over to stand next to Seb and Lawler.

There were three recruits left: Mia, Robinson, and the woman Mia had befriended—apparently, her name was Kayla. Bren started up another round, and Leigh watched with rising interest as Mia and Kayla shared a look, seeming to arrive at some silent agreement. Mia and Kayla both moved at the same time, rounding out on either side of Robinson.

"Come on, ladies, who wants some of this first?" The guy held out his arms, lapping up the cheers from his buddies on the other side of the ring. While the idiot was distracted, both Mia and Kayla moved at the same time, quickly and efficiently taking Robinson down to the mat. At first, the guy laughed, but when Kayla managed to flip him and then Mia stuck her knee in his back, the snicker turned into a litany of curses.

Beside Leigh, Seb cracked up laughing, while Bren declared Robinson out of the match. The guy bitched about the girls cheating all the way across the mat, where he took his place next to his buddies and then eyed Bren with a baleful expression.

"Stevie-boy isn't so chummy now," Seb commented. "Those girls better watch out. If he's like every other humiliated jerk-wad I know, he'll be looking for payback."

Seb was right. Robinson would definitely want to return his mortification in kind. "We'll keep an eye on him, but hopefully he'll be gone before he gets the opportunity."

On the mat, Bren oversaw the final match between Mia and Kayla. Though Mia was a good head shorter than her opponent, she had speed on her side and appeared to have an innate ability to predict her adversary's movements. An instinct like that would serve her well as a fighter pilot, if she made it through the program. And from everything he'd seen so far today—no, everything he'd seen of Mia starting with her selfless bravery on board the shuttle—she had the makings of a star fighter pilot if she was willing to push herself harder than she ever had in her life.

And what does that mean for you, exactly? Hadn't he been telling himself that he needed to hope she dropped out or failed the program sooner rather than later, so he could avoid the exact mess he found himself in today? What would happen if she made it into the elite force, under his command twenty-four hours a day?

Disaster.

When it came to her, cracks had formed in his outer defenses. The only way to deal with this anomaly would be to have her transferred out from his command. But, how fair was it to change the course of her career simply to avoid having to deal with her and keep his desire in check?

Yeah, it made him an all-round jerk.

The match between Mia and Kayla lasted for a few long

minutes, until Mia found an opening and took control of the situation, baiting Kayla into leaving her right side open. Mia slipped in and had the other woman down in another second.

Bren walked onto the mat as Kayla moved back and the crowd around them cheered.

"Okay, okay. Recruit Wolfe, as a final challenge, you get to take on me. And if you win, you get a much-coveted free pass on any upcoming unit within the training program. If you don't think you can pass a subject, or fail a test, then the free pass will be your second chance to successfully complete the training program."

A surprised murmur rippled around the crowd. Yeah, a free pass was a great thing for a recruit to have up their sleeve, but Bren offered the same to every new bunch of potential recruits. And in all the years he and Bren had been training together, he could count on one hand the number of recruits who'd beaten her to win the prize.

Mia simply retreated to the edge of the mat, waiting for Bren to call the match into action. The two women circled each other, then Bren went in low, no doubt to test Mia's range and reflexes. Despite Bren's steadily increasing challenges and attacks Mia managed to hold up her own.

Just when it looked like Bren would get the upper hand, Mia changed her tactics and got Bren off-balance. Right away, Mia took advantage of the opportunity and knocked Bren to the mat, claiming victory.

The crowd cheered, and Mia grinned as she offered Bren a hand up.

As his XO stood, Bren caught his eye. Of course, now she expected him to take on Mia in one final challenge. Of the few recruits that had bested Bren over the years, none had been able to take him when he'd gone up against them.

Just one problem: he didn't want to face Mia across the mat. It didn't really run with his plan of distancing himself from her.

However, he couldn't refuse, because Bren and Seb would wonder what was up with him. Instead of coming up with an excuse and fleeing, he shrugged out of his uniform jacket and handed it off to Seb, then unfastened the top few catches of his shirt.

"Congratulations, Wolfe, you've got yourself a free pass." Bren motioned to him, and Leigh found his feet taking him out onto the mat. "Now, if you can take down Captain Alphin, you get a fast track into the final days of the program, whether you pass the initial days or not."

An awed murmur rippled through the crowd. Yeah, it was an honor worth killing over, but not a single person had managed to win it yet.

He came to a stop in front of Mia, who appeared to be sizing him up.

"So, Wolfe, are you willing to take on the CAFF?" Bren shouted the last few words as the other recruits started cheering.

Mia nodded, her expression determined. But Leigh caught something else in the flash of her velvet-brown eyes, something entirely uncertain. Maybe he wasn't the only one who thought this was a bad idea.

Bren called to begin and a hush fell over the crowd, but he and Mia just stood there and stared at each other. A long moment went by, and then another, while he tried to decide exactly how he was going to do this and hold on to his sanity.

Mia shifted into a defensive stance, obviously not willing to go on the attack with him as she had with the others. Well, he could accommodate her there. The sooner they got this over with, the better for their agreement to keep their distance.

Leigh lunged at her, but before he could get her in a grip, she'd slipped out of his way. Damn, she was quick and light. Yeah, he'd seen it while observing her engage the other opponents, but experiencing it firsthand was another matter. He got her back in his sights and tried a few other moves, once almost getting the better of her. But each time, she managed to elude him. It didn't help that the feel of her silken, damp skin under his hands or coming up against her body was damned distracting.

Mia got underneath his arm and almost unbalanced him.

Concentrate, moron, or she'll end up being the first recruit to beat your stupid ass down.

Leigh regained his footing and turned the tables on her. Just as he'd wanted, Mia started dropping. Except, instead of tripping because he'd bested her, she seemed to be tucking into the fall…and taking him with her.

He couldn't get his footing because he'd overcommitted to the attack and propelled himself off-balance. They both hit the mat, Mia half on top of him.

Goddamn.

She'd actually done it—managed to put him down. A head-clearing dose of shock burst through him, and before Mia could pin him and win the match, he rolled, putting her underneath him.

Her wrists were trapped against the mat beneath his hands, her breasts pressing into his chest with each uneven breath she took and her hips cradling his.

The feel of her beneath him started tearing up the steady rhythm of his pounding heart.

"I guess you won." Mia shifted beneath him only the slightest bit, but it was enough to make his blood rush. Sucking in an uneven breath, he fortified his self-control and pushed to his feet, making sure he kept his movements efficient and calm as if it were no big deal. Every muscle in his body burning and tight, he sent Bren a nod, indicating she should move the recruits on to the next task, and then walked away from where Mia stood getting congratulated by her fellow trainees.

At the edge of the mat, Seb held out his jacket and shot him a questioning look. Leigh shook his head and brushed by his friend, not in the mood for chitchat. Unfortunately, Seb didn't take the hint, moving from where he'd been standing with Lawler to follow him. His buddy stopped him with a tight grip on his shoulder.

"Hey, man. What gives? I know she almost beat you, but that's nothing to get all huffy over. If you ask me, it looks like Recruit Wolfe has some real potential, despite her size."

Leigh couldn't help himself. He stole a glance across to where Mia listened to Bren explaining the next activity.

"Yeah. I'd say she's got a good chance of making it to the end."

Seb shook his shoulder before letting him go. "Then what gives, buddy? You've been a bigger hard-ass than usual the past few days."

"It's classified."

"*Pft.*" Seb sent him an exasperated look but then seemed to realize he wasn't joking. "Shut up. Really?"

A small trickle of guilt crept through him for lying to his friend, even if it was only a small lie, and one that was necessary. Yes, the situation with the traitor weighed on him, but a lot of his bad mood definitely came back to Mia and his inability to ignore his attraction to her.

"Things are complicated, and I wish I could tell you about it, but I can't. So I'm going to need you to step up and have my back, even if you don't know what that's going to entail."

Seb's expression lost the amused edge he usually had. "Of course. You know you can count on me."

"Good. Now, I've got to go deal with some of that classified stuff I can't tell you about."

Seb stepped back and inclined his head to him. "We'll hold down the fort."

He clasped his hands behind his back as he strode toward the hatchway. He ordered himself not to look back at Mia, repeating the command in his mind like a mantra. However as he reached the doorway, his gaze crept around, finding where she stood to the back of the crowd, listening to the lieutenant give instructions. She glanced over her shoulder and when he caught her gaze, his stupid heart bumped against the inside of his chest like he was a damned teenager.

Cursing at himself, he left the PT room, focusing his mind on the bigger issue of a possible mole in his squadron. Solving that mystery seemed easier than facing the fact that for the first time since enlisting with the UEF, his emotions might be totally compromised.

Chapter Eight

The dinner crowd had started trickling out of the mess-deck, some headed across the way to the common room, while others headed for the transit and likely, entertainments on commerce level.

Mia scraped the last bits of food off her plate and glanced up at Kayla sitting across from her, who'd managed to finish her meal in record time.

"You didn't have to wait for me." She set her utensils on the now-empty plate and added her cup to the pile.

Kayla shrugged as she stood. "I'm not in any hurry. Besides, there's safety in numbers. Steve looked pretty pissed about us taking him down earlier today. Not that I'm scared of the jerk-wad rich boy, but it might be better if we stick together for the time being to make sure he doesn't try to corner either of us."

Nope, Steve certainly hadn't been happy about Kayla and her beating him in hand-to-hand combat. Luckily, between classes for the remainder of the day and evening messdeck, they'd been able to avoid him. But it was hard not to notice the death glares he aimed in their direction whenever he got the chance.

Some of the other recruits had been talking about a get-together Steve and his buddies were having in charlie-two dorm. As much as the idea of winding down and getting to know the other recruits tempted her, she wouldn't be going anywhere near Steve voluntarily. Plus, when she'd told him earlier in the day that she planned on studying tonight, she hadn't been bluffing. They might have two weeks before that exam, but the sooner she could get those schematics memorized, the better.

She grabbed a bottle of juice and an energy bar on the way out of messdeck; she'd need it later when her overworked brain started sucking the life right out of her.

"I heard earlier today that the best place to study is in the media room," Kayla commented as they made it out into the passageway.

"Good. It'll probably be better than the dorms." While she and Kayla were down the hall from charlie-two dorm in bravo-one, there would probably still be noise from the party, plus other recruits hanging out in bravo-one who wouldn't be interested in studying.

They made a stop by the dorms to get their datapads and then headed for the media room. Inside the large space it was mostly quiet, like an old-fashioned library. There were a few people scattered around, either watching newsfeeds on low volume or with headphones, while others read or were having subdued conversations. An immediate sense of relaxation washed over her, taking away the tension she'd been walking around with since leaving Ophelei Academy a month ago to make the journey to the *Valiant Knox*.

"Now this is more like it," she murmured as they headed for a couple of short couches arranged on either side of a low table.

Kayla shot her a grin as they each took a couch. "You are *such* a nerd."

Yeah, she would totally own that. "Tell me about it. So explain how some computer psyche-eval assigned me to this fighter-pilot program?"

"Must have been a system failure." Kayla's grin widened. "Seriously though, you took down Lieutenant Brenner, so obviously you're not lacking in the appropriate skills."

"Only out of necessity." She looked down, tapping her datapad to life. "I've always been so much smaller than everyone else, and I know I look like a sixteen-year-old. I took extra combat classes back at the academy because I wanted to make sure I could look after myself."

"Then we have that in common, at least. Although I took extra combat classes just to make sure if people pissed me off, I could kick their asses. People like Steve."

Mia gave a short, distracted laugh as she searched for the file she needed, but then frowned when it opened. The schematics were all jumbled, and information seemed to be missing. She spent a few moments trying to sort it out then swore under her breath.

"I think my file is corrupted. I'm going to head back up to the ready room and see if I can download it again off the master datapad."

"No problem. I'll be waiting here." Kayla didn't look up from her own datapad.

She pushed to her feet with a low sigh, tiredness catching up to her. A cynical smile tugged at her lips for a brief moment. If she was tired now, just how exhausted would she be once they started the real training? She forced the thoughts from her mind as she made her way to squadron level. There was no use worrying what kind of physical toll the program would take on her; either she'd get through it or she wouldn't. It was as simple as that.

Except, the niggling question of what she'd do if she did wash out of the program stuck into the back of her thoughts like a burr and refused to dislodge, no matter how hard she tried to banish it. She didn't want to end up on the ground, particularly if it meant fighting on the front lines, which was what happened to most soldiers who failed fighter-pilot training.

Since she'd arrived on the *Knox*, she'd started getting the idea that she'd be satisfied living and serving on the battleship. On the heels of that vague sense of belonging, she chastised herself, because there was every chance those mushy feelings had something to do with a certain CO she shouldn't be thinking about in anything other than the most professional, platonic terms.

At this time of evening, squadron level was all but deserted, many of the rooms and less-used corridors powered down to auxiliary lighting. There wasn't the constant chatter and low din of people going about their duties, only the hum and buzz of the *Knox's* systems working in the background.

She took one wrong turn before finding the ready room they'd been in this morning, everything looking a little different in the half-light and without other crew members milling around.

As she stepped into the darkened room, she swiped her hand over the sensors, flooding the room with yellow-white light. She blinked as she moved forward, her eyes taking a moment to adjust to the brightness.

A figure loomed up in front of her, and she took half a step back as surprise jolted her system.

"Sorry, I didn't realize anyone else—" Her words cut off on an anxious half breath. Something wasn't right. The man wasn't wearing a UEF uniform, but dark pants and a black sweatshirt with the hood pulled up.

He lunged at her, and she tried to sidestep, but he clipped her shoulder, putting her off-balance and knocking her datapad out of her hand to smash on the floor. By the time she jerked out of his reach and regained her stability, he'd put himself between her and the door.

Though she couldn't see his features with the hood of his sweatshirt pulled so far down, leaving shadows to obscure half of his face, something about his body language made it seem as if he knew her, because he hesitated.

She held up her hands in a peaceful gesture. "Look, technically neither of us are probably supposed to be up here. I'll pretend I didn't see you, if you return the favor."

He didn't say anything, but took a slow step toward her. Something in his demeanor sent cold rippling under her skin and warning alarms in her head telling her she needed to get out of here *now*.

"Okay, I'll take that as a yes." Her voice came out slightly uneven as she resisted the urge to retreat. Instead, she took half a step forward, angling toward the exit.

The man lunged again, and this time she wasn't quick enough. He grabbed her arm, stopping her from sprinting for the door. With a vise grip on her elbow, he clamped his other hand onto the back of her neck and twisted until her arm was bent at a painful angle behind her.

She clenched her jaw against crying out, her breath cutting in and out too shallow, making her dizzy.

"I-I s-swear I won't t-tell anyone I saw you." Her words were choppy to the point of incoherent, and her captor made no indication that he'd either understood her or cared. He swung her around and she sucked in a deeper breath to ask him what he planned on doing with her. Before she could get the words out, he loosened his grip on her arm, but used the hold on her neck to smash her face-first into the corner of a nearby desk.

Pain exploded through her head, but not enough to put her out. In that second, as everything swam and agony pulsed through her skull, *God* did she wish she had blacked out. Maybe her survival instincts kept her conscious, because she knew if she passed out, she probably wouldn't wake up again.

Working on the instinct she'd honed through long hours of combat training, she twisted out of his grip, but lost her balance because of the way her brain was spinning from the impact with the desk. Still, she was free, and she scrambled toward the door. Glancing back, she saw the man hadn't come after her, but had pulled a gun. She froze using a nearby chair to keep herself upright while her head throbbed.

Oh God, he wasn't going to let her leave here alive.

Leigh stepped out of the transit on squadron level: his last refuge. Yep, he had totally been avoiding everyone—particularly Seb—since he'd fled the PT room earlier today, telling himself that he needed to start investigating the possible mole.

He'd spent a few hours in his office reviewing each member of his squadron, until his churning thoughts and a damned traitorous mind distracting him with Mia had nearly sent him on a long spacewalk with a short oxygen supply. He'd hit the gym, but Bren had come looking for him, so he'd headed back to his apartment. Except who had he seen lurking outside his door before he'd even stepped off the transit? Seb. Sure, the guy had been doing a bad job of hiding the prohibited bottle of whiskey he was holding, but even the temptation of taking the edge off his frustrations with some smooth liquor hadn't been able to change his mind about the conversation that would surely come with it.

So as a last resort, he'd come up to squadron level, intending to go over the notes for tomorrow's class, even though he'd done it fifty times already and knew the planned curriculum for the day inside and out.

As he turned down the passageway to the ready room, he frowned at the wide shaft of light breaking up the shadows of the corridor under auxiliary lighting. Before he stepped through the hatchway, his gaze landed on a datapad on the floor, the screen cracked and the outer casing broken. *What the*— He reached the hatchway, finding Mia with her back to him. Annoyance washed through him, because she shouldn't have been up here at this time of night, and he'd escaped here specifically to get away from everyone. He pulled to a stop when he saw the second figure in the room a few short steps away with a gun pointed at her chest.

A bolt of shock zapped through him. He dove forward on instinct alone, the sharp sound as the electromagnetic gun fired echoing through the room. He hit Mia and they went down, sliding into the row of desks. The shooter let off a few more rounds in their direction, and he dragged one of the desks in front of them to provide cover. A burning-chemical smell hit him as the outer side of the polymer-resin on the desks melted under the energy pulse.

But the shooter didn't seem as interested in killing them as he did in escaping. Leigh watched, fury lighting through him as the guy ran from the room, keeping him pinned down with a few wildly aimed shots. He waited a beat, then pushed to his feet and sprinted out into the corridor after him.

There was only one place the shooter would be headed—the transit-porter. When he came around the final corner, he saw the man slipping into the transit, turning to punch at the screen controls. The shooter saw him and brought the gun up again. Leigh swore and ducked back behind the corner as energy pulses pinged into the bulkheads.

After a second, he risked a peek around the corner to see the transit doors close. Jogging up to the door, he watched the display as the transit went down a level. He hit up his comm, getting an ensign on the ship-wide emergency line.

"This is Captain Leigh Alphin reporting condition code alpha-three. Gunfire on FP squadron level—I repeat, gunfire on level foxtrot-papa. I need the transit locked down and a MP unit on standby to apprehend the shooter."

The ensign confirmed, but even as he did, the transit had stopped and let the shooter out somewhere on port side of the level below him. He swore under his breath and put in another comm call to make sure the ensign had noted the transit stop and to get someone tracking the shooter straight-away. On a ship like this, there was no way that person would escape. Dark satisfaction rolled through him, since there was a very good chance he was about to find out who the traitor was in the FP squadron.

Now, for his other immediate problem. Mia needed to answer a few questions about what the heck she was doing up here at this time of night. He backtracked to the ready room, but when he walked in, he didn't see her right away, and for half a second, thought she'd also somehow escaped while he'd been distracted. But then he spotted a pair of boots from behind the clutter of desks and chairs where he'd taken cover.

His heart took a free fall as he realized she hadn't moved from when he'd tackled her to the floor.

"Mia?" Even as he shoved a desk out of the way and dropped down on his knees next to her, he saw the small puddle of blood that had formed beneath her.

His throat closed over, cutting off his breath. With an unsteady hand, he reached down and pressed his fingers into her neck. Her skin was warm, and a steady pulse registered under his fingertips. An exhale of relief burst out of his chest, releasing the rigidity that had set into his muscles when he'd thought the worst. She'd been hit in the left shoulder and had a gash above her right eyebrow.

He tapped his comm, putting him through to the same ensign he'd talked to a moment ago.

"This is Captain Alphin again. I need a medico response team to ready room one-four on squadron level, condition code bravo-orange."

"Yes, sir, right away." The ensign ended the comm after the clipped answer, and Leigh turned back to Mia.

The pool of blood beneath her had spread, and he swore under his breath. He sat back and pulled off the tank top he wore underneath his shirt. After quickly shrugging back into the shirt, he wadded up the tank top and pressed the material against the shoulder wound, trying to move her as little as possible in case of spinal injury.

The seconds dragged while the silence pressed in on him.

"Damn it, Mia, what the hell happened?" he muttered to distract himself from the seconds ticking by while he waited for help. Why had she been up here facing off with a masked shooter?

Her breath hitched and she shifted, derailing his thoughts. With one hand keeping his tank top against the wound, he set his other palm on her opposite shoulder to hold her in place. She seemed to be coming around, her face tensing into a grimace before her eyelids flickered.

"Mia, just stay still until the medics get here to assess you."

"Leigh?" She brought a hand up to press into her forehead, her eyes staying closed. Already, a purple bruise had started creeping from the edges of the gash along her hairline to darken the skin around her right eye and brow.

"Yeah, I'm here, Mia. I've got you." The words didn't exactly come out steady, and he swallowed down the tension in his throat.

Her grimace deepened and she shifted slightly beneath his hold. "Oh God, it hurts."

"I know it does, but I need you to stay as still as possible until the medics are here." Even as he said the words, he could hear footsteps from out in the passageway.

"Captain Alphin?" someone called out.

"In here," he threw over his shoulder. The *only room with the lights on, guys*. He would have thought their position would be obvious. A second later, a male nurse and sub-doctor rushed in, followed closely by Dr. Sacha Dalton.

"What happened?" Sacha shot at him as she dropped her emergency kit to the deck and got down on her knees on Mia's other side.

"She's been hit, high left shoulder. Not sure how the head injury was sustained." He hoped he hadn't done it to her when he'd pushed her down. He sat back as Sacha leaned forward and took over where he'd been pressing the now-bloody garment to Mia's chest.

The nurse handed him a cloth, and he distractedly wiped at the blood on his hands as he watched Sacha examine Mia and ask her a couple of questions.

Movement in the doorway of the ready room caught his attention and he glanced up to see Bren and Seb stepping into the room.

He pushed to his feet and tried to pretend he hadn't caught the slightly panicked look Mia had cast him. And then he had to clamp down on the urge to get back down on his knees and reassure her that everything would be okay. If he started acting like he had a right to comfort her, like he *needed* to comfort her, the disaster he'd been trying to avoid would come crashing down on them. It was far from his place to be the one offering her any kind of reassurance, no matter what familiarity had developed between them.

"What the hell happened?" Seb demanded as Leigh walked over to join his subordinate officers.

He shook his head to indicate they couldn't talk about it here and motioned for them to follow him. He stepped out into the passageway, well out of earshot from Sacha and her two attendants.

"I came up here to check the notes for tomorrow's class. When I got to the ready room, I found Mia facing off with some guy holding a gun. He took a couple of wild shots at us as he went for the door. She was hit. I chased him down to the transit, but I didn't get a good look at him, and he wasn't wearing a uniform."

He clenched his fists, belatedly realizing he'd slipped and said *Mia* instead of Recruit Wolfe. But neither Seb nor Bren seemed to notice.

"Do you think it was the squadron traitor Yang warned us about yesterday?" Bren's question effectively cut off the dark turn his mind had sucked him into.

"What other explanation could there be?"

"Wait just a second, did you say *traitor*? In FP squadron? That's impossible." Seb abruptly closed his mouth as the medics came past with Mia on a stretcher.

"I'll fill you in later," he replied as he half turned and cast a look over Mia. She had her eyes closed, and Sacha had wrapped a bandage around her shoulder and upper chest.

As the nurse and sub-doctor maneuvered the stretcher out of the ready room, Sacha stopped next to them.

"She's got a nasty gash on her head and the shoulder wound from the shooting, obviously. It looks worse than it is. The shoulder wound is superficial. We can repair that easily with a micro-laser. I'm going to admit her to med level over-night to monitor her concussion. I'll do a head scan just to be sure, but I don't think it's anything more serious. She should be fine for discharge around lunchtime tomorrow."

"What will this mean for her training?" Bren asked.

Sacha shrugged one shoulder. "Depends on your dictates, I suppose. I would recommend she abstain from any physical activity for forty-eight hours after discharge and then light activities for another seventy-two hours after that, keeping an eye out for any headaches or dizziness. If that means she's going to miss anything important to the agenda, then it's up to you whether you give her a medical exemption or simply cut her from the program."

Relief jolted through his system, clashing right into a stream of disappointment. This was it. He had a legitimate reason to decide right now that Mia couldn't continue any further with the program, and his issues with her would be solved. Except then he'd have to live with the guilt of taking advantage of an already bad situation she'd been thrown into.

"Thanks, Sacha. I'll contact you in the morning for an update." He sent her a respectful nod, which she returned as she left.

Leigh crossed his arms and turned back to Seb and Bren. This wasn't the first time they'd had to make a decision about an injured recruit over the years. But none of them had ever presented such a multilayered complication for him.

If this was any other recruit, one he had no knowledge of outside of the classroom, where would his decision fall? Because to be fair to Mia, he had to make the right decision for the right reasons, even if it meant leaving temptation in his path.

Chapter Nine

Mia settled against the pillows as the nurse ducked out of the room, leaving her alone at last. Not long after bringing her up to med level, Dr. Dalton had given her some painkillers, so at least her face, head, and shoulder didn't hurt as much any longer. But it hadn't helped the sleepy fatigue dragging at her. Unfortunately, she'd had to stay awake as a sub-doctor used a micro-laser to repair her shoulder and then positioned her for a head scan.

Next there'd been a visit from a pair of military police, one stern-looking female officer and her bored-looking male counterpart, who'd questioned her about being on squadron level at that time of night and the man who'd attacked her. The questioning had brought on a headache, her answers increasingly jumbled, while the female officer seemed to become impatient, as though they needed something from her. Whatever it was, she didn't have it to give. In fact, she'd been able to offer them very little. All she'd known for sure was her attacker had been male. Any other features or clues to his identity had been hidden beneath the dark clothes and hoodie he'd used to obscure his identity.

Dr. Dalton had eventually returned and shooed the officers away, then had a nurse come in to check her vitals. All she wanted to do was sleep away her aching head and hope she felt better in the morning. She didn't want to consider what this would mean for her spot in the FP program, though the thought had surfaced and refused to go away.

She half turned on her side, settling into her pillow as she dropped into a doze. But before she could sink into a deep slumber, she sensed someone nearby, jolting her from sleep.

She blinked open her eyes to find Leigh sitting next to her bed, his elbows braced against the edge of the gurney and chin resting against his hands. The sight of him sitting there made her heart skip a beat. And that was saying something, considering she was half doped-out on painkillers and swimming in exhaustion.

"Sorry. I thought you were asleep." The nearby lamp cast shadows across his intense expression.

She shifted so she could look at him without keeping her head on an uncomfortable angle. "Not quite. What are you doing here?"

A cynical smile flashed over his lips. "Can't the CAFF check in on an injured recruit?"

"If that's all this is...?" Regret that she'd questioned him pushed against the warm-and-fuzzies the painkillers had given her. The drugs had also apparently loosened her tongue, because surely she wouldn't have said such a thing if she'd been in her right mind.

He shoved a hand through his hair, his blue gaze appearing darker in the dim light. "I needed to know what happened. Why you were in that ready room and how you got injured."

She nodded, the action making her head throb. Even though she'd already been through this with the military police, she owed Leigh an explanation for different reasons. She took him through the events, from the media room until she stumbled on the masked man. "The last thing I remember is him smashing me face-first into a desk and then pointing a gun at me."

Leigh winced. "So he's responsible for your head injury. I'd thought that I—"

He glanced away from her, gaze troubled as he pressed a hand against his mouth.

"You thought that you what?" She reached over to take a sip of water from a cup the nurse had left nearby.

"Nothing, it doesn't matter." Leigh muttered a curse. "I chased him to the transit-porter, but he got away. They're trying to track him now."

She returned the cup to its spot on the trolley, feeling the weight of his regard. When she'd first opened her eyes after the attack and seen Leigh leaning over her, the relief that had flooded her body had been profound, every instinct telling her she was safe, that Leigh wouldn't let anything else happen to her.

She'd never been the sort of person who expected others to take care of her, which was partly why she'd taken those extra combat classes. So her weird desire to let Leigh protect her, along with the comfort and sense of safety he created within her, was totally foreign. Which was why it was probably a good thing this incident would see an end to her spot in the program. She couldn't deny any longer that she was feeling things for him that she shouldn't.

"This is the end for me, right? Dr. Dalton told me I couldn't do any thing physical for forty-eight hours after discharge and recommended light physical activity for another day after that. If I can't participate—"

"We haven't decided yet." He dropped his arm to rest on the edge of the mattress, his hand close to hers, but not touching. "We found your datapad in the ready room. It's smashed, but we still should be able to check the data files to backup your version of events. Ultimately, I could make the decision to cut you from the program, but in these situations, I always take the opinions of my team into account. Lieutenant Brenner, Sub-Lieutenant Rayne, and Sub-Officer Lawler will be deliberating on it tonight and giving me their thoughts tomorrow."

She nodded, though she didn't really think this "deliberation" made any difference—simply a stay of execution. She would miss vital training regimes in the coming days, so how could she possibly move forward with the program if she didn't work as hard as the other recruits?

"Well, thanks for coming to tell me." She dropped her gaze to the blankets, wishing she had the fortitude to tell him to leave, but not wanting to see him go until she had to, which was totally stupid. The stability of a permanent posting had to be all that mattered.

"I didn't come here because I wanted discuss your spot in the training program."

The intensity of his voice brought her gaze back up to him, like trying to resist the gravitational pull of a black hole.

"Then why did you come here?" She folded her arms across her middle, gripping the edge of the blanket as a small swell of apprehension rose within her.

"I need you to swear that what you told me about your attacker and why you were up in the ready room is the full truth, that you really don't know anything else. This is vitally important, not just to the squadron, but to the entire ship. If you know anything, if you're hiding something to protect yourself or anyone else—"

"I'm not." The words rushed out on a spurt of desperation that he would believe her.

Leigh's expression hardened. "This is the only chance you're going to get. If it comes out later that you held even the tiniest bit of information back, it will end badly. And I don't just mean getting sent off the *Valiant Knox*. I'm talking dismissal from the UEF and prison time."

This time, her heart pounded for an entirely different reason. Something else was going on here, more than just an intruder on squadron level waving a gun around.

"I've told you everything I know." Her voice came out low. "I wish I had more information. I want this guy found. You think I'm going to feel safe knowing that the person who shot me is walking around the ship?"

He sat forward, his gaze catching hers. "We will find him, Mia. Nothing else is going to happen to you. If you want, I can organize a MP escort for you until he's apprehended. But there's nowhere safer you can be than with the FP squad. Just don't go wandering off on your own again."

Her pulse skittered at his use of her name, at the way he stared at her with absolute certainty of the fact that she wasn't in danger as long as she was with the FP squadron. As long as she was with him.

She shook her head. "I don't need an MP escort. People are already going to be talking without adding a bodyguard to this ridiculous situation."

His lips kicked up for a second, in what she was coming to learn was the closest he ever got to smiling. "Yeah, if it was me, I wouldn't want a bodyguard either, but I thought I should offer."

"Thanks." The word came out a little awkwardly and then seemed to shift the tension between them. For a long moment there was silence, and she tugged at the edge of the blanket, trying to think of something to say.

"You should get some rest," he said at last, shifting forward to the edge of the seat.

"Wait." As he started to stand, she reached out and caught his forearm, stopping him from getting up. "If you all decide to cut me from the FP program, what's going to happen to me?"

She had to ask, even though she could already guess the answer.

Leigh's gaze became troubled before he glanced down. But by the time he looked back up, his expression was neutral and impassive.

"There'll be a position on the ground made available to you."

"On the battlefront?" Her worst fear, but if she ended up on the front lines, she would go knowing that she'd done everything in her power to avoid it. He didn't reply, and she took his silence as confirmation. "There's nothing else I can apply for, no other posting I could get?"

His gaze cut away from her. "Unlikely, here on the

Knox. You could take it up with ground command when you get there, talk with Commander Emmanuel or Colonel McAllister about other positions besides the front lines. But nothing has been decided yet, so don't start thinking the worst."

"I can't help it. I like to have a clear path going forward. And if that means I'm going to end up on the ground, then I want to be prepared for that eventuality. I'm not going to avoid thinking about it. I'm going to plan for every possible outcome."

"We have that in common. I'm always trying to plan things ten steps ahead." He looked back up at her, his expression a little less tense now. He reached up and covered her hand, where she still held his arm and hadn't even realized. She tried to pull out of his grasp, a small thread of chagrin slipping through her that she'd been sitting there holding on to him. But his hand tightened around hers, not letting her escape.

"Getting attacked like that, getting shot, it can mess with a person's head." His low words washed over her with an intensity that she wanted to ignore.

"You know this from experience?" She tried to make the words light, tried to inject some levity into the moment, because the way he stared at her, she could almost imagine he cared. More than a CO should for a recruit.

Switching grip on her hand, he reached up and flicked open the top catches of his shirt, tugging it aside to show a puckered scar, half the size of her fist, on his chest. "Third year after joining the squadron. We were providing air support to a unit of ground troops pinned down by a contingent of CSS twice their number. Some lucky bastard took my jet down with a surface-to-air launcher, and I ejected on the wrong side of the lines. A CS Soldier found me while I was still strapped into my parachute. I was literally tied down, couldn't do anything except lay there and watch him shoot me."

Though he was obviously fine and sitting here in front of her, the bottom had dropped out of her stomach. "What happened? How did you survive?"

"I was lucky that we'd just inducted a couple of new pilots, including this cowboy rookie, Sebastian Rayne. He landed behind enemy lines, against orders to rescue me, and got there just in time to take the CS Soldier out before he could finish me off. It wasn't the last time Seb disobeyed orders or saved my life, though I like to think I've returned the favor a time or two since."

"Sounds like you're lucky to have a friend like him." She'd never had anyone in her life that would risk themselves to save her. She could only guess what such loyalty and devotion would feel like.

"I'm lucky to have an entire squadron of people like Seb at my back, which is why the FP program is so tough. We need to know that those who join our ranks really want to be there and will do anything for their fellow pilots."

He lowered his head after he said those words and dragged a hand over his short hair as though something was weighing on him. She pressed her lips together over the urge to ask him if everything was okay. She had no right and knew he wouldn't tell her even if she did let the words spill out.

He blew out a long breath. "Anyway, if you need to talk, if it starts messing with your head, then I want you to know that you can talk to me. I'm here if you need me."

Maybe if he hadn't been holding her hand so tightly, she could have told herself that it was no big deal, and he would offer the same to any of the recruits or pilots in his squadron, because that's what a good leader did.

"Get some rest, Mia, and I'll come by to check on you in the morning."

She nodded as he let go of her hand and slipped out of the room, her chest too tight to form any words.

Maybe she was just seeing what she wanted to see in believing he regarded her as more than just another recruit. Because no matter how hard she tried to fight it, she couldn't help seeing him as more than just her CO. She could see the man underneath, and he was starting to chip away at the protective defenses around her emotions.

Leigh stood watching the double-shot espresso coffee trickling into his mug. There were only a handful of other extra-early risers on messdeck at this time of morning, and he wouldn't have been down here himself except after a restless night, he'd finally given up on the idea of getting any sleep.

Every time he'd closed his eyes, the vision of Mia lying bloody on the floor bombarded his mind. He couldn't work out why the image had imprinted itself on his brain and refused to budge. So instead, he stewed over who in his squadron could be the traitor and what it would mean for him and the rest of the *Knox's* crew if the UEF removed Yang from his post.

He dragged a hand down his face, whiskers he hadn't

bothered shaving off abrading his palm. His eyelids felt like they had sandbags sitting on them. He was used to shift work, so the tiredness didn't bother him as much as the multiple stress factors dragging on his shoulders.

The shooter hadn't been found yet. The MPs reported that no one had gotten off the transit after it had left squadron level. The only explanation had been that somehow the man had gotten off between stops, and he couldn't imagine how the guy had managed that without help.

Stanton, the Command Intelligence guy, had put in a request with Yang for deep background checks on all of the pilots in his squadron. He understood the need for a thorough investigation, and the notion had also crossed his mind. Yet he didn't want someone like Stanton running the checks, someone who didn't know or care about the squad.

Yang said he could stall Stanton, but not stop him altogether. The investigation would go ahead eventually, but Leigh planned to find the traitor before then. His squad didn't deserve to have their privacy invaded by CI just because they had one rotten pilot in their rank. Of course, he'd only managed to add more work to his already full schedule, because he didn't trust anyone else to run the checks. Not that he had much beyond the most basic skills to use when it came to this sort of thing. But he'd push through and hopefully find some clue as to who the mole, or moles, might be.

The coffee finished dripping and he reached out to wrap a hand around the hot mug, enjoying the sting of the burn for a moment before grabbing it by the handle and taking a quick sip. The dark, bitter brew hit the back of his throat and started waking him up, as if his body had decided to perk up now that a caffeine hit was imminent. He turned around and almost ran into Commander Yang.

"Another early start Alpha?" Yang reached by him to set his own mug under the coffee spout. Yang's posture was tight, his expression tense. The guy was all but tapping his foot as the coffee started pouring out.

"Honestly? Couldn't sleep. What about you?"

Yang snatched a quick glance around the near-deserted messdeck. "I've been down in the brig for the last hour. One of Stanton's agents uncovered another CSS mole on board."

A surge of shock mixed with anticipation rushed through him and shifted everything into hyperawareness like the caffeine hit he'd been looking for moments ago.

"Is it the guy who attacked Recruit Wolfe?"

Yang shook his head. "*He* is a *she*. Kerrin Hershel, one of the launch-deck maintenance crew."

"God*damn* it." Hearing a name was like taking a jab in the guts. He didn't know Kerrin all that well, but he did know her, had worked alongside her on his jet a time or two. "I want to talk to her."

Yang shook his head and reached down to take the coffee out of the machine.

"Sorry, Alpha, we're trying to keep this contained for the time being. Something like this can cause a close-knit crew to turn on each other. With my command already under the microscope, the last thing we need is everyone on board this ship suspecting their friends and making un-founded accusations."

"I'm not going to tell anyone, sir, but I need to know if she can reveal the identity of the mole in my squadron."

"Believe me, it's on our list of questions, but so far, she's not talking." Yang rubbed the back of his neck, tension lines bracketing his eyes and mouth.

"Maybe you just need a new face in there. Someone she's worked with. If Stanton is the one leading the questioning, you're not going to get anywhere. The guy's an uptight douche."

Yang's lips quirked in a small smile. "I can't disagree with you."

"So give me five minutes with her. If she's not talking now, and still not talking when I leave, then you haven't lost anything. But if I can get her to spill even some tiny detail—"

"All right." Yang held up a hand to stop him. "Stanton is not going to be impressed about this."

He sent the commander a grin. "All the more reason to do it."

Yang sent him an unimpressed look, but he could see the amusement in the CO's gaze. "Come on then."

They left the messdeck and headed down two levels, and then to the far, narrow end of the *Knox*. The entire end of the ship had been designed to detach and reattach to other battleships for easy and foolproof transportation of high-risk prisoners, all without them ever needing to leave their cells.

Yang led him to one of the interview rooms, where Stanton stood outside, arms crossed and a seriously peeved expression on his face.

"You told Captain Alphin?" If Stanton could have knocked him down with a glare, he'd be flat on the deck by now.

"Yes, Stanton. He's one of my most trusted officers, and considering you told us there's probably a mole in the FP squadron, he has a right to know what's going on here."

"What's going on is that the CSS will get their wish and we'll end up destroying ourselves from the inside out if word gets out about Hershel."

"Alpha knows the cost. He won't tell anyone."

Yang sent him a nod, so he stepped past Stanton and entered the interview room. He didn't know what he'd been expecting, but shock cut through him at the sight of Kerrin slumped in a corner and chained to the wall, face bloodied and bruised. Even from here, he could tell she was unconscious. Had Stanton worked her over? *Sick bastard*. She might be the enemy, and she might have betrayed them, but no one deserved to be tortured.

He ducked his head back out of the hatchway. "Can I get a bottle of water and some cloths in here?"

"No." Stanton replied shortly.

Yang shot the agent a glare and stepped forward. "Why—"

He looked into the room, fury tightening his expression as he rounded back toward Stanton. "What the hell is this? I wasn't even gone for twenty minutes."

Stanton stared at him, cold and emotionless. "We weren't getting the answers we needed."

Yang threw a hand out in the direction of the interview room. "And what, torturing her did?"

"Yes, actually. I got far more out of her in the last five minutes than I did in the entire hour before that."

Yang took an angry step forward. "This is my ship, and I will not have people on board tortured, no matter who they are."

Stanton's expression took on an almost bored edge. "I might be on your ship, Yang, but I don't answer to you. I answer to Command Intelligence. And they've instructed me to use any means necessary to find every single CS Soldier hiding in the UEF ranks. Orders that came to CI from your superior officers, I might add."

"If we lower ourselves to their level, then what are we really fighting for?" Yang's voice came out slightly uneven over the words.

"Your judgment in this matter is quite obviously compromised. Isn't that why the UEF sent in Lieutenant Prescott?"

The anger already stewing over Stanton's treatment of Kerrin snapped Leigh into fury at the agent's taunt. He lunged, but Yang caught him and shoved him back.

He shrugged out of Yang's grip and took a step away, clenching his fists over the tight urge to smash Stanton square in the face. "You disrespect the commander like that again, and next time you'll be eating my gun."

"Sure I will." Stanton shot him a smile, as though the threat genuinely amused him. "No one else is to see the prisoner. A specialized CI shuttle will be here to take her for further questions in an hour."

"Take her where?" Yang demanded.

Stanton's grin widened. "That information is classified."

Yang's shoulders tightened, as if maybe he was thinking about laying the agent out himself. "We need to know if there are any other CSS on board this ship."

Stanton examined his hand, and Leigh caught sight of some blood spatter on the man's otherwise pristine sleeve. "Oh, you *need* to know, yet you disapprove of my methods."

He clenched his jaw over calling the agent about a dozen different names, all beginning or ending with the word *ass*. "Just tell us, does she know who the mole in the FP squadron is?"

Stanton stared at them for a long moment, an inscrutable expression on his face.

"No," he said at last. "She doesn't know if there is a CS Soldier in your squadron. In fact, she doesn't know a single other CSS mole. It seems they've been smart in the way they go about their infiltration, keeping all the traitors isolated and ignorant of one another. That way, if they get caught like Hershel has been, they've got nothing to tell."

Leigh cursed, rubbing the tight muscles in the back of his neck. "Then we're no closer to finding out the identity of the mole in the squadron, or the person who attacked Recruit Wolfe."

Stanton looked past them, toward the interview room, expression smacking of anticipation. "We have ways of getting certain details out of people, things they don't even know they're telling us."

"What's that supposed to mean?" The agent's expression gave him the creeps.

Yang shook his head. "I don't think we want to know."

Stanton returned his gaze to Yang. "You're right. You probably don't want to know. How about you take care of your issues, and I'll take care of mine?"

"That's all well and good, but it's when those issue run together we've got a problem." Yang backed up a step and turned away from Stanton. "Come on, Alpha, we're not going to get any more information here."

He shot the CI one last glare before catching up with Yang. "Sir, I don't want to tell you how to do your job, but—"

"I know." Yang strode stiffly along the passageway, his expression furious. "But he's right. I've got no power over what Stanton or CI do, even on board this ship. The best I can do is go up to my wardroom and make some calls. Even then, I'm not likely to get any answers before the CI shuttle arrives."

"This is turning into a damn mess," he muttered. If Leigh didn't find the squadron mole, and soon, there was no telling what else Stanton might do. The way things were going, people would start turning on each other, and rampant suspicion would blow the ship apart.

Chapter Ten

Mia tapped her fingers against the edge of the datapad while she waited for the routed connection to go through, which would give her access to the *Knox's* main systems.

Most people would have said accessing the primary systems from a datapad would have been impossible. But most people didn't want to be an aeronautical engineer. Most people wouldn't have studied the specs of the UEF fleet's battleships like she had. Of course, battleship specs weren't available to just anyone, and when she'd been studying for an assignment and accidentally come across a pirated version online and downloaded it, she hadn't exactly been on the right side of the law. And she may have taken her extra-credit classes on cybersecurity a little farther than was technically legal, because the challenge of getting in and out places had been the kind of thrill she couldn't resist.

And she definitely wasn't on the right side of the law

right now. But she'd woken up in the small hours of the morning, and after replaying the attack in her mind, plus the conversation with Leigh, she needed to find out why the shooter had seemingly disappeared, maybe find some way to track him herself.

Because the idea that the person who'd tried to kill her was walking around the ship had settled like a low hum of noise in the background, keeping a constant shadow of apprehension lurking in the corners of her mind.

So she'd gone out into the hallway and lurked by the nurse's station until she could snag a datapad. She felt a little sorry for whoever the device belonged to, because although she planned to wipe the evidence of her activities once she was done, she wasn't an expert hacker and might leave a traceable footprint if someone went looking hard enough.

The datapad gave a low chime, indicating the connection had gone through. It'd been a while since she'd studied the specs for this class of battleship, so it took her a little longer than necessary to access the security logs for the surveillance on squad level. She watched the recording of the shooter running down the passageway, followed by Leigh a moment later. Her breath caught as Leigh narrowly avoided getting shot. She accessed the shooter's transit route, then brought up the camera feed for the passageway where the assailant supposedly got out.

However, when the doors opened on the level below, the carriage was empty.

Frowning, she switched to the in-transit surveillance feed. It showed the shooter firing at Leigh before the doors slid closed. After that, the man kept his head angled down as he concealed the gun beneath his clothes. The pictured flickered and the man disappeared. *Gone*.

In one screen shot and then not in the next after the slight interference.

Since she didn't believe in magic, the only explanation would be that someone had tampered with the footage. Leaning forward, she accessed all the transit-porter logs. The shooter's transit hadn't stopped and it was impossible to get off midtrip.

The challenge of solving this mystery had energized her, chasing the last of the aching fog from her mind. She cross-checked other things, like maintenance logs, and had been at it for about an hour when she found a clue. Someone had messed with the transit ID numbers. Halfway through the trip, someone had reset the system and the security feed had then tracked a different car.

All she had to do was work out what ID the shooter's transit had changed to, and she'd find his actual destination.

With a low thrum of excitement buzzing through her, she set to work tracing IDs until she found the feed she needed. She watched footage of an empty transit, where the picture flickered and the shooter appeared, as if from thin air.

"Got you," she muttered, leaning closer to the screen and willing the bastard to look up. Unfortunately, he kept his head down until the doors opened on one of the ship's lowest utility levels. Once she'd watched the shooter disembark, she switched the feed to outside, in the passageway he would have stepped into, but all she found was static. Someone had killed the cameras.

"Damn it." She slapped the edge of the table the datapad was on and then slouched back against the pillows. Just when she'd thought she was going to discover the shooter's identity, or where he'd gone, she'd hit a wall. But at least she'd worked out how he'd eluded the MPs. Of course, this meant he'd had outside help, and whatever his reason for being in the ready room, there was obviously something much larger going on here.

Her mind dredged up rumors she'd heard before arriving on the *Valiant Knox*, rumors that the explosion on the Ilari base had been an inside job, that the CSS had infiltrated UEF ranks. She'd dismissed the chatter as exaggerated, or simple speculation, because the idea that the CSS could have so successfully gained access to the UEF was as ridiculous as it was terrifying. But what if the rumors hadn't been simple gossip? What if there'd been some truth to it? What if something similar was happening on board the *Knox*?

No. Surely people would know if that was happening. She was letting her imagination run away with her. Getting a position on the *Knox* was hard enough even as a recruit or enlisted personnel of the UEF, let alone for someone with intentions of sabotage or betrayal. There were processes in place to make sure such a thing didn't happen.

"Did someone else already bring you a new datapad?"

She glanced up at the familiar voice in the doorway, so wrapped up in her thoughts that she hadn't noticed Leigh walk into the room. "According to personnel records, a new one hadn't been assigned to you yet."

He walked over, another datapad in hand, probably the one that had been assigned for her use. She started to slide hers, with all its incriminating information displayed on it, toward herself, but Leigh got to her and closed a hand around it before she could shut the program.

"Where did you—" He tugged the datapad out of her

hands, expression hardening as he looked at the screen. "What the hell is this?"

"I can explain." She reached out for the device but he kept it out of her range.

"I don't think there's any possible sane reason you could give for accessing the ship's main systems. Or why you even know how to do that."

Her heart thrummed against the inside of her chest. "Please, before you do anything, just listen. I know how to do it because I wanted to be an aeronautical engineer and studying ship specs was kind of a hobby. And as for the reason I did it, I was trying to find the shooter. I was accessing security footage and the transit-porter logs to see if I could track him."

His tense expression hadn't shifted, his impassive CAFF mask firmly in place as he stared at her. For the first time since she'd met him, she suddenly understood the reputation that preceded him.

"You were trying to find the shooter," he repeated, sounding far from convinced. "A job you should be leaving up to the MPs."

She lowered her gaze, the exact amount of trouble she was now in pressing down on her. "I know. I'm sorry. It was impulsive and stupid, but I thought I could get in and check without anyone ever knowing. I needed to know who he was."

"Well I hope that reasoning is enough after you've left the *Knox* and the UEF, because there's no way in hell you'll ever serve again. You'll be lucky if you don't end up in a military prison."

He started to turn away and desperation clawed into her

chest. "But I found him."

Her words made him freeze, his gaze coming back around to clash with hers.

"You mean you can identify him?"

"No. Well, I don't know. I worked out that the transit ID system had been scrambled and he actually went down to one of the lower utility levels. He had to have outside help to trick the system so flawlessly that no one would notice. I almost missed it myself."

"How could you— Never mind." He sighed, glancing down at the datapad before looking back up at her. "Show me everything."

He walked over and handed the datapad back to her and sat on the edge of the mattress, his shoulder and hip brushing hers, since the gurney wasn't exactly wide.

Her anxiety wound down a notch now that he didn't seem ready to run off and report her to Command Yang right this second. That didn't mean he wouldn't, but maybe she could convince him not to reveal her security breach, and in return she would offer to quickly and quietly leave the *Knox*. The thought made her chest tighten, so she pushed it away and concentrated on the datapad, showing him how she'd found the transit IDs had been scrambled, confusing the security feed, and then playing the footage of the shooter leaving the transit on the utility level.

"And what about this footage?" Leigh asked as she showed him the static when she tried to access the images on that level. "Can you fix it or find some other camera?"

She shrugged one shoulder. "I don't know. This is where I got up to when you came in."

"Okay." He crossed one arm over his middle and

dragged the other hand over his jaw, expression tense with contemplation. "What else can you do with this thing?"

She cut him a wary sideways glance, not sure how far she should be implicating herself. But she'd already been caught; it probably couldn't get any worse from here no matter what she admitted.

"Pretty much anything. Once you're into the main systems, everything becomes available, from personnel rosters to the ship's navigation controls."

He shifted, spearing her with an intense look. This close, she could see the slightly darker rim around his gray-blue eyes. "That's dangerous power to have. And anyone can do this from any datapad?"

"No, not just anyone." She shook her head. "They'd have to either be a consummate hacker, or know the specs of the *Knox* down to the last detail."

He tucked his other arm over his chest so both were crossed. "And which of these options best describes you?"

"I told you. I wanted to be an aeronautical engineer. I studied ship specs. Not just the *Knox*, but others, too."

His brow lowered. "I can't decide if I'm worried that your illegal activities started well before you arrived on the *Knox*, or impressed about how thorough you've been."

"Consider yourself impressed, because I'm assuming from your reaction that no one else managed to work out how the shooter escaped."

He didn't reply. Instead he sent her a look that was almost exasperated. "Close the program and hand over the datapad."

She gave a tight nod, anxiety wrenching through her once more. Her thoughts spun, trying to come up with a way to convince him not to report this major infraction, but knowing there was nothing she could say to save herself. He didn't owe her anything and if he failed to report her activities and it was discovered later, he could also face losing his posting.

Once she'd exited the main systems and then wiped the evidence as best she could, she handed it over to him, shifting to the side a little so she could face him.

"I got it from the nurse's station."

One of his brows arched upward. "Are you kidding? I'm not putting this back. If anyone works out what you did and traces it back to this datapad, you'll get some poor doctor or nurse in trouble, and they'll probably still find you anyway."

A small spark of hope flamed to life in her chest. "So you're not going to report me?"

He set the new datapad on the table and then stood. "Right now? No. Tomorrow? I don't know. This is serious, Mia. I need to decide how to handle it."

"I could quit the FP program and leave, if it would make things easier. I'm injured anyway. I might as well call it. That way, it wouldn't be your problem. You can pretend like you never knew about it."

His jaw tightened. "I can't do that, and you know it. And you are not leaving this ship, not with potentially dangerous knowledge of how to access the *Knox's* main systems. If the enemy got their hands on you— Well, that's a scenario I don't even want to imagine."

His words sent a mild shock jolting through her. He was right. If she got captured by the enemy and they worked out what she knew, it was the kind of information that could bring down the ship. A few years younger and a lot more naive, she hadn't ever considered the larger implications of learning those ship specs; she'd just been feeding her thirst for knowledge and told herself she'd have an edge if she ever got the opportunity to apply for some kind of aeronautical engineering position.

"Okay, I won't go anywhere." Her voice came out a little uneven, and she swallowed down the tightness in her throat.

Leigh's gaze softened just a touch as he stared at her. "I'm not trying to scare you, Mia, I was just stating a fact. And nothing has been decided about your position in the FP program. I haven't talked to Bren or Seb yet. So there are several conversations that you and I need to have, but right now, I need to get to class."

She nodded and then winced when the sudden movement caused her headache to return.

Leigh reached out and touched gentle fingers to the side of her face, making her freeze and her lungs stall. His gaze roamed over her as he traced what she assumed was the outer edge of the bruise. She hadn't seen it herself, but the nurse who'd come to check on her earlier had said it was spectacular.

"You look like hell. Whoever that guy was, he sure did a number on you. Are you feeling any better?"

"Just a headache," she managed to force out through the tightness in her chest, almost sounding like herself. If the words were a bit strangled, hopefully he'd assume it was her sore head.

"And your shoulder?" His hand dropped to the edge of her gown. "Do you mind?"

She shook her head, pulse picking up as he pushed the material to the side, revealing the pink scar from where the micro-laser had repaired the internal damage, as well as the layers of muscle and skin.

"It looks good, but you'll want to be careful for a few weeks. When it happened to me, I would think it was fine and then something would make it pull and it'd ache for a day or two after."

"Thanks. I'll keep that in mind." Yeah, her voice definitely wasn't sounding all that composed anymore.

His fingers lightly skimmed along her collarbone as he returned the gown to rights, and she tensed against a shiver she could feel creeping up on her. His hand lingered on her shoulder for a moment before he stepped back again.

"I saw Dr. Dalton on my way in here. She's going to discharge you just before the end of forenoon watch. After that, I want you to head up to your dorm. Get some rest and don't go finding any more trouble."

"Okay," she muttered, only just managing to resist rolling her eyes.

"What was that, Recruit?" Though the words were formal, there was a definite light glint to his gaze. Was he actually teasing her?

"Sir, yes, sir." The reply came out sounding more like a question.

He gave a single nod, one side of his lips lifting in a small smile that made him look nothing short of adorable. Her stomach flipped over, and if she had been alone, she would have definitely slapped herself. Had she really just thought that the legendary, hard-assed Captain Alphin was adorable? That concussion must have really scrambled her brain.

"Very good. I'll be down to check on you later, so I better find you exactly where you're meant to be."

Before she could confirm that she would do as he'd said, he spun on his heel and strode out of the room. Once she was alone, she blew out a long, uneven breath and sank back against the pillows.

Being around that man was like stepping onto a roller-coaster. He could go from intimidating to charming in the space of a heartbeat. Her entire future with the UEF was in his hands. But for some reason, that notion didn't terrify her as much as it should have. Maybe that was stupid, having this inexplicable, blind trust of a man she hardly knew, feeling that for some reason, he would do everything in his power to protect her. He didn't owe her that; he didn't owe her anything. Right now, the only thing she could bring him was that trouble he'd told her to stay out of.

But something had sparked between them, and no matter how many times she told herself it was one-sided or it meant nothing or it was all in her imagination, the more time she spent with him, the more she was starting to think that she wasn't the only one fighting whatever these feelings were.

Chapter Eleven

The dorms were quiet and deserted as Leigh walked along the passageway, not that he expected anything different in the middle of the afternoon when all the recruits were off at their training session. But he expected to find at least one person here. And she better not be doing anything that even remotely looked like trouble, or he'd be busting her down to the ground before she could even think about flashing those dark eyes at him.

Accessing the ship's main systems. *Christ.* If he didn't already know she was too brave and smart for her own good, he would have thought she was a complete moron, pulling a stunt like that.

He should have gone right up to the command center to report her, because what she'd done had been nothing short of a major security breach. But then he'd started thinking. Yang had already said that Stanton kept more information to himself than he revealed, and though Leigh had checked in again on the progress to find the shooter, Yang had told him that they still weren't any closer to finding how the shooter had disappeared. Which either meant Stanton knew and didn't want to share, or he and Mia now had information that no one else did.

His gut told him not to trust Stanton. With Mia and her skills, he had a way to do the background checks on his pilots without needing Stanton and could run his own investigation into the shooter and the identity of the mole in his squadron, which obviously had to be connected.

Though the idea had occurred to him while Mia showed him what she'd found, his sense of loyalty, the part of him that had always been a good soldier and trusted the system, balked at doing something so blatantly outside of the rules he'd lived his entire adult life by.

As he stopped in front of the hatchway to Mia's dorm room, the low drift of music came through the door. He knocked to announce his presence, but then swiped a hand over the door control after only waiting a moment.

"Don't get up," he called as he ducked around the door. But Mia was already halfway across the room. She shot him a rueful smile, then switched directions and went to turn down the music.

Instead of the usual recruit uniform, she had on a pair of dark leggings and a maroon and white Ophelei Academy T-shirt. Her feet were bare and her golden hair was loose around her shoulders, apart from a few shorter strands she'd pinned up in the front, keeping them out of her face. She looked relaxed, casual, and too damn tempting.

He cleared his throat, forcing his wayward thoughts to get back on track.

"I hope I wasn't interrupting anything." He stopped in the middle of the room, casting a glance over the six bunks, all of them neat except one on the far end left rumpled, with a datapad sitting in the middle.

"I was actually reading a book. Like, a book I picked myself, not one I'm required to read for classes. I can't remember the last time I did that." She walked back over to her bed and plonked herself down on it.

With no other option, he followed her over and sat on the opposite bed, facing her. "Is it the manual specs of an armored class transport or something?"

Surprise flashed across her face before she gave a short laugh. "No. It's a crime fiction."

He clenched his jaw over the urge to grin back at her, intrigued by a slight tinge of color in her cheeks.

"And how are you feeling now?" he asked to distract himself from how easy it was sitting here exchanging light banter with her.

She tucked back a strand of hair. "Fine. The headache is gone and my shoulder only has a slight ache, like a pulled muscle or something."

He clasped his hand between his knees. "That's good, because I've talked to Bren, Seb, and Lawler. As long as you're feeling confident to continue, we'd like you to keep your place in the program. It will mean some extra work to make up the session you missed today, but I get the feeling that won't be a problem for you."

"I'll handle it." She looked genuinely surprised by his words. Maybe because after he'd caught her this morning, she'd been sure he was going to kick her out. And by all rights he should have. If it weren't for the fact that he had a mole in his team, he would have definitely given her marching orders.

But the fact was, if not for the traitor, she wouldn't have been attacked and wouldn't have had a reason to access the *Knox's* systems. Or so he chose to believe. With those sorts of skills, some people would have done it just because they could, but he didn't think Mia was that type of person. She'd had a genuine reason to take such a huge risk and hadn't done anything other than try to find clues about the shooter.

"And about what you saw me do this morning?" she asked, her features tightening with wariness.

He shifted forward, his shoulders tensing. This was where things got complicated, and he was about to take a huge risk that could end badly for both of them. But he figured Mia had already thrown herself into the deep end of a treacherous risk and he might as well take advantage of it. This way, he could try to protect her if they were found out. He didn't want to examine exactly why he felt the need to make her his responsibility. Yeah, he couldn't ignore how intelligent and daring—and if he were being completely honest—how goddamn sexy she was, but he'd never done anything in his life for any other reason than duty. And, he assured himself, that was what this also came down to—his obligations. She'd almost been killed under his watch. He had to find the traitor and protect his people, even if that meant going outside the regulations to achieve his ends.

"I've put a lot of thought into what you did," he started, choosing his words carefully. "And the way I see it, you have nothing left to lose. So the classified information I'm about to tell you cannot be repeated; otherwise I will see you buried."

Her eyes widened a touch, and his conscience kicked him with a vicious jolt of guilt at threatening and possibly scaring her. But this was even more serious than the fact that she'd accessed the ship's primary systems. This could get them both killed or dishonorably discharged and dumped in prison.

"I've been given reason to believe there's a CSS mole in the fighter-pilot squadron."

"So it's true? The CSS have infiltrated UEF ranks? I heard rumors, but I didn't believe—"

"It's true." A small swell of dismay washed through him that apparently gossip about CSS moles had spread so far already. No wonder the UEF were so hot and bothered about reviewing Yang's command. "There could be as many as a dozen on the ship right now. There are people working to find them, but my only concern is for my squad."

She crossed her arms, expression somber. "Why are you telling me this?"

"Instead of reporting what you did this morning, I want you to use your skills to help me find the mole in my squad or identify the shooter, since I'm pretty sure they're going to turn out to be the same person."

She took a deep breath, seeming to process what was no doubt an unexpected request. "This is asking a lot. I mean, accessing the systems one time for an hour was a risk I was willing to take on the gamble I wouldn't get caught. But this will require me to spend hours searching all kinds of data and accessing all kinds of stuff, going in and out over multiple sessions. It will increase the risk of getting caught by an infinite amount."

"I know. I thought it all through before I came here,

which is why I want you to use my datapad. That way, if someone does pick up the activity, it'll come back to me."

A cynical half smile tilted her lips up. "And will anyone believe that you had the necessary skills to do something like this?"

He shrugged. "I'm sure they won't. But they won't ask, and I won't tell. There's a chance I'd be able to use my standing and years of service to get out of it lightly, whereas you would take the complete fall. But that's only if we get caught. Obviously my preference is that we don't. And there's one other thing."

"One other thing *besides* the questionable activities you're already recruiting me for?"

He ignored that bit of sarcasm, even if it had been meant in good humor. "Can you get around the *Knox's* security system to say, break into someone's apartment without leaving a trace?"

"Of course." She didn't hesitate in her reply, as though it should have been obvious she could do that as well. "Don't tell me the CAFF is considering a little B and E?"

"CI have a mole in custody, but she's not talking, or the agent in charge is keeping us in the dark. Either way, I want to get into the traitor's apartment to see if I can find any information, particularly the identity of the mole in my squadron."

She pushed her hair back, expression serious, but contemplative. "And what if I don't agree?"

"Truthfully? I don't know. Not agreeing isn't really an option."

"I see." She shifted, angling herself away from him as she glanced off across the room.

The fact that he wasn't really giving her a choice made him feel like a bastard, but this was bigger than either of them.

Voices in the corridor caught his attention, and he glanced over his shoulder at the door. "Are you expecting company?"

"Oh yeah," she said, as though she'd only just remembered. "Kayla said she'd come and check on me in between sessions."

"Great," he muttered, pushing to his feet. He glanced around the room, but already knew what his only option was.

"What are you doing?" she asked as he walked by her bed.

"Hiding."

She stood, incredulity crossing her features. "Are you serious? Why?"

He went over to the cupboard and pulled open the door. Only just enough room to squeeze himself in. He turned to look at her, finding that she'd come over and stopped only a step behind him.

"Besides the fact that no one can know we're working together on uncovering the traitor, how do you think it's going to look when your friend walks in and finds you alone in your dorm room with your CO?"

"Oh." That hint of color was back on her cheeks again. "Of course. That would look bad."

"So let me hide already." He gently pushed her back and shut himself in the cupboard just as the door across the room opened.

"Hey, Mia." Kayla's cheery voice was muffled by the closed door. "How is all that rest going?"

"Boring," Mia responded, sounding like she'd moved away from the cupboard. "How have the sessions been? Have I missed anything interesting?"

"Two washouts, Steve being his usual jerk-self, and Captain Alphin being in a foul mood."

Foul mood? Yeah, he'd been a little distracted and short-tempered because he'd been trying to work out what to do about Mia, but he'd been far from a foul mood. If those recruits thought that was him on a bad day, they hadn't seen anything yet.

"Really?" Mia had responded, her voice rising a notch. "Well, maybe he had a good reason."

He could have almost rolled his eyes. Teaming up with Mia to find the traitor wasn't going to get him very far if the girl didn't learn how to play it cool.

"Or maybe he's just an uptight son of a bitch," Kayla replied breezily. "Either way, he made Lewis cry this morning."

Lewis had *cried*? Well, the guy had failed to grasp the most basic concept in engine components, what did he expect?

"You're kidding," Mia's voice was heavy with disbelief. "Like actually full-on cried?"

"Well he wasn't sobbing like a baby, if that's what you mean," Kayla replied, a hint of amusement in her tone. "But I saw a few tears when he thought no one was looking. He was one of the washouts. He just quit after the last session with Lieutenant Brenner. Who, by the way, is almost as much of a hard-ass as the CAFF. The two of them could make adorable little hard-ass babies together."

Mia gave a small laugh, but it sounded forced.

"Well, enjoy the snacks I brought you." Kayla's voice shifted, as though she'd moved across the room. "I've got to get back before the next session starts. Don't want Captain Hard-Ass giving me extra drills to run or something for being late. I'll catch you at messdeck tonight."

Mia murmured a good-bye, and then the door opened and closed. Leigh waited, making sure the coast was clear. But before he'd decided it was safe to come out, Mia had pulled open the door. With one hand on the knob, she set her other hand on her hip.

"So, Captain Hard-Ass, I hear you've been making people cry."

Her sheer audacity blew him away. He couldn't ever remember anyone having the gall to say something like that to his face, with maybe the exception of Seb, who treated everyone like that.

He stepped forward and leaned against the doorframe. She didn't move back, leaving less than a few scant inches between them.

"I've got a reputation to maintain. Making people cry is a staple of hard-asses everywhere."

"I see," she replied with a perfect amount of gravity. "You know, I'm starting to think this whole tough-guy thing is just a routine."

"Really?" They'd strayed into forbidden territory; even this light flirting could end in trouble. But the more he got to know Mia, the more intrigued he became. He could honestly say he'd never met a woman like her before, never been tempted into doing things he knew were wrong. But it felt reckless in a way he liked a little too much. Maybe he'd been living by the rules, set in his ways for too long. Maybe he was having some kind of early midlife crisis. Whatever it was, he couldn't find the will to pull himself into line.

She nodded in response to his one-worded question. "Yes, I do. I can see you, Captain Alphin, and the truth is you care more than you'd like anyone to believe. You care enough to put your own career at risk to help the people under your command. Not many men would go to those lengths."

"Don't go making me out to be a hero. You forgot the part where I blackmailed you into helping me."

"Well, I didn't say you were perfect." She grinned, and her smile hit him right in the middle of his chest.

Every muscle in his body locked up and it was all he could do in that moment to hold himself still. Because he wanted to kiss her. Right here, right now. Push her up against the wall and get himself all over her until she moaned for him.

She seemed to sense the sudden shift in the air between them because her smile disappeared, and she started to move—closer or away, he wasn't sure. *Goddamn it*. Maybe if she'd just stayed still another second, he could have got a handle on himself. But as it was, the warm, sweet scent of her hair or whatever it was that smelled like nutty vanilla, was all he got on his next breath in. And then his hands were on her hips, and he was pulling her up against him.

Her arms went around his shoulders, one of her hands landing on the back of his neck as he leaned in and closed his mouth over hers. Sensation tore through him, the flood of everything he'd been pushing away since the first moment he'd met her. The feel of her against him, the taste of her lips, it was like a dose of profound relief, even as an undeniable, heated exhilaration flashed through him.

But this hadn't been his intention when he'd come here. And this couldn't happen between them. With that thought, he managed to gain control of his common sense and break the kiss.

He took an unsteady breath as he released her and eased away. "That shouldn't have happened."

She nodded, though a little uncertainly. "No, you're right. I'm sorry. I don't know why I did that—"

She started to turn, but he caught her upper arm, stopping the movement.

"It was my fault. Don't blame yourself. Let's just keep it professional from now on, okay?"

"Of course." Her cheeks were flushed, whether from the kiss or embarrassment, he couldn't tell.

He took a couple of steps toward the door, since he swore he could still catch the scent of her. Or maybe some of it had rubbed off on him when he'd had her up against him. Either way, it was tempting him right back around to what they shouldn't be doing.

"Meet me tonight, after everyone in your dorm has fallen asleep." He went over and picked up her datapad. With a few quick taps, he'd entered the contact number for his personal comm. "Send me a message when you're ready and I'll come find you."

She nodded, avoiding his gaze. "Okay. If you're sure this is the path you want to take?"

"I'm sure I've got no other option," he muttered in return, walking over to the door. "Get back to resting, and I'll see you tonight."

He sent her a short wave before walking out into the

passageway. He strode through the dormitory in an unhurried, steady pace, and then got on to the transit. As the doors closed, he let his shoulders drop as he dragged a hand over his face. *Christ.* Had he really just kissed one of his recruits? In all the years he'd been serving on board the *Valiant Knox*, he'd never, ever had a slip up like that before.

He wanted to blame it on the stress of everything that had happened in the past week—the traitor in his ranks and getting shot at. But he got the feeling this particular type of insanity stemmed from the temptation of Mia and nothing more. He had to get a handle on this. Bad enough that he'd coerced her to work with him on illegally accessing the *Knox's* systems to find the traitor in his ranks. Forming any kind of intimate relationship with her would be like committing career suicide. He might as well take the CAFF insignia pins off his shirt and vent them out the nearest hatch, because kissing a subordinate was pretty much doing the same thing.

He shook his head at himself and straightened his posture as the transit arrived on squadron level. That kiss hadn't happened. It was as simple as that. He'd had one lapse in control. Considering his sterling fourteen years serving on the *Knox*, he was going to chalk it up to being overdue for some kind of small infraction and forget about it.

His comm chimed a little before twenty three hundred. Leigh set aside the reports he'd been writing on his datapad and leaned over to grab the device where he'd left it on the coffee table.

As expected, the message had come from Mia, letting him know that everyone in her dorm room had fallen asleep, and she was ready whenever he was. He sent back a reply to say he'd meet her in an hour at the dorm transit.

Truthfully, he was itching to go grab her right now and get to Kerrin's apartment as soon as they could. And though it was late and most people would be in bed, aside from the skeleton crew who ran the night shift, there was still a chance they could run into someone. If they left it until closer to midnight, hopefully they'd minimize the possibility of getting caught.

It had occurred to him earlier today that Stanton had more than likely already removed any possible evidence from the apartment. But he needed to see for himself, needed to at least go through the motions so he could be satisfied that he'd covered every angle and done everything possible to find the traitor in his squad.

The following hour trickled by with frustrating slowness. He couldn't concentrate on his reports anymore, knowing what he was about to go and do. He was nervous like a rookie facing his first battle, worried about getting both himself and Mia caught. Sneaking around and breaking into people's apartments wasn't in his skill set, and there was a very good chance this hunt for the mole could fail spectacularly before it had even begun. In the end, he took his datapad, left his apartment, and made his way up to the recruit dorms after only forty minutes, sending another message to Mia to let her know he was on his way.

When the doors opened on the dormitory level, Mia stood waiting. He waved her on, then tabbed the transit screen to close them in.

"Here." He handed her his datapad. "The first thing you'll have to do is find out which apartment Kerrin Hershel lives in."

She nodded, her expression far more somber now than it had been when he'd talked to her earlier this afternoon. Maybe the gravity of the situation had sunk in. Or maybe she was having second thoughts about helping him. Whatever the case, he needed her committed, needed to know he could rely on her.

"Look, Mia, I know that I all but strong-armed you into helping me today, but I want you to know that I wouldn't have done that if I had any other choice. It's okay to have cold feet or be nervous about what we're doing, but I need to know you're with me a hundred percent."

She looked up from his datapad, seeming a bit more together now. "I'm not worried about what we're doing. I spent half the afternoon thinking of all the ways a CSS mole—or several moles—could totally screw us. Most scenarios ended with the *Knox* exploding into a gigantic fireball. I'm not going to lie, it completely freaked me out. I am so with you on this."

He hadn't realized how tense he'd been about securing her agreement to work with him until he heard the words, causing a coil sitting in his guts to unwind. He hadn't let himself think too closely about the fact that he'd coerced her into cooperating since he'd left her dorm that afternoon, but apparently the guilt for it had still been sitting heavy and thorny within him. But if she was here because she was just as concerned for the welfare of the *Knox* and everyone on board, then no matter what happened from here on out, he could trust that she would be doing everything in her power to keep their secret and protect the integrity of this little mission they'd embarked on.

His datapad chimed in her hands, and she glanced down at it again. "Kerrin Hershel lives in apartment one two seven on the beta housing level."

Leaning past her, he punched the destination into the screen.

Neither of them said anything else as the transit took them down into the apartment levels of the ship, tension tightening through his shoulders the closer they got to their destination. When they arrived, he held up a hand to indicate she should wait and stuck his head out of the transit to check if anyone was in the corridor. Just as he'd hoped, it was empty.

"Come on, it's clear." He exited, Mia just behind him, and they hurried down the passageway until they found a door marked with one two seven.

As they stopped in front of it, Mia had already turned her attention to his datapad, biting her lower lip while she concentrated, a strand of her golden hair falling forward from the messy bun she had it shoved into.

Just when he'd started lecturing himself about not getting distracted by the way her teeth dragged over her full lower lip, the door clicked open, and Mia sent him a satisfied grin.

"I did that in half the time I thought it would take."

"Let's celebrate your breaking-and-entering skills later." He set a hand on her upper back and ushered her inside, stealing one last glance up and down the passageway to make sure no one was watching them. It was only after the door closed behind them that it hit him.

"Goddamn it, I didn't consider the security feed in the corridor." There'd be footage of them entering this apartment. Shit, he was not cut out for this kind of sneaking around. Never mind Mia slipping up. At this rate he was the one who was going to get them into hot water.

"Oh, I can take care of those easily enough. I'll just scrub them or replace the footage or something." Mia walked farther into the apartment, casting a curious look around. The apartment was identical to every other apartment on the ship, but of course, Mia hadn't seen any other living space except the dorms.

"You might want to do it sooner rather than later. Stanton could have people watching this place for all we know."

She glanced over her shoulder at him. "Stanton?"

"He's a Command Intelligence agent, one of the senior ones." Leigh went over to the hall table and yanked open the single drawer. Empty. Well, that probably wasn't a good sign. Frustration started crawling up the back of his neck as he went over to a desk on the adjacent bulkhead.

Mia dropped onto the couch. "Okay, you look for whatever it is you came here for, and I'll get to work on the cameras so there's no trace of us even coming onto this level."

Putting Stanton and his worries about getting caught out of his mind, he focused his effort on searching every square inch of the apartment. Unsurprisingly, the place had been cleaned out, no evidence that anyone had even lived here as recently as two days ago. The frustration at yet another failure to get any answers had set into his muscles with taut heat. He slammed the bathroom cabinet door, making it swing back out again. CI had been thorough, not leaving a single scrap of paper or personal item behind.

He'd already considered the possibility before they'd come up here. Still he was disappointed and irritated about the lack of any clues. He checked the time on his personal comm as he left the bedroom, finding it was just after oh one thirty. He headed back into the main room and went over to drop on the armchair adjacent to where Mia sat on the couch.

He dragged a hand though his hair as fatigue caught up to him all of a sudden.

"Find anything?" Mia lowered his datapad to her lap.

He shook his head. "What about you? Did you get the security feed sorted out?"

"We're good to go. And I started a program that's going to mine UEF personnel files and put together profiles on all the fighter pilots in your squadron. If anyone's trying to hide anything, hopefully this program will find it."

"Efficient." And impressive. At this rate, he might be able to out the bastard traitor in his squad within a matter of days. For the first time since Yang had told him there might be a mole under his command, he felt like he'd gotten some footing back.

"I hope you don't mind me saying, but you look really tired." An edge of something too close to sympathy entered her expression as she stared at him.

His first impulse was an automatic urge to deny it, but he caught himself.

"It's been a long couple of days." The words came out slowly, because he wasn't used to being so candid, especially with someone he was only just getting to know.

"I've only know about it for a few short hours, and it's already doing my head in. I can't imagine how much worse it must be for you, especially since you're in charge of everyone." She reached up and set her fingers on his shoulder, smoothing downward over his biceps in a comforting gesture, but then seemed to belatedly realize what she'd done and snatched her hand away again.

Instead of doing something totally moronic like revealing he enjoyed it when she touched him, he shifted, angling his body away from hers as she avoided his gaze.

"Yeah, it hasn't exactly been a highlight of my career," he muttered. Yet strangely enough, until a second ago, he'd felt more relaxed sitting and talking with her about it than he had in ages. Maybe it was simply because he'd been able to share the burden with someone. Or maybe it was the way she looked at him with those expressive, dark eyes.

Whatever the case, things were straying too far toward personal again, when he'd vowed this afternoon that after that slip up with the kiss, things between them would stay platonic and professional. Opening up to her about exactly how this situation weighed on him wasn't exactly conducive to staying detached.

Voices echoed in the passageway and Mia straightened, casting a worried look toward the door. He shifted to the edge of the cushions, holding his breath until the conversation faded again, whoever had been out there moving on.

Maybe if they'd found something, it would have almost been worth getting caught. But since this had been a bust, he didn't want to face Yang or Stanton for a gamble that had gotten him nowhere.

"Come on." He stood up, sidestepping past the coffee table. "We better get out of here before our luck runs out."

Chapter Twelve

Mia stifled a yawn behind her hand, trying to get her brain to keep up with Captain Alphin's lecture on survival skills. The daily, early morning, rigorous drills before the session definitely hadn't helped her exhaustion levels. After she'd gotten back from the little midnight mission with Leigh the night before, she'd spent another few hours on his datapad, working a few kinks out of her program before she was completely happy with how it was running.

Using Leigh's datapad was a little weird. Every time she logged onto the device and the screen background appeared—it showed a younger Leigh, Sub-Lieutenant Rayne, and two other men she didn't recognize—she had a moment of total surrealism, feeling like she was invading his privacy somehow.

Although technically he had all but coerced her into helping him, she could honestly say that even if he hadn't held her illegal activities over her, she still would have agreed to help him. Yet, she worried whether or not she could come through for him without getting them both caught…when she wasn't distracted by the incredibly stupid mistake she'd made before he'd left her dorm room. God. She'd kissed him. Sure, he'd said that it had been his fault, but that was just him being all noble and responsible.

She had no idea what had possessed her in that moment. Actually, she totally knew and didn't want to admit it. She'd been fighting it, denying it, ignoring it. And what had that gotten her? In that moment, when he'd stood there looking down on her, his gray-blue eyes sparking with humor, the forbidden thrill of flirting with him chasing through her, she'd gotten ambushed by all the ways she'd tried not to notice him, and all logic had abandoned her brain. Somehow, she'd ended up against him, and then she'd pulled him into that kiss.

But holy mother, what a kiss it had been. It had lasted no more than a second or two, but it had burned her from the inside out in a way she wouldn't ever forget.

And it had mostly been fine. Despite a brief explosion of butterflies in her stomach, she'd thought she had herself well in hand until she'd walked onto the transit. Seeing him had triggered some kind of auto-response, causing a sensory recall of the moment she'd been up against him with his mouth on hers. Yeah, in that millisecond she'd been far from the logic of everything wrong with a relationship between them, instead swamped by exactly how exhilarating it had been and the deep gouging need for more.

How much of an idiot could she possibly be? Things were already dangerous and complicated. Adding any kind of personal feelings to the mix was just asking for things to get messy.

On top of it all, this morning's drills had nearly killed her, and the following session had dragged as she'd fought the exhaustion from staying up so late the night before. She hadn't been able to find anything, either. Maybe the answer was in the actual transit car the shooter had used to escape. In the end, she'd only gotten three hours sleep before getting up again to skip breakfast and drag herself straight to class.

Now that the lecture was finishing, she hoped to grab a quick lunch and a quick nap before the class went into the PT room for the afternoon's drills and practical activities on survival. At some point she needed to tell Leigh her idea, but had no idea how she was supposed to arrange that. She supposed he would find time to see her when he could.

Her name being called pulled her attention up from the admittedly poor notes she'd taken over the morning.

"Recruit Wolfe, since you spent half of the morning yawning through my lecture, you can stay behind and explain to me exactly which parts of survival training you found so boring." Leigh's voice had an aggravated edge to it, and though she assumed he was actually keeping her behind to ask her if she'd found anything, she could almost believe from his harsh tone that she really was in trouble.

"Sir, yes, sir," she replied as Kayla sent her a sympathetic glance.

She walked to the front of the room and stood by the lectern as the other recruits filed out, while Leigh stood nearby looking pissed. Her heart skipped a nervous beat. Maybe he really was angry that she'd constantly yawned all morning. But she'd done her best to conceal it.

Once the last recruit left, he walked over and swiped a

hand over the door control to close it. When he turned back to her, he no longer looked angry, and she breathed a silent sigh of relief.

He walked back toward her. "From how tired you look, I'm assuming you were up late last night working on the project instead of getting that sleep I ordered?"

She nodded. "I'm sorry. I wasn't going to put so many hours in, but I guess once I got going, time kind of slipped away from me."

"Then am I right in assuming you found something?"

A small kernel of excitement lit up within, the same one she'd gotten last night that had kept her working so late. "I tried to pick up the shooter's trail, but the utility levels are like a maze. The security camera coverage is pretty poor. There wasn't much chance I was going to find him, which is exactly why he picked there to disappear. So I focused on finding whoever helped him by messing with the transit IDs and cameras."

"And?" Leigh leaned against the lectern, staring at her expectantly.

"Well, I didn't find who it was, but I was thinking maybe if you checked out the transit car the shooter got into, you could see if it had been tampered with at the source."

"Less than twenty-four-hours in and you've already got us a lead." He seemed more than a little impressed as he stared at her. "We've got an hour until the afternoon session starts. Let's go track down that transit and see what we can find."

He pushed off from the lectern and started to step past her. "Wait, you're going right now? And you want me to come?"

He shrugged one shoulder. "You're all in, aren't you? And since we're looking for one specific transit car, I'm thinking I'm going to need your skills."

The kernel of excitement turned into a full surge of anticipation. Really, this wasn't meant to be fun, it was serious and dangerous, but the idea of sneaking around the ship with Leigh was apparently enough to quell any anxiety she might have felt.

"Okay, let me duck up to my dorm room to get your datapad."

"I'll meet you at the transit near the gym in ten minutes. Now wipe that smile off your face and start looking like you're about to cry because I just reamed you for yawning through my class this morning."

She tried to settle her face into a more serious expression, but failed miserably.

Leigh shook his head at her, but a grin kicked up one side of his lips. "You are terrible at this. Remind me to give you a few lessons in keeping things under wraps later."

Him smiling at her like that definitely wasn't helping her put on a sad face, because she felt nothing but buoyant at the sight of his amusement over her apparent lack of acting skills.

"Off you go, we're on the clock."

"Okay, okay." She turned away from him, and as she approached the door, she took a settling breath, making a more concerted effort to appear miserable. Luckily, she didn't see any of the other recruits as she navigated the squadron level and went down to the dorms. She grabbed the datapad and made it back to the designated meeting spot well before ten minutes were up, but found Leigh already waiting for her.

"So how do we find one specific transit car?" he asked as she stopped in front of him.

"Well, for a start, we're better off not doing it here where anyone can see us. I think we should backtrack. If we head down to the utility level where the shooter got off, I can start there."

He pressed the button for the transit and the door opened right away.

"By the way," he said as they stepped on to the car and he put in the lower utility level as the destination. "If anyone asks, I kept you in the ready room by yourself to complete a report on survival skills as punishment for your lack of attention while I went and had lunch. We didn't spend more than two minutes together."

"Got it." She moved to the rear of the transit and leaned against the back wall. It would take a few minutes to get to the bottom of the ship.

Leigh came over and leaned next to her, kicking one boot over the other in a pose that was about as relaxed as she'd ever seen him.

"So aeronautical engineering, huh? What's the lure?" His shoulder brushed hers as he glanced down at her.

"I like knowing how things work, down to the last detail. I like to take them apart and put them back together. I love the idea of finding new ways to make things work better. What about you? What's the lure of being a fighter pilot? It's pretty dangerous. Besides being on the front lines, the fighter squadrons have the highest mortality rate."

He shifted his gaze to focus on the transit doors. "I wasn't meant to be a fighter pilot, according to the computer psyche-eval, anyway. It pegged me for a leadership track, which would have put me behind a desk for most of my career. Maybe I could have done some good in that sort of role. But I wanted to wake up every day knowing I was making a difference right in that moment by simply being where I was, not pushing papers and playing politics."

She studied his profile, surprised at this revelation. He was such a great fighter pilot, had literally become a legend of the UEF, she couldn't believe he'd ever been assigned to anything else.

"So how did you end up on the *Knox*? I didn't think there was any way to circumvent the computer eval."

"So few people are singled out as leaders at such a young age, it doesn't come without its perks. I told them I'd happily take a brass role, but I wanted actual experience behind me, not just what I gleaned from reading reports. They were more than happy to put me anywhere I wanted to go, and joining the FP squadron on the *Knox* seemed like the hardest and fastest way I was going to learn the real cost of this war."

If she hadn't been impressed with him before now, that little revelation would have sealed the deal. He could have gone off to a UEF ivory-tower office somewhere far from the front lines, had a cushy future of money, privilege, and women, yet instead he'd chosen to put his life on the line. Not just once, but day after day.

"No wonder everyone around here thinks you're such a hero."

He finally looked back at her, shadows in his eyes. "No one except Commander Yang knows where the computer eval assigned me. And I'm no hero. If you knew how many good men had died on my watch—" He released a harsh breath, shaking his head. "I'm not a hero, Mia. Hell, if it was humanly possible to do any more I would, because every single one of those pilots I lost burned a place into my soul."

He pressed a hand against his mouth as if to stop himself from saying anything else as he avoided her gaze.

Her heart ached for him, for the things he clearly struggled with but hid from the world. Why had he revealed this to her, especially if Commander Yang was the only other person who knew about his true posting? But she pushed the questions aside and shifted to face him, her heart skipping a beat when she set her hand on his shoulder.

"You didn't get those men killed, Leigh; the war did. And maybe if you weren't the CAFF, the number of people dead would be twice as many. I'm sure you've saved far more."

His chest expanded as he took in a deep breath. "You know, I'm not sure if I can be friends with someone who is so blatantly optimistic and sensible. It's kind of scary."

"Friends? Is that what this is? See, I thought it was some weird situation where my CO was blackmailing me into doing all sorts of dreadful things." Her hand tightened a little on his shoulder. It was the only way she could stop herself from sliding it up to his neck, to getting closer to him and repeating the same mistake she'd made last night. Apparently the temptation of him when they were alone really damaged her common sense.

He braced one of his hands on the wall just above her head and leaned the slightest bit closer to her. "So you're innocent in all this? Is that what you'll tell them if we get caught?"

"Yeah, I'm totally going to throw you in front of the ship to save myself." She let herself slip just a little closer, the warmth of his body and light woodsy scent of him rippling through her in tingling waves.

"Well, then, I'm glad we know where we stand with each other," he murmured. He tilted his head, the movement nearly indiscernible; she would have missed it if she hadn't been watching him so closely. His gesture promised what she'd been yearning for and her breath caught, the buzz within her intensifying in anticipation of his lips touching hers.

A chime sounded above them and Leigh glanced away as the transit doors opened. He cleared his throat and shifted back from her, leaving a swirl of cool air where his body had been.

The deflating disappointment was almost enough to make her groan. Instead, she tightened her grip on the data-pad and reminded herself why she and Leigh were alone in the first place. And it certainly wasn't to have some heart-to-heart or any other kinds of personal interactions.

"Come on. Let's see what we can find," he said as he headed out of the transit.

She nodded, since her vocal chords had apparently forgotten how to work, and followed him out into the passageway.

As expected, the lighting was set down low to auxiliary only, while a quick scan on the datapad revealed there wasn't a single other soul on this level.

"Okay, we're all alone down here, so we don't need to worry about bumping into anyone." Turning to the screen inset in the bulkhead next to the transit doors, she set about linking into the system.

"We might not need to worry about bumping into anyone, but what about the security feeds?" Leigh asked from right behind her, the sound of his voice so close, startling her, since she'd been focused on getting the datapad to connect with the transit station.

"I put the feed for the utility level on a loop. If anyone checks, it'll show the same empty corridor from ten minutes ago. I also used a similar transit ID scramble like the traitor did to cover any evidence that we even came down here."

"Smart," he murmured, which sent a small swell of warmth through her. Clearly, she enjoyed his approval more than she probably had any right to. Giving herself a mental slap and a stern reminder on why she was here, she returned her concentration to the datapad, taking a few long minutes to slip seamlessly into the system, connecting with this transit-porter so that no one in the command center would pick up the activity.

Leigh moved from behind her to lean against the bulkhead, arms crossed but appearing alert, even though she'd told him there was no one else down here. Maybe that was part of what made him so good at what he did—he was always ready for action, no matter the circumstances.

It didn't take long to run a diagnostic. The tampering definitely hadn't been done from out here.

"This is a dead end," she said, not quite able to keep the disappointment out of her voice.

"It was probably always a long shot." Leigh didn't sound too worried about the fact that she hadn't found anything. "Did you still want to find the transit car the shooter got onto?"

"Already on it." While she'd been checking the station, she'd also called down the exact transit car the shooter had used to escape.

After another few silent moments, the transit chimed and the doors opened, revealing a car that looked like every single other transit operating on the *Knox*. She switched the datapad connection over to the screen inside and stepped in, Leigh following behind her. As the doors closed, she ran a quick override command so that the car couldn't go anywhere while she ran the checks.

"Is this going to take long?" Leigh asked, picking a new wall to lean against. "We've got to get back before the next session starts, and I heard they were serving burgers at mess-deck today."

"Depends on if I find anything," she returned distractedly. Except her stomach pinched at the thought of a burger. Damn, she hadn't been hungry until he'd mentioned food.

A slight anomaly popped out at her. If a transit failed to respond to a call-up, another one quickly took its place. But this packet of data was too big for a simple routine glitch.

"I think I found something." She tried to keep the excitement out of her voice since this could still turn out to be nothing. But the fact that she might have a clue was just too damn exhilarating.

"What is it?" Leigh shifted closer, his chest brushing her shoulder as he leaned in to look down at the datapad. "All I see is a bunch of numbers and letters."

The dismay in his voice would have been funny if she hadn't been so hooked into unraveling this mystery.

"It's system coding. If you know how to read it, this can tell you all sorts of things about how the *Knox* is running."

"I'll take your word on it," he returned dryly, shifting back again.

She didn't reply as she isolated the packet of data and

begin extrapolating the information. However, the screen flickered, the various tabs scrambling together.

"Uh-oh." The transit car shifted up with a sudden jolt and she threw a hand out to keep her balance.

"And I'm assuming *uh-oh* means—"

The lights cut out, the transit grinding to a halt and powering down with a lowering hum. The blue-white glow of the datapad screen didn't go very far in the pitch-blackness, and she glanced up at Leigh.

"That's what uh-oh means."

His expression was exasperated as he glanced around the darkened space, not looking the least bit worried about the fact they were trapped in a powered-off transit car and nobody knew they were down here.

"Crap," she muttered, stepping over to the screen next to the doors. She pressed the emergency call icon on the otherwise blank screen but, of course, nothing happened.

Leigh moved over next to her. "How long will it take you to get this transit back online? We've only got forty minutes until the next session starts."

She glanced down at the datapad in her hand. "I don't know if I can, not from in here any way."

"Okay, so we'll put a call out for someone to come and get us." He shoved his hand into his pocket and pulled out his comm.

"That won't work."

"Why not?" He tapped at the screen, adding an extra glow to the darkness.

"Because comm and datapad signals are usually routed through the transit screen during a trip. There's no signal getting in here." Somehow, she had to find a way to reboot the system, which was next to impossible with the transit car powered off and no access to the outside.

He frowned, beginning to look a little unimpressed. "Then what usually happens when people get stuck in a transit car? Everyone knows it happens every now and then."

Frustration and apprehension had started chipping away at her calm, making it harder to keep her thoughts straight, to find an answer to this problem.

"Usually people get stuck from anomalies or malfunctions that stall the system. The transit cars never power down like this. Plus an alert will be sent to the central maintenance station."

Leigh slipped his comm away again. "So someone will know the transit car is stuck. Can we get out before they send a team down to check it out?"

She lowered the datapad and spun to face him. "Weren't you listening? I said I don't know if I can get us out at all, let alone before the maintenance crew turns up."

Leigh reached up and set his hands on her shoulders. "Don't freak out, Mia. Just stay calm, we'll work something out."

"I'm not freaking out." Though, really, she kind of was considering that her screwing around with the system might have got them trapped in here indefinitely. So she forced a slow breath to fill her lungs. "Sorry. It's just dark in here and with the power off, I'm not sure if we're getting a fresh oxygen supply. Plus if a team of maintenance officers find us in here, how are we going to explain that?"

Leigh didn't look the least bit ruffled, either about their possible lack of air or them getting caught. "We'll just tell them we were heading from squad level down to messdeck when the transit malfunctioned and we didn't even know we'd ended up down in the utility levels."

Some of the tension leeched out of her at his totally logical reasoning. "Oh, that makes sense."

"Yeah, it does. Now, before you do anything else, how about you work out whether or not we're going to be able to keep breathing?"

She nodded, lowering her head to turn her attention back to the datapad. He squeezed her shoulders reassuringly, then let his hands slip down her arms as he stepped back.

Putting all other thoughts out of her mind, she tried to revive the connection with the transit car screen, not aware of time passing. Except after a little while, her legs started aching from standing in the same spot. Glancing up, she found Leigh had sat down on the floor, his long legs stretched out in front of him, one boot kicked over the other and hands clasped over his stomach.

With a sigh, she joined him on the floor, crossing her legs and setting the datapad on her knee while she stretched her fingers.

"How is it looking?"

She picked up the datapad again, checking the progress of the latest connection route she'd run. "Ask me something else."

"Will you have us out of here in the next ten minutes before the afternoon session starts?"

She sent him an annoyed look. "That's not helpful."

"Sorry." The expression on his face didn't appear at all repentant, despite his apology.

Above them, the lights came on to half strength, while a whoosh of fresh air cycled down.

Leigh straightened from where he'd been slouched against the bulkhead. "Have you done it?"

She shook her head, chewing on her thumbnail as she started a secondary program. "No, I got basic power up, but the main controls are still offline."

"You'll figure it out, Mia." The quiet confidence in his words had the opposite effect from what he'd probably intended, bringing the panic up again.

"But what if I can't? What if we're stuck here for hours—"

He reached up and cupped a hand over her collarbone, at the base of her neck, effectively cutting off the trepidation spinning through her.

"If you can't get us out, it doesn't matter. Eventually the maintenance crew will find us, especially once the next session starts and people notice we're missing. And before you can start worrying about it again, no one will have any reason to question us when we tell them we got on at squad level and the transit car malfunctioned."

"I'm sorry." The words just kind of blurted out, even though she had no idea what she was apologizing for.

"There's nothing to be sorry about, except maybe my empty stomach." He sent her a half grin, letting her know he wasn't really put out by this situation. Amazing. Even in a situation like this, one that most people would be angry, frustrated, or anxious about, he was as calm as ever. It forced her to reassess her own nerves and keep her composure. "Is there anything else you can try?"

"I am running another diagnostic program that will hopefully restore the full connection. But it could take a few minutes, or it could take an hour."

"Since you got half the lights back on and the airflow going again, we're not in any immediate danger. So why don't you put the datapad down and take a quick break? Maybe the answer will come to you if you're not stressing so much."

With a sigh, she set the datapad down on the floor, despite her brain telling her she had to keep working the problem until she found a solution. She leaned back against the wall and Leigh shifted to sit next to her, their shoulders not quite touching.

"There. Is that better?"

"No," she replied grumpily, but then immediately realized how ridiculous that sounded. She glanced up at Leigh to see an amused glint in his eyes and couldn't help breaking into a laugh, relieving some of the tension within her. "Clearly I'm not the best person to be stuck in a transit with."

"Truthfully, I could think of worse people to be stuck in here with."

Maybe his statement had meant to be flippant, but somehow it ended up creating a different sort of tension in the air between them. Just the same way things had gone before she'd given into the stupid impulse to kiss him yesterday afternoon.

Like then, all rational thought was quickly evaporating from her mind as she stared up at him, tempting her toward things she shouldn't want. She'd promised herself she wouldn't slip up like that again. But sitting here, closed in the transit, the lighting dim above them, no one aware they were down here together, it became harder by the second to stick to her resolve to stay detached from him.

Though she'd mostly put the kiss out of her thoughts

straight after it had happened and had kept herself busy since, now it was all she could think of. And she couldn't see him as her CO anymore, couldn't see a man who should be forbidden to her. All she could see was his gray-blue eyes, lit with an intensity that sent an answering warmth swelling within her.

Chapter Thirteen

Leigh forced a slow breath on himself, hanging onto the threads of his tenuous control with every last shred of determination he possessed. Maybe he should reassess his last statement—Mia was the worst possible person he could have gotten trapped in a transit with. Especially considering the way she was looking at him right now, a definite gleam of desire mixed with a hint of curiosity, like maybe she was wondering exactly what it would be like if they shared more than just a brief kiss.

He'd been absolutely adamant yesterday that despite the fact they'd be working in close quarters while uncovering the mole in the squadron, nothing more personal would develop between them. But apparently he wasn't as strong as he'd thought and that resolve had failed in less than twenty-four hours, because *goddamn* did he want to kiss her again. Not just for a stolen, rushed moment like yesterday afternoon. He wanted to *devour* her. And take his time doing it.

"Mia—" he started, but had no idea what he wanted to tell her. It should have been something along the lines of all the reasons why they couldn't, because apparently he at least needed a reminder. But the words got lost in translation somewhere between his brain and his mouth.

She tilted her head, and he could all but see her mind working behind those expressive dark eyes. Maybe he didn't know her that well, but he got the feeling she never did anything without considering every angle first. Right now, she was definitely turning something over in her mind, something he probably didn't want to know about if they were going to get out of this transit without crossing a big fat line or two.

Shifting onto her knees, she got closer to him, that damn inquisitive glint in her gaze almost his undoing. He set his palms flat against the cool floor, the only way to stop himself from reaching out and yanking her against him.

But if she could see the struggle going on within him, she seemingly wasn't going to give him any quarter. She leaned in, and the next breath he took was nothing but her and that nutty-vanilla scent she favored. On her hair or skin, he couldn't tell, but whatever it was, it'd started driving him crazy, so damn mouthwatering—

Her lips touched his, the contact almost featherlight, but it echoed through his entire body. His hands contracted into fists against the floor, every muscle catching fire with an intensity that left him fighting for air.

She increased the pressure of her mouth, her hand coming up to cup his jaw. It was too much, so far past the line. But hell, it wasn't anywhere near what he wanted. He brought a hand up, only as far as her lower back, and pressed her closer, even as he deepened the kiss, maybe taking a little more than what she'd initially offered. But God, she had him so wound up. If anything, he'd only encouraged her into further recklessness as she knelt up and hooked a leg over his, then settled in his lap.

Oh yeah, that was a problem. And somehow his hands had ended up on her ass. Hell, he was so screwed. But he didn't care, not when she was all over him like nobody's business.

The transit jolted and Mia gasped, breaking the kiss, but grabbed onto his shoulders. The lights flickered again, but then returned to full strength. Leaning over, Mia retrieved the datapad where she'd left it on the floor.

"I've got a connection, but the control files are all screwed up. There are entire packets of data missing."

"What does that mean?" He shifted his hands to her hips, which was probably only marginally better than having them on her ass. He probably should take his hands off her altogether, but since she was still sitting on top of him, he was just going to go with it.

"It means some of the control icons either won't work, or they'll do something completely different. So if you put in one destination, you might end up somewhere else. Or trying to open the doors might make the lights go out again."

"But despite that, you can get us out of here?"

"It's more likely now, yes." She slipped off his lap, attention riveted on the screen of the datapad.

Leigh stood, taking a moment to adjust his pants since he had some swelling issues that had left him more than a little uncomfortable. He went over to the screen of the transit.

"Don't even think about touching that screen," Mia said as she stood. "It'll just confuse things that are already messed as hell."

He fought a grin at her ordering him around, but she didn't notice. The doors clunked, and he glanced over to see them start to open, only to slam shut again. But from the glimpse of outside he'd gotten, it looked like they were just beneath a floor.

"Can you get the transit to move, Mia? We're just below the lowest apartment level. At least that's what it looked like."

She shook her head. "I tried that first, but it doesn't seem like this thing is going anywhere. If I can get the doors to stay open, do you think we can climb out?"

He hadn't gotten a clear enough look, but between the two of them, he didn't see any reason why not. "Sure. Get the doors open and I'll give you a boost."

The doors clunked two more times before opening and stopping halfway. There was only just enough room for him to get his shoulders in.

"I think that's the best I can do." She glanced upward, brow creased as though she really wasn't impressed with her own effort.

"Come on then. If we hurry, we might make the beginning of the session before any of the recruits start wondering why the CAFF is so late for class."

"And what about me?" she asked as she stepped closer.

"You're going to arrive fifteen minutes late, and I'm going to dress you down in front of the entire class. I haven't made anyone cry today. Maybe you could shed a few tears."

She glared at him as he bent his knees, bringing him

down to her level and then linking his fingers palms-up to provide her a foothold.

"You know, I'm starting to think this situation is much more beneficial to you than me." She set a foot in his hands and hoisted herself up, catching the edge of the floor above them.

As she pulled up, he gave her a push, helping her scramble out. Once she'd cleared the opening, he backed up as far as he could, then took a run up at the door and leaped at the last second. He only just managed to grab the lip, but it was enough. He took a moment, drawing in a breath before tensing his muscles and hauling his body weight up to get his forearms on the edge of the floor. After that, it was easier to heave himself the rest of the way up.

He took a second to catch his breath and then stood. "Guess I won't need to go to the gym today after that little acrobatic routine."

But Mia wasn't paying him any attention, instead staring down the passageway. "I think someone's coming."

He glanced over his shoulder, and sure enough, could hear voices somewhere farther down the hallway. "Come on, there's another transit on the starboard side of this level."

She nodded, setting off in the opposite direction. He checked his watch to find the afternoon session had started exactly three and a half minutes ago. He'd never been late to a single session or meeting in his life. Hopefully Bren wouldn't question him too closely about it, despite the fact it was so far out of character for him. In the past few days, he'd come to realize there was a lot of truth in the old saying "first time for everything."

The following evening, Leigh stepped through the doorway into Harley's, the bar on commerce level favored by most of the military staff for after-shift drinks. When he'd first earned his wings, he'd spent a fair bit of time here with his fellow pilots, blowing off steam and generally having a good time. But in the last few years, since becoming the CAFF, the occasional after-shift tradition had become less and less frequent.

Truthfully, considering the day he'd had—no make that the *week* he'd had—he could definitely use an hour or two in this bar tonight taking the edge off. He'd just never expected the invitation to do so would come from Commander Yang.

As he let the low lights, raucous conversations, and underlying, near indiscernible rhythm of a song he couldn't identify wash over him, he forced some of the tension from his shoulders. He felt like he'd been walking around with a bowstring yanking his neck and shoulder blades tight ever since he'd escorted the damaged troop transport onto the *Knox's* deck a week ago.

But sneaking around with Mia and getting stuck in that damn transit yesterday had really jacked him up. Admittedly, he'd had no patience to deal with the recruits today, not when the need to find the traitor was slowly but effectively eating away at his control. And riding him even worse had been the fact that he'd gotten Mia involved in this situation as well. She'd fallen a little behind in class and was clearly tired. He should never have pressured her to participate, putting her spot in the FP program in jeopardy, but he'd seen an opportunity and taken it, ignoring the risk of collateral damage. Now they were too far in. If the traitor didn't already know they were after him, he might soon figure it out. The only way to keep Mia safe was to let her work up those profiles and find the mole.

He scanned the shifting crowd, finding Yang sitting in a far booth across from another man. As he got closer and found a clear view, he recognized Cam slouching in the opposite corner.

He slid in next to the colonel, where they'd already ordered him a beer.

"Seriously, McAllister, if you love being on the *Knox* so much, why don't you just ask Yang to find you a posting?" He slid the beer a short way across the table toward himself, using a napkin to wipe at some of the condensation before he picked it up and took a long swallow.

Cam sent him a flat look. "Like I told you, I prefer to keep my boots firmly planted in the dirt. Though, I have to admit, you guys have better beer up here."

He saluted with his half-empty glass, then took a gulp.

"So is that your reason for this visit, our superior beverages?"

Cam nodded toward the commander. "Yang got me back up here, ask him."

He glanced over at the CO, who was nursing his own glass, looking like he'd taken less than a sip of the beer.

"There are things I wanted to discuss with the two of you."

"And it couldn't be done in your wardroom during office hours?" He took another quick sip of beer, the ice-cold bitter beverage going down smooth. He'd definitely need a second pretty soon. "Not that I'm really complaining about the venue choice."

An annoyed expression flitted across Yang's face. "No actually, it couldn't be discussed in my wardroom, not unless we wanted every word recorded and analyzed by Lieutenant Caleb Prescott."

"The guy they sent to review your command?" he asked as Cam muttered a few choice insults.

Yang nodded. "He's being very thorough, I'll give him that."

"Its just more bureaucratic bullshit," Cam put in. "They're not going to pull the deck from under you, not without some serious backlash. You're a war hero, people aren't going to like hearing they gave you back command of the *Knox*, only to change their minds."

Yang glanced down at his glass, his expression mostly blank, but Leigh caught the shadows of doubt in the CO's gaze.

"We're not here to talk about that." Yang focused on them, features now set into stern lines. "I want to keep you both in the loop about the CSS infiltrations. You two are the only ones I fully trust right now—my direct link to what's going on in the ranks. I need full disclosure, no matter if you think your suspicions might be groundless, or that the truth might be worse when it's revealed. The whole thing is obviously bigger than just the *Knox*, but this ship and the people on it are my first priority. No matter what UEF or CI mechanisms might be going on around us, my only concern is the welfare of those who serve under my command."

A smolder in Leigh's chest blazed with every breath he took over the secrets he held. For the first time in his entire career, his loyalties tore him in two different directions: protect Mia or offer the full disclosure Commander Yang expected and deserved.

The only thing that kept him from blurting out the truth was that coming clean would give Yang one more complication to bear on his already strained shoulders.

"Have there been further developments from Stanton?" His voice came out a little rough, so he took another swallow from his beer to wash down the remaining tension.

"Stanton hides as much as he reveals. I'm not sure he's telling me anything of real value, anything that can really help us. He sent me a dossier of information, most of it pertaining to things I'd missed in the past year and a half as a POW. Things like the Pontifex becoming increasingly reclusive. In fact, he hasn't been seen in public for several months."

The Pontifex was the man who acted as a figurehead to the CSS. Everyone knew him. Ronald Martin, once UEF Governor of the Brannon System until he'd declared the three planets under his jurisdiction a sovereign state and made himself Pontifex—religious leader of the CSS—which started the war that had spanned two decades.

"Well, he had to slow down eventually. The guy must be in his seventies by now." Leigh couldn't remember clearly.

"Sixty-eight, according to the intelligence report Stanton gave me," Yang answered.

"Anything else?" Cam finished his beer and set the empty glass down, then tapped on the screen inset in the tabletop to order another.

Yang shook his head, expression annoyed. "Nothing. A lot of the reports are contradictory, so it's hard to know what's factual and what's misinformation."

"How so?" The tension crept back into his neck, brought on by the fact that this subterfuge stuff was beyond his patience. Give him an enemy to face in the open, something to aim his jet at. Sneaking around for crumbs of information in the shadowy corners of this war wasn't his thing.

"Like despite the fact that the CSS are seemingly ramping up the scale and intensity of their attacks, they're running out of skilled pilots and experienced soldiers."

"This war could have been over with in a matter of months if we'd gone in hard from the first," Cam muttered.

"We all know the deal, even if we don't agree with it." Yang's expression became shuttered. As commander, he couldn't be too vocal if his opinion didn't fall into line with what the UEF mandated. "The UEC still have to answer to the Galactic Alliance for Health Treaty Organization, and they can only get away with spending so much money, and delegating a certain percentage of the UEF resources to this war, all in the name of GAHTO protecting the citizens. This is technically classed as a peacekeeping effort, after all."

Cam crossed his arms. "Yeah, and what has two decades of war brought them? I wouldn't think too many of Ilari's citizens feel like they're being protected."

Leigh said, "But where does the CSS infiltration of our ranks come into it? Their actions in recent months defy all patterns of the previous two decades."

Yang inclined his head. "That's the question I have no answer for."

A waitress walked over and set a couple more beers on the table. Leigh finished up the one he'd been holding, and handed the empty glass off to her. No server-droids in

Harley's. That was one of the things people loved about it—old-fashioned service from an actual person.

Leigh took the second beer and passed a glance between the two guys sitting at the table with him, both looking pensive. Between the bombing on the Ilari base a few weeks back, the CSS infiltration of their ranks, and the UEF breathing down Yang's neck, he felt like he was hearing a whole lot of noise but couldn't see where it was coming from. As though he'd been shut in a dark room with the volume turned way up.

Whatever the case, there were a number of outside factors coming at them like meteorites. The only thing he knew for sure? The *Valiant Knox* was smack-bang in the middle of the impact zone.

Chapter Fourteen

Mia hummed along to the music swelling in her ears, tapping her finger against her knee in time to the beat as the datapad in her lap ran a search, building a profile on one of the fighter pilots in the squadron. This was the fourth she'd done and had almost gotten used to the fact that she was prying into every facet of these people's lives to see if they had any possible connection to the CSS. It seemed so wrong, but this was important to Leigh. The other reason—which probably should have been a bigger concern, considering she'd gotten stuck in a transit yesterday—was that they needed to find the traitor before someone got killed, especially Leigh or her.

She glanced up at the time display in the corner to see it just creeping past midnight. Letting the datapad rest in her lap, she stretched her arms toward the dark controls in front of her, gaze running over the cockpit of the fighter jet she was sitting in. A few days ago, she never would have considered sneaking up to alpha level launch deck after hours, but compared with all the illegal things she'd done in the past couple of days, this infraction seemed small.

Maybe she'd promised not to wander around the ship by herself, but she'd needed somewhere quiet to work, somewhere she wouldn't be interrupted.

The profiles mostly built themselves, so she'd also run checks on the *Knox's* systems one by one, beginning with the transit system, to see if she could pick up any anomalies or signs of tampering. She needed to know if what had happened in the transit really had been a coincidence, or if it had been some kind of ambush.

But what exactly would a traitor hope to achieve by trapping them?

Not being able to solve that particular puzzle had definitely made her moody, and the last thing she'd felt like doing after evening messdeck tonight was socializing with the group in her dorm.

Besides, since Leigh was her every-other-thought at the moment, she'd developed this nearly debilitating fear that she was going to let something slip in front of Kayla or one of her other fellow recruits and give away exactly how far beyond inappropriate her relationship with him had gone.

God, she couldn't believe she'd been so brazen. She'd definitely initiated the kiss this time, no question about it. And she'd climbed on top of him like a total hussy. Maybe the oxygen levels had gotten far lower than she'd realized and it had affected her judgment. That was the excuse she'd decided to go with.

The aftermath had left a jumble within her. Until now, the fact that Leigh was her CO had kept her emotions mostly reined in. But now she had so much real life experience to feed her clearly senseless imagination. Her self-control had shut up shop and abandoned her. More than a few times in the last thirty-two hours she'd imagined finding Leigh alone and letting herself get lost in him, no matter how reckless or career-endingly suicidal it was.

A stinging dose of guilt burned through her, however, because even thinking about taking things to that level worsened her confusion.

Everything was such a mess, and the more time she spent with him, the deeper her feelings for him grew.

But one issue was plainly apparent. She was totally screwed.

Even if she happened to get through the program and ended up posted under Leigh's command, she would never be able to separate her feelings for him, never see him as just her CO. It was too late for that.

Maybe if she could just get through the rest of the training program, she could ask for a posting elsewhere—one not on the front lines—instead of staying in the FP squadron. She'd never heard of it being done before, because most people would give their left arm to be in the squad, but surely it was possible? She had no idea what that would mean for her career, but putting distance between Leigh and her seemed like the most important detail in this equation.

With a sigh, she pulled the headphones out of her ears, the music starting to grate on her nerves. Actually, everything was getting on her nerves. She had this tension inside of her that she didn't know what to do with. It had kept her awake half of last night, kept her wired, and continuously sent her thoughts off into a million different directions at once.

"I feel like I should be surprised to find you here, but somehow I'm just not."

She jumped at the low voice above her and looked up to see Leigh leaning against the open edge of the cockpit. With her music going, she hadn't heard him climb up the side.

She pressed a hand to the middle of her chest, willing her heart rate to settle. "You scared the hell out of me. What are you doing here?"

"Shouldn't I be asking you that?" He braced his arms along the edge of the hatch. "You do realize this is my jet you're sitting in?"

She glanced down at the dark control screen, but of course it didn't have an ID tag anywhere that read *Captain Leigh Alphin*. Out of all the jets on the launch deck, how on earth had she managed to end up in his? She'd simply picked this ship because it had been off to the side, one of its wings half under a tarp for repairs.

"No, I didn't know." She looked back up at him, the tension within her climbing as she took in the way he stared down at her.

"So what are you doing up here?"

She tapped the datapad in her lap. "I started on those profiles for you and was running some system checks, searching for anomalies. Obviously I couldn't do that in my dorm room."

"So you decided to sneak into a restricted area instead?" He didn't sound incredulous or annoyed, just mildly curious, maybe even a little impressed.

She shrugged. "I figured I was already so screwed if I got caught, it wouldn't matter in the scheme of things. I couldn't think of anywhere else I wasn't likely to be found. I suppose you're annoyed because you told me not to go off on my own after what happened in the ready room a few days ago."

"You're a big girl. You make your own decisions. Plus,

you beat Lieutenant Brenner on the mats. In most situations, I'm sure you can hold your own." He lowered his chin to rest on his forearm, gaze shifting to the datapad in her hands. "So have you got anything yet?"

She glanced down at the screen; it was certainly a lot easier concentrating on the information, especially considering where she'd been letting her thoughts drift earlier. And recalling that sent a flush of heat through her chest, making her heartbeat pick up speed.

"Not yet. Building a complete profile is time consuming, so it's probably going to take me a few days to get through the entire squadron. And despite what happened on the transit yesterday, all of the *Knox's* systems seem to be working like they should so far."

"Anything I can do to help?"

She tilted her head back to look up at him with a half smile. "Sure, if you suddenly learned how to navigate these systems yourself without leaving a trace."

"And what if I did?" Although he didn't smile, she could see a spark of amusement in his eyes.

"Then I guess you wouldn't need me anymore."

"Well then you're lucky that I've still got no idea how to do any of that tech stuff, and I definitely still need you." He clambered higher on the side of the hatch. "Scoot forward."

She met his gaze, not quite sure what he was getting at. Sure, it seemed like a simple enough instruction, but what could he —

"Come on. Don't stare at me like I'm the crazy one, since you thought this was such a good place to hide out. Scoot forward and make room for me."

While the fighter jets usually only took one pilot, they

had been designed to fit two in an emergency. She shifted forward in the seat, coming closer to the controls, while Leigh dropped in behind her and stretched his legs out on either side of her thighs.

His arms closed around her, hands joining hers where she held the datapad.

Her heart stuttered at having him so close, at the feel of his body around hers, but she turned her attention back to the datapad with staunch determination to act as if practically sitting in his lap was no big deal.

He murmured, "Show me some of what you're doing. Maybe I'll be a quick study."

Mia glanced over her shoulder, stealing a quick look at Leigh's profile. "Okay, so I've opened the personnel files for a start. I've already completed several profiles, and I've got a program currently building another." For the next few minutes, it was easy enough to focus on the datapad, showing him how a few of the processes worked and how she accessed the information.

"You've really got this covered," he said at last, sounding impressed. "Maybe you should be aiming to join Command Intelligence instead."

She made a face, not that he could see it since he was sitting behind her. "No thanks. I don't actually enjoy all this sneaking around and working in the shadows. I'm doing it out of necessity, believe me."

His hand loosened on the edge of the datapad, skimming lightly up her arm until he reached her collarbone, brushing some strands of hair off her neck and leaving tingles in wake of his touch. "In case I haven't said it already, thank you, Mia. You didn't have to help me, especially after what happened yesterday."

She half turned, wishing she could see his face. "You're welcome — "

He cut off her words, taking her mouth in a sudden, forceful kiss.

She melted, just immediately liquefied into a boneless heap against the cradle of his arms around her. His lips against hers made the tension she'd carried the past few days snap free. The relief was acute, rushing through her like fuel running off a spark.

If she'd known all she needed was for Leigh to kiss her, then maybe she would have given more serious consideration to the idea of finding him alone somewhere. Instead, he'd found her. All that pressure within her, it had been everything she'd pushed down when it came to him; the truth of just how much she wanted him, how deeply she'd come to care for him.

This was the last thing they should be doing. Hadn't she just told herself how messy things already were? Yet after everything that had happened, her views on right and wrong had taken a drastic turn. And she couldn't imagine being anywhere other than here with Leigh, like all the resistance against her feelings had been pointless, because this had been inevitable.

She twisted her body, rotating to press herself flush up against him. And then somehow she managed to maneuver her thighs over his legs, his large hand on her butt helping her slide into his lap.

Oh yeah. This was what she wanted, Leigh up against her with no chance of escaping and the likelihood of them being caught almost nonexistent. Still, the knowledge of just how forbidden this was sparked an extra thrill in her already rushing blood.

She rubbed herself against him, unabashedly taking this moment for all it was worth before one of them came to their senses. Leigh groaned, his hands tightening where he held her hips. And then his fingers were tugging at her shirt, loosening fasteners with careless haste. Her shirt gone, her undershirt and bra didn't stand a chance. Leigh had them off and her breasts bared to his roaming hands in a matter of moments.

Getting rid of everything between them seemed like a great idea. She grabbed the edges of his uniform jacket and pushed, until he sat forward enough for her to shove the garment down his arms and out of the way. And then his shirt had to go, and she fumbled over each catch, since she couldn't bring herself to stop kissing him long enough to concentrate on one task at a time.

As she parted the sides of his shirt and got her hands on his muscled, heated flesh at last, Leigh started working the fastenings on her pants. They were definitely in the way. She ached to feel the rigid length of his erection pressed against her core, to relieve the throbbing that had started the second his lips had touched hers.

Unfortunately, to get out of her pants, she had to stop kissing him. She held her breath, certain he would end this as soon as he got more than a second to think about what they were doing. But his gaze roamed her body, leaving tendrils of fire licking under her skin in the wake of his heated gunmetal-blue stare. Emotion avalanched onto her from all directions. As much as burning desire had overridden the reservations she'd clung to, the man Leigh had proven to be destroyed any hope of keeping hold of her heart. He trusted her, respected her, protected her time and again.

As she sank back toward him, not a stitch of clothing on any longer, Leigh yanked her up against him, his mouth finding the tip of her breast with unerring certainty. She speared her hands into his short hair and let her head drop back, giving him free rein to lave his tongue over her nipples, followed by the decadent scrape of his teeth.

"*Mia*," he murmured against the base of her throat, his deep voice sending a cascade of shivers down her spine. "Take me, Mia. Take all of me and do whatever you want."

Her heart clenched, even as her feelings for him swelled, leaving her in dangerous territory where she knew without a doubt, she was already more than halfway in love with him. Would she be so ready to put herself in danger, to sacrifice her spot in the FP program to protect him, or even be here now, risking everything for one moment of euphoria with him, if she weren't?

Leigh dropped one hand, the back of his knuckles brushing the sensitive insides of her thighs as he unfastened his pants. She let one of her hands fall to his shoulder, preparing to take him exactly where they both wanted to go, but at the last second, her courage failed her.

Were they really about to do this? They couldn't come back from here. Once they were joined, once they were bared to each other and shared that moment of definitive completion, everything would change. Probably for the worse.

But then Leigh cupped her jaw, bringing her face closer to his. In his steady, intense regard, she saw through every insulating layer he'd built around himself, saw the man beneath who had nothing beyond his career, and what it meant that he would risk it all to be with her for this short time they had.

The last little piece of her resolve cracked and fell away. She shifted forward, keeping his mesmerizing gaze as she took him inside of her and let him slide home.

Pleasure rippled through her, and it was all she could do not to lose herself to a hard and fast climax. Leigh set his hands on her upper thighs, just below her hips and gave her the pace, taking control of the moment, despite the fact that she was on top of him.

She let him build a steady rhythm, wrapping her arms around his shoulders and holding on for dear life as the momentum built inside of her. He tilted her face and caught her mouth in an impassioned kiss, the sheer emotional depth behind it spearing straight into her soul. The final onslaught ripped her over the edge, and she cried out against his mouth.

Leigh clamped her harder to him, and she experienced the shuddering release overtaking him in every place their bodies touched, even as she felt the hot spurt of him coming deep inside her. She'd had sex before, but none of those encounters had been anywhere near as intimate as this single moment, where she realized that *this* was what people meant when they talked about making love.

She sighed as he loosened his hold on her a little, breaking the kiss, but resting his forehead against hers. For a long moment, they simply breathed together, and with every pound of her heart, a contentment the likes of which Mia had never experienced before spread through her, like the rosy glow of summer sunset.

Too soon, reality began creeping back in, along with the slight chill of the air against her damp skin. But she couldn't let him go, not yet. She sank against him, her limbs shivery and limp. Leigh altered his hold on her until they were hugging, with her cheek against his chest and his arms wrapped securely around her.

Okay, so she'd get up in a few minutes, once she was sure her legs would cooperate. And if she slipped into a sated doze, then he'd surely wake her up in a little while.

She tightened her embrace and let her thoughts fall into comfortable silence.

The pins and needles in his hand were starting to get critical, but Leigh didn't want to move, enjoying the slight, sweet-scented weight of the woman on top of him.

Mia.

His heart skipped a rushed beat, and he lifted his free hand to run a light stroke over her mussed golden hair. He couldn't remember the last time he'd felt this exact depth of peace.

It was a far cry from the head-aching stress he'd been walking around with all week. Since the incident in the transit yesterday, he'd had a sense of things being incomplete. Like there was something he needed to do, he just couldn't work out what it was. He'd put it down to the lingering adrenaline in his system and the stress of knowing there was a traitor hiding in plain sight.

When he'd come up to the alpha level launch deck, he hadn't been looking for Mia. He'd had no clue she was up here. He'd been planning to do some maintenance on his jet, get his hands dirty and shut his mind down with a menial task, something that had worked well for him in the past.

Instead, he'd found temptation sitting inside his jet, and all the reasons for resisting his attraction to her had simply fallen away, leaving him with the certainty that in that moment, Mia had been the only thing he needed.

Now, he felt like the pressure had lifted and he could breathe again, like when the cool fresh air had flooded into the transit car yesterday. The relief inundating his system at finally giving into his need for Mia had been much the same.

With a slight shift and a reach forward, he tapped the screen of the jet and glanced at the clock display in the corner. Oh one hundred.

Damn it, there was a night patrol due to come through at oh one thirty. They probably didn't have much time—sometimes the night patrol ran late, but occasionally they ran early. The last thing he needed was to be found half naked in a fighter jet with one of his recruits even more naked and perched on top of him. Yeah, his career would never come back from that.

He'd have to wake her up and get them out of here, but the last thing he wanted to do was go back to an empty bed alone. For half a second, the totally insane thought of taking Mia back to his apartment crossed his mind. Except there was no way of getting her there without someone seeing them, even at this time of night. They'd get caught, and then he'd be hearing from Commander Yang later today. And then probably be looking for another posting. However, while he had Mia in his arms like this, he couldn't dredge up as much concern for the prospect as he should.

"Mia." He whispered her name against her ear, smoothing a tangle of hair from the side of her face. "Wake up, sweetheart. We can't stay here any longer."

She murmured, but simply snuggled deeper into his hold, her face in the crook of his neck, plump lips brushing his collarbone.

Treacherous pleasure trickled beneath his skin, seeping downward and pooling in his groin.

"Mia." He stroked her back and told himself he was trying to wake her up...and not thinking about starting all over again.

Okay, he totally did want to start up all over again, despite the fact that they could get busted at any second. The only thing worse than being caught naked with one of his recruits? Being caught naked *and* in the middle of making love to one of his recruits.

"What time is it?" Mia grumbled, before yawning.

"Oh one hundred."

She sat back, gaze all sleepy and grouchy as she looked at him. "Couldn't you just let me sleep for another half hour?"

He grinned at her as she pushed her hair back and fumbled for the elastic, which had slipped free to tangle in the ends of her silky strands.

"Sure, if you wanted to be found sleeping naked on top of your commanding officer by the night patrol."

"That would make us both bigger idiots than we already are." She frowned and caught her hair up, the movement doing interesting things to her beautiful breasts. He had no idea when or if he'd ever get the chance to be with her like this again. That, of course, was the only reason he sat forward and kissed a line across the top of her chest, then spanned his hands between her shoulder blades and pressed her closer.

"Leigh." She sighed, her fingers sliding into his hair,

sending a shudder down his spine.

He caught a nipple between his lips, and knew he was lost. It didn't seem to matter that he'd just been thinking how catastrophic it would be if they got caught, he wouldn't be leaving the cozy confines of this jet until he'd stolen one last moment of pleasure with his Mia.

His Mia. No one else's. *Just mine.* After the attack a few days ago and then finally giving in to his desires tonight, that one notion had become achingly clear. He had no clue how this would all end—actually he did: in disaster—but no matter what happened, he would protect her. And maybe, just maybe, he could find a way to keep seeing her.

"We can't; we've already risked too much." Mia rocked against him, her body telling him what she wanted, despite her words to the contrary. "We should get out of here while we still can."

"I can't let you leave. Not yet. Not until—" He caught her mouth, plunging recklessly into a consuming kiss that stole the very breath from his lungs.

Mia kissed him back, desperation edging into the frenetic movements between them. Leigh tilted his hips forward, urging her up and then bringing her back down. He groaned as she enveloped him to the hilt, and then started to ride him with an unbearable cadence.

Last time, he'd taken control of the moment, but now, he couldn't have been more content to give her free rein. He took his time to touch and memorize every dip, plane, and curve of her luscious body. But the suspended stretch of time between beginning and end couldn't last.

She shortened her tempo and the ecstasy burning through him intensified. As she moaned, her body tightening up all over, he had no hope of drawing things out any longer. Even while he let go, he felt Mia shatter around him, making it all that much better.

"Oh God." Mia sank against him again, lowering her forehead to rest on his shoulder. "We shouldn't have done that again. Or at all."

A prickle of disquiet pulsed through him, but he shoved the unpleasant sensation away and cupped her face, urging her to look at him.

"Mia, I know this was unexpected and beyond complicated given our situation, but I have no regrets." He stared into her soulful, velvet eyes and swallowed down the other words crowding his throat, words about feeling and emotions. He'd never been very good at expressing those kinds of sentiments. And when things were so new, uncertain, and definitely forbidden, he couldn't bring himself to say anything that might get her hopes up.

Mia stroked a hand down the side of his face. "No regrets."

He nodded and leaned up to kiss her briefly, sweetly, and nowhere near as deeply as he wished he could. Not if they wanted to get dressed and out of this jet before the night patrol came by. He broke the kiss, but held her for a moment longer and finally let her go.

Mia slid back, groping for her bra that was hanging half over the open edge of the cockpit. He took a moment to refasten his pants, then helped her retrieve the rest of her clothes and get dressed.

"You leave first," he murmured, once she was decent again. With her gaze all bedroom eyes, her hair in a sexy tousle, and clothes irreparably rumpled, anyone who saw her between here and her bunk wouldn't need half a guess at what she'd been up to. With any luck, no one would see her, and then there wouldn't be any speculation as to whom she'd been with.

"I'll see you at oh six hundred. Get back to your bunk and snooze for a few hours." He helped her up, so she was steady.

"If I sleep in and miss the start of the lesson, you better not put me on laundry duty again because it's half your fault," she grumbled as she climbed over the side of the jet.

"Hey, I was just going to do some routine maintenance on my jet, you're the one who came up here to lie in wait for me. And I won't put you on laundry duty, I'll put you on CAFF duty, and you can't begin to imagine how torturous that is."

Guilt slipped beneath the gratification he was rocking. He'd keep an extra eye out for her today and make sure her exhaustion didn't cause her to mess up. If that meant he was playing favorites, then screw it. He owed her for all the extra work she'd done, if nothing else.

She paused on the outer side of the jet and sent him a sweet smile, one that speared right through the middle of his heart. "Bye, Leigh."

Before he could catch his breath long enough to reply, she'd slipped out of sight.

He blew out a long breath and dragged a hand down his face. For better or worse, he'd just taken his whole life and tossed it out the hatch, exposing it to the destructive vacuum of space. But never mind that, right now he had to find his shirt and get out of here before the night patrol came along and wondered why the CAFF was sitting half dressed in his fighter jet.

Chapter Fifteen

Leigh paused at the threshold of the ready room as his comm beeped. His heart skipped a beat as audio identified the caller as Commander Yang. For half a second, a sense of doom rushed through him, thinking that somehow, someone had found out about Mia and him, leaving him wondering where the hell he was going to end up posted once Yang finished raking him over the coals. But instead of imagining the worst, he took the message ordering him up to the command center.

Ah, hell. As he turned on his heel, he sent a message to Bren, asking her to take over the morning session with the recruits. Of course, Bren might be taking over every class for the rest of the training program while he settled into his new role as grunge monkey in the bowels of the *Knox*.

By the time he'd arrived outside the commander's wardroom, he'd worked up a damned decent cold sweat beneath his uniform. Getting caught seducing one of his recruits would be a humiliatingly inglorious end to what had been a pretty kick-ass career he'd made for himself in the UEF. But he'd known the risks, and he'd gone ahead with it anyway.

The commander's assistant, Command Officer Olivia McAllister—a datapad-wielding sentinel outside Yang's office, who also happened to be Colonel Cameron McAllister's sister, motioned him straight through the open door of the wardroom. With a short breath, he clasped his hands behind his back and straightened his spine as he stepped into the room. If he was about to get taken to task over his relationship with Mia, then he sure as hell was going to own it.

Except Commander Yang wasn't alone. Stanton was already seated in front of Yang's desk.

"Sir." Leigh stopped and saluted as the door whooshed shut behind him.

"Alpha." Yang motioned across the desk. "At ease, take a seat."

"Thank you, sir." He went over and lowered himself into the only other free chair in the room, next to Stanton.

"Has there been a development about the person who attacked Recruit Wolfe?" He tried to set himself into a relaxed posture, as if the answer wasn't vitally important to his peace of mind.

Yang leaned back in his seat, bracing an elbow against the armrest. "Not in terms of identifying him, but we may have confirmed the intel that suggests there is a mole in FP squadron."

"How?" His stomach churned heavy and slow, as though he'd had rocks for breakfast.

"Stanton's had an agent looking into what our mystery person might have been doing in the ready room before

Recruit Wolfe interrupted him. It seems they were trying to send out the schematics of our V-29s and other sensitive information on training and squad movements from your master datapad on an encoded, almost untraceable comm line. We've got no way to tell how much this person sent or where it ended up."

"But I've got assets on the ground looking into it," Stanton put in. "And then there's the matter of the V-29 fighter jets themselves."

Stanton's expression took on a suspicious edge, and Leigh tried not to shift in his seat, since the agent seemed to be examining him.

"What about them?"

"The first-shift maintenance crew were doing a routine check of the logs this morning," Yang took up. Leigh turned his attention back to his CO and hoped to hell he wasn't looking as guilty as he felt. "And they noticed that logs show you were on launch deck last night, between midnight and oh one hundred?"

He nodded, trying to make the movement confident, like he had nothing to hide. "Yes, sir. I often do routine maintenance on my jet, no big deal."

"So you didn't see anyone else while you were up there; otherwise I assume it would have been reported, as protocol dictates?" Stanton pressed.

He looked over at the agent, and from the terrier-like gleam in the guy's gaze, got the sense that the agent possibly knew far more than he was letting on.

"No, I didn't see anyone else," he returned, working to keep his words slow and calm. "Why? Was there evidence of someone else there last night?"

A grim shadow passed over Yang's features. "After the maintenance crew noticed your logs had been accessed, they decided to do a full check of the fleet. They found four of the jets had been tampered with."

He straightened in his chair, shock zapping through him and making the rock sensation in his guts that much worse. "Tampered with?"

Yang dragged a hand across his lower jaw. "To the point that if anyone had taken those jets out, they wouldn't have come back alive or in one piece."

"God*damn*." Leigh braced a fist against his mouth as the implications sank razor-sharp talons into him. He could have lost four pilots only a few weeks after a dirty firefight with the CSS that had seen one of his men killed and one permanently benched from his injuries.

And the person responsible for that was hiding right under his nose.

A burning kind of ferocity seethed through him. "Could Kerrin have done this before—"

Yang shook his head. "All of the jets were thoroughly checked over immediately after Kerrin was detained. This has been done within the last twenty-four hours."

All they seemed to be doing was taking blows. How the hell were they ever going to get the upper hand? "We have to find the son of a bitch responsible before he hurts someone else."

"On that we can all agree." Yang leaned forward again and clasped his hands on the neat surface of his desk. "So I need you to think, Alpha. Did you see or hear anything out of the ordinary when you were up on launch deck last night? Anything that might not have even seemed important at the time. It could be the clue we need to out the bastard."

He clenched his jaw, casting his thoughts from when he'd arrived on launch deck to when he'd walked over to his jet and found Mia sitting inside. Of course after that, his attention had shrunk to a single focus. Had the traitor been up there tampering with the jets while he'd been distracted with Mia? The thought left a trail of frost through his veins. For half a second, he considered telling Yang the truth. But with the stakes getting higher every day, he needed Mia's skills to find this bastard now more than ever. For a moment, Mia's presence in his jet struck him as entirely suspicious. But he dismissed the ridiculous thought just as quickly. It couldn't have been her; she definitely hadn't attacked herself in the ready room.

Finally, he shook his head. "I'm sorry, sir. Off the top of my head, I can't think of anything that seemed out of place. But I'll keep it in mind, and if anything comes up, you'll be the first to know."

Yang sent him a respectful nod. "Thanks, Alpha. If you can spare a little more time, the maintenance chief wanted to go over the condition of the jets with you."

He pushed to his feet. "Yes, sir, I'll head straight up. I'd like to check for myself that the rest of my squad is going to be safe out there in the black."

"Dismissed, Captain." Yang saluted him, and he returned the gesture before turning on his heel to stride out of the room.

He'd have to be dead not to notice the suspicious glare Stanton sent him as he exited the wardroom. Did the agent think he had something to do with the mole, or worse, that *he* was the mole? It would make a twisted kind of sense, because who would ever suspect the CAFF of being CSS? But in a thousand years, he would never consider joining the religious zealots who thought piety and living an honest, good existence meant keeping people in poverty and denying them the opportunity of a better life.

As he left the command center, he let his shoulders drop, though tension still hummed through him. It would take all day to do the most basic checks of every V-29 in service on the *Knox*. Though he trusted the maintenance crew, he still needed to see for himself what kind of tampering had been done and how the repairs were coming along.

However, as soon as he could find a few spare minutes, he needed to track down Mia and ask her if she'd heard or seen anyone else on launch deck last night. A jolt of cold nausea hit him. Hell, she was probably lucky whoever had tampered with the jets hadn't found her, because they might have finished what they'd started the night before in the ready room.

Whoever it was, once he found them, they were going to wish they'd never infiltrated his pilots.

Mia covered her mouth with her hand and yawned for the millionth time, the chatter going on in the PT room battering her already aching head.

"I'm sorry, Recruit Wolfe, are we boring you again today?" Lieutenant Brenner asked as Mia stepped up to grip the weights of a nearby machine.

"Sir, no, sir. I stayed up to late last night, sir."

Brenner eyed her more closely.

"Studying, sir. I was trying to make up for the classes I missed, sir." A rush of heat flared through her.

The lieutenant nodded and then moved off to set another recruit up at a weight station.

"You *so* weren't studying."

Mia turned to where Kayla was pushing and pulling against the weights in the machine next to her.

Kayla shot her a mischievous look. "Don't think I didn't notice how late you came back to your bunk last night. Just please tell me you weren't with a-hole Steve."

Mia glanced away as the heat in her chest crept up her neck, leaving her face burning. "I wasn't with Steve."

Kayla made a sound of relief. "I knew you were smarter than that. So, come on, spill. Who were you with?"

She concentrated on meeting the weight requirements with each set. "I wasn't with anyone. I really was studying and then I fell asleep. I woke up with a crick in my neck and decided I better get back to my bunk."

"Pft!" Kayla finished her set. "I understand why you'd want to keep it quiet. It's easy for a girl to get a reputation around here. But I wouldn't ever tell. You can trust me. Just let me live vicariously through your apparently exciting love life. I can't remember the last time I had a guy get me off good and solid."

A laugh ambushed her at Kayla's choice in words, and her new friend sent her a grin.

"I wish I could tell you something exciting happened, but I really was glued to my datapad. You want to know where I was? I snuck up to port level alpha to get another look in one of the fighter jets."

Kayla shot her a glance that was part scandalized, part

admiring. "You didn't! Score one for Mia. I didn't think you had that kind of rebel inside of you."

What would Kayla say if she knew the truth of what else she'd been doing in that jet? And with whom. One of the other recruits called out to Kayla, who sent her a quick wave when she crossed the PT room.

As Mia walked over to the next testing station, she glanced around. And if she was searching for a certain head of coffee-dark hair, an unmistakable swagger, or the intense regard of gunmetal-blue eyes, well, it was her weakness. After last night, she was willing to wear the flaw.

She hadn't seen Leigh since she'd left him in the jet. He hadn't made an appearance at messdeck, hadn't been present for role call and review of the previous day's activities, and hadn't joined the other instructors when they'd moved onto another round of rigorous physical testing.

As the day wore on, tendrils of anxiety had started creeping in under her calm belief that the two of them had gotten away with their assignation. What if someone had seen them and reported it to Commander Yang? What if, even now, Leigh was up in the command center, trying to explain what had led him into seducing a young recruit? What if they shipped him off in disgrace and she never saw him again?

Panic clamped around her chest, but she made herself breathe long and steady to release to tightness. If the worst really had come to pass, surely she would have heard about it by now, surely they *all* would have heard about it by now.

So instead of giving in to the gnawing urge to ask one of the other instructors where Captain Alphin was today, she forced herself to concentrate on each task. She was already tired; adding any more distraction was just asking to wash out.

The instructors organized for a meager lunch to be delivered to the PT room, and the break was too short. Her limbs burned, head felt heavy, and body worn down in a way she'd rarely experienced. But, despite her lack of sleep, she didn't seem to be faring any worse than the rest of the recruits. The endless drills and demanding regimes were pushing everyone outside their limits. On top of all that, they still had to learn and retain the theory, not to mention pass random tests on any of the subjects they'd covered since training had begun. Already that morning, three people had given up and made the choice to wash out.

As the instructors announced that lunch was finished and ordered activities to resume, amongst a quiet chorus of groans and mumblings, the CAFF finally made an appearance, striding into the gym with his usual don't-mess-with-me walk and stopping next to Lieutenant Brenner, no doubt for a report of the day's proceedings. However, he wasn't looking his usual impeccable self. His uniform was definitely on the rumpled side, streaked with dust, while a smudge of what looked to be engine grease smeared his jawline. Yeah, he was looking rumpled, but in a sexy, getting-his-hands-dirty-with-some-hard-work way, which only made her breath that much harder to catch as she recalled exactly where he'd had those hands last night.

"Recruit Wolfe." At Lieutenant Brenner's call she straightened, training her gaze ahead and not letting herself focus on anyone. "The CAFF requires your presence in ready room one one."

Her heart bumped against the inside of her chest, and

she strove to keep her expression neutral. What the heck was Leigh playing at? Singling her out in front of everyone and then taking her off for a private chat was not the way to keep their relationship secret. Nonetheless, she sent a respectful nod to the lieutenant, then clasped her hands behind her back and followed Leigh across the mats, feeling like every gaze in the room bored into her.

They crossed the hall and entered the ready room directly across the way, the lights flickering on as they entered. As the door slid shut behind her, she came to a stop and glanced over her shoulder. Leigh took a moment to enter what she assumed were his officer codes, meaning no one would be getting into this room unless he wanted them to. Her pulse accelerated from fast to light speed, but she determinedly ignored the foolish organ. He wasn't going to try anything here in the middle of the day. At least she *thought* he wouldn't…

"What's going on?" She looked back at him to find he'd let his CAFF mask slip and transformed into the Leigh she'd been with last night. He rubbed a hand over his jaw, looking stressed and a little tired. Her heart squeezed for him, and she only just resisted the urge to go over and put her arms around him. "Do you really think it was a good idea to pull me out of class after last night—"

He shook his head. "No one has any reason to suspect anything. I told Bren I'd been in a meeting with Yang this morning and needed to ask you some follow up questions about your attack, which is actually true."

Her ribs contracted around her lungs for a long second. "So last night…?"

He sent her a smile that didn't quite reach his eyes. "It

seems we got away with it, if that's what you're worried about. But we've got another problem."

"Okay." She walked over and leaned against the front of a desk.

Leigh blew out a short breath. "I need to know if you saw anyone else or heard anything on the launch deck last night before I got there."

She shook her head. "I think I was the only one there, but I did have my headphones in and music on, so I guess I can't be sure. Why?"

He glanced away from her and paced a few steps, his expression becoming more haunted. "I got called up to see Commander Yang and a Command Intelligence agent, Stanton, first thing this morning. Several of the jets were tampered with, possibly last night. If the interference hadn't been found and those jets had been taken out, I'd have another couple of dead pilots on my hands."

She pushed upright, stepping forward to intercept his pacing. "I'm sorry, Leigh. I can't imagine what you must be feeling right now, being responsible for all those pilots. I'll get those profiles done as soon as I can and hopefully something will turn up. In the meantime, you have to find a way to maybe distance yourself, because if you burn out, you won't be any good to anyone."

He sighed, scrubbing a hand over his hair. "You're right, but it's just so damn frustrating, like we're playing one step behind and losing ground every second."

"We're not losing ground. We'll find him, I'm sure we will." She stepped closer to him, feeling like her reassurance wasn't enough, wishing there was some way to make this better for him. Obviously, the best way to help him was to finish building those profiles and discover who the traitor might be.

"Come on, you better get back to class. And I've got to get back up to the launch deck to finish checking over the jets with the maintenance chief."

"Is that where you've been all morning?" She reached up and wiped her thumb over the smudge on his jaw, his short whiskers abrading her skin, but in a way that gave her a buzz.

"Yeah, getting grungy beneath the engines of the V-29s to make sure my pilots are all safe next time they're out in the black."

Her chest squeezed around her heart, breaking up the steady rhythm. Not many CAFFs would do that kind of work themselves. No matter which way she looked at him, Leigh was one of the most caring, dedicated men she'd ever met. And every day she fell that little bit harder for him.

With her hand still on his jaw, she went up on her toes, leaning against his chest to set a teasing kiss just next to his mouth. She went to move back, but his arms clamped around her, keeping her trapped up against his chest.

"What was that, recruit?" The demand was in that scary CAFF voice he was prone to using, but it didn't do anything except turn her on.

She sent him an impertinent grin. "Sir, I believe I just kissed you, sir."

"Wolfe, if you're going to go around kissing your CO, at least make sure you do it properly."

Before she could reply, his hand closed around the back of her neck as he pulled her up the few inches separating them and caught her mouth beneath his. The kiss wasn't demanding or hard, instead his lips moved almost gently, leisurely over hers, as though he was learning and memorizing the almost palpable force flowing between them.

The kiss deepened, and the energy changed, amping up as his tongue slid against hers, sending a muscle-weakening shudder rocking through her.

Leigh pulled back suddenly, swearing on the unsteady breath he blew out.

"We have to stop now; otherwise I'm going to start thinking it's a good idea to take you on that desk while a class of recruits and my XO are right across the hall."

He let her go, and she took her own uneven breath, smoothing her hands down her uniform. Her clothes weren't any worse off than when she'd walked in here, but she definitely felt rumpled and more than a little flustered from that heady kiss.

Leigh seemed to take a moment himself, then clasped his hands behind his back and walked over to push the door release. She set her posture as she marched back across to the PT room, trying to look as impassive as possible. At the doorway, Leigh waved to Lieutenant Brenner and then stepped back to let Mia pass.

She didn't look up at him as she went by, but the shock of his hand brushing her hip sent a pulse of heat through her. She couldn't help glancing back over her shoulder at him, and the gleam in his gray-blue gaze stalled her breath.

She tore her gaze from him and made a beeline for Kayla on the other side of the room. She'd never thought having any kind of relationship with him would be easy; in fact she'd been set against it until last night. And the awareness of everything that could befall him if they got caught was a constant niggle in the back of her mind. Sure, he didn't seem that worried, but she was horrified by the censure and criticism he'd face if their relationship became public knowledge. And the worry over the traitor had just doubled as once again, the mole proved to be aiming to kill. As if Leigh's day-to-day duties weren't dangerous enough, knowing he had someone working against him from the inside made ice form in her chest.

She had to get working on those profiles, build them more quickly, before the traitor made another move. Because next time, they might not be lucky enough to find the trap before it snapped closed.

Chapter Sixteen

Another day had gone by and Mia was about ready to throw the datapad in frustration.

She was no closer to finding the mole—her program had completed three more profiles that revealed the pilots to be exactly who they said they were, with no dark secrets in their pasts. And, her torturously slow but thorough checks of the *Knox's* systems hadn't turned up anything out of the ordinary. She couldn't believe what had happened in the transit was just a coincidence, yet she couldn't find any proof of tampering either.

She glanced over the notes she'd taken for the day's class, some of them sadly incomplete because she was so damn distracted—by her need to find the traitor and the man currently standing in front of the class. If she weren't careful, she'd end up washing out of the program and find herself on the ground. Besides it being rather hard to access the *Knox's* systems and help Leigh from down there, she also sure as hell didn't want to get posted on the front lines.

A reminder icon flashed in the corner of Leigh's datapad, and she automatically reached out to tap it up, even though she'd been strict about not snooping through any private files. But what if it was something important he'd forgotten about because he'd given her his datapad?

The reminder appeared in the middle of the screen. *Meeting: squadron officer's wardroom, nineteen hundred hours—to discuss appropriate usage of fighter jets while docked on launch deck.*

Anyone else reading the reminder would have thought nothing of it, but considering where she'd been the night before last... She glanced up, looking directly at Leigh for the first time all day. It'd been easier to keep her thoughts straight by simply taking her notes and pretending he wasn't even in the room.

The recruits all had their heads down, concentrating on some task she didn't have the first clue about since she hadn't been listening. Leigh held the ready room's master datapad, which was obviously how he'd sent the reminder to his own device. When he caught her eye, he sent her a subtle nod, his lips kicking up on one side for a brief moment.

A message for her. Her heart tripped over itself and then sped into double time. He wanted to meet in the officer's wardroom at nineteen hundred. Probably to check how her profiles were going. Better that was the only reason he wanted to meet her.

A swell of heat rushed up her chest as she dropped her gaze back to the datapad. Though her body might have other ideas about what it wanted to be doing while she was alone with him, her last shred of common sense sternly warned her that the more times they were together, the more likely they were to get caught.

No matter how good it had been, all logic was telling her it wasn't going to end well. Whether they got caught or not, they didn't have a future, especially since she'd firmed up her decision to ask for a position elsewhere once she made it through the rest of this program. They were over halfway through, and she still had that free pass up her sleeve. If she could just hold out for another week, if she could just stop herself from getting in any deeper with him, then maybe they'd both come out of this unscathed. Well, mostly anyway. She'd probably never see him again once she transferred to another unit, but she couldn't take any chance of ruining his career.

The last hour of the class slowed to a crawl because she couldn't help checking the time every few minutes.

For the second day in a row, Steve waited for her when she stepped out of class. Yesterday he'd asked her out again, if a girl could call an invitation to join him in his bunk after midnight a date. She so didn't have the patience to deal with him again today. Gaining Kayla's attention, she pointed Steve out, and luckily her friend seemed to get the hint, putting herself between them and then steering her to the outer side of the crowd, making some loud announcement about going to get an early dinner on commerce level instead of eating at the messdeck. The distraction worked, as a couple of others asked to join in. They'd managed to move off before Steve could approach her, though from the look on his face, he hadn't liked being thwarted.

Early evening didn't go any faster. She was distracted at the impromptu dinner at one of the fast-food joints on commerce level and then distracted when she hung out with Kayla and a couple of the other recruits at some bar. Finally, just before nineteen hundred hours, she came up with the excuse that she was still trying to catch up on the sessions she'd missed and made her escape.

The officer's wardroom—off-limits to subordinates without express permission—seemed like a strange place for Leigh to ask her to meet. What if one of the senior fighter pilots like Lieutenant Brenner or Sub-Lieutenant Rayne or Sub-Officer Lawler came by and found them? Despite her misgivings about the meeting place, she trusted Leigh so none of the rest mattered.

She arrived on squadron level, the corridors deserted like the night she'd come up here and been attacked by the shooter. Except this time, the lights were still on, which meant there still must be FP personnel somewhere. She passed the darkened ready rooms, heading for the room at the end of the passage. The datapad in her hand chimed and she glanced down to see a message from Leigh, telling her he was running a little late, but to wait for him.

The lights were on in the officer's wardroom and the door was open. She passed a quick glance over the central conference table, the amenities bar on the far wall, and the viewport showing the very edge of Ilari and the star-dusted blackness of space beyond.

She went to sit on the long couch set in front of the viewport, deciding she might as well get on with the profiles while she waited for Leigh. However, she'd only just tapped the screen to life when she heard footsteps. She glanced up, but the person appearing in the doorway wasn't Leigh. Steve Robinson stopped when he saw her sitting there, his expression cold enough to leave shivers tracking over her flesh.

"What are you doing here?" She set the datapad on a nearby table and stood.

A calculating gleam in his gaze, Steve said, "Following you. Now it's your turn to tell me what you're doing here."

Her mind flashed with a second of intense panic, because Steve was the last person she wanted to see. He was the type who would use her relationship with Leigh for maximum damage.

"I'm behind since I missed out on those sessions. Captain Alphin and Lieutenant Brenner wanted to speak to me about it, and I'm sure they'll be here any second."

Steve stepped into the room, his movements unhurried. "Really? That's interesting, because I know for a fact that Captain Hard-Ass, along with Brenner, Lawler, and Rayne, are playing their weekly poker game in the common room, and everyone knows they'll be there for hours. So what's your real reason for being here, Mia?"

Is that what had Leigh running late, a *poker* game? Just how did he plan on getting out of that without raising suspicions, if he was playing with the other three instructors?

Well, no matter what, she had to get rid of Steve. He strolled farther into the room, rounding the end of the table.

"See, I've started getting a little curious," he continued when she didn't reply. "You're kind of antisocial. I mean, first you don't want to hang out with me, and in the last few days you always seem to be off on your own studying."

He reached the end of the conference table and stopped a handful of steps away from her. Something in his demeanor, in the way he stared at her, set alarm bells off in her mind.

"You got me. I don't want to be friends with anyone. I'm more interested in beating you all out for a spot in the FP squadron." Never mind getting rid of Steve, she didn't want to stay in this room with him any longer. She'd have to arrange to meet Leigh another time. Stooping down, she picked up the datapad. "So, sorry, but I've got more of that studying to do."

She went to step past him, but he grabbed her arm, his fingers biting into her biceps hard enough to bruise. "We're not finished talking yet."

A trickle of fear skulked through her, but anger washed it away. "Let me go."

"Not yet. Not until we've agreed to some terms, because the way I see it, you owe me for the free pass you picked up on day one. I could have beat you and Kayla easy, but I was trying to be a gentleman."

She scoffed and yanked her arm out of his grip, wrenching her shoulder in the process. "A *gentleman*? That's about the last word I'd use to describe you. I don't owe you anything, so get out of my way before I decide to comm the MPs and make a complaint about you harassing me."

He held his arms out wide, conceited grin spreading over his features. "Go ahead. Call the MPs. I'd love to hear your explanation about why you're in the officer's wardroom."

Damn it, he'd called her bluff and from the expression on his face, he knew it.

"Whatever. Just leave me alone." She sidestepped, intending to make for the exit, but he grabbed her shoulder, forced her back around, and shoved her up against the table. The edge rammed into her lower back with bruising force. Ignoring the sharp kick of pain in her lower spine, she dropped the datapad and pushed against his hold. Dread mixed in a tempest with fury, billowing through her in hot and cold waves.

"Let me go, or this isn't going to end well for you."

Steve's grin turned into a leer as he kept hold of her shoulder and grabbed her wrist. "Actually, I think it's going to end very well for me. Maybe not so much for you."

She twisted her arm out of his hold and aimed a fist for his face, though she didn't get much momentum behind it because of the way he clutched her. Still, it surprised him enough to loosen his grip, and when her other hand was free, she shoved him and followed with a second punch to the jaw, leaving her knuckles aching.

But it wasn't enough to completely dislodge him and he came back at her, hitting her in the face hard enough to make her head spin, and this time throwing his whole body weight against her in a crushing hold. Blood trickled from a cut on his lip.

"You *bitch*. Now you owe me for that, too." He changed his grip on her, twisting her around and forcing her face-down on the cold surface of the desk with a hand biting into the back of her neck. With his other hand, he reached down and grabbed the collar edge of her shirt, giving a sharp yank, causing fasteners to pop free and the material to rip. She screeched, bucking against him, but he only plunged his hand into her hair, yanking the strands at her scalp until her eyes watered.

"Don't think I won't knock you unconscious and do you anyway." He leaned down, hot breath in her ear, making her want to gag. "It's easier, but not as fun."

Oh God. Had he done this before? For a blind second,

absolute terror surged through her. But then the anger returned, sharper and more desperate. She would not be another one of his victims. She snapped her head back, connecting with his face. While he was still reeling, she used her hands against the edge of the deck to propel herself backward, knocking him off-balance. She turned and, before he could regain any footing, kicked out at his groin. Her foot didn't quite connect as hard or on target as she'd hoped, but it was enough to send him to his knees. She went to dash past him, but he reached out and grabbed at her legs, tripping her into the chairs by the table. One caught her in the ribs, another scraped the edge of her jaw. But she didn't let it slow her down. She kicked at his hold, but missed completely and nailed him in the face—couldn't have knocked him better if she'd been aiming for his head.

He let her go and she scrambled up, collecting Leigh's datapad from the floor at the last second and sprinting out of the room and down the passageway. She didn't stop running until she'd reached the transit. Glancing over her shoulder, she repeatedly tapped at the screen, knowing it wouldn't bring the transit any faster, but doing it anyway.

The seconds rattled by, and she glanced several times between the display and the passageway behind her, sure Steve would emerge any moment for a second try.

An aftershock of panic rocked through her as various injuries started to ache. She wrapped an arm across her burning ribs, where she'd caught the chair as she went down, forcing herself to breathe slowly. She felt a trickle over her jaw and used her sleeve to wipe at the ooze of blood from a small split on her cheek where Steve had hit her.

She should report this. She *had* to report this. But if she did, everyone would want to know why she'd been in the officer's wardroom.

Frustration pulsed through her, because she hated the idea of Steve getting away with it, even though he technically hadn't done anything except knock her around a bit. But his confession that he'd done it before made a sick kind of fury twist up her insides. She burned to do something; she just didn't know what. Her situation with Leigh and the fact that his career was on the line kept her hands tied.

The transit finally chimed as it arrived and she started to step toward the doors, but froze as she realized someone was already in the car.

Leigh stood there, hands clasped behind his back, waiting to get off the transit. Shock flashed across his features when he saw her, and he closed the distance between them in a few short strides, reaching out to pull her into him.

"Mia! What the hell happened?"

She grimaced as he grabbed her bruised arm in the exact same spot Steve had held her. For a second she clenched her jaw, indecision riding her. Part of her wanted to let everything gush out, knowing he'd make it all better simply by hugging her and telling her she was okay. But another part of her didn't want to tell him the truth. Leigh was an honorable man, considering all that had happened between them, he obviously cared about her somewhat. She didn't want him to go after Steve on her behalf, because that would only raise the suspicions about their relationship they were trying to avoid.

Except Leigh didn't deserve her lying to him. More than that, she couldn't lie to him, she just wasn't that sort of person.

"Steve Robinson. He followed me up to the wardroom." She wanted to ask if it had really been a poker game keeping him from arriving sooner, but she pressed her lips shut over the pointless question.

An unholy wrath sparked in Leigh's gaze the likes of which she'd never seen before. Truthfully, it scared her a little.

"Did he—" He swallowed the end of that question, but she knew what he was asking. His gaze roamed over her and when it caught on her ripped shirt, his grip on her shoulders tightened a fraction, his features hardening with lethal rage.

"He tried, but I fought him off."

An unmistakable relief passed over his features, his hands gentle on her shoulders. "Damn it, I'm sorry. If I hadn't been late—"

"Please, it's not your fault. Just forget about it. I doubt he'll be game enough to try again. I just want to get back to my room and get tidied up before anyone else sees me."

Leigh let her go and moved back, shoving a hand through his hair. "Forget about it?" His voice was hoarse. "He hurt you, and you want me to *forget about it*?"

She reached out and grabbed his forearm. "It's not worth it. He isn't worth it."

His gaze focused on her with burning intensity. "But you are. You're worth it. He's not going to get away with this."

He stepped past her, but she grabbed his arm to stop him.

"Wait, what are you going to do?"

Leigh cracked his knuckles, the cold fury in his gray-blue eyes telling her the answer she feared.

"Go back to your dorm, Mia. I'll come find you when

I've dealt with Robinson." He gently pulled his arm from her grip and steered her onto the transit, then hit dorms on the screen and stepped out again. The doors slid closed, cutting him off from sight.

Oh God, this was bad. Right in that second, she had no idea what Leigh might be capable of. She couldn't let him kill Steve, even if the guy probably deserved it. She knew what she had to do, even though it was probably going to cost a lot. Maybe everything.

Hand shaking, she accessed the transit screen and changed the destination. The short trip seemed to take forever, but finally she arrived on communal level and headed for the common room where Lieutenant Brenner, Sub-Officer Lawler, and Sub-Lieutenant Rayne were apparently playing poker. She just hoped they were still there. As she entered, she tried to keep her head down, but there was probably no way to disguise the state she was in.

She reached the table where Lieutenant Brenner and Sub-Lieutenant Rayne were playing poker, though Sub-Officer Lawler wasn't at the table.

Lieutenant Brenner dropped her cards to the table when she glanced up and saw her standing there.

"Wolfe, what the hell happened to you?"

She took an anxious half breath, pretending she didn't realize everyone in the room was staring at her. "Can we talk, but not here? It's urgent—"

She'd hardly finished saying the words before the lieutenant nodded at Rayne and the two of them stood, escorting her out into the passageway.

"What's going on?" Brenner asked, once they came to a stop.

"You need to get up to squadron level, right now. Captain Alphin has gone after Steve Robinson and I'm worried he's going to—" She couldn't even finish the sentence; she'd never seen someone so coldly furious as Leigh had been before the transit doors had closed.

"Is Robinson the one who did this to you?" Rayne demanded.

"Yes, but it doesn't matter right now; we have to stop Leigh before he does something—" She closed her mouth as soon as she realized she'd slipped up and used his first name. A flash of realization crossed Brenner's face, before she glanced at Rayne with a grim expression.

"Come on, Seb. Wolfe, you, too."

She nodded, guilt and acid-like trepidation burning through her that she'd given everything away. But if it was a choice between outing their relationship and stopping Leigh from doing something that could ruin his life in an even worse way, then there was no question. She followed Brenner and Rayne back to the transit, hoping they didn't get there too late.

Chapter Seventeen

By the time Leigh reached the wardroom, his icy rage had worked itself into a hard lump sitting square on the middle of his chest. Didn't matter if Robinson was still there or not, he would scour every inch of this ship until he'd found the bastard.

As he went to step into the wardroom, Robinson came limping out, using the back of his hand to wipe the blood on his mouth. Cold satisfaction rippled through him. Looked like Mia had kicked his ass. But the guy still needed a hard lesson in manners.

Robinson glanced up, eyes widening a second before Leigh closed the distance between them, grabbed a fistful of Robinson's shirt, and shoved him up against the bulkhead. He hauled back, putting every ounce of burning fury behind the fist he smashed into the a-hole's face. When he went for a second blow, Robinson threw an arm up to block him, and clocked him in the side of the head with an elbow.

Although Leigh staggered slightly, the blow didn't faze him. He took it and then went in for more, because if the guy was going to hit him back, that made this a fair fight. And never let it be said he didn't fight fair.

He caught the front of Robinson's shirt, and this time when the guy brought his elbow up, Leigh blocked the hit and retaliated with a strike in the gut. Robinson doubled over as far as Leigh's hold on him would allow. He half lifted Robinson and thumped him back into the wall.

"What's wrong, Robinson? Can't fight back against someone stronger than you?"

He hooked in a left punch, messing up the side of Robinson's face that had been untouched. Leigh hauled back, intent on aiming for the bastard's intact nose, but someone got hands under his arms and jerked him away.

Robinson slumped to the floor, pressing a hand against the side of his face.

"He attacked me out of nowhere!" Robinson yelled, pointing a shaking finger at him.

Leigh yanked out of the hold on him with a violent wrench, glancing over his shoulder to see Seb staring at him with an expression that landed somewhere between incredulous and horrified.

Bren brushed by him and knelt down next to Robinson, grabbing his chin and tilting his head, apparently examining the guy's injuries. Didn't anyone care about Robinson trying to rearrange his teeth? Leigh worked his jaw back and forth over the ache as he glanced at Seb again.

"For God's sake, stop looking at me like that." He turned away, his gaze homing in on Mia, where she stood near one of the ready rooms.

Leigh stalked the short distance down the corridor and stopped in front of her. She started to retreat, but he latched a hand onto her arm to stop her from going anywhere. The rapidly forming bruise and blood smeared across her jaw made his rage bubble up all over again, but he locked his muscles against moving. Bren and Seb wouldn't let him get near the sonuvabitch again anyway.

"Are you all right?" He touched a finger to her jaw, tilting her head up slightly.

She nodded, her expression determinedly calm, yet he didn't fail to notice the wetness on the edges of her thick lashes.

Though he'd told himself to detach, that he wouldn't allow himself anything except the most impersonal contact in front of others, that hint of tears broke the last resolve within him. But instead of going back over to pound Robinson into a bloody pulp, he pulled her against him, wrapping her into a tight embrace. He felt her take one shuddering breath and then another, as though within the safety of his arms, she could let go of the composed mask she hid behind. He lowered his head, resting his lips against her hair, and squeezed her tighter for a second, hoping she got his silent message that everything was okay.

"We need to talk."

He looked up to see Bren had stopped beside him, her gaze slowly moving back and forth between Mia and him.

He had to let her go, but his arms weren't willing to unclamp their hold on her. However, Mia shifted, gently pushing to put some distance between them.

"I'm fine; you can go." She stepped out of his hold and shot him a tremulous smile that was probably meant to be encouraging.

Despite not wanting to leave Mia in the vicinity of the coward who'd just assaulted her, he trailed Bren a short distance along the passageway, not letting himself even glance at Robinson. Or hear whatever rubbish the guy was yacking at Seb. He didn't quite trust himself not to lose it again if he laid eyes on the bastard's smarmy face.

Leigh shook his head at himself. What in the hell had happened to his much-prized self-control, to the legendary calm-under-fire persona of Alpha? Robinson touching Mia had been like striking the match that burned it all to the ground.

Bren walked a few steps ahead of him, taking them over to the nearest ready room. As soon as they'd entered the hatchway, she rounded on him.

"What the hell was that? You almost beat that recruit unconscious."

Leigh flexed his aching fist; a glance down at his hand revealed a busted knuckle. "Yeah, I did. That's what I do when I find out a guy tried to rape a woman, no matter who he is."

Bren went rigid at his words. "Are you telling me that Robinson—"

"No." He blew out a hard breath. The image of Mia when the transit doors opened fired him up all over again. "Mia said he didn't. But he could probably be charged on grounds of sexual assault. We might also be able to pin him with intent to rape."

Bren moved to lean against one of the desks. "This is a mess. Robinson is claiming he didn't touch Wolfe, that you simply came up here and started attacking him without provocation."

Leigh threw out an arm in disbelief. "You saw her, the condition she's in. There's no doubt that he did something to her."

She rubbed the back of her neck in an agitated movement. "That's all well and good, Alpha, but it's her word against his, and you coming up here to beat the hell out of him isn't going to help matters. You've probably only made things worse."

A frosty thread of apprehension crept through him. "What do you mean?"

Bren shrugged. "Robinson wants to put in an official complaint against you. He says he never touched Mia, and you used excessive force in dealing with a simple misunderstanding."

"A simple misunderstanding?" He gave a short, disbelieving laugh. "I don't think I misunderstood things when I stepped out of the transit and saw Mia all bruised and bloody. *Jesus*."

Was the bastard actually going to get away with this? He couldn't even use the security feed as proof—he'd had it turned off earlier for the planned meeting with Mia, which wasn't unusual when classified or sensitive material was being discussed.

Bren speared him with a weighted look. "Leigh, we've dealt with some serious crap over the years, but I've never seen you lose it like that before. What is going on with you?"

"Nothing is going on with me." Leigh dragged a hand down his face, groping for his equilibrium. Once this got back to Commander Yang, there'd be any number of people taking a closer look at things, and if they discovered even a hint of what happened between Mia and him—

The consequences were too numerous and thorny to even consider. God, could he have screwed things any better for himself?

"It's her, isn't it? Mia. That's why you lost it. If it had been any other female member of the crew, yeah you would have been pissed. But what I saw in there…you were possessed."

He glanced at his XO. No point saying anything when the truth was probably written all over his face.

"I've known you a long time, and I couldn't help but notice the way you've been looking at her in the last few days." She held up a hand. "I'm not judging. I'd started wondering if the heart in that chest of yours would beat for anything other than duty. I'm not going to mention this to anyone, despite what happened just now. I'm sure I don't have to remind you that she's fifteen years younger than you, and under your command. I know you're smart enough not to let anything happen between you and one of your subordinates."

Ah, hell. He didn't deserve Bren's loyalty and couldn't bear to look at her right then.

"You *are* that smart, right, Alpha? Please tell me you haven't been fooling around with one of the recruits entrusted to your care. Are you *trying* to commit career suicide?"

"I haven't been fooling around with Mia," he managed to say with a straight face and perfect amount of sincerity.

No, he hadn't been fooling around with her, but he sure as hell had made love with her. Twice.

Bren blew out a sharp breath and then stood. "Thank God. Then we can totally contain this."

"As long as Robinson is out of the program, I don't care."

Bren sent him an unimpressed look, but before she

could answer, the ready room door opened. Seb and Lawler walked in, followed by Commander Yang.

This had gone up the chain already? Despite the pulse of trepidation pushing through him, Leigh decided to take it as a good sign. Things would be taken care of quickly and quietly, which meant minimal trauma for Mia.

"Captain Alphin, you've made a mess out of this." Commander Yang crossed the room with his usual uneven gait and paused to lean an elbow on the lectern. "There are protocols when it comes to this sort of thing, and I don't remember beating the hell out of the alleged perpetrator being one of them."

"You have my apologies, sir. I lost my head for a minute. It won't happen again." Especially once he didn't have to see Robinson's smug face any longer.

"You better make sure it doesn't, because even though I'm sure you're hoping otherwise, Recruit Robinson will be staying in the FP program for the time being."

The fury he'd been working to tamp down snapped out of its restraints and tore through him with a dash of incredulity to round it out. "Sir, you can't allow Robinson to remain in the program after what he did. What kind of message does that send—"

"And what kind of message would it send to have my CAFF beat the crap out of a recruit before booting that recruit from the program? I've spoken to both Wolfe and Robinson and I'm getting two completely different versions."

Leigh grabbed in a long breath, using the cool air to stuff the antagonism back down. "Sir, how many years have you known me? When I tell you that Robinson assaulted Wolfe, then you can take that to the bank."

Yang sent him a faintly sympathetic look. "I know, Leigh. But this isn't about whether or not I trust in you. This is about what will hold up if it went as far as a court martial. You didn't see the assault take place. It's her words against his. And if you didn't realize, Steve's father just happens to be Admiral Richard Robinson."

Leigh swore. "Of course he is. Someone who is that big an a-hole wouldn't be just anyone's kid."

"I don't think the admiral will take too kindly to his son getting the spit beat out of him by a superior officer who also happened to be his CO," Yang continued. "And personally I don't need a visit from that kind of brass. So yes, despite my own opinion on the subject, Recruit Robinson will be staying in the program until such time as he washes out on his own, fair and square."

Leigh rubbed the back of his neck, where agitation burned high. "So that's it then. He puts the moves on one of the female recruits against her will and gets off totally free?"

Yang straightened from the lectern and crossed his arms. "Robinson has received a behavioral warning from me personally, and will need some kind of attitude adjustment, which I'll leave up to you and Lieutenant Brenner to impart. Robinson will own whatever responsibility you bestow upon him until the end of the program, or he drops out. Hopefully that should take up too much of his time for him to even think about any out-of-hours activities."

Leigh forced himself not to grin. In other words, Yang was giving Bren and him free license to make Robinson's life a living hell until he either quit, or—as unlikely as it seemed—completed training.

"Yes, sir. Thank you, sir."

Yang sent him a short nod. "Next time, Alpha, follow the damn rules to the letter. The only reason I'm not slapping you with your own infraction notice is because of your pristine record up to now. Don't make me change my mind."

"I won't, sir."

Yang bid them all farewell and then disappeared out into the passageway. For a moment, silence stretched, but then Seb turned on him.

"What the hell was that?"

Leigh crossed his arms, only just stopping himself from rolling his eyes. "I just had this conversation with Bren less than five minutes ago. She can fill you in. Meanwhile, I'm going to go see Ace about my jaw and hand."

He walked out of the room, ignoring Seb's bitching, and took himself down the passageway to the transit-porter. While he waited for the transit to arrive, he cast a short glance around.

Where was Mia? She'd told him she was fine, but he needed to make certain for himself. Unless he could get her alone, however, he knew she wouldn't admit to any kind of weakness.

Unfortunately, if they ended up somewhere by themselves, he had firsthand experience of what would become of his self-control. After everything that had just happened, and with Bren knowing some of the truth, the last thing he should be doing was risk being caught alone with Mia, even if he managed to keep himself in check and not touch her. The rumor mill would be spinning at light speed over this event and simply talking to Mia could easily add fuel to the fire.

So, no matter how his chest ached at the knowledge of

her earlier distress and his longing to comfort her in every way he could think of, he was going to have to totally cut himself off from her for a few days, just until the heat died down.

And during that time, he probably needed to take a long hard look at what exactly he was doing to himself.

Chapter Eighteen

Mia sat in one of the plastic utilitarian chairs in the passageway just outside the quarantine airlock doors on med level. Commander Yang had insisted she come down here for a checkup, despite the fact she must have told four different people she was fine. But when the commander of the *Valiant Knox* gave an order, a person had absolutely no choice but to follow it.

Going to get checked out had been all well and good, until she'd arrived in the ER and found Steve being treated for the injuries Leigh had inflicted on him. At the sight of him bloodied, with his face already turning interesting shades of black and blue, she'd spun and marched right back out again, but had only made it as far as these chairs before her legs gave up on her. She couldn't have gone much farther anyway, not until one of the doctors cleared her per Commander Yang's mandate.

Sitting there alone was not helping regain any of her

composure. She could only worry about what this situation may have exposed. Leigh's reaction to her being attacked and her slip up in using his name in front of Lieutenant Brenner may have revealed there was more going on between them than a simple CO-recruit relationship.

She'd started chewing on her thumbnail not long after sitting down, something she hadn't done since she was a kid. But no matter how many times she told herself to stop it and lowered her hand, she ended up doing it again when the dire thoughts got the better of her. Since she still had Leigh's datapad, she'd even tried getting back into the diagnostics she'd been running, but her brain wouldn't cooperate.

Across the passageway, the transit doors whooshed open, and the current subject of her problems strode out of the lift. His gaze landed on her, a range of emotions flashing across his face before his expression became neutral.

He glanced up and down the corridor, then crossed over and dropped into the chair next to her. Mia's lungs stuttered, making it hard to draw a full breath as she stared at him, this man who'd become everything to her so quickly, including her possible downfall.

He took a short breath, not directly meeting her gaze. "I know I asked you already, but are you really all right?"

She nodded, crossing her arms tight over her chest instead of giving into the urge to collapse into Leigh's arms so he could make everything better. It wasn't his responsibility, nor should it be, considering their respective roles.

"I'm fine. Yes, he hit me and intended to—" The words cut off, her mind refusing to acknowledge the fact Steve had admitted to attacking others, let alone voice it to Leigh. "But I got away before he could do anything worse."

She shuddered, forcing down the thoughts on exactly how things could have gotten worse if she hadn't managed to fight him off. "I'll just be glad when he's gone. I don't want to have to see him again, even if that makes me a coward."

"About that…" Leigh cleared his throat and then rubbed the back of his neck. "Robinson hasn't been thrown out of the program."

"*What?*" A surge of anxiety-driven bile burned the back of her throat, and she covered her mouth with her hand.

Leigh rotated in his seat to face her more fully. "I'm sorry, Mia. If it was up to me, he'd already be off the ship and headed for grunt work down on Ilari. Unfortunately Commander Yang came to the conclusion that Robinson couldn't be removed from FP training without it causing even bigger problems."

"How? That doesn't make any sense." Her words wavered, and she clenched her fists, trying to contain the churning emotions.

"Well for a start, Robinson's father is an admiral, and there are too many ways to count how he could make this worse for us. Plus, Robinson is claiming I used excessive force when dealing with him." Leigh's expression became frustrated as he shook his head.

While the feminine side of her had found more than a little gratification over the way he'd punished Steve for what he'd done to her, the pragmatic side of her had to agree that, yes, Leigh probably had used excessive force. But she wasn't about to tell him that.

He lifted his gaze and caught her with an intense regard. "I don't want you to worry about this. I'm sure Robinson will wash out soon, and in the meantime, Bren and I will be filling all his spare time with the worst muck work we can come up with."

She blew out an uneven breath. Somehow, she had to get up tomorrow morning and face Steve at oh six hundred roll call without embarrassing herself by having a total panic attack. True, he hadn't really hurt her, but he'd scared her and made her feel powerless. And she didn't want to relive those horrid sensations in front of the entire class.

"Mia."

Leigh's voice held power over her and just her name in that deep huskiness was enough to soothe her fracturing calm. She looked up at him, focusing on his face like a lifeline.

"I will be there, I promise. If Robinson so much as looks at you in a way that makes you uncomfortable, you only need to say the word, and I'll come down on him so hard, he'll be wishing he'd left when he'd had the chance."

"I don't want you to get into any more trouble over me." The vow bolstered her nerves, even as a swirl of concern for him swept through her.

He leaned a little closer to her. "I told you already, you're worth it, Mia."

Her heart tripped in her chest, and she wished she could touch him, pull him closer and kiss him, show him her gratitude and burgeoning emotions through her actions. But she dared not even touch his hand when they were sitting out in a passageway where anyone could come along at any moment.

"But if anyone found out about us…"

Leigh scrubbed a hand over his short hair. "In that regard, I have to agree. Questions are being asked. It might be better if we have minimum contact for a few days."

He sent her a guarded look. Did he think she would be upset over his suggestion? No. If staying away was the best thing she could do for him, then he didn't have to tell her twice.

"I agree."

"You do?" He leaned back from her a little, arching one eyebrow.

"What did you expect me to say? That I couldn't live without you, and not to abandon me?"

He gave a short laugh and rubbed his jaw, where a purple-blue bruise had started forming. "Well, yeah, my manly pride would have liked to hear something like that."

She sent him an exasperated glare. "I think I can do without you for a couple of days."

He stared at her for a long moment, his gaze heating. "Really? Because I don't know how I'll get through even a few hours without you. We've been through a lot together this week and I've gotten used to knowing you're here if I need you. For professional purposes only."

"Of course." But she knew what he really meant. Her heart smashed into the insides of her ribs, and she clenched her fists against her sides to stop from reaching for him.

The airlock doors whooshed open, preventing her from replying. One of the doctors walked out, glancing between her and the datapad he held.

"Mia Wolfe? Sorry to keep you waiting."

Leigh stood. "I'll leave you to it. Ace, have you got time to take a look at my jaw and busted knuckle when you're done here?"

Sub-Doctor Moore tilted his head and glanced at Leigh's bruise, then gave a low whistle. "That's going to come out in some beautiful colors. Still isn't half as bad as the other guy looks, though. You really went to town on him, Alpha."

Leigh glanced at her, some of those violent shadows rising in the depths of his gaze. "He got what he deserved. I'll wait in one of the triage cubicles for you."

Before either she or the doctor could respond, Leigh stalked away, disappearing through the airlock doors.

Sub-Doctor Moore sat down next to her. "Well, this has been an interesting day. I've know that guy for over ten years, and I've never seen him smash the ever-living hell out of someone before, even when he was a hotheaded recruit."

Mia crossed her arms, unsure whether the doctor's comment required some kind of response.

But he didn't seem to notice her lack of reply as he typed on the datapad, then glanced back up at her. "So, how about I take a quick look at your face? It looks like you're only going to have some very light, superficial bruising. However, Commander Yang has ordered a full physical. Sorry. It might take a few minutes. There are some questions to answer, and then we'll have to go into the ER so I can give you a quick, full body scan."

She nodded, knowing the only way to get herself out of here faster was to cooperate. Exhaustion dragged at her, both physical and mental. Right then, the only place she could think about going was her bunk for at least ten hours of uninterrupted sleep.

Mia woke up with a start, her heart pounding, mind churning. But not because she'd had a bad dream, or relived Steve's attack, but because her brain had just ambushed her with an answer.

She rolled over and groped for Leigh's datapad where she'd left it on the nightstand after returning from med level the night before. She blinked her eyelids wider to wake herself up a little more, the glow of the screen making her eyes ache for a moment until they adjusted to the brightness. The clock in the top left corner read oh three seventeen. She should have been a zombie at this time of morning, especially considering all the late nights she'd had recently. But the idea that had jerked her from sleep worked more effectively that half a dozen coffees.

Pulling up the diagnostic system she'd been navigating, she started an entirely new data check. After only a few seconds, the datapad chimed with a result.

Holy hell, she'd done it. She sat up straighter, clutching the datapad tighter as she read the information scrolling down the screen. All this time, she'd been searching for *what* the traitor had been doing inside the *Knox's* systems, and hadn't thought to search for *where* he might have operated from. She might have found the answer in a little used maintenance station on echo launch deck.

Swinging her legs out of bed, she tabbed up a message and sent it to Leigh's comm. It wasn't until after she'd already hit send that it occurred to her she'd either wake him up, or he simply wouldn't get it because he was sleeping. So what should she do? He'd want to know about this right away. What if he didn't get the message until he woke up for the morning's sessions? Could she really sit here for the next two hours waiting? Well, it wasn't like she had a choice; she couldn't exactly waltz down to his apartment and knock on the door.

The datapad flashed with a return message telling her to meet him at the same dorm transit as last time. She jumped up, throwing on the first clothes she could lay her hands on, and then shoving her feet into her boots and hurrying down to the transit-porter. After that, she got to cool her heels for another ten minutes. Just how long did it take the guy to get on some clothes and catch the transit up here anyway?

When the doors finally opened, it revealed Leigh in full uniform, his hair damp as though he'd showered and dressed for the day. Although her heart went into a slow flip, and a trill of excitement sung through her body at the sight of him, she must have had a rather peeved look on her face, because he glanced down at himself.

"What's wrong?" he asked, sounding a tad defensive.

"You actually showered. That's what took you so long?" She stepped onto the transit and tabbed in echo launch bay as their destination.

"I figured whatever this was, I probably wouldn't be going back to bed. And since inconvenient things—like getting stuck in a transit car—tend to happen when I'm with you, I thought I might as well get ready in case I have to head straight to class from wherever we end up. What's this all about anyway?"

She practically wanted to bounce up and down with excitement, but she managed to contain herself. "I found where the son of a bitch slipped up. If this pays off, we might actually be able to identify him."

Leigh raised both eyebrows. "Are you serious?"

"Hell yeah." She couldn't help but let a self-satisfied grin surface. "I worked out that someone's been regularly accessing a maintenance station down on echo launch bay, including the exact time when the guy who shot me got on the transit and disappeared. I'm hoping that if I can access the data at the station, it'll not only tell us what he's been up to, but also give us a clue as to who it is."

"Damn it, Mia, this is incredible." He started to shift forward, as if he was going to grab her, but then seem to catch himself and think better of it.

She dropped her gaze away from him, since in that second, she'd wanted to throw herself into his arms and maybe enjoy a little victory hug. But it was only a few short hours ago that they'd agreed to put some distance between themselves. They were together now only out of necessity in finding the mole. Any contact, even something as innocent as a hug, would put a huge dent in her resolve to protect him from the possible fallout of their relationship.

The transit arrived on echo launch level, saving either of them from coming up with any small talk to cover the awkwardness. Echo launch deck was the least-used level on the ship, storing engine parts, disused or spare ships and shuttles, and was hardly ever accessed by crew. Logically, that should have made it easy to find who'd used the maintenance station, but she assumed the person had covered their tracks, just like she planned on doing for Leigh and her.

She didn't look up from the datapad as she ran the information to find which maintenance station the shooter's accomplice had utilized.

"So what are we looking for?" Leigh asked, his voice echoing slightly in the empty space.

"We're headed for delta-three bay."

Leigh glanced around then indicated the right passage.

"This way."

Delta-three bay turned out to be a bit of a dumping ground, and they had to clamber over engine and ships parts crammed into the space. Once they stood in front of the maintenance station, she tabbed the lights a little higher.

As she brought the station on line to see if she could glean any clues about the last person to use it, Leigh took a seat on a nearby engine block.

"Seems like a lot of trouble to get in here when the mole could have accessed the systems from anywhere, right?"

She watched information scroll across the screen. "Probably, which is why I'm hoping we can find some clues here that I couldn't access remotely."

Except what she was seeing made no sense. According to station logs, this machine hadn't been used for months. She rechecked the datapad to make sure she hadn't gotten the bays mixed up, but the logs confirmed this exact location had been used. So which one was telling her the truth?

"This is going to take a little longer than I anticipated." She set the datapad down and got to work pulling up more information on the station.

"How much longer?" Leigh checked his watch. "Mess-deck starts serving breakfast in less than an hour."

"I don't know. It depends on what I find."

He pushed to his feet and paced the short distance they had between the machinery. She sent him an exasperated glance, causing him to stop.

"What?" he asked, almost sounding defensive.

"You pacing like a caged tiger isn't going to make me work any faster."

"Sorry." He walked over to lean on the opposite side

of the console, which was even more distracting, damn him, because now his hands were in her peripheral vision and her mind didn't want to do anything except imagine exactly where he could put them.

She gave herself a mental slap as a small section of information jumped out at her. But before she could confirm the notion that had started forming in the back of her mind, a dull clunking sound echoed through the bay and she froze, glancing up at Leigh.

"What was that?"

He looked past her, an expression of dawning realization on his face. "The atmospheric doors. Mia, run!"

He'd barely finished saying the words before he took off, leaping the engine block he'd been sitting on, then scrambling over a hull section and disappearing from sight.

Her heart thumping with apprehension, she grabbed Leigh's datapad and followed after him, clearing all the obstacles they'd navigated on the way in. Only to find Leigh standing in front of the inner hatchway now closed and blocking them from escape.

He went over to the control screen, but it was flashing a red error message. A hydraulic hiss started from somewhere behind them, deeper in the bay. Leigh slapped a frustrated hand over the uncooperative screen.

"What's happening?" She didn't know why she asked, when she really didn't want to know.

Leigh stepped back, shoving a hand through his hair, expression tense. "Venting. The outer doors are opening."

"Into *space*?" Her near shout echoed over the increasing hiss.

He looked over at her, features grim. "If we don't get out

of here—"

"It was a trap."

It all made sense. The station had shown her the real information, instead of the baited information she'd found using Leigh's datapad: if anyone tried to track the traitor's activities, they'd get sucked into oblivion.

Maybe she'd gotten too close to something with those system checks, or maybe she hadn't covered her tracks well. Either way, the mole had turned the tables on her and she'd walked them into this snare without a second thought.

"What are you talking about?" Leigh stepped closer as the air around them started whipping into a frenzy, the vacuum increasing.

"We walked into a death trap." Around them, smaller, lighter pieces of debris were picked up and tossed around. They only had a few minutes, if that, to find a way out of this bay before everything got sucked out into space.

Chapter Nineteen

Adrenaline-driven fury washed through Leigh once he grasped what Mia had told him. But with the very air getting sucked out from around them, starting to drag anything that wasn't bolted down, they didn't have time to discuss the particulars. The inner atmospheric doors had already been closed by the time he'd reached them and the control screen was a loss. He'd already tried putting in his officer codes to override it, but got nothing except an error message.

He dashed over to a cabinet and pulled it open, grabbing a pry bar as the rest of the tools on the shelf succumbed to the increasing vacuum, falling to the deck and skittering past his boots. He returned to the doors and jammed the end into the gap. He glanced over at Mia, who still stood where he'd left her, working at his datapad. Probably trying to find a way to stop whatever protocol was about to vent this bay.

A light but sharp piece of debris flew by her head and

she didn't even notice, just about giving him a heart attack. Beyond her, past the stacks of engine and ship junk that were starting to whine and shift, a seam appeared in the outer launch hatchway. They only had a minute or two left.

"Mia!" he yelled over the increasing noise. "Get over here."

She hurried over, hunching against the whipping air. "Leigh, I can't help you with that, I'm trying to override—"

"I know. Just get down next to the door and keep doing whatever you're doing."

She didn't even look up at him again as she crouched down and pressed herself against the hatchway. With a tense half breath that was getting short on oxygen, he rammed the bar harder into the seam of the atmospheric doors and pushed, putting all his weight against levering. It was probably a lost cause, but he had to do something. He wasn't going to stand there counting his sins until the outer hatchway finished opening and sucked them into space. Still, vehemence washed hotter through him when shoving against the bar got him exactly nothing. He took another breath, this one feeling like it burned his lungs, as there was even less atmosphere to suck in.

Goddamn it. He did not want to die like this. Without enough oxygen, it was like his muscles just decided to pack it in. He lost his grip on the bar. It clattered out of his hands and spun across the deck as the vacuum got stronger.

He dropped down, covering Mia with his body and locking his hands into the metal grate of the floor. She was still working the datapad, her expression burning with determination, but edged with fear. Christ, even a second before what would no doubt be a horrifically painful death, she was still fighting. Most people, even seasoned soldiers, would have given up by now.

He leaned into her. Somehow, even with the failing oxygen and pulling burn of the vacuum wrenching at him, he could smell the now familiar nutty-vanilla on her hair. Or maybe it was just his imagination taking him to a better place.

Either way, he buried his face in her hair, his muscles stinging as he struggled to hold on for both of them. Just as his fingers started loosening on the grate, Mia grabbed onto him.

"Leigh, I did it!"

He barely heard her over the rushing roar, but as he looked up, the hatchway in front of them cracked open. Unfortunately, this created a new problem, as a burst of air cut through the gap, almost blasting what little grip he still had. At least they had something to breath now, and as he gasped a sharp inhale of air, Mia grabbed onto the edge of the doors, pulling herself through.

He risked letting one hand go to help push her out, fighting the rushing air to get himself hooked onto the edge of the door. She seized him under his arms, helping to haul him through. For a second he thought they were both going to slip and tumble back in, but he found a hold with the toes of his boots and pushed with his legs, launching himself over the threshold. They collapsed onto the deck on the other side and Mia slapped at his datapad lying on the floor nearby, snapping the doors closed.

In the sudden silence, his ears started ringing, his head throbbing from the pressure. For a long moment he let himself lie there, sucking in deep lungfuls of air and thanking whatever deity was out there in the universe for the fact they were both still alive.

Holy hell, he'd had some brushes with disaster over the years, but he didn't think he'd ever been that close to certain death before. He rolled to the side, looking down on Mia lying next to him, her eyes closed as her chest rapidly rose and fell.

"Are you okay?" His throat felt stripped raw, and he swallowed over the dryness.

She opened her eyes and slowly propped herself up on her elbows. "Physically, yeah, because clearly I'm not dead. Psychologically? I'll tell you in a couple of years."

He gave a short laugh of relief, knowing exactly what she meant.

She blew out a jagged breath and flopped back onto the deck again. "Oh God, we almost died. I walked us right into a trap. How could I be so stupid?"

"Hey." He caught her hand as she swiped it over her face. "How were you supposed to know? You were just doing exactly what I asked you to do. If this is anyone's fault, it's mine. I should never have gotten you involved in this."

She opened her eyes, lashes damp as she stared up at him. "Don't blame yourself. You've got enough on your plate without adding this to it."

He cut his gaze away from her sincere expression, focusing on their joined hands. No matter what she said, it wouldn't make him feel any less responsible for nearly getting her killed. "I think we should take this as fair warning. I don't want you looking for this guy anymore."

She let go of his hand and sat up. "I'm not going to let this scare me off. We have to find him, if only because this proves he's willing to kill anyone to keep his identity secret. Considering he set this trap, he obviously knows someone is looking for him."

"Which is exactly why you need to leave this alone. You've nearly been killed twice now. It's too dangerous."

Her expression became stubborn. "And what about you? Are you going to leave it alone? Because the way I remember it, I wasn't the only one who got shot at last week and almost vented just now."

"It's my squadron. My people, my responsibility. I can't just stand by and leave it to someone else to take care of."

"If you're not giving up, then neither am I." She tipped her chin up, her obstinacy as infuriating as it was admirable. He wanted to be angry at her for not stepping back like he asked, but instead he felt humbled that she wanted to stick with him despite the danger. He also wanted to kiss that damn stubborn expression right off her face, but they'd made a pact to stay away from each other. They may have narrowly escaped getting sucked into space, but that didn't change the fact that he was still her CO and had already taken things between them way into forbidden territory.

He sighed and ran a hand over his hair. Despite it being fairly short, he could feel it sticking out all over the place. From what he'd learned of Mia, he got the feeling that she'd continue with this mission whether he wanted her to or not. At least if she worked with him, he could make sure she stayed out of harm's way.

"Fine," he agreed reluctantly. "But we're not tracking the shooter or his accomplice directly any more. Keep running the background checks and building profiles on everyone in FP squad instead. We'll just have to hope we can pinpoint the traitor that way."

For a long moment she stared at him, and he could all but see her mind working the angles, probably trying to figure out if he was playing her.

"Okay, but only if you promise not to go chasing any leads by yourself as well. You told me not to wander off on my own, so now I'm telling you the same thing."

A smile tugged at his lips, washing away some of the tension. He shouldn't have been so charmed by her apparent concern for him, but after nearly being vacuumed into oblivion, he was going to give himself a break.

"Come on. We need to get ourselves looking respectable and back up to squad level for the morning's session." He pushed to his feet, held out a hand, and helped her up.

Her gaze shifted upward and she reached up and ran her fingers though his hair, sending a shiver spearing down his spine.

"Yeah, people are definitely going to be suspicious about what you've been up to." She grinned.

"Yeah, well you look like you were on the losing end of a fight with a hair dryer."

She gave a surprised laugh and socked him one in the arm. "Hey, you're not supposed to say stuff like that to a girl."

He rubbed his arm as they set off toward the transit. "Somehow, I think you can take it."

She cut him a considering sideways glance. "I already know I can take it."

Maybe it was the leftover adrenaline, but his body flash-heated, and he was sure he could see something more in her gaze than just friendly banter. He clenched his fists and focused his gaze ahead, not letting himself look at her.

Yeah, those urges ripping hard and fast through him were just the aftereffects of almost getting killed. Riding a high like that, the downturn was always going to be difficult to keep a rein on. So he was just going to keep his hands to himself and run battle drills through his mind until they got back up to squadron level and could go their separate ways.

Chapter Twenty

Mia filed onto the troop transport with the rest of the class, the recruits more animated today at the news they were taking a trip down to Ilari. Leigh had explained earlier it was to show them the reality of the war they were fighting, because in the air or on the ship, it was easy to forget the cost being paid on the ground.

Considering the shadows she saw in his gray-blue eyes sometimes, and what he'd told her about the men he'd lost over the years, she could say without a doubt that Leigh, at least, never forgot the true price of this war.

Since agreeing to help him find the traitor in FP squad, she'd been getting some hard and fast lessons in this herself, not the least of which had been almost getting sucked out of a launch bay two days ago.

She still couldn't believe how close she'd come to simply not existing any longer. But worse was the paranoia that the mole would work out who she was and get to her or Leigh before they could find him. She'd started looking twice at everyone, even her fellow recruits, scrutinizing the way they talked or how they acted. It was damned exhausting being so on edge all the time.

Those last few moments in the launch bay kept replaying over and over. At first, she hadn't been able to believe it was really happening, and started using Leigh's datapad to override the command in a bit of a daze. But when he'd ordered her to crouch down near the doors, the hard, grim expression on his face rammed home that they were seconds from getting sucked into space.

She admired him for trying to pry the atmospheric doors open, even though the double reinforced hatchway had been designed to withstand the vacuum of space. In that last second, when he'd given up and sheltered her with his body instead, it had been like an explosion of too many emotions inside her. But his protection had bolstered her resolve, because she'd been determined that would not be the last moment they spent together.

Seeing him only in class the past two days had been harder than she'd anticipated. Not because she missed him, or wanted him in a way that left her muscles knotted— though both sentiments were true—but because she'd fallen so far for him that she'd become anxious of giving her feelings away, or slipping again and using his first name.

Whenever they'd had to interact, she'd kept herself locked down and distant, only speaking when absolutely necessary.

The whole sneaking-around thing was just too hard; she had no idea how people managed to do it. She couldn't lie to save her life and keeping what she'd shared with Leigh, as well as the extracurricular assignment, under wraps proved to be almost harder than the FP training program.

Mia also had to work hard to avoid Steve, who acted like he'd done nothing wrong. Most of the other recruits, however, having heard she'd bested him again, would shoot her a thumbs-up when she passed. Apparently Steve had won no new friends since coming into the program, but she still hated the additional scrutiny when all she wanted was to be left alone.

Running the last of the profiles took longer than she'd anticipated, too, and she still had three more pilots to go. She'd left the program instructors—Bren, Seb, and Lawler—until last, since they seemed to be Leigh's core group of officers. She hated the idea that the traitor could be one of them, so she had avoided their profiles until she couldn't any longer. Worse, the program had stuttered when filling out a complete profile on one of them the night before. The blanks in the report made her suspicious, and she'd planned to dig deeper today until she'd found out they were heading for the ground and wouldn't need their datapads. The delay was frustrating. She wanted this whole situation to be done with, wanted to find the traitor and concentrate on completing the program, so she could request a transfer and end the exhausting charade that she was all peachy.

On the shuttle, she took the closest seat to the door available, a slight cold shiver tracking through her as the memory of her last experience on a troop transport pushed up in her mind. Kayla squeezed past her to sit in the window seat she'd left vacant, carrying on a one-sided conversation about the flight simulators they were due to start in two days.

When Steve boarded, she averted her gaze, but then a

wave of anger swelled up within her. Every time that exact billow of antagonism toward him washed over her, it got stronger and harder to ignore. If she weren't so caught up in the profiles, getting through the FP program, and pretending like she wasn't half in love with her CO, she actually might have started entertaining the notion of vengeance, even though she generally wasn't a vindictive person.

As Steve passed by the row she and Kayla were sitting in, she looked up, letting the anger into her expression. Damn it, he didn't even look at her.

"Whoa. Lucky you don't have psychic powers, or I'm pretty sure Steve would have just exploded into a fireball."

She focused on Kayla, feeling a little sheepish. "Sorry, it's just that seeing him is making me angrier every time."

Kayla gave her hand a quick squeeze. "Hey, you don't have to explain it to me. And don't think I haven't considered spitting in his morning coffee or throwing a dumbbell weight at his smarmy face in the gym a time or two."

She breathed out over a laugh at Kayla's ideas for revenge.

However, her amusement was short lived as Leigh, Lieutenant Brenner, Sub-Lieutenant Rayne, Sub-Officer Lawler, and one other pilot boarded before the hatchway slid silently closed.

"Buckle in and settle down, recruits. We'll be on the ground in around ten minutes." Leigh announced as the other instructors found seats and the transport vibrated to life with a low rumble.

The only empty seat close to the front was to her right, on the aisle end of the row. As Leigh took a step, she turned to look out the window, heart thumping against the inside of her chest. Some of it had to do with the anticipation mixed with the apprehension that he'd sit next to her. But she had to admit part was because the transport had started moving and her last experience on a shuttle hadn't exactly been fun. She nearly laughed aloud at that, albeit hysterically—a potential fighter pilot afraid of flying.

However, all of that got lost as she sensed him dropping into the seat beside her—she was so hyperaware of him, she could have sworn the very air around her changed to become thick with static as he settled next to her.

"Are you okay?" The words were murmured so low, she nearly missed them under the noise of recruits' conversation.

Despite her earlier determination not to look at him, her gaze was drawn to his profile, like a moon trying to defy the gravitational pull of a larger planet. It was useless to resist.

"I was concerned you might be nervous, considering how your last flight in a transport ended," he continued, not looking directly at her as he spoke, his expression impersonal. But there was something in his tone, something she couldn't fail to miss now that she knew him so well.

Her heart stumbled over a few beats. He'd thought of the possibility she might be afraid. She hadn't even realized it was going to be in issue herself until she'd been faced with boarding a few minutes ago.

The transport started moving, making her stomach kink, but she forced out a slow breath. "I'm okay…now."

He gave a single nod, his gaze sliding over to consider her briefly, nothing but warm affection in his eyes. "Just think of something else, and we'll be on the ground in no time."

She took another breath, the air catching when a gentle pressure registered on the outer side of her thigh. Leigh had shifted his leg outward so that it rested lightly against hers. His hand was just above his knee in what looked like a relaxed pose, but two of his fingers almost imperceptibly stroked in short movement up and down her lower thigh.

Okay, thinking of something other than being aboard a transport was not going to be a problem, not when his illicit, secretive touch rippled through every cell in her body with a thrill.

God, this was torture. If he'd been any other boyfriend, they could have held hands, she could have leaned in to him, let him wrap his arm around her and hold her tight until they landed, found comfort in being able to relax into his hold. Instead the way he almost not touched her soothed, but wound her tighter, both with longing and the trepidation that if anyone looked really closely, they'd give away the truth.

She'd never imagined that one day she might fall so hard and fast for someone, only to need to pretend like she didn't feel anything at all for him. It was ridiculous when she thought about it. The one man she shouldn't want, and she couldn't stem the emotions blooming higher and brighter within her every hour.

Neither of them said anything else for the rest of the trip, but it was a case of not needing to. Despite the impossibility of their situation, Leigh had made sure she'd known he was here for her. Simply sitting next to her had been enough, his light touch an extra thrill that had distracted her from the tight anxiety in her stomach.

As the transport touched down, Leigh stood at the front of the shuttle. "Recruits, attention front and center. Listen closely, because I will not be repeating myself. Despite the fact that we've landed in UEF-held territory, we are close to the front lines and it will be dangerous. The occasional team of enemies does get through and will take any UEF soldier they find on their own or in small numbers for their Enlightening Camps. This is not some academy field trip where you can goof off or push the boundaries. Down here, if you make a mistake, it will cost your life."

The other instructors joined him, and the hatchway opened and they stepped out into the weak, cloud-filtered sunshine. There wasn't much chatter as people left their seats and filed out of the transport, the mood subdued by Leigh's words.

"Well, this will be interesting," Kayla muttered as they shuffled into the aisle.

"They're right though. We need to see the realities of war. Some of us more than others."

Kayla glanced back over her shoulder with a flat look. "I get the feeling there are *some people* who will still be imbecilic assholes no matter what they see."

Yeah, *some people* being Steve and his buddies. They'd probably never see the death and destruction, only the glory of beating back the enemy.

When she stepped outside, it took a second for her eyes to adjust to the glare, despite it being overcast. One of the side effects of always being on a ship or station, a person's eyes became a little more sensitive to actual sunlight.

They'd landed in a wide intersection of what looked to be an abandoned city. Some of the buildings looked mostly intact, but crumbled with age, while others were bombed out or damaged from bullet holes or energy blasts.

Leigh and the other instructors had walked over to stand

in front of a structure with a half-destroyed sign: the Brannon system Earth consulate and GAHTO headquarters.

Their footsteps echoed as Mia followed Kayla and the other recruits over to the cracked sidewalk. She'd watched media-vids of abandoned cities, but had never seen one firsthand. It was eerie imagining that once people had gone about their everyday lives here until war came. How many people had died on the street in front of this very building?

"Does anyone know the significance of where we are right now?" Leigh asked the group over the quiet murmurs.

"This is where the war started, where the self-appointed Ponitfex, Ronald Martin, ordered the first attack on the UEC," Kayla spoke up.

She shot her friend a surprised look.

"What? So I've got brains as well as beauty," Kayla muttered.

Mia bit her lip over a laugh as she returned her attention to the instructors.

"Recruit Dawson is correct," Leigh answered, clasping his hands behind his back. "This is where the first act of war was perpetrated. Martin felt that the UEC and Earth were exerting too much influence on his people, who strove to live a more simplistic life, rejecting the most advanced technologies and getting back to nature. When the Brannon system was founded by immigrants from Earth two hundred and fifty years ago, these ideals worked and the people thrived and existed quite well. But as time went by, the leaders began to resent any interference from the UEC."

Leigh paused, glancing over his shoulder at the half-destroyed building behind him. There wasn't a sound from the group, as though everyone was holding their breath while the wind whistled through broken windows and the far-off hum of a ship rumbled.

They'd all studied this back at the academy, but reading the facts and standing in the spot where it had actually happened were two very different things. A shiver rippled down her spine, sending goose pimples over her skin. She'd never been superstitious, but in that moment, she could almost swear the atrocities that haunted this place were touching her.

"Twenty years ago, the UEC and GAHTO sent in a team of aid workers with food and medicine after a storm flooded this city. Instead of accepting help, Ronald Martin dropped a bomb on his own city, killing the aid workers and many Ilari citizens. He declared the Brannon system to be a sovereign state and that any UEC, UEF, or GAHTO presence would be dealt with swiftly and by deadly force."

Mia's stomach went into a slow churn, unable to imagine what those people must have gone through.

"So, now that you've seen for yourselves the ruins of this war, you'll be moving on to face your final test of survival training." Leigh indicated toward the transport they'd flown down, and Mia glanced over her shoulder to see Rayne and Lawler had been unloading packs while the CAFF had been talking.

Oh, that couldn't be a good sign. She shared a worried look with Kayla.

"You'll each be assigned a pack, all of which are stocked with identical supplies. The UEF Ilari base is northeast of our position. You've got two nights and two days to make it back there. Those who don't walk through the gates within that time frame will be cut from the program. Your packs also have emergency beacons. Only activate it if you are in an extreme medical emergency or want to quit the program."

A ripple of low, anxious murmurs passed through the group of recruits. Okay, this might be a problem. If she spent who knew how long hiking to the Ilari base, it was going to delay her finishing the final profiles. Plus, if she was traipsing around down here, it gave the traitor more of an opportunity to work out who'd been tracking him and take out Leigh and her separately. How could Leigh think this was a good idea? But then her logic reined in her apprehension long enough to remind her that he probably hadn't a choice. He couldn't just pull her out of what probably amounted to an important aspect of FP training with no concrete reason—one he could share with anyone else anyway.

Leigh motioned to the other three instructors and then the four of them walked back toward the transport.

"Wait!" One of Steve's buddies spoke up. "You're *leaving*?"

Leigh paused and looked back at them as the two pilots and two other instructors boarded the transport. He shot a cutting grin at the recruit who'd questioned him.

"It wouldn't be much of a test in survival if we showed you the way and lit your campfires for you now, would it? Just make sure you don't accidentally walk west, or you'll find yourself on the CSS side of Ilari. And if that happens, no matter how many times you press your emergency beacon, no one will be coming to get you."

With that, Leigh gave a short salute and disappeared inside the transport. The hatchway slid closed and the shuttle lifted off with a low swirl of dust a moment later.

The group of recruits broke into a surge of noisy disbelief and questions.

"They can't just leave us out here!" someone yelled. "What about GPS and holomaps? How the hell are we supposed to know which way is northeast?"

For a long second Mia couldn't breathe, her lungs too tight and ribs contracting. She was down on the ground, only a few miles from CSS held territory, with no type of security and no immediate help if anything went wrong. Without Leigh's datapad, without actually being able to do anything to find the traitor, she felt like she'd been stripped of weapons and marched onto the battlefield.

What better opportunity to get rid of her than an exercise like this? Accidents happened. Or she could just disappear without a trace, assumed captured and killed by the enemy.

With dread growing inside her like a thick, black cloud, she watched the transport disappear over the buildings. She wasn't exactly an expert at direction, but it seemed the shuttle had gone in a northeast direction, and logically it made sense that the instructors were going to kick back at the Ilari base for the next two days while they waited to see how many recruits turned up.

"We are so screwed," Kayla muttered.

"Some more so than others."

She passed a gaze over the remaining recruits standing around. Maybe the stress of the last few days was really starting to get to her, because the thought occurred to her that maybe she should have been running profiles on the people in this class. But that was ridiculous, wasn't it? How could any of them be a mole, when the troop transport had been attacked, it? It made no sense that the CSS would fire on a vessel carrying one of its own people.

On the other hand, everyone had their price. What if the

traitor paid someone to take care of her—

She shook her head at herself and stepped forward, walked over to the pile of packs, and grabbed one off the top. She tossed it to Kayla, who had trailed her, and then grabbed a second. She was getting ridiculous with the conspiracy theories. Yes, she possibly was more exposed down here, but there was safety in numbers, so she'd just make sure she stuck with a large group at all times. No point in standing around worrying about things. The sooner she got moving, the sooner she could walk into the Ilari base and put this latest test behind her.

Chapter Twenty-One

Mia glared at her aching feet, hating the combat boots that obviously weren't designed for walking long distances. If she'd given in to the discomfort, she could have quite happily stopped to set up camp two or three hours ago, but she'd pushed on. The more ground she could cover today, the better off she'd be in the long run, because tomorrow would only get harder, not easier.

Though the physical side of things presented a muscle-straining challenge, this situation was more a mental game than anything—seeing if she could push herself, keep motivated, and succeed. Instead of thinking about how far she had to go or how long it would take or how cold or hot it might get or where she'd find water to refill the bladder in her pack, she'd simply started living in the moment, putting one foot in front of the other, picking a landmark in front of her, and concentrating on getting to it before finding another goal.

Being so hyperaware of everyone around her had been an extra drain. She'd shamelessly listened in on more than a few conversations today and a couple of times even found herself searching the landscape for an ambush or sniper, becoming more and more convinced that if the traitor knew who she was and planned on trying anything, it would be while she was out here. Not that she'd probably be able to see it coming anyway; she didn't exactly have any experience being a ground soldier, so she had no idea what kind of signs would indicate the enemy were nearby.

When Kayla and she had set off, most of the recruits had scrambled to follow them, no doubt the pack mentality kicking in for everyone that they'd be better off sticking together. At first, most people had seemed somewhat relaxed and chatty, though not totally jovial. This wasn't some academy camping trip after all, just like Leigh had said.

Kayla and she had chattered for a while, but as the day wore on, they'd become quieter as their group grew smaller and some people fell back. Others had stopped altogether. She'd taken note of every single person as they'd broken off from the group, and then started looking even more closely at those keeping up, trying to pick out anyone who seemed extra nervous or overly interested in her.

Now, the sun was dipping toward the horizon behind the clouds and a glance around revealed eight others beside Kayla and her, none of whom were Steve or his friends. Thank God for small favors. At least she wouldn't have him and the other Ackerly assholes to worry about tonight. It was going to be bad enough fighting her exhaustion from walking all day to stay awake. Because no way was she going to fall asleep out in the middle of nowhere, giving anyone the opportunity to walk up and kill her in her sleep.

"That looks like as good a place as any to camp." Kayla pointed ahead to an old barn or shed next to a small stream in the overgrown field they were crossing.

Mia nodded, too tired to reply, and switched directions slightly, headed for the structure. The clouds had been steadily thickening over the afternoon, and the scent of rain had been in the air for the last half hour, a slight humidity making the hike more uncomfortable. It would definitely rain tonight, maybe even storm. Finding an actual building to shelter in pretty much seemed like luxury at this point.

The small group they'd formed all trekked over to the barn. It wasn't huge, but could have fit their entire class of recruits inside if everyone had kept up. Instead, the ten of them would have plenty of room to spread out or lie down.

In the fading light, it was hard to see much, but obviously they weren't the first people to use the barn for shelter. Down the far end, where a hole in the roof let in the last of the day's light, there was a blackened spot surrounded by stones where fires had previously been set. A couple of old crates and other things had been arranged in a loose circle to form a ring of mismatching seats. Maybe previous recruit classes had done the same hike and found the barn like they had. It gave her hope that they were on the right track and hadn't spent the day walking in the wrong direction.

A couple of recruits were already making their way over to the pit, grabbing bits of wood to make a fire. Everyone in the group who'd made it this far probably could have been considered the top performers in the class. They were all hardworking, seemingly honorable people who took their duty to the UEF seriously. She hated to think that any of them could be a traitor, but her paranoia and mistrust had taken her off the rails hours ago. She was just going to believe her OTT suspicions of everyone and everything would keep her alive until she got back onto the *Knox*.

She set down her pack and crouched to unfasten it so she could assess the food situation. A cursory check earlier in the day had revealed some MRBs—meal replacement bars. They were chewy and definitely on the unappetizing side, but had the required nutrients for soldiers in combat or troop movement situations when a five-star meal wasn't the first priority. But she hoped that somewhere in the bottom of the pack, there might be something a little more substantial. She wasn't a fan of preserved foods, but right now she'd even take a plexi-can of baked beans over another MRB.

Her search efforts were futile—she found the emergency beacon, a basic first-aid kit with the usual antiseptic wound-healing gel and other items to treat minor injuries, a paper-thin thermo sheet for sleeping under, enough MRBs to last about a week, and not much else.

She pushed the pack aside and stood, walking the perimeter of the barn, assessing the structure in the rapidly fading light. If there was going to be a storm tonight, she didn't want to end up crushed under a beam if the dilapidated barn couldn't hold up. However, she didn't exactly have a degree in architecture. The best she could do was check none of the support posts looked rotted while she tried not to think about her growling stomach.

By the time she'd done a lap, most of the recruits had moved to sit by the rapidly catching fire in the pit. Some grimaced their way through MRBs, while others like her had decided that staying a little on the hungry side was preferable.

One of them, Granger—who had turned out to have a lot of hiking and camping experience and had sworn all day they were definitely heading northeast—seemed to be trying to untangle something, while Nicka sat next to him, holding part of it up.

Curiosity got the better of her and she rounded the fire to get a closer look. It seemed to be some kind of netting, but it was definitely in a mess.

"What did you find?" she asked, sitting down next to Nicka.

The other girl gave a quick shrug. "Looks like junk to me, but Granger says he might be able to catch something in it."

"Catch something?" She glanced over at Granger, who had his head bent over a knot, trying to work it free.

"Something to eat, like a fish or one of those bunny-raccoon things that we kept seeing in the fields today," Granger clarified.

She leaned forward and grabbed the net from him. Since her fingers were more slender, she had the tangle undone in a matter of moments.

"I'll take an order of fish, but you're on your own with the rabboon."

He sent her a grin as he separated what had actually been two nets tangled together. He tossed one in her direction as he stood.

"Then you're on fishing duty, Wolfe."

Without waiting for her to answer, he turned and headed out into the slanted golden light slicing in under the cloud cover.

She studied the net, then glanced over at Kayla, who had kicked back on the ground, leaning her back against one of the crates and using her pack as a pillow.

"Feel like a spot of fishing?"

Kayla shook her head and held up her half-finished MRB. "No way. I might eat fish, but I don't want to see it alive before I do so, and I definitely don't want to have anything to do with gutting or de-scaling."

"Suit yourself," she muttered, turning to trail Granger outside. He'd moved off into the field, wading through thigh-high grass, holding the net up, ready to trap the first unsuspecting rabboon he came across. She took a moment to cast a searching glance across the landscape, looking for any signs that there might be other people around. For half a second she considered turning around and heading back inside with the excuse that she didn't want to or couldn't catch fish after all, but the lure of something other than an MRB to eat proved too hard to resist. She'd just make sure she didn't go too far.

With her heart skipping a beat or two, she turned toward the stream, the gently flowing water reflecting the last orange streaks of the sky and dark gray of the clouds. The water was literally crystal clear and not very deep; she could see the rocky bottom.

Were there even fish in a stream like this? She walked to the edge and set down the net, taking a moment to wet her face and drink from her cupped hands. Somewhere in the distance, grass birds were calling back and forth, while insects chirped in the last of the day's humidity. The peacefulness of it all struck her quite suddenly.

Like almost all of earth, her home state was one big city.

The few vacant stretches of land were nothing but dusty, barren dirt. Though Earth still maintained around twenty billion inhabitants and acted as the central government to all the far-reaching systems and planets that had been colonized over the last few hundred years, the original birthplace of human beings had long since seen the death of Mother Nature. The only examples of what had once been a gloriously green world were now housed in special biospheres with carefully maintained mini-ecosystems, like living museums.

But she couldn't let the novel tranquility lull her, not when she'd been getting closer and closer to finding the traitor.

With a short sigh for her aching muscles, Mia grabbed the net and stood, turning left and trekking along the bank, looking for anything that might pass for a meal. Even some kind of fresh water crustacean would probably be better than the MRBs. She'd been going along for about ten minutes and was considering giving up when the stream widened and deepened slightly. With the light almost gone, and stray droplets of rain beginning to fall, it was hard to see much, but a large school of fish darted up and splashed out of the water.

With an excited burst of energy rushing through her, it was simply a matter of throwing out the net, drawing the string to close it and then tugging it into the bank. Without much effort at all, she'd caught seven fish.

"I should have guessed that you'd be the one out here catching everyone else's dinner."

She shot to her feet, the voice familiar, but still zapping her system with acute shock.

"Leigh—I mean Captain Alphin! What are you doing

here?" He stood on the opposite bank, arms crossed and leaning against a tree trunk. She glanced back toward the barn in the distance, but didn't see anyone else, not the other recruits or instructors.

"It's okay. There's no one else around to hear you calling me Leigh." His lips quirked in a short smile. "As to what I'm doing here? Monitoring and assessing, mostly. There's somewhat of a gray area legality-wise when it comes to taking a class of green recruits and dumping them in the middle of nowhere to find their own way to base. As long as we're within a mile or so of you at all times, the brass can't say we put you in undue danger or whatever crap they come up with."

Suddenly the day's walk took on a whole different light. "So you never actually left us?"

It had all been a ruse, another test for them to pass or fail. Of course, she'd already known it was a test, the parameters just hadn't been what she'd thought.

"For all intents and purposes, yes, we did leave you. We maybe didn't go as far as you thought."

The heavy knot of tension she'd been carrying unwound a little. All day, she'd stressed about the traitor making an attempt on her, but the entire time, Leigh had been nearby.

"So where are the other instructors?"

"Checking in with the rest of the recruits, since you're all fairly scattered. You and the others did well to get this far. I don't think any of the others found shelter, so they'll probably spend an uncomfortable night getting rained on."

Even as he spoke, a few more drops splashed down from the sky, the wind picking up slightly.

"Do you have any idea how much I freaked out after

you left? Since the incident in the launch bay, I couldn't help thinking—"

"That if the traitor knew you were the one who'd been tracking him, what better opportunity to get rid of you than while you were off the ship?"

Her shoulders drooped a little, his words effectively cutting off the indignation she'd built up. If Leigh had considered the possibility, then maybe she wasn't so paranoid and crazy after all.

"I've been snatching glances behind me all day. The possibility that I'd started going nuts had crossed my mind." She felt a little silly admitting it, and if it had been anyone else but Leigh, she wouldn't have said a word.

His expression took on a grim tightness. "It's not crazy to be on alert like that Mia. That's how a good soldier survives. I'm sorry. You don't know how much I wanted to talk with you before now. I almost said something on the transport down here, but I couldn't be sure we wouldn't be overheard. I'm just glad you're smart enough to see the danger."

"Yeah, well I wasn't the only one in that launch bay, so I hope you're taking precautions as well."

His lips kicked up in a half smile that didn't reach his eyes. "You don't have to worry about me. Just watch out for yourself until your boots are back on the *Knox's* deck. Speaking of which, I should probably get back. I'm supposed to be reporting the recruits' progress." He sounded as reluctant as she felt. Which was ridiculous. Did she want to stand around out here in the dark and get rained on? Unfortunately, if the answered featured her getting to spend a few more minutes with Leigh, then obviously she wasn't as sensible as she'd always believed.

Despite the fact that he was more than ten feet away and the stream separated them, just seeing him had brought a profound measure of comfort. Comfort and a sharp, surprising surge of longing.

The last few days, she'd been able to keep from examining how deep her feelings ran and how she craved his touch, because there'd always been other people around and the danger to both their careers outweighed the reward. However, now they were most definitely alone and her body was waking up, despite the aches, tension, and exhaustion from the long day.

"You know, we're lucky that this stream is keeping us apart," Leigh said, his voice pitched low. "Because I definitely would have tried to kiss you by now, even though we're meant to be keeping things under wraps. But if you keep looking at me like that, I'm going to decide wet clothes and the possibility of getting caught aren't enough to stop me."

"Looking at you like what?" She could have slapped herself as the words practically oozed out, all husky and definitely asking for more than the simple question she'd voice.

Leigh pushed up from the tree and walked to stand at the very edge of the opposite bank. "Like you're remembering how you stripped me naked and took me on one hell of a ride in that jet. Like maybe you're thinking about doing it again."

Well, she hadn't been until he'd said it, but she sure was now. Oh God, temptation had never looked so good—in clothes or out. Even though she'd vowed she wouldn't put Leigh's career at risk, the idea of wading across the stream and giving into the desire swelling through her, like a jet-propulsion system heating up, was about to overtake all of her resolve. Fine tingles ran over her skin, leaving a rippling warmth that pooled in her stomach. Delicious anticipation made her muscles tighten with hunger for him, to experience again the rapture of having him inside her, of the way he could satisfy her deeper and more profoundly than she'd ever thought possible.

Leigh slowly reached up and unzipped his flight jacket. "We both know the risks, and we both know exactly what happens when we're together. Just say the word and I'll be over there and all over you before the sound has even finished leaving your lips."

The jacket open, he reached up and started on the fastenings of his shirt. Her throat seized, the back of her mouth going dry. She wanted to, *God*, how she just wanted to yell, *Yes!,* and strip out of her own clothes, maybe meet him halfway and let the water cool her oversensitized skin, even as he set fire to her from the inside out.

But the word had gotten trapped somewhere between her brain and her tongue, no doubt blocked by the small kernel of sense trying to tell her that if one of the other recruits came looking for her and instead found her naked and rolling around with the CAFF...yeah, that scenario was the stuff of nightmares.

Except her traitorous body didn't want to listen to cool logic. Before she'd even realized what she was doing, she'd reached up and unzipped her own jacket. Leigh stopped working on his own shirt to stare at her, his gaze very definitely dropping down to her chest. In this post-sunset gray twilight, it was hard to see much, and very soon, neither of them would be able to see anything at all.

"Your turn. Unfasten your shirt." His voice came out

with a rough edge and a very definite tone of command. Maybe she would have been annoyed about any other guy ordering her around, but she'd already come to terms with the fact that Leigh being high-handed only turned her on.

Her fingers weren't exactly steady as they caught the clasps, but in a few moments she'd undone every fastener.

"Show me." This time his words were low, almost inaudible, but a shiver raked down her spine, as though he stood right next to her and had whispered in her ear. She parted her shirt, revealing nothing but the singlet she usually wore underneath. He made a frustrated noise, but it turned into a groan as she tugged the singlet up before he told her to do so. He went down on his knees in the grass, gaze raking over her with an intensity that left her aching, but gave her a rushing thrill at the simple power she held over him.

"I want you naked. I want to see every bare inch of you."

A short laugh escaped her, both because of the way his words washed through her, leaving tingles and the absurdity of their situation.

"And how do I explain needing to activate my beacon in order to be evaced out of here from exposure?" She tugged her singlet back down.

Leigh frowned at her, a definite thwarted gleam in his gaze. "It's not that cold. And I could be persuaded to come over and warm you up—for medical reasons only."

"Wolfe! You better not be lost because I'm totally not coming to find you." Granger's voice carried on the rising wind, and she glanced over her shoulder. It was so dark now the barn was little more than a hulking form in the field, and she couldn't make out where Granger was.

When she looked back at Leigh, he'd risen to his feet and

started refastening his shirt. "Good night, Mia, remember to stay alert and stay strong. Whatever tomorrow brings, I won't be far away."

Before she could reply, he'd shifted back from the bank and slipped around the tree, disappearing into the night shadows.

She blew out a long uneven breath, wishing she could dispel the tension from her limbs just as easily. Leigh had her all wound up—though to be fair, it was half her own fault. She didn't have to play along with the game he'd started.

With hasty movements, she righted her clothes, the stray raindrops forming a drizzle. She scooped up the net with the fish, where she'd dropped it on the bank earlier, and hurried back toward the barn. As she walked in, she found the rest of the recruits crowded around Granger, who was arranging two skinned rabboons over the fire.

"I hope you're also an expert at preparing fish, Granger, because I wouldn't have the first clue where to begin on these." She walked over and set the net down next to where he crouched in front of the fire.

"Good job, Wolfe." Granger turned to flip the net open, then glanced up at her with a grin. "I can teach you, if you want."

An automatic refusal sprang to her lips, because like Kayla had said, while she might enjoy eating fish, the idea of actually cutting them up and cooking them made her squeamish. But while she didn't ever plan on finding herself in the situation where she would need to catch and cook her own food, it would be a good skill to have.

She nodded and Granger's grin widened. "Knew you'd be up for it."

By the time they had the fish cooking on the fire and smelling delicious, the clouds had opened a steady downpour, drumming above them in a lulling rhythm.

Everyone ate, and at Granger's insistence she even tried some of the rabboon. It didn't taste bad, but it definitely didn't taste like chicken; it was much gamier.

They organized a couple of recruits to take turns keeping watch, and after so many late nights working on the FP profiling, she was glad no one asked her to volunteer. After that, people began dozing off.

Mia moved to sit next to Kayla, getting her thermo sheet out as a definite chill chased away the last of the day's warmth. Where was Leigh right now? He hadn't said anything about finding shelter for himself. She hoped he wasn't stuck out in this downpour like the rest of the recruits apparently were.

As she closed her eyes, her mind filled with him and the last words he'd spoken to her—that he would be nearby if she needed him. For half a second, she felt a little guilty. That Leigh was looking out for her, even at a distance, made the notion that she had another full day's walk ahead of her tomorrow that much easier to endure.

Chapter Twenty-Two

Mia gasped awake as someone kicked her in the thigh, sending pain shooting into her hip. She half rolled, only to come face-to-face with the barrel of an old-fashioned assault rifle. Shifting her gaze beyond the gun, she found herself staring up at a dark-robed soldier, patch announcing his allegiance to the CSS pinned to the middle of his chest. He had a hood pulled up over his head and material obscuring the lower half of his face, but she could see his eyes, and they glared down at her with malice.

"Get up," he growled, kicking at her again.

The last time she'd faced a hooded attacker in the ready room on board the *Knox* whammed her from nowhere, stealing her breath as disorientating dizziness cut through her. Around her, Kayla and the eight other recruits were also being dragged from their sleep and thrust onto their knees in a tight group in the middle of the barn, including the guy who should have been on watch. So much for having a guard.

Though, considering the number of CS Soldiers surrounding them, a lookout who'd actually stayed awake wouldn't have made much difference.

She'd tried to stay awake most of the night herself, but eventually exhaustion had gotten the better of her.

Her captor stepped forward, grabbing her shoulder and half of her ponytail, which he yanked painfully. He jerked her up and propelled her over to the rest of the recruits. She landed on her shoulder awkwardly, but she'd barely gone down before he roughly pulled her up to kneel.

He stepped back with the others to form a circle around them.

"In the name of his holiness, Pontifex Ronald Martin Benedictus, you are being detained for the crime of trespassing on the sacred lands of Ilari," one of the robed men spoke up. "You will be sent to the nearest Enlightening Camp for reeducation. At any time, you may choose to repent and join our holy war to rid our system of those who perpetrate and extol the evil seductress that is technology."

The man gave a single nod. The rest of the robed figures stepped forward, grabbing up recruits and hustling them toward the door.

As two sets of hands clamped onto Mia, wild disbelief washed through her in a numbing wave. *No.* This couldn't be happening. They weren't in CSS territory; they were only a few miles from the UEF base. How could such a large group of CSS be here and have found them?

But the answer was obvious, the move she'd been terrified of since yesterday. The traitor didn't need to reveal himself or get his hands dirty to get rid of her. All he had to do was tell his people where she was and the rest took care of itself. No one would realize that a group of captured recruits resulted from the sole intent of eliminating her. Oh God, every one here was going to be tortured and possibly killed, and it was all her fault.

Leigh had said he'd be nearby. Surely he must have seen them, even now be getting reinforcements— A slice of heart-spasming cold sliced through her. Unless this patrol had found Leigh and—

She couldn't finish the thought, her stomach cramping and legs giving out as they reached the barn doorway. Her captors didn't give her a second to find her feet, just kept dragging her until she scrambled and got some footing.

Outside, the early morning sunlight blinded her, the rain and clouds from the night before blowing away to leave the world all sparkling and too bright. After blinking her eyes a few times, her gaze came into focus on an ancient, clunking shuttle set down in the field a little way off from the barn. The ship had to be at least three hundred years old, some of the earliest tech of its type. It looked like it belonged in a museum, not actively used in a war.

Ahead of her, there was a commotion. Granger had broken free of his captors and gotten his hands on a gun. His actions spurred two other nearby recruits who started fighting harder to pull free.

Granger brought the gun up to aim at the nearest CS Soldier, but the leader came up behind him, pulling a sidearm from beneath his robes.

"Granger!" She yanked against the soldiers holding her and one of them clipped her in the side of the head, sending her mind lurching as a shot rang out. By the time everything stopped spinning and she could focus again, Granger was lying on the ground and everyone had frozen in place.

"Resistance is a sin, and you will be punished for it," the leader announced over the silence, then returned the assault rifle to its owner.

Two CS Soldiers hefted Granger between them. From here, she couldn't tell if he was dead or unconscious, but he definitely wasn't moving.

No one else struggled or made even the slightest noise as they were marched over to the shuttle. Mia couldn't draw a full breath, her heart thrumming too hard and too fast. She couldn't decide if she was closer to throwing up or passing out. Either way, fear was beginning to get the better of her.

The CSS Enlightening Camps were the stuff of horrific nightmare. Built, fortified, and guarded so well the UEF found it impossible to send in rescue teams. The few times they'd tried, both the rescuers and rescuees had ended up dead. That Commander Yang had survived and escaped, after eighteen months in prison, had given him near-god status.

Once they were inside those walls, no one would be coming to get them. They would either die there or endure what would probably amount to months of torture while the UEF negotiated their release. She didn't know how she'd hold up under those conditions. What she could tell was the enemy had the power to bring down the entire *Valiant Knox*. This was exactly what Leigh had been worried would happen if she ended up on the front lines and got captured. Another wave of pulse-pounding wooziness assaulted her, tipping her farther toward losing her grip on things and passing out.

The wide rear hatchway of the shuttle stood open. They were led inside, then forced to their knees and chained to the bulkheads, five on one side and four on the other. The metal grate flooring bit into her, the plexi-cuffs chafed her wrists. She'd ended up across from Nicka. Despite a few stray tears trickling down her cheeks, Nicka looked more angry than afraid.

The soldiers carrying Granger came in last and dumped him face down in the middle of the aisle. Mia leaned forward, casting a careful look over him. When the rise and fall of his back registered, the relief that surged through her was acute. He wasn't dead, just unconscious. However, he still might not survive if he didn't get medical attention. Unfortunately she couldn't see his wound, couldn't even tell where or how much he might be bleeding.

The leader strolled in, hands clasped behind his back. "Before we take off, I'd like to give you all one final opportunity. Give me some valuable information about the UEF, the *Valiant Knox* and its inner workings, swear allegiance to his holiness and you will be free of your restraints to join us right now."

No one said a word as the leader paced up and down the line, most people keeping their heads bowed or gazes averted.

"Remember, it's not your lives you are risking, it's your eternal souls." The leader turned on his heel and walked back along the aisle, stopping in front of Nicka who stared at him with blatant loathing.

"How about you, my child? Would you like to absolve yourself of your sins?"

"*My sins*?" Nicka all but spat. "What about *your* sins? You bastards killed my brother! I will never join you, but when I get my wings, I will drop a few bombs on your house, you psychopathic son of a—"

The leader backhanded her, sending her crashing into the bulkhead. But it didn't put her down. She straightened and spat blood on his too-shiny boots.

With a nod and an outstretched hand, someone gave the leader a dark bag.

He leaned down over Nicka. "I see we have our first candidate for reprogramming when we arrive at camp."

Opening the bag, he dragged it over Nicka's head, despite the way she cursed and fought him the whole time. Several other soldiers stepped forward, and the rest of the recruits were subjected to the same treatment.

When one of the soldiers stopped in front of her, Mia couldn't look any higher than his shins. She closed her eyes and gasped through her rapidly tightening throat. The rough material of the bag settled over her head and face, scratchy and dusty-smelling. It drew taut around her neck and for a terrifying second, she imagined it tightening until her air was cut off and she was strangled. But then the soldier moved away from her, leaving it secured so it wouldn't come free easily, but not so tight that it affected her breathing.

Panic had scrambled her mind. What was she supposed to do? How was she supposed to deal with this situation? No answer came to her, no instinct to follow or recall of instructions from classes in the past few weeks, just blind, numb terror that she was probably going to die. Worse than death itself, she would almost certainly be tortured first. The fear of betraying the UEF, the *Valiant Knox,* and Leigh pushed down on her with suffocating intensity. She would do everything in her power to keep the information to herself, but she didn't know how much torture it would take to break her.

Though shock had initially frozen her, it was starting to melt away, allowing too many sharp emotions to cut into her. Tears began trickling from the corners of her eyes, wetting her face and the bag covering her head.

Somewhere inside her she had to find the strength to endure, to face whatever came next. It would be easy to give up. If it was only her life on the line, maybe she could have. But it wasn't just about her; it was about the safety of Leigh and everyone else on board the *Valiant Knox*.

The notion that he might have been captured, or *worse*, crept into her thoughts, but she pushed it away. The only thing that would get her through this was the small kernel of hope that Leigh had avoided the patrol and gone for help. That he and the rest of the FP squadron would intercept this shuttle before they got to the Enlightening Camp.

Fortifying her mind, she blocked out everything else, concentrating on the chance that help would find them. In the dark, under the thick hessian bag, hope was the only thing keeping her together.

Chapter Twenty-Three

Leigh stood in parade stance next to Seb and Lawler trying to look relaxed, despite the fact his inside were churning like he'd eaten a plate of five-alarm chili from that Mexican place on commerce level of the *Knox*.

The second shuttle of recruits was touching down, the one with Mia on board. Another fifteen recruits stood on the damp earth of the training yard, bags still over their heads, each stiller and more silent than the last. Four had already been led off by Bren and booted from the program after they'd taken the bait, proving themselves weak of character and ready to sell out to the enemy at the slightest provocation.

Most years, he didn't care too much more about this section of testing than any other. As far as he'd been concerned, it was one more requirement to be fulfilled. Besides, it had been done to him the year he'd completed the FP training program, and he'd survived just fine.

But other years, there hadn't been a certain golden-haired recruit who had him tied up in so many emotional knots, he was starting to have trouble working out which way was up or down. He'd wanted so badly to tell Mia last night what she'd be facing today, but to be fair to her, all of the other recruits, and the whole damn FP squadron, he'd kept his mouth shut, despite knowing the fear and panic she'd have to suffer. And this year, with traitors in their ranks, he, Seb, and Bren had agreed to go a little harder on the recruits, to see if they could shake anything loose. Maybe it was a stretch to think any of these recruits, who'd only just arrived in the Brannon System, could be traitors, but these days, he was suspicious of everyone. And after almost getting sucked out of a launch bay, he'd decided there was no such thing as being too careful.

The old junker of a shuttle they'd confiscated from the CSS a few years back jolted down with a *thud* and whine of tired metal. He winced as Seb muttered something about putting the thing out to pasture before it killed someone. The ancient shuttle was pretty much a death trap waiting to happen, but it had served them well in testing recruits and inserting small teams of UEF soldiers into CSS-held territories over the years.

The rear hatchway of the shuttle opened and Cam strolled out, hood pushed back. He stepped aside and watched as the soldiers he'd handpicked to help him in this training drill led nine recruits out and carried one other.

Leigh walked over to join him, gaze brushing over Mia as he passed her at a distance.

"What happened to that one?" He nodded toward the recruit being carried.

"Fought off two of my men and laid hands on a weapon. I used a dark-round on him." Cam stripped the CSS robes off and chucked them back into the shuttle. "It was impressive. If he happens to flunk out of your high and mighty FP regime, send him my way. I'll gladly add him to one of my specialized teams."

He sent Cam a grin, though he wasn't exactly feeling it. "With any luck, he won't flunk out."

Cam nodded toward the recruits being led over to the others already waiting to form a second line. "None of this lot caved. They all kept their mouths shut. The dark-haired girl, the one with the small scar on her chin, she put up a good fight, too, though you might want to check her anger issues. Said something about her brother being killed."

He made a mental note of it. "Thanks, I'll make sure we cover it when she's debriefed."

"I've got to get back, but thanks for the morning's entertainment. And good luck. Seb's taking odds on how many walk-outs you'll get from this, so I'll be checking in later to hear the results."

"Seb should know better than to gamble with you. In fact, he should know better than to gamble with anyone by now."

Cam gave a short laugh. "What would we use for beer money every week if Seb didn't gamble?"

"Good point." He glanced over his shoulder at the sub-lieutenant in question, directing the last of the recruits into line. "I better get to it."

Cam sent him a salute, then called his men into formation.

Leigh returned the salutation, watching for a moment as Cam led his team toward the few intact buildings left in what had once been the main base on Ilari. Major operations had shifted to the secondary base after the bombing a few weeks ago. As of now, what had once been a thriving headquarters for troops and other necessary functions had been reduced to the skeleton staff of a minor outpost.

Leigh strolled over to Seb, who now stood waiting in front of the lined-up recruits. Lawler and a couple of his fighter pilots began untying the recruits. Some immediately yanked the bags from their heads, while others seemed hesitant to move and waited until it was done for them.

As they were all uncovered and took a moment to comprehend where they were, he forced himself not to look directly at Mia. If he did, if he saw any of the fear or hurt in her gaze, he wasn't entirely sure it wouldn't break him.

A ripple of exclamation passed along the line of recruits and Leigh stepped forward. "At ease, recruits."

The group immediately fell quiet, no doubt any fight or defiance scared right out of them.

"As you may have worked out by now, you were not captured by the enemy, but have proven that you can hold it together when faced with such a prospect."

"This was a *test*?" a recruit demanded, one of Steve's buddies. Besides him, Steve and one other Ackerly alumni hadn't washed out yet. "What in the hell kind of test do you call that?"

"The kind where I make sure you won't give us up to the enemy the first second you face any real kind of danger." The same question got asked every time, and his answer always remained the same. It might have been cruel, but it had been necessary. "You're welcome to register your disapproval with Commander Yang as you're leaving."

"You're damn right I'm leaving!" The recruit stomped out of line. "And I'll be taking this up with UEF command. This is unconscionable! You can't just go around making people think they've been taken by the CSS."

"Go right ahead. Others have tried and yet here we are, doing the same thing with each new FP class."

The recruit swore and stalked away, toward the buildings.

"Anyone else feel they were treated unfairly or unduly, I will remind you that this is war, and this is a reality you may face one day."

For a moment no one moved, but then three other recruits broke away to follow the first across the training yard.

The others shifted uneasily, but he didn't say anything until the four who'd quit had left.

"The rest of today will be considered downtime. You'll all be given an appointment for individual debriefing, but otherwise the mess hall, showers, and other amenities are yours for the next few hours. We'll be returning to the *Knox* at seventeen hundred. The transport will be leaving from the launch pad on the hour and if you're not on board then, I'll assume you've decided to take a ground posting instead. Recruits, dismissed."

"Wait, sir." Leigh froze as Mia called out. His determination not to look directly at her got whitewashed by the simple sound of her voice, and his gaze had landed on her before he could even think about resisting.

Her skin was a little pale, damp tracks down the side of her face and hair a tousled mess; she looked just as hard-done-by as the rest of them. But looking at any of the other recruits didn't make his heart squeeze.

"Sir, what about Granger? He was shot." Her voice

came out carefully even, but a slight tremor betrayed the truth of her turbulent emotions.

"Granger is fine," he answered, working to keep the tone of his voice impersonal. "He was hit with what we call a dark-round. It's specialized training ammo that renders a person unconscious on impact. He's probably waking up in the field-med building right about now. Hit the showers and get some food, recruits. This is the only downtime you'll get for the rest of the training program."

He stepped back and turned toward Seb before Mia or any other recruit could start questioning him. His mood was rapidly darkening, and he didn't feel like playing guidance counselor to any recruit's bruised emotions right now.

"Did we lose more or less than you expected?" Seb asked as he joined him to watch them head off toward the buildings across the yard.

"I hadn't given it too much thought. I suppose between the walk-outs and the four who caved, we probably cut the usual number."

Now that he was no longer standing in front of the group of bedraggled recruits, he let himself search out Mia, watching as she walked next to Kayla, though her hand rested on the shoulder of another girl... Nicki? No, Nicka. The recruit Cam said had also put up a fight, but might have issues.

But the question of Nicka's suitability for the program dropped away as his gaze returned to Mia. He'd sworn to take care of her, and no doubt in the aftermath of this harsh psychological test she'd definitely be in need of comfort. Yet he was still bound by duty and limited in what he could do for her. Part of him wondered if he might not be better simply staying away and not put either of them in the path of temptation like he had last night. By all rights, he shouldn't have made any contact with her the evening before, let alone led her into taking any kind of risk of them being caught. Yes, he'd needed to make sure she was aware of the danger to her, that she was watching out for herself. However, giving even the slightest credence to the flame that had kindled between them was beyond stupid.

But any illusions of control he'd hung onto might as well have all the consistency of space dust when he was alone with her. Worse, it seemed he didn't *want* to stay in control. He'd found a heady, dangerous freedom in the things he felt when he was around her, the sensations becoming almost addictive.

"Is everything okay with you?" Seb's quiet question jolted him and he half turned to look at his sub-lieutenant.

"Fine. Why are you asking?"

Seb's expression wasn't giving anything away as he shrugged. "You just seem a little extreme lately. Well, extreme for *you*. Maybe not as buttoned down as you've been in the past. I mean, I'm not complaining. Half the *Knox* are convinced you're really some AI-borg with no actual feelings. It's an interesting change to know you can lose it like the rest of us every now and then."

He sent Seb an unimpressed frown. "Good to know my apparent emotional breakdown is a validation of your own shortcomings."

Seb grinned. "Is that what this is, some emotional breakdown? And here I just thought you had the hots for one of the recruits."

Cold shock zapped him like electrified razors. "What have you heard—"

"Nothing." Seb laughed, lightly punching him in the upper arm. "Geez, don't have a coronary. No one has said anything. But I'm not stupid. You get a certain gleam in your eye when you look at Wolfe. I only noticed because I know you so well. And I'm not judging. I can't say I haven't lusted after a gorgeous new recruit a time or two myself over the years. Just do yourself a favor and wait until after the FP training program is finished if you're going to hit that."

"Because if she ends up under my command, it would be slightly less wrong than getting involved with her while she's still a recruit?"

"Exactly." Seb's grin widened. "Anyway, it's technically only wrong if you get caught. Don't get caught, and you won't have a problem."

"Thanks for the advice," he muttered dryly.

"Whenever you need it. Now I need some breakfast." Seb saluted and then sauntered off across the yard to catch up with Lawler.

Leigh let the short conversation with Seb roll over him as the new, unfamiliar quietness of the base pressed around him. A slight breeze swirled through the training yard, bringing with it the lingering chill of last night's rain and the lone call of a bird. After years of everything being so routinely the same, it had all suddenly started shifting and changing—from the varying dynamics of the war they were fighting with the CSS to his own personal battle in making sense of the chaos Mia had brought into his life. But in a way, it was a welcome chaos after so long living the same existence of responsibility, duty, and control.

However, nothing could exist in chaos for long, and though they were only days from completing the FP program, a sense of impending disaster had formed in the back of his mind like heavy storm clouds. Probably because he couldn't believe no one else besides Bren and Seb had noticed his interest in Mia, especially after his response to the Robinson incident. Apparently, his strict, duty-bound professionalism had served him well. No one had even considered the CAFF might have started an inappropriate relationship with a recruit.

Worrying now was pointless. He shook his head at himself. Standing out here, giving himself a psychoanalytical once-over wasn't helping matters. Despite the fact that staying away was definitely the better idea, and he should concentrate all his resources on ferreting out the traitor, he had to find Mia and make sure she was okay. She'd just been through what probably amounted to the scariest hour of her life. Only the real CSS storming the base could have kept him from getting to her.

He headed for the amenities building. Some of the recruits had gone straight to the mess hall, but Mia wasn't among them. A few had found the bunks, but she wasn't in there either. He headed for the shower block, passing a couple of recruits, but not seeing her face in the small group.

As he rounded the last corner, Kayla stepped through the doorway of the female locker rooms. Unlike on the *Knox,* with its limited space and unisex change rooms, the base had the luxury of separate amenities.

Kayla was finger combing her short hair, but paused when she saw him. For a second, she seemed to be having some kind of internal debate, a range of emotions flashing through her gaze, chief of which appeared to be anger. He wasn't surprised or upset about it. He'd be more astonished to find a recruit who *didn't* hate his guts at this point.

From previous experience, he'd spend these last few days of the program receiving pissed-off glares from the recruits who hadn't washed out. And whatever last tests or requirements he put them through would be met with more hostility.

But he wasn't here to be their friend; he was here to turn them into first-class fighter pilots. They could hate his guts all they wanted. When they got their wings and flew out into the black, their chances of surviving were that much better.

"Mia is still in the shower. She's been in there for a while. But if you're thinking about checking on her, there's still one other recruit in the change room."

Her words pulled him up short. Did she know something of his relationship with Mia? He wasn't sure how he felt about that. Not worried, because if she was going to report it, surely she would have done so already. But maybe apprehensive—the more people who worked out the truth, the worse things could end up.

"Thanks, Dawson." Playing it cool and detached seemed like the best option.

"Sure," she muttered, stepping past him.

No doubt the fallout from this year's torture test was going to be worse than usual. But between Commander Yang being captured and imprisoned for a year and a half, and the fact that the CSS had well and truly infiltrated their ranks, it was more imperative than ever that he ensure the pilots he accepted into the squad were fully prepared and aware of what they possibly faced in this war.

Leigh scrubbed a hand over his face, then leaned against the opposite wall of the changing room, settling in to wait as long as it took for Mia to come out.

However, patience was one the virtues he'd recently lost. He was tapping his foot by the time the door opened to reveal the other recruit Kayla had said was still inside. She paused when she saw him, a flash of confusion crossing her features, then she saluted and continued down the hall.

He tracked her until she rounded the far corner, then pushed off the wall and walked across to the change room door, hesitating for a slight moment as he pressed the door open. Glancing up and down the corridor, he made one last check there was no one around to see the CAFF sneaking into the women's locker rooms and entered.

There was no one in the open area of benches and a few lockers, but he could hear water running, so he crossed toward the tiled alcove where the showers were situated.

Steam rolled out to meet his boots as he stepped onto the slick tiles, but he paused before rounding the wall to the shower stalls.

"Mia?"

She murmured an answer he couldn't hear over the hissing water. Sidestepping, he grabbed a towel from a stack in the nearby metal shelves and headed for the stalls, walking into a wall of steam.

Mia stood leaning against the tiles underneath the angled spray of a showerhead. Her skin was reddened where the water had tracked over it. With a curse, he reached over to tab the water off, the back-spray almost too hot to bear.

As soon as the water cut out, she started shivering, wrapping her arms around herself. She glanced up at him, eyes shadowed with a lingering glaze of shock as he flicked the towel around her damp shoulders.

"Sorry, I just couldn't get warm. The water wasn't hot enough."

"The water was plenty hot enough, believe me." With the towel folded securely around her, he pulled her against his chest, closing his arms tightly around her.

She shuddered violently, grabbing the front of his shirt as she pulled herself closer to him. "Leigh, it was so horrible. I thought I was never going to see you again. I thought I was going to be tortured into saying things that would betray you all. You can't imagine—"

"I know." He lowered his head to rest his cheek against her wet hair. "I know, because we do the same thing with each new group of recruits. I know because they did the same thing to me when I came through the FP program. It's a baptism by fire, and I never hated the process until today."

She raised her head to look up at him, leaving their faces only inches apart.

"What happened when you got taken?"

The distant memory of that morning had always hit him in the guts for a long time. It'd been the most terrifying thing he'd ever experienced in his entire twenty-one years to that point. But the stab of recollection had dulled, and unfortunately he'd since experienced far worse in battle.

"I suppose I was already somewhat of a leader, even back then, just like the computer-eval had reported. I tried to negotiate for them to take me and leave the other six who'd camped out in that barn with me, not realizing they'd already captured the rest of the class. All that earned me was a punch in the face and the taunt that I was worth nothing and would be worth even less by the time they were finished with me. If I hadn't been scared before then, for some reason that threat rammed everything home. My bravado was topped off by me throwing up on the boots of my captor, which I didn't live down for the rest of FP training. Or for years after. There are still a handful of people on the *Knox* who remember it and like to bring it up every now and then when they think I'm letting the CAFF power go to my head."

The last of the distracted glaze left her eyes as she stared up at him, disbelief entering her expression. "You actually threw up? You're not just making it up to make me feel better, are you?"

"Do you really think I'd make up something so embarrassing? If I was trying to make you feel better, I would have come up with something more romanticized, like I cried manly tears of frustration at the plight of my fellow recruits."

That earned him a small laugh, ending with her relaxing into his hold and the shivers finally subsiding. "Truthfully, I can't imagine you doing either. You always seem so in control."

Now it was his turn to laugh, the sound hollowed with cynicism. "*In control*? Mia, since you walked in to my life, I've never been more out of control. Do you really think I was anywhere near *in control* that night we spent together in the jet, or when I nearly beat Robinson to a pulp for touching you? My mind, my body, my very soul are in chaos."

Her expression shuttered, and she lowered her head again.

"I'm sorry," she mumbled.

He caught her chin and urged her to look back up at him. "Don't be sorry for anything, because I can tell you that I'm not."

"How can you say that?" She stared up at him, her

expression troubled in a different way now. "Isn't any of this getting to you? This is a disaster. The sneaking around and the lying, not to mention having to pretend like I don't feel anything for you. Do you know how hard that is? How many times a day I almost slip up? How many times I've imagined saying *to hell with it* and kissing you in front of everyone? How, whenever anything happens, good or bad, the first person I want to tell is you?"

He tightened his hold on her. "I'm fighting the exact same impulses. You're not alone. I'm going through the same motions each day."

She pushed out of his hold, wrapping her fingers into the folds of the towel at her chest to keep herself covered. "Then why the hell are we doing this to ourselves? Nothing can come of this. Nothing was ever going to come of this. You're going to be my CO, or if not, I'm going to end up somewhere that's not the *Knox* and we'll never see each other again. Either way, there's no hope for us to end up together."

"That's not true." Her words had lit a fire in his chest, one that was blackening his heart and spreading out through his limbs with painful intensity. "We talked about this. You can get a recommendation for a different post—"

"And truthfully, what are the chances that post will be on the *Knox*? Everyone knows if you're not going into a specialized team like the FP squadron, how hard it is to get a post on a ship without years of other training first."

"Hard, but not impossible." He took a step toward her, but she backed away. He clenched his fists, locking down his muscles to stop himself from reaching for her. "Mia, I know this morning was tough, but you just need some down time—"

"No." The single word was brimming with determination. "Its not about this morning, it's about everything else. We should never have started down this road."

His pulse surged, straining, as though his heart was having trouble pumping blood. "What are you saying?"

Her gaze dropped away from him. "I care about you too much and this is only causing us pain. So I can't do this anymore. I *won't* do this anymore."

The heat inside him extinguished leaving him numb and cold. "Are you really sure this is what you want? Because I was willing to fight for you, Mia. To fight for us."

She looked back up at him, sorrow in her dark eyes. "That's the point, isn't it? We shouldn't have to fight for it. You ever think that while we're putting all that energy into trying to make something work that so clearly can't, we're missing the universe telling us it's not meant to be?"

He clenched his jaw, wanting to argue that sometimes the fight made the victory that much sweeter, or the battle was what made a person worthy of the prize, but he knew Mia well enough to realize she wouldn't be swayed by hollow clichés. And he respected her too much to stand here and talk her out of the decision she'd so clearly made. If this was what she truly wanted, then he would give it to her, because at the end of the day, the thing he wanted most was for her to be happy. And if she was happier without him, then whatever feelings he had about the end of their short, not-quite-relationship weren't important.

"Okay, Mia." The words came out quietly, but didn't give away the turmoil ricocheting around inside him. "Good luck with the rest of the FP program, though you don't need luck, you'll do fine. And whatever comes after that... I know you'll be brilliant, no matter where you end up."

He stepped back, and when he caught the sheen of tears in her eyes, had to turn away with a silent curse, before he caved and went begging on his knees to change her mind, to let him take care of her. Because more apparent than his weakness for her was the fact she was right. They'd already attracted attention to themselves after the incident with Robinson, and Bren at least knew he was emotionally compromised when it came to Mia. If they kept on this path, the most likely result would be the destruction of both their careers. As much as he didn't want that for himself, he wanted it even less for her.

Though he hadn't recently done all that much thinking with his upstairs brain when it came to her, he had to admit that he'd been arrogant enough to start believing maybe they could get away with this. She'd been right in making the call to end it because the balance of risk for her wasn't worth it. He'd already established himself in the UEF and would mostly be able to weather it if the truth had come out. But she would be ostracized; she'd have no recourse except to take a ground posting. The thought of her down on the front with the hardened troops who held the lines, the danger she would face, it terrified him in a way he'd never thought possible. He couldn't risk it.

He strode out of the change rooms, not seeing anything as he tried to get a handle on the smolder in his chest slowly working its way upward, charring his heart and then singeing his throat, blocking off the next breath he tried to take. Halfway down the corridor, he picked a random door on the left and slammed through it, finding himself in an empty training room, dim and dusty after only a few weeks of abandonment.

Leigh leaned back against the door, trying to force air into his aching lungs as he slid down to a crouch. It felt like someone had reached into his chest and yanked out a few important arteries, leaving his heart drowning in its own blood. He lowered his head to his hands as the burn he'd been fighting reached his eyes, making them sting.

He and Mia had never really had anything, if he was going to be brutal about it. Nothing but a couple of illicit assignations and a handful of private conversations. So technically, he hadn't lost anything despite the yawning, dark vacuum inside him that told him otherwise.

Somehow in the short time he'd known Mia, she'd struck deep within him and he'd let her get closer than anyone in his entire life. There were subjects he'd talked about with her that had made him uncomfortable to deal with in the past. But with Mia, it had all been so easy and comfortable.

Whatever it had or hadn't been, it was over now and he needed to get on with pretending like his insides hadn't been lasered to a pulp.

He dragged both hands over his face, pushing away the ache in his eyes and sniffing down the tightness in his throat. With a long, slow breath in, he pushed to his feet, settling his CAFF mantle back in place and turning his mind to the debriefings and the regime for the last days of testing.

Finally back in control, he set his shoulders and stepped out of the room, leaving everything that had happened behind him.

Chapter Twenty-Four

She'd never thought she'd be so glad to see her bunk. Mia tiredly followed Kayla into their dorm room and went straight over to flop onto the bed. Her whole body hurt with a dull ache after spending all day walking yesterday, but her exhaustion was more mental than physical. She'd already been on edge about the sneaking around she'd been doing with Leigh—both in trying to find the traitor and their more personal moments—so the brief terror this morning, thinking she'd been captured by the enemy, had sapped what little energy she'd had left.

That kind of heart-attack-inducing fear made a person reevaluate life, and a couple of facts had become blatantly clear to her. One, she couldn't continue her relationship with Leigh any longer, even though it hadn't been much more than a single night together. And two, she sure as absolute hell did not want to be a fighter pilot.

As soon as she got the two final squadron profiles

finished and completed FP training she would be requesting a transfer to a nice, safe, boring desk job somewhere. She wasn't cut out to be a hero and she definitely wasn't cut out for battle. Truthfully, now that she'd gotten a taste of it, she had no idea how Leigh lived with such responsibility day after day. Her respect for him had ballooned, while the things she shouldn't be feeling deepened even more.

But she had to be strong. Ending things had been the right decision. What had developed between them could end in nothing but hurt. It was better to cut it off now and lessen the pain, rather than getting in deeper and being devastated when the inevitable end came.

Rather than dwelling, she rolled over and reached out to retrieve Leigh's datapad from the drawer in her nightstand.

"Don't tell me you're going to study now." Kayla's tone was drenched with disbelief.

"I need a distraction." She didn't glance up as she tapped the datapad to life and keyed in Leigh's code.

"So let's head down to commerce level and catch a movie. Or better yet, get a beer at Harley's. Studying is not the answer tonight, not after what we went through."

"I'm still catching up—"

"From that one day you missed?" Kayla got up and came over to sit on the edge of her bed, expression landing somewhere between suspicious and annoyed. "Just how much extra work could they possibly have given you? Surely you've made up for it by now. You've spent twice as long glued to your datapad as anyone else."

Yeah, the excuse was wearing thin, but it was still the best one she had. "Actually, I'm just about done. If I put in a few hours tonight, it'll be finished and I won't have to spend any more time looking at this datapad."

Kayla reached out and set a hand on her forearm. "Seriously, Mia. Leave it tonight and do it tomorrow. Give yourself a break."

It would be so easy to head down to commerce level and relax, have a few beers, take the edge off. But while she did that, the traitor could be making his next move. Despite what happened between them personally, Leigh was counting on her to get this done, not blow it off to get tipsy in a bar.

She dropped her gaze back to the screen of the datapad, feeling like she had betrayed Kayla somehow. "I'm sorry. I just really want to get this done. If I finish up soon, I'll come find you."

Kayla dropped her grip with a long sigh as she stood. "You know where I'll be."

She watched her friend walk out of the room, leaving her in peace, but with a deep sense of loneliness.

She blew out a hard breath and returned her concentration to the datapad. Once she got the program running on the last two pilots, she returned to the one she'd been stuck on for days, the one with too many holes. It had fully pricked her suspicions, but she wouldn't go to Leigh unless she had infallible proof.

Widening the search parameters, she started checking for other information she hadn't included for the others, like high school and hospital records. A note in the pilot's high school files caught her attention.

Sub-Officer Nolan Lawler had been diagnosed with a rare blood disorder, which could be an ongoing issue. For a second she felt bad that such a nice guy had such a terrible disease, but then another thought occurred to her. Weird that she hadn't seen any mention of it in his UEF personnel file. Pulse picking up slightly, she accessed the med records for various tests all candidates went through when joining the UEF.

The blood test Lawler had after joining the UEF and coming to the *Knox* showed no sign of the disease. In fact, his blood type was totally different than that listed in the med records from high school.

A shot of excited disbelief ripped through her. She tightened her grip on the datapad. Lawler wasn't really Lawler. He was somebody else. This was it, the evidence she'd needed. She'd found the traitor. But *Lawler*? He seemed like such a dependable and unassuming guy.

Out of all the instructors, none of the recruits ever had a bad thing to say about him, and clearly he had Leigh's trust. Her stomach churned, making her feel sick. This was exactly what she'd been afraid of. How was she supposed to tell Leigh something like this?

Switching tabs on the datapad, she pulled up the comm system to send a message to Leigh, thinking about how she should word it. No doubt as vaguely as possible, but she still needed him to realize it was crucial. All communications on the *Knox* were routinely and randomly monitored, and she didn't want anyone to question why a recruit personally messaged the CAFF so often. But this was too important.

She typed the message with an unsteady hand deciding to get straight to the point. *Where are you? Need to see you now. Urgent.*

After scooting to the end of the bed, she started tapping her foot against the floor while she waited for a reply. If he was in a meeting, it might be hours before she heard from him. The datapad gave a soft chime and a new message appeared.

Was just heading back to my apartment. Where are you?

She pushed to her feet, typing a quick message as she walked. *Dorms. Heading out now, meet you halfway.*

As she reached the end of the passageway, another message arrived. *Already on the transit, wait there for me.*

She arrived at the transit, glancing around the deserted passageway. Only about a third of the recruits who'd started the FP program remained, and it seemed like none of them had stayed in the dorms tonight. Maybe they'd all gone down to Harley's like Kayla.

The transit arrived with a ding and she stepped closer as the doors opened to reveal Leigh. Though it had only been a bit over an hour since she'd last seen him on the transport that had brought them back to the *Knox*, her heart gave a little kick.

He exited the transit and crossed his arms, expression locked down.

"What's going on, Mia?" He stopped in front of her, leaving an impersonal amount of distance between them.

Her heart gave a painful squeeze at how detached and cold he seemed toward her. But it had been her decision to end things, and they had more important issues to worry about right now. She held out his datapad.

"I found him. Running the profiles worked. Nolan Lawler isn't really Nolan Lawler. I found blood tests that confirm it."

If she hadn't known him so well, she would have missed the utter devastation in his eyes before his expression hardened. "Then who the hell is he?"

She shrugged one shoulder, her heart aching for a different reason now. She hated being the one to tell him this. And in that moment, she regretted that she'd so effectively cut him off, because she wanted nothing more than to comfort him. "That I can't tell you. But there's no doubt he's an imposter. It's all right there in the files."

Leigh skimmed through the evidence she'd put together.

"Got you, you son of a bitch," he muttered, dark fury flashing across his features before he looked back up at her. "You came through. And now it's time for you to get out of this mess."

She crossed her arms. "You don't need to tell me twice."

He gave a short nod. "I need to get this information to Commander Yang. Thanks, Mia. I know you won't ever get any public recognition for what you've done, but you've saved the lives of my pilots, and that's something I can never repay."

A surge of self-conscious gratitude at his words stopped her from replying. Instead she simply nodded and then watched as he disappeared back onto the transit with a quick wave.

So that was it. She helped him find the traitor and all she got was a quick thanks. Not that she expected any sort of commendation or reward, but after everything they'd been through together, he could have at least made his appreciation a little more personal or sincere. Although, what did she think his response would be after telling him a few short hours ago that things were over between them?

She sighed and rubbed a hand over her face, deep tiredness dragging at her now that everything was done. She was relieved at this finally being over, but a weird pang tightened her chest, because it also meant she didn't have a reason to see Leigh outside of sessions anymore.

Now that she no longer had the shadow of espionage or an inappropriate relationship with a superior officer hanging over her head, she could give her full attention to finishing the FP program and consider what other posting to apply for once the training was over.

Except, with the end in sight and the reality that she would walk away from Leigh once and for all weighing down on her, she realized that she couldn't imagine going day after day without seeing him, even if they couldn't have any type of personal relationship. For half a second, she considered staying in the squad just to be near him. But then remembered the whole death-defying danger aspect, leaving an anxious chill creeping through her. No, fighter pilot wasn't the career for her, and taking a position just because of her feelings for Leigh would be foolish and irresponsible.

Maybe her overtired brain simply needed a decent night's sleep and everything would look lucid and clear in the morning.

With heavy steps, she returned to her bunk, quickly changing and the burying herself under the blankets, sinking into the peaceful relief of sleep.

L eigh clasped his hands behind his back, locking himself down as he waited for Commander Yang to review the information on his datapad. He wanted nothing more than to find that backstabbing bastard Lawler and take a pound of the guy's flesh for the four pilots that could have been killed when he'd tampered with the jets, and an extra pound or two for the times Mia had almost been killed. Not to mention the fact that they'd been more than just a CO and pilot, they'd been friends. Seb, more than anyone, was going to be devastated when he heard the news. However, instead of letting his fury drive him, he stood in front of Yang's desk, following due process.

At last Yang sat back in his chair, clasping his fingers tightly, expression contemplative, but edged with tight anger.

"Looks like you're right, Alpha. Lawler had to be the traitor in the squad." Yang speared him with a knowing look. "And it's amazing that you knew how to work the *Knox's* systems so well to find all of this information."

"What can I say, sir, I have hidden talents."

"Uh-huh," Yang returned dryly. "More like a hidden source, but what I don't know, I can plausibly deny. So yeah, let's just believe that you've got the skill to do this kind of hacking."

"That's very wise of you, sir."

One side of Yang's mouth kicked up in a grin. "So, what's your play on this?"

"Actually, I hadn't thought that far ahead. I brought this straight to you as soon as it came to light." Because mentioning that really he wanted to find the guy and beat the ever-living crap out of him wouldn't help the larger situation at hand.

Yang sat forward and reached out to tap at the datapad set in the recess on his desk, opening a comm line. "Olivia, can you get me the current whereabouts of Sub-Officer Nolan Lawler?"

Olivia confirmed, and a moment later, reported that he

was in the larger gym on communal level.

Yang stood and rounded the desk. "Let's go have a chat with Lawler before we bring Stanton in on this. We need to know who his accomplice was."

Leigh followed Yang out of the command center and down to the communal level. Anticipation rushed hot through his veins, clashing with the ice-cold ache of betrayal, along with relief that his squad would no longer be in danger. They could finally get the answers they'd been seeking these past weeks.

In the gym, they found Lawler at the weights with two other guys from the FP squad. They all stopped what they were doing and saluted—more for Yang's benefit than his own—as they approached.

Leigh searched Lawler's face for any signs of guilt or subterfuge, but he appeared the same as he had every day since joining the squad four years ago. Looking at him now, however, made him sick to the guts.

"Lawler, we need to have a word."

"Of course, sir." Lawler grabbed up a towel, not looking the least bit worried and sent a wave to the other two pilots, before they went back to working out.

Lawler didn't say anything as they led him out of the gym and up to squadron level. If he was worried, he certainly wasn't showing it. But then again, he'd apparently had them all fooled for years.

Yang led them into one of the smaller ready rooms on squad level, and as Lawler walked to the middle of the room, Leigh noticed Yang locking the door with his own officer codes. Even he wouldn't be able to get out now. Not that he wanted to go anywhere until he'd gotten some straight answers from Lawler.

"Take a seat, Sub-Officer." Yang indicated the single large table, skirted by half a dozen chairs.

Lawler nodded and then sat, leaning back in the chair and crossing his arms. "What's this all about?"

Yang moved to sit across from him, but Leigh was too wired to sit.

"It's recently come to our attention that you suffer from a rare blood disorder, Lawler." Leigh braced his hands against the edge of the table adjacent to Lawler and leaned in. "See, we're going to have to address this issue, reassess your suitability for the FP program. I can understand why you'd want to hide something like that. It can really damage a guy's career."

"I don't have any blood disorder, so wherever you got that information, it's wrong. You can get a doc in here and test me right now." Lawler looked a little annoyed, but still not worried.

"Then you must have had some miraculous kind of recovery in the past ten years, because according to the records we have, it seriously impacted your sophomore year of high school," Yang said, tone conversational as though they were discussing nothing more interesting than the weather.

Lawler passed a slow look between the two of them, then abruptly shoved to his feet and ran for the door. Unfortunately for him, he didn't get any farther and slammed a fist into the hatchway when he realized he was trapped.

"Did he really think he could make a run for it?" Leigh shot the question at Yang, who almost looked amused. "Obviously he's not that smart after all."

Leigh stalked over and grabbed the back of the guy's

shirt, yanking him away from the hatchway and steering him over to the table. He threw the guy back into the chair and then clamped a hand on his shoulder to stop him from getting up again. It was all he could do in that moment not to let the fury loose and snap the guy's neck.

"You sure as hell aren't Nolan Lawler. So who are you?" The cold violence in his tone came out crystal clear, and for the first time, Lawler actually looked concerned.

But the guy tipped up his chin, putting on a tough front. "Torture me all you want. I'm not telling you shit."

Leigh let him go with a rough shove and rounded the table to stand next to where Yang was still seated. "We don't torture people, not like you sick CSS sons of bitches. But you will talk, because if you don't, then we're going to send you back to your own people with a nice explanation about how helpful you are."

Fake-Lawler wasn't looking so smug anymore, in fact, he'd started looking a little pale.

Leigh dragged the chair out next to Yang and sat down. They needed Lawler to roll over on his accomplice to see this situation resolved. "Now, I don't know how accurate those rumors are, about what the CSS does to their own people who betray them. But even if just a fraction of that is true, then I sure as hell wouldn't want to be in your shoes right now."

Chapter Twenty-Five

Mia's steps were measured as she left the transit on squadron level and headed along the passageway toward the officer's wardroom. She'd seen Sub-Lieutenant Rayne at messdeck, and he'd told her she could find Lieutenant Brenner up here.

Despite going to bed early, she'd slept the night away deeply and soundly, as though her body was trying to catch up on all the sleep she'd missed in previous nights. However, when she'd woken up, she still hadn't been sure what kind of transfer to request. All of the work she'd done for Leigh had made her realize she'd never be suited to Command Intelligence, and while she still wanted to be an aeronautical engineer, usually a person needed a few years experience serving on ship before moving into such a position. That would be her ultimate aim, but she wasn't sure what to do with herself until she'd gained the necessary background. Still, a little voice kept telling her that staying in the squad might be the answer.

She didn't want to be a fighter pilot. So why this lack of enthusiasm about cutting the ties? She had a feeling it came down to two things that shouldn't influence her decision. First off she was more than a little competitive and quitting had never been her play, even though requesting a transfer after graduation technically wasn't quitting.

Secondly, stupidly, it came back to Leigh and the trepidation that after giving up her spot, she'd leave the *Knox* and never see him again. He hadn't been hers to begin with, so the fact that she'd gotten so attached to him was no one's fault except her own fool self.

So she had to organize a transfer, work out where she wanted to go, and how to get there. This morning. Right now. Because the two reasons dragging her footsteps weren't good enough to keep her here. She only wished there was some way to get out of the day's sessions, because after the final exam, the remaining recruits would be taking their maiden solo flight in a jet. Maybe flying a jet would be fun, but maybe it wouldn't be. Truthfully, she didn't want to find out.

She arrived at the officer's wardroom to a closed-over door. She tabbed the call icon on the inset screen and waited for Brenner to let her in. The hatchway cracked open and she pushed through, but had only taken two steps into the room when she stopped short.

Lieutenant Brenner was nowhere to be seen, but Leigh was standing next to the conference table, coffee in hand, a brief flicker of surprise crossing his features.

Her damned heart flipped out before simply stopping altogether, making her next breath impossible to find. Every time she saw him, her physical reaction to him became stronger. Her heart tried to tell her she'd made a huge mistake in ending things with him, becoming louder and more insistent every time. It was exactly why she needed to get away from him, before she did something stupid, like decide Leigh and everything he made her feel was worth the destruction of both their careers.

"What are you doing here? Class starts in a less than half an hour."

She clasped her hands behind her back, glancing around the room as if it might give her some clue as to where Brenner had gone.

"I'm here to see the lieutenant." The reason didn't matter as a more pressing issue took over her thoughts. "What happened with Lawler?"

There were shadows in his gaze that hadn't been there a few days ago, new lines of tension and strain around his eyes and mouth, as though this whole situation had started taking a physical toll on him.

"I can't tell you. I'm sorry. But you were right, he betrayed us all."

She wanted to press him for details, wanted to ask if he was okay or there was anything she could do for him, but she'd given up the right to any of that days ago.

"So, do you know where Lieutenant Brenner is?"

Leigh set the coffee down and leaned against the edge of the table. "She just got called up to launch deck. I'm not sure why. But I doubt she'll be back before you need to be in session to sit the exam. Is there something I can help you with?"

She hadn't wanted to have this conversation with him,

but there was no point in skirting the issue, he'd find out eventually anyway. She took a deep breath, pushing her shoulders back a little. "I wanted to talk to her about a possible transfer, instead of taking a spot in the squad after training is complete."

Leigh's expression gave nothing away as he stared at her for a long, silent moment.

"We both know it's the right thing to do," she continued after the silence started getting to her.

"Maybe. Maybe not. Its not a question of what's right, it's a question of what you want. Do you want to be a fighter pilot, Mia?"

The sound of her name, inflected with the slightest hint of intimacy, deflated the indifferent bravado she'd held onto. She let her shoulders drop as she glanced away from him.

"I don't think flying is my thing, but I'll admit, I don't like the idea of quitting. Not to mention I have no idea where to go from here because even if I get another posting on board the *Knox*, it'll be years, if ever, before I get anywhere near aeronautical engineering."

From the corner of her eye, she saw him straighten and step toward her, sending her heart into an erratic pound. The closer he got to her, the harder it was to remember why they were supposed to be staying apart.

"Then don't quit. At least wait until the end of the day. See if you pass the exam. Take the maiden flight. If you make it into the squadron, you could look at transferring in twelve or eighteen months when you've got some solid experience. Or maybe you'll get into that jet and it'll be like coming home. You'll know you're exactly where you're meant to be."

"Is that what it was like for you?" She shouldn't be

asking; she didn't need to know anything more about him to feed the feelings she'd been trying to fight, but her weakness for him continually overrode her logic.

He gave a quick half smile that didn't quite reach his eyes. "Yeah. I'll never forget the first time I slid into the cockpit and launched out into the black. It literally stole my breath. Until recently, I never thought anything else would feel better than that moment."

Her breath caught as he took another step closer to her. Was he talking about— No, she'd already set her resolve when it came to them; she couldn't let anything sway her, particularly the gleam in his gray-blue eyes as he stared at her.

"Leigh, we already talked about this. I don't want either of us to get hurt, and we both know that's the only way this is going to end."

He ran a hand over his hair, and for the first time, his control slipped, expression showing the conflict raging within him. "I've always been confident in every decision I've made, never second-guessed myself, never regretted a single moment, even the ones that saw my men killed in action, because I always knew that when it came to the bigger picture, I was doing the right thing. But I don't know what the right thing is when it comes to us, Mia. I know what's right according to UEF policy, but what feels right, deep down where it counts, is in total contradiction. Plus this thing with Lawler— What am I supposed to do with all that?"

Her heart clenched, because she understood exactly what he was saying. Keeping her distance from him seemed the right thing to do, but it hadn't *felt* like the right thing. It felt wrong to the very depths of her being. But it wasn't like they had a choice. Yes, transferring from the program would mean he wouldn't be her CO anymore and technically their relationship would no longer be in violation of UEF regulations. But wherever she ended up probably wouldn't be somewhere she could see him often enough to maintain any kind of relationship. Or, say she made it into the squadron and waited a year or two for a possible transfer. Then what? Did she want to spend every day of the next year like she had these past weeks? She couldn't imagine holding up the charade for over a year.

So she had to remind herself for the millionth time, what was the point?

"I should go." She half turned, but that was as far as she got before she stopped again, indecision freezing her in place. And then they were just standing there, staring at one another, silence stretching between them.

Leigh's gaze darkened, and she took a step back. If she gave in this time, there would be no going back. For better or worse, they'd be stepping off a ledge into the unknown, a yawning cavern where she couldn't see the bottom. Maybe they'd find a soft landing, but the fear of jagged rocks waiting to tear them apart was definitely winning out.

Except Leigh was staring at her with more emotion in his gaze than she'd ever seen from him and it was slowly but surely breaking down her resolve.

"Don't look at me like that." She held up a hand to fend him off, but he closed the distance between them to catch her hand and flatten her palm against his chest, over his pounding heart.

"Why not?" His voice had dropped a little lower.

"You know why not."

He crowded closer to her. "Yeah, I know why not. I've done everything in my power to give you what you asked for, and I've hated every minute of it."

She swallowed, allowing him to tug her closer. Her heart trembled, and she couldn't resist as he cupped her cheek, his gaze roaming over her face. "Leigh—"

"I miss you." His voice had dropped to a whisper.

All of the emotion she'd been keeping at bay rushed in like the ocean tide, sweeping all resistance from its path, because she felt exactly the same way. She ached all over, and nothing would soothe the hurt...nothing except Leigh.

Mia surged up against him, catching him around the shoulders, even as her lips found his. Leigh stumbled back a step, but held onto her, hauling her tighter against him. His hand slid around to the back of her neck and clamped on as he kissed her deeper, almost desperately, until shivers cascaded down her spine in a waterfall of desire.

There was no controlling this moment, nothing made any sense as she succumbed to the furious twist of desire inside of her. Nothing existed beyond Leigh, with his body up against hers.

He turned them and urged her backward until something hit the backs of her upper thighs. *Desk*. Even as she registered the object, he was lifting her, setting her down, and pressing into her.

Mia wrapped herself around him, gasping as his lips slanted away from hers and laved a hot path down her neck. She needed to feel his skin, warm beneath her hands. The top two fasteners of his shirt slipped free beneath her fingers, but before she could get any farther with them, Leigh took over, yanking at the material until the catches popped free.

As he shrugged out of the garment, she reveled in the sensation of smoothing her palms over his firm, muscled flesh. She ran her hand up the strong column of his neck and then pulled him in for another heart-stopping kiss.

"Your turn," Leigh murmured against her mouth, tugging her shirt free of her pants. But, instead of getting the garment off her, he slid his hand up underneath it, skipping lightly over her skin until she was shuddering.

He hooked a finger between her breasts and into the catch of her bra, releasing it with a simple flick. Her breath stuttered into nothingness as he eased his palm underneath a cup and molded her sensitive flesh with his fingers.

"*Leigh*." She wanted so much more, but didn't have words as the rough pads of his fingers rasped over her nipple.

Mia pulled him in closer, opening her thighs to bring him up against her very center. *Oh God*, it felt so good as he rocked against her, the length of his erection hot, even through their clothes.

Leigh grabbed the top fastener of her pants, his movements hurried and forceful, giving hint to the desperation swelling between them.

The solid *thud* of the wardroom door slamming closed jolted every cell in her body. Leigh broke their kiss and glanced over his shoulder, swearing under his breath. He shifted back, and Mia caught sight of Steve Robinson standing just inside the door, staring at them with an expression of gratified malice.

Chapter Twenty-Six

Goddamn it. Of all the people on this ship who could have caught them, it had to be Steve Robinson.

Leigh met Mia's horrified gaze as he straightened, slipping his hand from beneath her shirt. Moving away, he kept a steady hold on her shoulder as she slid down from the desk. There was no way he could turn around to face Robinson yet, not until he got himself under control. He would have thought the imminent demise of his life as he knew it would have been enough to cool his ardor, but apparently not.

"I knew it." Steve gave a short, vindictive laugh. "I've been watching the two of you, waiting for the slip up. I knew something had to be going on. But this...? Well, I couldn't have made up anything better. I never thought I'd be so happy I had to come up here to get my day's extra duties from Brenner."

Mia had gone pale, and she stared up at him with unconcealed panic. Yeah, this was bad, but right now, he was more pissed off than alarmed.

He bent to pick up his shirt, buying himself more time as the last of his heated blood started draining from the region of his groin.

"This doesn't concern you, Robinson, so I suggest you forget you ever saw anything and get lost." He shrugged into his shirt and turned to stand partly in front of Mia, re-fastening the few catches that hadn't been damaged in his haste to get himself naked with her.

"Or what? You'll beat the hell out of me again? No way. You *owe* me, Alphin, for every hour of crap-ass grunge duty I've pulled for the last weeks."

Leigh pinned Robinson with a hard stare, one that usual-ly sent recruits scurrying for the relative safety of anywhere that wasn't in his vicinity. Unfortunately, the guy didn't take the hint.

Robinson took several steps forward. "So here's how it's going to work. No matter what happens in the next couple of days, even if I fail some of the final exams, you're going to make sure I pass, got it, Captain?"

"No, actually, I don't." He'd cop to the mess he'd made with Mia, but he wasn't going to give this bastard one second of power over him.

Robinson's expression darkened. "Its simple. You make me a fighter pilot or I tell every single person I see between here and Commander Yang's office exactly what I found you doing."

"I'm not going to make you a fighter pilot, Robinson. That's something you either earn or don't, on your own."

Steve smashed a fist against the nearby bulkhead. "Didn't you hear what I just said? I'll tell everyone your secret!"

Leigh slapped a bored expression onto his face, even though his heart hammered against his ribs. Part of him wanted to bow to Robinson's demands, if only to protect Mia. But he couldn't do it, even if it meant annihilating himself in the process. He'd made all the choices that had led him to here and had to live with them. Plus after everything that had happened with Lawler, now more than ever, he couldn't saddle his tight-knit squad with a substandard pilot.

"Go ahead, and see where it gets you."

Robinson swore, then slammed back through the door.

Mia grabbed onto his arm. "Leigh, he wasn't bluffing. He really will tell everyone. We have to do something."

He dragged a hand down his face, feeling light-headed for an unsettling moment. "I know he will, but I wasn't going to stand here and let him blackmail me. Robinson is a bully, and I can't let a guy like that through the program if he doesn't get there on his own steam."

She stared at him with an expression of disbelieving horror. "So instead you're going to let him *destroy* you? Leigh, this will end your career. You might be court-martialed. You could wind up in a military prison."

He caught her face in his hands, cutting off her panic with a short kiss.

"I told you before, it won't come to that, Mia, trust me. Everything will be fine."

Okay, so he had no way of knowing that for sure, but it sounded reassuring, which was exactly what he needed for her.

She grabbed the front of his shirt, moisture in the edges of her lashes. "Are you sure? How do you know?"

"Because I found you. And I can't believe that anything

that makes me feel like this is a bad thing. Yes, I'll have some explaining to do to Commander Yang, and I'll probably be looking for another posting, but none of that matters in the end."

A tear escaped and slipped down her cheek. "But it does matter. This is your whole life we're talking about here."

"No, Mia, it's not. It's just a job. I've recently started seeing that there are more important things in life than my posting."

"Oh my God." She dropped her head against his chest, a short sob escaping.

He shushed her, cradling her against him, wanting to protect her from every bad thing in the universe, especially the censure their relationship would bring once Robinson spilled his guts.

"I'm sorry," she mumbled against his chest. "I'm sorry, I kept telling myself this was going to end in disaster, but I couldn't stop myself from falling harder for you every day since we met."

He cupped her jaw and lifted her face to his, her velvet eyes sparkling with tears.

"Mia, you have nothing to be sorry for. I don't regret anything. Trust me when I tell you things are going to be okay in the end."

He slowly lowered his head to hers, taking her lips in a tender, unhurried kiss, until he felt her relax in his hold.

"Now, we've got a class to get to, and you've got your maiden flight to take today. I don't want you to worry about anything else."

She nodded, wiping her eyes with the sleeve of her shirt. Unfortunately, no matter how much he reassured her, he couldn't do anything about the anxious shadows in her gaze until after they'd gotten through the fallout of Robinson blabbing.

He pulled her in for one more quick kiss and then let her go before his libido decided that since they'd already been caught, finishing what they'd started couldn't possibly get them in any more trouble.

Instead, he told her good-bye and headed down to crew level, making a quick stop in his quarters to change into a new shirt. But then, since he was most definitely still half standing at attention, he put himself into a cold shower, forcing himself to disconnect from all thoughts of what he'd been doing with Mia.

He should be considering what the hell he was going to do with himself once Commander Yang canned his ass and booted him from the FP squadron. Grunt work on Ilari—that was the most likely scenario in his immediate future. But none of that mattered. As long as he had Mia, he'd work out the rest.

If someone had told him a month ago he'd be willing to give up his career—the single thing that had driven him since joining the UEF—for the sake of a woman, he would have laughed in their face and then probably slapped some sense into them.

Except here he stood, suffering through a cold shower, at the precipice of falling into the unknown, and he was strangely calm about it all.

By the time he'd spent long enough under the icy spray to give himself hypothermia while killing off the last of his damn lust and then gotten himself dressed again, time was cutting close to oh six hundred.

He hurried back up to squadron level and strode into the classroom right on oh six hundred on the dot.

Mia sat in the front row, her expression tense. Nicka sat on one side of her, while Kayla sat on her other side, shooting glances over her shoulder where Robinson held court in the far corner of the room, conversation buzzing. When Leigh stopped next to the lectern, the room fell silent.

Hell. Robinson hadn't even waited an hour. Even though he'd taken the guy's threat at face value, part of him had thought the kid would wait and make some kind of announcement at a moment that was guaranteed to cause maximum damage. Instead, the bastard had come in here and started shooting off his mouth to all of the other recruits.

Leigh clasped his hands behind his back and clenched his fists. "Find your seats, recruits. We've got an exam to get through if you even want to think about flying a jet later this morning."

Tense silence reigned as the recruits sat down, while Robinson grabbed a desk in the back, shooting him a triumphant grin.

Leigh ignored him, explaining the exam before starting the clock.

As soon as he could get away, he'd head up to the command center to see Commander Yang. The truth would be better coming from him, rather than Yang hearing it third-hand off some random crew member.

The two hours allocated for the exam dragged by while Leigh paced restlessly at the front of the room. He half thought about calling Bren or Seb to take the class for him. Now that he'd be coming clean, he was impatient to get it over with. But Seb had taken the news of Lawler hard and requested some personal time, while his XO was busy with other duties.

Still, he sent Bren a message to meet him on port level alpha. She'd have to take the recruits out on their first training flight, despite the fact that he'd done it with every new class of recruits since becoming the CAFF.

"Time is up, recruits." Leigh grabbed the master datapad, where results of the tests were downloading. He skimmed the list looking for one name in particular. Damn it, Robinson had passed, though only by the thinnest margin. He'd held out one last hope that the guy wouldn't succeed.

"O'Connor, Brooks, and Gibson, you haven't scored the required mark so you won't be joining us for this morning's training. You'll have one last chance to re-sit the exam tomorrow, and if you fail that, then you're out of the program. Everyone else, on your feet, you're about to take your first flight."

Usually this was the point where the successful recruits cheered, and while there were a few exclamations, for most part the mood remained subdued. In fact, most of them seemed more interested in crowding around Steve as they headed out into the passageway.

Leigh led the recruits down the corridor to the transit, the chatter behind him swelling.

"Hey, Mia," one of the recruits called out. Leigh glanced over his shoulder to see it had come from Carson, the only one of Robinson's buddies who hadn't washed out. "I heard you've been getting some personalized tutoring from the CAFF. Is that how you managed to pass all the tests and make it this far?"

A few of the other recruits laughed nervously, as Leigh

slowly turned to face them. "Have you got something you need to share with the rest of the class, Carson?"

Carson shared a smug look with Robinson, and Leigh clenched his fists over the urge to smash both of their heads together.

"No, sir. I was just commenting on how *talented* Wolfe is."

Robinson snickered, and Leigh swallowed down scorching rage as all his muscles hardened like rock. He'd made the choice not to give in to Robinson's blackmail. This was the fallout he had to take. The only thing he could do now was protect Mia from the worst of it.

"I can see why you'd be impressed, Carson, since she's got more smarts in her little toe than you've got in your entire brain. If you happen to make it through this program, you might want to keep in mind that Wolfe or any of the recruits standing here might be the pilot you need to get you out of a tight situation. Alienating any of them by shooting your mouth off is just one more way to get yourself killed." That shut the moron up. He glanced over at Mia. "Recruit Wolfe, front and center."

She shot him a worried look as she stepped in front of him. The transit-porter arrived and he ordered the recruits to pile in, waiting to go on last. Once inside, he put himself between Mia and the rest of the recruits. They could say whatever they wanted to him, but he wouldn't let them insult Mia.

They arrived at port level alpha, and while he assigned each recruit to a jet with the help of the deck crew, he kept Mia at his side, leaving her until last. He walked around the far side of the ship, putting them mostly out of sight.

Mia crossed her arms as she stared up at him. "Leigh, what are we going to do? Everyone knows."

He helped her into her flight jacket, though her movements were hesitant.

"Right now, you are going to take your maiden flight."

"I'm serious. Maybe I shouldn't go."

He shook his head. "Why? There's nothing you can do here. Take the flight and no matter what happens, you get through the next four days and graduate, okay?"

She latched onto his arm. "Don't talk like I'm never going to see you again."

He slid an arm around her waist. "Like I keep telling you, Mia, things will be okay. I'm going up to see Commander Yang to sort it out."

"But what about the training flight?"

He smoothed a hand along the side of her face and cupped her chin, tilting her head up a little. "This is more important."

"Alpha?"

Leigh glanced over his shoulder to see Bren standing behind him, a hard expression on her face.

"Just one second, XO."

He turned back to Mia. "Just remember everything you've learned and don't think about what's going on back here."

She nodded, though her gaze was still troubled. He pulled her in, grabbing her up for a swift, hard kiss. What did it matter who saw them now? The truth was out and would be all over the ship by evening messdeck.

He pulled back and stared down into her soulful brown eyes. "Fly safe and come home to me."

Her grip tightened on him. "Good luck with Commander Yang."

He nodded and then let her go, watching as she climbed up the side of the jet and disappeared into the cockpit.

"Alpha, what the hell is going on?"

Leigh turned to Bren, slowly reaching up to unpin the insignia on his collar that singled him out as the CAFF. "I need you to take the recruits on their maiden training flight."

He reached out and took Bren's hand, setting the pins in her palm. She glanced down at them, appearing confused for a moment. But when she looked back up at him, her expression was downright horrified.

"Leigh, no—"

"Apparently I wasn't as smart as you thought I was, Bren." He shot her the ghost of a smile. "Though, where Mia was concerned, I never stood a chance. Take care of the kids for me. I've got to go face up to my choices."

He went to walk past her, but she stopped him with a hand on his arm. "You're serious about her, right? I mean, this isn't just some sordid affair?"

He cared deeply for Mia, but everything was happening so fast, he hadn't stopped to exactly define what it was he felt for her. All he knew was that he needed her in a way he'd never needed anyone else.

"They can take my post, and they can throw whatever kind of punishment they want at me, but I'm not giving up Mia. Not without one hell of a fight."

Bren's expression softened. "Then you're doing the right thing. Good luck, Leigh."

He sent her one last nod and left the flight deck.

The walk up to the command center was the longest and

loneliest trek he'd ever taken in his life. A quiet sense of doom clawed into the back of his neck, along with a definite sense of paranoia, because he could have sworn people were looking at him differently and whispering between themselves as he passed. Surely the story couldn't have gotten this far already? If it had, he was royally screwed.

In the command center, Leigh got waylaid by Olivia.

"What can I do for you, Captain?"

"I need to speak with Commander Yang right away." Before Yang heard God-knew-what version of events from somebody else.

Olivia glanced down to look at the datapad on the pristine desk in front of her. "You'll need to make an appointment. The Commander is still catching up after his absence. How about the day after tomorrow at—"

Leigh braced a hand against the edge of the desk. "No, I need to speak with him *now*. It's important and it definitely can't wait."

Olivia glanced up at him and then sat back in her chair. "Well, you'll at least have to come back later. The commander is currently in a subspace conference with Admiral Watson."

Frustration simmered through him and he rubbed his nape, where that sense of impending doom dug deeper. "How long will it be before he's finished?"

An annoyed expression flitted over Olivia's face. "I don't know. Five minutes or five hours. Take your pick."

Leigh blew out a long breath. "Do you mind if I wait?" Because he sure as hell wasn't going to head back out into the ship and pretend like he wasn't the subject of everyone's conversations.

Olivia shrugged. "Suit yourself."

Leigh walked over to the far bulkhead, where a cushy couch had been arranged next to a slim table, both a lot fancier than the furniture he usually sat on down on squadron level. He took his personal comm out of his pocket and started going through the messages and emails he'd neglected since FP training had started.

Nearly an hour went by, before Olivia took a comm call.

"Captain Alphin, Commander Yang wants to see you now."

Leigh stood, cold apprehension slicing through him. Not *Commander Yang* will *see you now*, but *Commander Yang* wants to *see you now*. He swallowed down his trepidation and nodded to Olivia, then made his way past the desk and through the doors into the commander's wardroom.

Commander Yang stood behind his desk, personal comm up against his ear. His expression was blank—scary blank—as Leigh walked in and saluted him, then fell into parade stance in front of the desk.

Yang ended the call and slowly lowered the comm to his desk.

"Captain Alphin, I've just taken a very interesting call from Captain Phillips. I assume there's something you want to tell me?" Yang crossed his arms, expression formidable.

Leigh swallowed and nodded. "Yes, sir. I'd appreciate it if you could possibly disregard whatever it is you've heard until after I've spoken my piece."

Yang gave a single nod, but his impassive expression didn't alter.

Leigh explained his relationship with Mia, right from day one, including the fact that she'd been the one to find the traitor. He left almost nothing out, apart from his most private moments with her. When he was done, Yang stared at him for a long moment then sighed.

"You've made a real mess of this, Alpha."

He nodded. "I am aware of that, sir, and I won't make excuses for myself. I don't regret the methods Wolfe and I employed to find the traitor, but when it came to my personal feelings, my judgment in this matter obviously failed me."

Yang's posture relaxed a little and he moved around the desk to lean against the front of it. "And this morning in the squadron officer's wardroom, was that a matter of you not thinking straight?"

A wave of chagrin rose within him, and incredibly, heat blazed along his cheeks. God, was he actually blushing like a damn schoolgirl?

"I can't explain what happens when I'm with her. I tried to hold out, but then I saw her this morning and... I don't know. It's like any ideas about staying in control are just obliterated."

The commander sighed. "You know, at the very least I'm going to have to demote you. You can't remain the CAFF after this."

He clenched his clasped hands tighter at his lower back. "I understand, sir. And I agree with your decision."

Yang raised a brow at him. "Just like that, you're going to give up your position, piss fourteen years of exemplary service out the hatch, and accept a black mark against your name, all without a fight?"

Leigh shrugged. "What am I really fighting for? I'm not losing out, because at the end of the day I'll still have Mia, and that's the important thing."

"Uh-huh." Yang sent him an exasperated look. "You

want to tell me again how you can't explain what it is about her that obliterates your judgment?"

Before he could answer, the door to the wardroom opened and Captain Phillips strode in. Had Yang called him in here so the two of them could decide his final fate? Despite his insistence that none of it mattered, a quiver of anxiety shook him.

"Sir, sorry to interrupt you." Phillips stopped a few steps away and saluted. "But I've just received a report that you need to hear right away, both of you."

Yang nodded. "Go ahead, Captain."

Phillips glanced at him, and in that one expression, Leigh felt the solid floor drop out from beneath his feet.

"It's the recruits' training flight, sir."

Leigh latched a hand onto the captain's arm. "What happened?"

"The CSS infiltrated the safe zone and cut the group in half. Lieutenant Brenner ordered the orphaned recruits to head for the secondary base on Ilari, but they didn't make it. Four planes down behind enemy lines."

"*Who*?" The word came out at not much more than a hoarse croak, because he already knew.

"Snyder, Dawson, Robinson, and Wolfe."

His grip slipped free from where he'd been holding Phillips as he turned to brace both hands against the edge of the desk, sucking air like there was no oxygen in the atmosphere any longer. *Mia.* Down behind enemy lines. God help him. He should have taken the flight this morning like he did every other year. But he'd been so fixated on doing the right thing. And now...now... His ribs felt like they were banding around his vital organs, choking him, one besieged heartbeat at a time.

Someone grabbed his shoulder. "Alpha—"

"I'm fine." He shut down his emotions and shrugged out of the hold, turning to find Yang staring at him with concern. "I'll be fine. But I need to get on the ground, *now*."

"Sub-Lieutenant Rayne is already on deck organizing a response party," Phillips reported.

"I thought Seb was off duty."

Phillips shrugged. "He was until he heard about what happened."

Seb probably wasn't in the right frame of mind to be involved in a situation like this, but selfishly, he wasn't going to pull the guy out, not when he needed every resource available to get Mia back in one piece.

"Clear the air space and shut down the other ports for immediate emergency launch," Leigh told Phillips. But as he went to step by the captain to run like hell for the launch deck, Yang stopped him.

"Alpha, technically, I can't let you leave the ship."

He swung around and speared the commander with a disbelieving stare. "Sir?"

"You're no longer the CAFF. As of this minute, you don't even officially have a posting until I work out what we're going to do with you. You know as well as I do that no one except members of the FP squadron can take out a V-29."

Leigh swore. "Then I'll take a goddamn shuttle. I don't care, as long as it'll fly between here and Ilari."

"Leigh, you're not hearing what I'm telling you. Without any kind of clearance, you cannot leave this ship. My hands are tied. You know the protocols as well as I do."

"Sir, it's *Mia*. I can't just stay up here while she's out there—"

Yang's expression hardened. "You think I want this for you? There's nothing I can—"

Leigh pointed an unsteady finger at him. "Don't tell me there's nothing you can do, Yang. What exactly would *you* be doing right now if it was Sacha down there?"

Yang's posture tensed. "Sacha is the mother of my baby. I love her more than life itself."

"Then I'll ask you again," Leigh replied quietly. "What would you do if it was Sacha down there?"

Yang glanced away from him, a muscle pulsing in his jaw.

"You better have found me a new posting and given me clearance by the time I make it to alpha level; otherwise you'll have to add defying a direct order and ship theft to that charge sheet you'll be writing later."

Leigh didn't wait for Yang or Phillips to say anything else before leaving the room and sprinting for port level alpha like his very existence depended on it. It was apt, because if anything happened to Mia, his life would never be the same.

Chapter Twenty-Seven

Mia scrunched down behind the half-collapsed wall of the church. Her first flight was a catastrophe—enemy ships had invaded the safe zone, forcing her and three other recruits to make a run on the Ilari base. They'd been within sight, when some kind of ground-to-air weapons system had taken them out. She, Kayla, and Steve had all ejected, but Snyder had gone down with his plane.

Mia took another quick peek over the crumbling stones out to the ruined graveyard. Four CS Soldiers stood around Steve, who sat on a toppled gravestone. For some reason, she found it hilariously ironic that she was hiding from a bunch of religious fanatics in a destroyed church. Or maybe that was the near-hysterical panic talking. She braced her shaking hands against the dusty flagstones beneath her, trying to subdue the tremors.

She didn't know how she'd ever get her fingers to remain steady again. Since the torture test had brought the reality of this war crashing down on her, she knew exactly the level of terror she'd experience if the CSS captured her. This wasn't another test with a safety net she couldn't see.

The front lines were only a few clicks east of their position but Steve hadn't wanted to hunker down, make sure their encoded GPS trackers were on, and wait for a rescue party like they'd been trained. Instead he'd dashed out from the meager cover they'd found, right into a CSS patrol. From what she'd overheard, they were waiting for a transport to take Steve to the nearest Enlightening Camp.

At first they'd started to make a run for it. But guilt at leaving Steve behind had pulled her up short. Kayla wanted to keep going and find somewhere farther from the patrol, stating Steve was the idiot who'd dismissed their training and gone off on his own, so he could live with the consequences. But for whatever stupid, *stupid* reason, despite how much she loathed the man, she couldn't leave him. He'd be consigned to a cell at one of those facilities where the CSS broke a person down until they either joined their cause or died.

So she'd convinced Kayla to go back with her. However, it had turned out they'd been lucky to leave the church when they had. The patrol had been searching the old ruins, because no doubt Steve had broken in two seconds flat and told the CSS where they'd been hiding. She had no idea how he'd survived the torture test earlier in the week.

Once the patrol finished, they found a new hiding spot in the building and tried to figure out a plan.

"We're not actually considering this, are we?" Kayla whispered from beside her. "I mean, for a start, this is *Steve* we're talking about, the guy who outed you and Captain Alphin this morning. Plus, we don't have any weapons, and we're not battle-trained."

She focused on Kayla, who was drinking some of their emergency water supply. "He's one of us. If it was you out there and Steve wanted me to leave you, I know what you'd be saying about that."

Kayla shot her a dry look. "It wouldn't be me out there, because I'm not dumb enough to disregard basic training."

Mia huffed a short sigh and held a hand out for the bladder of water. "Fine, you and I both wouldn't be dumb enough. That still doesn't change the facts. We can't just walk off and leave him."

Kayla sighed and pushed a hand through her tangled hair. "Okay, okay. You're right. I'd never forgive myself if we just gave up on him. But that still doesn't help the little detail of us having no weapons and no clue how to rescue a moron."

"I think our only option is distraction. One of us makes a lot of noise, while the other goes in for Steve."

Kayla shook her head. "They'll just split their party. Two will stay behind to watch him."

"You're probably right. But there's got to be some way to distract all of them."

They spent a few minutes discussing the pros and cons and then settled on a plan.

They moved to the opposite end of the church, hiding on either side of the splintered doors. A bit of noise brought two of the soldiers over, just as they'd hoped.

Mia stared at Kayla as the crunching of boot steps over gravel came closer. Her heart pummeled the inside of her chest, making it hard to draw a full breath.

The barrel of a gun appeared through the door. The

owner of the weapon followed and turned as he got inside, coming face to face with her. But, before he'd even met her gaze, she'd gone in under his gun arm, forcing it up as she propelled him back toward Kayla. Her friend swung a thick chunk of wood they'd found into the back of the man's head, knocking him face-first to the floor.

Mia didn't wait to see if he was conscious or not. She fell to her knees and grabbed the gun, pivoting in a crouch to line up the other soldier stepping through the doorway.

Her shot found its mark in the dead center of his chest — all that target practice at pre-mil training had paid off. As he fell, his finger on the trigger of his own gun let off a round, but it went into the exposed rafters above them.

Kayla scrambled for the gun. Then they both sprinted back to their original hiding spot to regroup.

"Okay. Now we have weapons," Kayla panted in a whisper.

Mia glanced over the wall. One soldier had remained behind to watch Steve, while the other had set off toward the source of the shots. Overhead, the rumbling whine of a ship closing in sent a spurt of cold fear shooting through her. Well, more fear than she'd already been feeling. Ever since she'd realized she was going to crash behind enemy lines, she'd held a surreal kind of hyperawareness that any second now her life could be over. Which begged the question, why the hell was she risking it for a complete jerk like Steve Robinson?

Once that ship landed there'd be reinforcements. And when that solider found his possibly dead buddies... Well, if she didn't want someone she hated to end up in a POW prison, then it would be an understatement to say *she* didn't want to end up there herself.

"Our window is closing, if we're going to do this…"

Kayla tightened her grip on the gun and gave a resolute nod, her expression grim.

They crept out from the protective shadow of their hiding spot, moving toward the CS Soldier who was staring off in the direction his companion had gone. A shout came from the far end of the church—the bodies had been discovered.

Hell, she'd wanted to be closer than this. A swift glance at Kayla, and she brought the gun up. They both shot at the same time, taking out the single guard. Sprinting the remaining distance, Mia kept her gaze focused along the church as Kayla motioned for Steve to run. For a moment the guy simply stared at her in confusion, then glanced at the soldier they'd just shot. Finally, he got to his feet and came toward them. Obviously shock was making Steve's moronic tendencies worse than usual. Which didn't bode well for this rescue attempt. The other guard appeared from the far side of the church and almost without thought, Mia squeezed off another few rounds. He crumpled in a heap.

While she waited a few long breathless moments, she caught sight of the reinforcements coming in from behind Kayla and Steve.

"Come on, we've got to go now!"

The CSS didn't hesitate. They opened fire and Mia ducked, returning a few halfhearted shots. But, she didn't plan on holding this ground, and the number of soldiers shooting in their direction left them at four-to-one odds. The only reason the three of them weren't full of holes was because the soldiers weren't in range yet. But that would change in about two seconds.

Steve hesitated yet again. But he was close enough for her to grab his arm and propel him into motion. Kayla fell into step, and they headed out past the church and deeper into the ruins of the city. Here was where their plan got a little hazy. They needed somewhere to hide, but unfortunately, the soldiers pursuing them probably knew the crumbling buildings far better. Their head start wouldn't last long. They needed to find shelter. Quick. It had to be somewhere clever, somewhere the soldiers would never bother to look—

She skidded at the next bombed-out street corner. "Guys, this way."

Kayla immediately switched directions, while Steve stopped.

Idiot. Jackass. Total jerk bastard. But, whatever. Kayla and she had saved his useless hide once. If he didn't follow them now, she wouldn't attempt rescue number two.

After a long moment, Steve followed them. Mia picked a path leading off at an angle from the pursuing soldiers, then altered her direction again. At the next change in direction, even Kayla hesitated.

"Mia, where are you taking us? This is going to lead right back to—"

"Where we started?" She puffed, breath starting to get short. "I figured the soldiers wouldn't search where they've already been."

Kayla shot her a grin. "Brilliant."

Steve muttered something behind them, but kept up as they rounded on the church, slipping right back into the first place they'd hid. Except as they knelt, another transport ship touched down in the decimated graveyard.

"More reinforcements?" Kayla shot her a worried look.

"Maybe we should have gotten as far away from here as we could when we had the chance."

"I'd say that was a given." Steve shot her an angry glare, taking a swig from the water bladder.

"Gee, I'm so glad I risked my ass to save you." Mia swiped the water back before he could go and drink it all on them. Who knew how long it would have to last?

Steve continued glowering at her, but didn't reply as he slumped against the wall.

Mia risked another look, to see the door of the transport lifting open. She couldn't read any identifying marks—the landing had kicked up too much dust.

Hunkering down, she offered Kayla the water and tried not to second-guess her decision to come back here.

"I think there's someone coming," Kayla whispered, bringing up the gun she still held.

Yes, there seemed to be something, some disturbance, that told her someone was getting close to their position. She crept to the end of the wall, keeping the gun out. As she reached the end, a shadow spilled across the dusty floor and her heart pounded to a stop.

She grabbed in a short breath and surged up and straight into a counterattack, as though the person had known she was hiding there. As she swung the butt of the gun around, the man caught her wrist and pinned her up against him.

"*Mia.*" The husky whisper made her freeze, and she looked up to meet a familiar, hard, gunmetal-blue gaze.

"Leigh!" She released her death grip on the gun and snagged her arms around him, relief pouring through her in blood-tingling waves.

For a short second, he returned the embrace, then

hustled her back to where Kayla and Steve waited.

Leigh and Steve exchanged hateful glares, and then he nodded at Kayla.

"Snyder?" he whispered.

Mia shook her head, and Leigh swore under his breath. He crouched and half unzipped his leather jacket, not the flight jacket she was used to seeing him in. Instead, he was wearing the protective battle gear of a ground soldier, holstered and strapped with enough weapons to turn him into a one-man army. In short, he looked deadly and so gorgeous it battered her heart.

He pulled out what looked to be three small protein bars and handed them around.

She made a face as she took it, her stomach roiling too uneasily to eat anything. "No offense, but I don't exactly have an appetite right now."

He reached over and ripped the foil open, his fingers brushing hers. "This is a combat bar. It'll regulate your blood sugar, plus it has a chemical compound to mitigate the affects of an adrenaline high or extreme anxiety. You'll feel better if you eat it. I promise."

She took a small bite, her mouth too dry as she chewed, but forced herself to swallow and take another bite.

"So, what, the mighty Captain Alphin doesn't need one?" Steve scowled and dropped the bar to the ground at his feet.

"This isn't my first firefight, kid. Plus, the three of you have already been on the ground for over an hour. I've used them plenty of times before during prolonged battle situations. This isn't about pride, this is about smarts."

"Yeah? And you think you've got it all worked out?"

Leigh's expression hardened into one she'd never seen before—this was the legendary Alpha people spoke in awed tones about.

"I'm not going to waste air arguing with you, Robinson. Eat it or not, I don't care. But if you want to get off the ground alive, you will shut the hell up and do exactly what I say. And if you put the rest of us in danger, I'll shoot you myself."

Steve's glare got even darker at that. And then suddenly he moved, sidestepping to grab Kayla and her gun. He wrapped one arm around her neck, but pointed the gun outward. Mia froze as the barrel aimed at her chest. At this distance, she wouldn't survive a single bullet from that caliber weapon.

Leigh started to step in front of her, but Steve moved faster until the nozzle was against her breastbone. "Stop right there, Alphin, or your piece of ass stops breathing."

Leigh held his hands up in a supplicating gesture. "Fine. I'm holding my ground. Now tell me what the hell this is."

Steve sent him a cutting grin. "Since you've got it all worked out, *sir*, you tell me."

"Whatever your problem with me is, you don't need to put Mia or Kayla between us." An edge of frustration entered Leigh's hard tone.

"This isn't about you or either of these stupid bitches. This is about me getting a promotion, about proving I've got what it takes to move up in the ranks."

Leigh gave a short, humorless laugh. "You're going the total wrong way about getting a promotion, buddy."

Steve didn't seem fazed by Leigh's taunting. Instead his expression seemed too satisfied. "I'm not talking about the

UEF."

For a second, confusion flashed through Leigh's expression, but it didn't last long as comprehension dawned in his gaze, bringing a furious light with it.

"*You*." Leigh's tone came out icy and infuriated. "You were Lawler's accomplice."

Steve smirked. "You really don't have a clue. Lawler was covering for *me*. I was the one who stole the intel from the master datapad on squadron level. I was the one who tampered with your jets. Lawler was just making sure any evidence of my activities couldn't be traced. I heard he nearly sent the two of you on a spacewalk without a suit."

"But you were on the transport with us when the CSS tried to shoot us down the day we arrived on the *Knox*," Mia blurted out, her need for answers winning out over the fear in that moment.

Steve sent her a look as though the answer should have been obvious.

"They weren't trying to shoot the shuttle down; it was to divert suspicion. Who would suspect anyone on board might be CSS when they attacked the transport?" Steve smirked at Leigh. "It totally worked. And it was a bonus that you were so distracted by this slut you had no idea what was really going on."

By the way Leigh clenched his jaw, it seemed that barb had hit a little too well.

"So you had it all over me. Bravo." Leigh lowered his hands a little. "I don't want anyone to get hurt, Robinson, so I'm giving you one chance to let Kayla go, lower the gun, and walk out of here. Take the out, because you won't get a second."

Steve shook his head, not looking the least bit concerned about the situation.

"You really think I'm going to walk away from the opportunity of handing over the legendary Alpha? I'm sure my superior officers would love to have a chat with you."

"Not going to happen."

"Oh yeah? I don't see how you've got any say in the matter." Steve pulled the nozzle of the gun away from Mia's chest, but before she could take a breath he switched his aim to line up Leigh and let off a round.

Leigh half spun from the impact and landed against the crumbling wall, then slumped to the ground.

"Leigh!" Her scream echoed off the remains of the church as she rushed over to drop down beside him, not caring if Steve shot her as well.

Even as she grabbed his shoulder, he started to roll over and get himself upright, leaning against the wall. He reached up to clamp a hand over the wound in his shoulder, breath short.

"It's okay." His voice came out choppy "It's just a flesh wound. He's not going to kill me. It'll piss off his superior officers."

Steve walked over to stand beside them, thrusting Kayla down next to Leigh and shoving the end of the gun into the side of Mia's face. "He's right. I don't want him dead, just manageable. You on the other hand, I could quite happily fill with bullets."

Leigh clenched his jaw, spearing Steve with an infuriated glare. "So help me, if you touch her—"

"What?" Steve bent at the waist and braced one hand against his knee, bringing his face level with hers, though he was looking at Leigh. "What are you going to do when you're lying down there bleeding, and I'm the one with all the control?"

Leigh didn't reply, but closed his hand tighter around the wound until his knuckles were white, contrasting with the dark blood seeping through his fingers.

"That's what I thought." Robinson smirked and straightened, lessening the pressure from the gun. "Now, Mia, be a good little slut and strip all his weapons. Try not to enjoy yourself too much though."

She hesitated, glancing at Leigh as fear wound tighter within her. When she didn't move fast enough, Steve grabbed her arm and propelled her into Leigh's chest. He blew out a sharp breath when she jostled his shoulder. With careful movements, she leaned back and glanced down at the guns in their holsters. She didn't want to take them, because if Leigh still had a weapon they had a chance of getting out of this. But Steve was back, this time pressing the gun into her shoulder blades.

"Hurry up, or I'll shoot you and bring Kayla over to do it instead."

"Do what he says, Mia," Leigh said in a low voice.

Clenching her teeth, she flipped open the holsters and drew the guns out, tossing them aside.

"And the rest." Steve stabbed the nozzle of the gun harder against the middle of her back. "I'm smart enough to know the bastard has more than a few spare weapons stashed elsewhere."

At Leigh's murmured instructions, she found and removed two other guns and one knife.

"Now secure both of them." Steve tossed down some

plexi-reinforced cable ties that landed in Leigh's lap.

With sick anxiety expanding within her, she sent Kayla an apologetic look then tied her hands and Leigh's. Without his hand holding the wound, blood flowed more freely down his arm, wetting his jacket sleeve.

She turned to glare up at Steve, the traitorous bastard. She should have listened to Kayla and left him with that patrol, who apparently hadn't been holding him captive. He was one of them.

"If you want to hand Leigh in alive, at least let me bandage his shoulder; otherwise he's going to bleed out."

For a second Steve simply stared at her, and then he shrugged. "Do what you need to keep him alive."

She turned back to Leigh and pressed a hand against the wound. He sucked in a sharp breath, beginning to look a little pale in the dim light.

"There's a small field medic kit inside my jacket, left side."

She nodded and kept her left hand pressed against the injury while she pushed his jacket aside and reached in, searching for the pack. It turned out to be a slim vacuum-sealed kit with a few painkillers, bandages, tweezers, and a small scalpel. She paused as her fingers brushed over the blade and glanced over her shoulder. Too busy glaring at Leigh, Steve wasn't paying attention. With a half breath and a prayer she didn't get caught, she slid the scalpel into the sleeve of her jacket and went back to pulling out bandages.

For the moment, she concentrated on tightly wrapping the wound to staunch the flow of blood. When she went to fashion a sling to minimize Leigh moving his arm, he caught her hand and shook his head. Obviously he didn't want to be incapacitated.

She bit her lip against saying anything, knowing it would be pointless. Leigh would take any risk to save Kayla and her, including sacrificing himself. But she wouldn't let him do it. She wouldn't let him be some big hero simply to see them safe. Somehow, she had to find a way out of this before Steve did something stupid, or more CS Soldiers arrived. And now that she had a weapon, she just needed to bide her time and strike when Steve least expected it.

Chapter Twenty-Eight

L eigh flexed the numb fingers on his injured arm. Hell, he wouldn't be holding a weapon in that hand any time soon. Mia sent him a worried glance as she finished with the bandages and sat back. She'd wanted to put his arm into a sling, which was the best thing to do according to basic field medics. Even though his hand felt next to useless, he wanted it free so he wouldn't be hampered if he had to make a move. Well, as free as it could be considering his wrists were cable tied.

"Finished playing doctors and nurses now?" Robinson reached down and grabbed Mia's braid at the base of her neck, using it to pull her up.

He clenched his fists, barely resisting the urge to leap up and wrap his hands around the guy's neck. The only thing keeping him down was that damn gun Robinson kept pushing at Mia, and the fact that a bullet moved faster than he could.

Still, every single time Robinson touched her was one more broken bone he planned to inflict once he got the upper hand.

Robinson yanked Mia a few steps away then shoved her down to the dirt-strewn flagstones.

"You and I have some unfinished business and this time your tough guy sugar daddy won't be coming to save you. But he does get a front row seat. Think he'll enjoy watching as much as he does when he gives it to you?"

A sharp stab of disgust and dread sliced through him, numbing the pain from his shoulder wound. "You think that's going to make you the better man, Robinson, by forcing yourself on a woman who doesn't want anything to do with you?"

Robinson sent him an arrogant smirk over his shoulder, reaching down with one hand to unbuckle his belt. "That's just it. I don't want to be the better man. I want to be the man who does whatever it takes to get what he wants. And I want this haughty, frigid bitch to realize that I don't like being told no. She should have given it to me when I wanted it, because what did running off to the CAFF get her?"

Steve finished unfastening his pants and looked back down at Mia, greedy anticipation in the gaze he raked over her. Mia stared up at him, her features blank, but he could see the panic on her face.

Goddamn it, he was not going to sit here and watch that sick bastard rape her. Not while his heart beat in his chest. He started yanking desperately at the cable ties, hard enough to cut into his wrists.

Crouching down, Steve swapped the gun for the knife Mia had tossed to the side earlier.

"Are you going to undress for me, or should I just slice your clothes off? Got to say, that idea really gets me going." His voice had thickened, and Leigh clenched his jaw at the sick sensation surging through him.

Mia didn't move, but a definite stubbornness had crept into her expression. Steve shifted forward to loom over her, setting the tip of the knife in the middle of her chest. He thrust lewdly against her and then groaned. "Oh yeah, I'm going to enjoy every second of this, you uppity whore."

Leigh cursed, pulling harder at his wrists, but all he managed to do was make his hands slippery with blood as the rigid plexi cut into his flesh.

"I'm warning you, Robinson, if you hurt her, I will end you. It might not be today, but on my life, I will hunt you down and slit your throat. Only not before I make sure you piss yourself in terror first."

The threat made Robinson pause and glance over at him.

Suddenly Mia moved, though from the angle she was sitting at, he couldn't see exactly what had happened. Steve reared back, clutching his neck. Mia used her legs to shove him off, then scrambled away as he collapsed to the ground.

She hurried over to crouch in front of him, and Leigh leaned sideways to see blood bubbling from a wound on Steve's neck. Mia cut his wrists free, her hands shaking and splashed with blood, the sharp scalpel in her fingers making short work of the cable ties.

When his wrists were free, he reached up and wrapped a hand around the back of her neck, pulling her into him as potent relief rushed through him so hard it made him light-headed, like the ground beneath him was tilting. Or maybe that was all the blood loss.

However, before he could take a full breath and let it sink in that she was really okay, she'd slipped out of his grasp to free Kayla.

Leigh pushed to his feet, taking an unsteady step as his brain tried to catch up with the whole idea of standing. He walked over to Steve, who had shuffled back a few feet, one hand clutching uselessly at his neck, the other still gripping the knife. Leigh got down, kneeling on Steve's forearm until he released his grip on the blade.

He picked it up and reached over to grab a handful of Steve's hair. "I made you a promise I intend to keep."

Steve shook his head frantically, eyes going wide. He tried to speak, but the words got lost in a garble as blood dribbled from his mouth. Leigh fisted the knife and swiped it across traitor's neck, then let him fall back to the ground.

As Robinson's body went limp, it didn't lessen the woozy, disgusted churning in his guts. The guy would have died from the wound Mia had given him. He'd just expedited matters and made sure Mia wouldn't feel like his death was on her hands.

Yet he couldn't purge the image of Robinson thrusting against her from his mind, no matter how much he tried to force it away. The churning in his stomach intensified and he pushed up from the body, stumbling three steps before falling to his knees again, retching as the contents of his stomach emptied. It was a long moment before he could suck in a full breath and gain some control over the spasms.

A palm touched his shoulder and he sat back. Mia gave him the bladder of water, and he took a mouthful, rinsing his mouth and spitting it out before taking a longer drink.

"Are you okay?" Her voice was low with concern as she took the water back.

He wiped his mouth with the bottom of his shirt. "I'm fine. But we need to get out of here before Steve's buddies show up." He shifted closer to her, his hand slipping up to cup the side of her neck. "Are *you* okay?"

He urged Mia to tilt her head to the side, cataloging every little scrape and bruise she had. When they got back onboard the *Valiant Knox*—and they would, he refused to believe anything else—he was going to take her home to his apartment and kiss every single contusion better, love her with his body and soul until they forgot this day ever happened.

She nodded again, the relief in her eyes obvious. "I'm okay. We're okay."

He wanted to kiss her more than he wanted to breathe, but he needed to keep his emotions in check until they weren't trapped behind enemy lines. Instead, he grabbed hold of Mia's arm, helped her to her feet, and passed both her and Kayla a gun, then collected his discarded weapons. He led them out from their shelter to make a run to the armed personnel carrier he'd flown down. It only sat four, and wasn't nearly as maneuverable as a fighter jet. But Seb and the rest of the squadron should keep the CSS in the area busy while he evaced them out of there.

At the far end of the church, he paused and crouched down, searching the open area between the crumbled building and where he'd set the ship down.

One of the patrols had returned. Six men. He cursed under his breath as they spotted the transport bearing the *Valiant Knox's* ID markings. It had been a calculated risk bringing one of their own ships behind enemy lines, but he'd gone for firepower over stealth.

The six CS Soldiers fanned out, alert and looking for them. It was only a matter of time before they radioed for help.

He turned to where Mia and Kayla were crouched just behind him. "I'm going to lay down cover fire. Make a run for the mausoleum. When you get there, I need you to return the favor so I can get across the open ground."

"What about your shoulder?" Mia asked, her tone even, but he caught the fear beneath the careful words.

"My shoulder will be the least of my worries if we get caught. I can still shoot a gun, so we'll be fine. Don't think about anything except getting low and running as fast as you can."

She nodded, her features settling into an anxious, yet determined expression. Turning from her, his heart bumped over an uneven rhythm as he brought his gun up. He'd been on the ground plenty of times and had to lay down cover fire for his fellow soldiers. But he'd never been so on edge, never been so tied up in knots about making sure they got out of this in one piece.

"Ready back there?" He lined up the soldier he thought would present the most threat.

He gave them a go, putting pressure on the trigger of his electromagnetic pulse gun to fire off several rounds as the girls sprinted out from the corner of the church toward the mausoleum. He didn't let himself follow their progress, instead concentrating on taking out as many of the patrol as he could until they found shelter. He nailed three guys, cutting their number in half and putting the odds a little more in their favor. But it wouldn't last. Another patrol would turn up here any second. News of a UEF transport on the ground would spread fast.

Mia and Kayla made it to the mausoleum, one of the few remaining intact structures in the graveyard. The two of them laid down fire, keeping the last three CS Soldiers pinned as he pushed up and sprinted, dodging fallen headstones and other debris. As soon as he made it, he tapped the girls on the shoulder.

"Come on, we need to keep moving." He put himself out in the open on the opposite side of the mausoleum, but the three soldiers stayed down, probably because their backup was only seconds away. Once the girls reached the ship, he sprinted the remaining distance, ignoring the way his energy flagged. He didn't want to think about how much blood he might have lost from that damn shoulder wound.

Inside the transport, he snapped an order for them to strap themselves in. He dropped into the pilot's chair and hit up the controls, the comms first of all.

"Seb, this is Alpha. I'm on the ground and have secured the targets. Bring on the rain."

"You took your sweet time, Alpha. I was beginning to think I'd have to drag my ass down there to rescue the rescue party. At ready and willing to blow these monkey-assed bastards into dust."

Leigh quirked his lips at his friend's usual irreverence, but considering his current condition, wasn't exactly in the mood for belly laughs.

"Waiting on your go." He replied into the comms, then disconnected. A few beats of silence went by until he heard the low, vibrating boom of jets entering the atmosphere, followed by the high-pitched *whirr* as the fighter squadron closed in on their position.

"Here comes the rain." He shot Mia a smile, and she returned it a little uncertainly. A few seconds later, the city lit up with incoming weapon fire a few blocks down from them. "That's our cue to move. Let's haul ass, recruits."

A few seconds later, they were lifting off—straight into a firestorm.

The CSS had rallied ships from nearby and actively engaged the fighter squadron. Leigh juiced the engines and opened up the weapon's system, cutting a rough and ready path through the action to make higher atmosphere. The small carrier took some hits. One chunk of ship engine almost smashed them in half, but he saw it and banked aggressively to get out of a collision path, breaking a double sweat at the pain in his shoulder. They literally scraped by the debris, leaving him wondering what kind of damage might have been done to their hull.

Higher up, the smoke and streaks of weapon fire cleared to show a watery-blue sky. However, the carrier's warning system continued bleeping at him. He checked the screen and then tabbed up communications.

"Seb, I've got one insistent bastard on my six, take care of that, will you?"

Seb swore, his breath short. "Because I've got nothing better to do right now. Hold out for ten and I'll be there."

Leigh dropped some sudden altitude and then set into a weaving path, one without repeating patterns to avoid being blown out of the ether by the CSS ship dogging them. Just as Seb had promised, right on ten ticks of the clock, he closed into range and opened fire, forcing the pursuing ship to cut off and fall back into defensive maneuvers.

"Thanks, Seb, I owe you one."

"Give me back the money you swindled off me last week when we played poker, and I'll call it even."

Leigh blew out a relieved breath as the carrier hit lighter atmosphere. "Deal. But only because we both know I can win it back again next week."

Seb muttered a bunch of curses at him. "I'll catch you back on deck, Alpha."

Leigh cut the comm and switched over to autopilot as they left Ilari's gravity and headed for the graceful lines of the *Valiant Knox*, lights flickering serenely in the distance.

He swiveled in his chair to catch a look at his passengers. Kayla had her eyes closed and Mia was staring at him with wide eyes.

He ran a hand over his hair. "Uh, sorry, it got a bit hairy back there. Are you okay?"

"I will be in about ten years," Kayla muttered.

Mia reached down and unclasped her belt, then slowly shrugged out of the harness.

And then it hit him. She was here, and she was safe. They'd made it.

Leigh shoved himself out of his seat and ended up on his knees in front of her. He grabbed her shoulders and yanked her up against him.

"My God, Mia. Do you know how terrified I was?"

She laughed against his chest, though the sound was suspiciously watery.

"You were terrified? What about me? I've never been so frightened in my entire life. When Steve shot you, it was even worse than how petrified I was a few days ago during the torture test." She pulled back a little and stared up at him with a searching, soulful gaze. "I can't do it, Leigh. I wasn't cut out to be a fighter pilot."

He shook his head. "Then we'll find something else for you. But right now, it doesn't matter."

She sniffed, tightening her hold on him. "I love you, just in case you haven't worked that out already."

He gave a short laugh. "I love you too, so don't ever, *ever* do anything like that to me again. I don't think I could take it."

Before she could answer, he caught her mouth in a consuming kiss, one that soothed the last few ragged edges of his heart.

Chapter Twenty-Nine

Leigh grimaced as he settled back against the gurney, hardly getting his head down before Ace whipped out a pair of scissors and started cutting away the bandage Mia had secured on his wound, followed by the sleeve of his jacket and shirt.

As Ace examined the injury, murmuring something to a nearby nurse, Leigh glanced down to see Mia hovering near the curtain and from the look on her face, he guessed she wanted to be near him, but didn't feel like she belonged. Plus the habit of hiding their relationship had no doubt become ingrained.

One of the nurses tried to shuffle her out, and he pulled away from Ace.

"Alpha, you need fluids and this wound needs repairing—" Ace began in an overpatient tone.

"Not unless Mia stays."

Ace hardly spared a glance for the nurse facing off in

front of Mia. "Let her stay if it means Alpha will keep still and let me microlaser his damn shoulder."

Mia stepped around the nurse and came over, a wary expression on her face. But when he reached out and took her hand, some of the tension left her. He brought her fingers to his lips, and she reached up with her other hand to smooth her fingers through his short hair, expression gorgeously intimate, telling him without words everything she was feeling.

Like the first day he'd met her, after he'd carried her out of the damaged shuttle and taken her to the deck triage, when she'd opened her eyes and looked at him, his heart went into a free fall, but this time he didn't fight the exhilarating sensation. Instead, he let it wash through him and thanked whatever higher powers ran the universe these days that he'd met her and they'd survived the CSS and Robinson to make it back to the safety of the *Knox*.

"So I guess the rumors are true." Ace poked a needle in his shoulder, and he grimaced before shooting a glare at his buddy.

The sub-doctor didn't look the least bit repentant about stabbing him without warning. "It'll go numb in a second and then you won't feel a thing. As for your brain and whatever damage made you annihilate your career, well, that I can't do anything about."

"I didn't *annihilate* my career. I just made a different choice." He tightened his hold on Mia and cast her a short look to see how she was taking Ace's comments, however her expression wasn't giving anything away as she focused on where Ace had started applying the microlaser to repair the tissue.

They were probably going to face more than a few

comments over their relationship in the coming days and weeks.

The curtain shifted, and he looked up to see Commander Yang and Bren standing at the end of his bed.

"Alpha, glad to see you made it back on deck in one piece. Mostly."

He sent his CO a respectful nod, since he couldn't salute while Ace was patching up his arm.

"We need to debrief. In private." Yang cast a look from Ace to Mia, and might as well have said *get lost*.

"Yes, sir." Ace smoothed a healing gel over the work the microlaser had done and then stood. "For what it's worth, Alpha, I recommend you stay overnight for observation. But since I know you so well, I'll tell you to at least stay in that bed for a few hours and let the fluids and the gel do their thing. Come on, Recruit Wolfe, let's check you out."

Mia dropped his hand and glanced down at herself. "The blood isn't mine. I think most of it is Leigh's and some is probably—" Some of the color she'd regained since they'd returned to the ship drained from her face, and Leigh reached out to grab her arm, worried she might topple over.

"Don't think about it. You did what you had to, and you didn't kill him, I did. Don't let it haunt you, Mia, or he wins anyway."

She nodded and started to step away, but he tugged her closer to the bed again, reaching up to pull her down to kiss her too briefly and too innocently, but considering their audience, it was probably brash of him to even do that much. She sighed against his lips, the sensation rippling through him on a low shudder. God, he wanted to get her alone for even just five minutes to reaffirm they were both really okay and soothe the last echoes of panic that he might have lost her. But duty had to come first.

He let her go, and when she straightened, a flush of color had spread across her cheeks. She avoided Commander Yang's gaze but sent Leigh a smile filled with the promise of *later* as she let Ace lead her from the triage cubicle.

Bren stepped out of the curtain for a moment, and when she returned, she sent Yang a nod before falling into parade stance with her hands clasped behind her back.

"The immediate area is secure, sir."

"Thanks, CAFF."

Leigh resisted the urge to wince. No doubt Yang had purposefully addressed Bren that way to remind of him his demoted status. He reached over and tabbed at the remote to raise the head of the gurney. There were some conversations a man shouldn't take lying down, and he got the feeling this was going to be one of them.

"So, Alpha, Stanton is rather unimpressed that you failed to bring the other traitor back alive for questioning," Yang started once he was upright. "Personally, I'm happy to commend you for a job well done. I have no doubt that Robinson got what he deserved."

While he agreed with the sentiment, it didn't lessen the weight on his conscience that he'd taken a life, even if the guy had been a scumbag traitor.

"I don't understand how someone like Robinson was CSS. He was an Ackerly graduate. You said yourself that his father is an admiral." He hadn't thought much about it until he'd arrived back at the ship and started trying to put all the pieces together into a picture that made sense.

Yang nodded, his expression grim. "The admiral has

been suspended, pending an investigation into the entire family. I've just come from a linkup with Stanton. Intel came to light that the CSS may have been recruiting certain personality types straight out of the academies. However, the source of the intel was questionable and at the time it seemed utterly ridiculous. Now, however—"

"It's an appalling reality." Leigh clenched a fist against his thigh. To think CI or Stanton might have had information that could have stopped all this before it started and hadn't acted on it... But there was no use going down that road. It only led to pointless anger.

"Stanton said he'd put a specialized team onto it, whatever that means. Seems to be his answer for everything at the moment."

"And the rest of the recruits?" How could he trust anyone he brought into the squadron now, knowing the CSS might have already gotten to them before they even arrived in the Brannon system?

"We've got extra screening in place, but that's not your concern anymore."

Right, because he'd handed his CAFF insignia over to Bren and been kicked out of the FP squadron. Yang might as well have slapped him with that one. Hell, what if they were about to bust him down to Ilari? Despite constantly reassuring Mia that everything would work out fine, for the first time, the notion that it might not stabbed into him like razor-sharp icicles.

He swallowed down the words crowding up his throat; they would probably make him sound like he was begging and he'd already decided he would face the consequences of all the choices he'd made. The least he could do was take it with dignity, and by the hard expression on Yang's face, the man had already made up his mind and wouldn't be swayed, no matter what anyone said.

"Protocol dictates I should not only strip you of rank, but remove you from the FP squadron and send you to the ground."

"Yes, sir, I understand." His voice came out rough as the resolution to take this without a fight wavered for a moment, his stomach dropping as though he'd done a high-altitude triple barrel roll in his jet. If he wasn't flying anymore, it would leave a huge hole in his life, one he didn't know how he would ever fill.

"However." Yang drew the word out and a small spark of hope kindled within him. "Dependable pilots are apparently difficult to find, and the number of people on board this ship I actually trust are even harder to find. Plus, with this war at a tipping point, it would be insane to waste a pilot of your skills on the ground. Therefore, the decision has been made that you will retain your position on the squadron, but you'll be starting at the bottom again with the new recruits who graduate this current class. That being said, I can't have you and Mia flying together. I'm sorry, I know it's unfair, but Mia won't be continuing with the program. It's the price to be paid. We need you on the squadron more than we need a green pilot."

The news probably wasn't that surprising when he thought about it. And it didn't hit all that hard, considering Mia had already told him she didn't want to be a fighter pilot. What did leave him cold was the idea of Mia being the one who ended up on the ground.

"Sir, I understand all of your reasons for not having the

two of us in the FP squadron together. And while I know you've probably already made a decision in terms of where Mia will be going, I'm asking you to do me a favor and keep her on board the *Knox*, get her a position with the deck maintenance crew or in aeronautical engineering. You know what she's capable of, what she did for us. We wouldn't have uncovered Lawler without her. If you can't afford to waste my skills, then you definitely can't afford to waste hers. I know it's asking a lot, since we both know you don't owe me a damn thing."

Despite the fact he'd been determined not to beg for his own fate, apparently Mia's outcome was a totally different matter. He'd lay open a vein if it meant keeping her safe, keeping her on board the *Knox,* and maybe making some kind of future with her.

Yang stepped forward and clasped him on his good shoulder for a long moment.

"That's not entirely true, Alpha. You've worked your ass off since the first day you stepped foot on the deck of the *Valiant Knox*, going above and beyond to protect both the people on board and the pilots you flew with. I'm not making any promises because my influence isn't what it used to be, but I'll see what I can do to keep her on board. "

He reached up and gripped Yang's forearm, finding it a little hard to breathe through the emotion surging through him. "Thank you, sir."

Yang nodded and stepped back from the gurney. "Now get that rest Ace ordered. I need you in fighting form and back on deck ASAP."

As Yang stepped toward the curtain where Bren still stood waiting and silent throughout the conversation, the last conversation he'd had with his CO surfaced in his mind about the lieutenant coming to review Yang's command. Is that what the commander had meant when he said he didn't have as much influence these days?

"Sir, what about your situation?"

His question brought Yang up short, and the commander glanced back over his shoulder.

"I called in just about every damn marker anyone in the upper echelons of the UEF owed me and managed to get a stay of execution, that's all." Yang sent him a short, grim smile. "They're reviewing the decision to review my command. If that's not the best example of the UEF's bureaucratic BS, I don't know what is."

"What does it mean in the long run?"

"It means I'm on the clock and time is running out. Eventually the review will go ahead. The revelation that we've got traitors in our ranks has rattled some cages, and the sentiment is that the *Knox* may no longer be a secure asset."

"And just what do the men upstairs think the answer to that might be?" Even as he asked the question, he got the cold sense that he already knew the answer.

"Best-case scenario, I'm removed from command and the new CO they bring in strips down and restructures the entire crew. Worst case scenario, they pull the *Knox* out for redeployment in a noncombative system."

"Either way, we're screwed." He swore under his breath. Didn't seem like much point in worrying about where he or Mia would end up once this review went ahead because in the end, the UEF brass were going to mess with the entire ship. Frustration blustered through him as if he were standing in the hot slipstream of a jet.

"They can't do that. We've been holding this line for years. We've lost good men and sweated blood for the cause. If they do this, all they'll achieve is giving the CSS one more advantage, because whoever they bring in won't know the fight the way we do—"

"You don't need to tell me any of that, Leigh. I'm living it every second," Yang replied quietly.

His aggravation was doused by his chagrin at forgetting, even for a second, that Yang had recently been a CSS POW.

"My apologies, sir."

Yang held up a hand. "You're not the one in the wrong, here, but that's not something I can say outside this room without shoving myself off the crumbling precipice I'm standing on. We've got time, Alpha, and I intend to use the full capabilities of this ship and its crew to put a serious dent in the CSS efforts and prove we're not compromised."

"Then I'm with you, sir, one hundred percent." He lifted his arm and gave a crisp salute, despite the aching pull in his shoulder where the gel was healing his flesh.

Yang returned the salute. "Now get some rest, Alpha, and I'll see what I can do for Wolfe."

As Yang walked around the curtain, he caught his XO's gaze. No, not his XO anymore, his *CO*. Damn, that was going to take some getting used to. Bren took a couple of steps closer to his bed.

"Congratulations, by the way." He sent Bren a smug grin. "How's being the CAFF working out for you so far?"

"After losing four recruits on a training flight and then engaging the CSS in a heavy-atmo fight so you could rescue your girlfriend? Just peachy."

"Don't let all that power go to your head." His grin widened as he repeated the words Bren had often spoken to him.

But apparently the new CAFF didn't see the funny side of it. "Screw you, Alpha. I never wanted this, and you knew it. You could have handed the pins on to Seb."

"You outrank Seb. And you really want a cowboy like that running the squadron?" He affected an exaggerated shudder. "We'd be reduced to playing beer pong to work out the shift schedule and he'd have us flying missions with no other objective besides poking the hornet's nest."

She dropped her gaze with a short sigh. "Yeah, you're probably right, but I still can't get my head around it. What if—"

"Theresa Brenner, you will be fine." He reached over and wrapped a hand around her forearm, giving an encouraging squeeze. "In fact, you'll do better than fine. You'll be legendary and I'll be in the background supporting every step you take."

"Thanks, but call me *Theresa* again and I'll give you a black eye." She covered his hand with hers for a moment, then moved away. "I better get back. Someone's got to oversee the last few days of the training program."

She sent him an unimpressed look to let him know what she thought of yet another of his responsibilities falling to her, then saluted him and left the triage cubicle.

Leigh sank back against the pillows and glanced down at his shoulder, covered in the blue-tinted gel, containing nano tech that healed flesh and left hardly a scar. The wound wasn't very deep, so the job would be done in maybe half an hour, and then he could see about getting out of here to find

Mia so they could go back to his apartment and *rest*.

Three hours later, Leigh headed up to the dorms, well aware of the looks he was getting as he headed toward Mia's room. After everything that had happened, he could honestly say he didn't give a damn about what anyone else thought of him or his relationship with her. It wasn't anyone's business how much he loved her. The only thing that mattered was that they'd found each other and both survived Lawler's and Steve's betrayals.

He'd barely laid knuckles on the door when the hatchway opened, revealing Kayla. She grinned when she saw him and stepped back, hastily saluting as he passed.

Mia had been sitting on a nearby bed with Nicka, cards littered across the blankets. Both girls stood as he approached, but before Mia could go saluting him as well, he grabbed her up against him.

"Mind if we go somewhere to talk?"

"There's still two days of FP training left. Is that a good idea?" Color bloomed on her cheeks, since she and the other two girls could probably guess he didn't exactly have conversation on his mind—not one featuring many words anyway.

Except he wasn't going to hide the way he felt about her any longer. He'd done enough of that in recent weeks. Plus, ever since she'd left his triage cubical on med level a few hours ago, an agitated desperation to see her again had been steadily building, as though he needed to make sure once and for all that she was really okay.

"It's a *very* good idea." Yeah, that definitely came out sounding like it had a whole other meaning behind it. He couldn't help grinning as Kayla and Nicka giggled to themselves. "I'll explain everything if you come with me."

"Go on, Mia," Kayla urged. "All you've been doing since you came back here is mope and talk about how worried you were about your man. I don't know about Nicka, but I'm sick of hearing about it."

Mia sent her friend an unimpressed look as the two girls laughed again.

"Fine." She sighed, sounding put out by his request. "But if this gets either of us in trouble, I'm blaming you."

He leaned in, catching her smart mouth for a quick kiss. "We already established last week that you can blame me for whatever you like."

He tugged her hand, leading her out of the room as she waved to her friends. Out in the corridor, he tucked her into his side, hoping she wouldn't be too upset by the stares or whispers going on around them. But if she noticed, she didn't react as they got on to the transit and he took them down to his apartment.

Once they stepped through the door, Mia seemed to relax, and he hadn't realized until then how tense she'd actually been. He hated that their relationship was being scrutinized and would probably be the most popular gossip on the ship for a while, but eventually people would get used to seeing them together and the scandal would disappear. He didn't know what kind of posting Mia would end up with, but he trusted that Yang would do everything in his power to make sure things worked out for them.

"So this is your place, huh?" She actually sounded a little

nervous as she stepped away from him, gaze trailing over the photos, medals, and other personal items he had on display.

"Would you like a tour?" He walked up behind her, wrapping his arms around her waist and then leaning down to nuzzle her neck. "This is the main room, where you'll find the usual couch, armchair, and media-screen. Over there is the kitchen. Down the hall to the left is the bathroom and storage. But most importantly—"

He shuffled her into a walk, running his hands over her hips, up her ribs to her breasts as they reached the doorway. She moaned, sinking into him, her ass pressing against his rapidly hardening erection.

"This is the bedroom." He kissed his way up her neck, and she tilted her head back, giving him easier access to her mouth. He caught her lips in a brief, heady kiss, then pulled away slightly. "You better remember where that is."

"Maybe you should show me why it's so important to remember." An impertinent grin kicked up her lips as she turned in his arms, her fingers going to the fasteners on his shirt.

He bent in and hooked an arm under her legs, then picked her up and carried her over to the bed. But instead of laying her down, he set her on her feet and then took a step back to shrug out of his shirt. His boots and pants came off next, with her watching every move he made, a fascinated gleam in her eyes that made him want to groan.

He sat down on the edge of the bed, setting a hand on each hip to bring her closer. She threaded her fingers through his hair as he started on her shirt, taking his time and enjoying every new sight revealed to him.

Once she was naked, he pulled her on top of him, but

she'd hardly settled in his hold before he flipped them, putting her beneath him where he'd dreamed of having her.

For a long second, she stared up at him, her gaze showing him everything she felt in that moment, and it was more than any woman had ever given him. He didn't know what he'd done to deserve her, but he was going to spend every day being thankful for it.

He leaned down, covering her mouth with his, plunging them into a kiss that flirted with desperation and lured him toward abandoning all sanity. He wanted to get lost in the rapture, and now there wasn't anything standing between them or holding him back.

One of his hands skimmed down, over her hip, along her thigh to wrap around the back of her knee. He hooked her leg around his waist, tilting her hips up as he pushed forward, her breath catching as he joined them together in a single stroke.

Her hands tightened on him, bringing him in closer as she kissed him more deeply, feeding the frenzied momentum building within him. He soaked in every second of sensation and reveled in the relief of being with her under no pretenses or secrets. More profound than the passion building within him was the emotion that accompanied it. No one had ever made him feel like this before, and as a sense of empowerment filled him, he wanted to get on his knees and succumb to whatever she desired.

She broke the kiss, but her teeth lightly scraped his jaw, sending a hotter surge of ecstasy though him. She kissed her way over to his ear, her fingers tugging his hair with a gentle pressure.

"I love you." Her words weren't much more than a

breath, but it was the most powerful thing he'd ever heard, taking the last of his restraint and fracturing it into a million pieces he'd never get back.

He pulled her tighter against him, burying his face in her sweet-scented hair as he groaned at the liquid fire of pure euphoria burning through his veins, scorching outward and upward until he was nothing but heated sensation and incandescent emotion.

Mia sighed against his shoulder as he relaxed against her, his limbs becoming heavy even though his heart was still racing. Maybe he was going sappy since he was getting toward midlife-crisis age, but that had been the single most profound moment of his life.

"I love you, too," he murmured against her neck, and he sensed, more than he saw, her smiling.

"Good. Then you won't mind if I sleep here for a few hours before I head back to the dorms where everyone stares at me like I'm *that girl* who slept with the CAFF to get herself through FP training."

He leaned back, her words effectively killing the buzz he'd been enjoying. "Don't worry about what anyone else thinks, even if they're moronic enough to say it to either of our faces. I love you. You're my everything now, which is why you're not going back to the dorms. You're staying here."

Her brow creased with a concerned expression. "Is that allowed?"

"Its fine, Mia. So quit stressing over it. Close your eyes and get some sleep so you can get through the last two days of the program."

He pressed a kiss into her forehead, before pushing up and going to sit on the edge of the bed to retrieve his clothes.

"Wait, where are you going?"

He yanked up his pants and then leaned over to kiss her one more time, while pulling the blanket up to cover her. "I've got a few things to take care of. I'll be back in a little while."

She nodded, yawning as she rolled over and settled under the covers, looking too perfect all curled up in his bed. He shook his head at himself and stooped down to collect his shirt before he could start getting any ideas about joining her.

He needed to go check in with Seb. He hadn't found the chance to really talk to the guy since the truth had come out about Lawler. Plus, he needed to write a report for Bren and Yang about what had gone down with Steve while the details were still fresh in his mind. He might not be the CAFF anymore, but he still had duties to attend.

Epilogue

"You risked yourself to save *him*?"

Mia glanced up from the ebook she'd been reading as Leigh dropped his datapad on the cushions next to her.

After he'd left his apartment the evening before, she'd had a nap and then helped herself to his shower. She'd even decided that she might as well help herself to his clean clothes before she'd gone into the kitchen and fixed herself a snack. She was hungry, but besides the fact that she didn't want to face the crowded messdeck and the probable stares aimed her way, she was loath to leave the comfy confines of Leigh's apartment. Especially since he'd said he'd be back soon. But soon had turned out to be midnight, and by then she'd returned to his bed and had fallen into a light doze. She'd only been half awake when he'd climbed in with her, and she'd let him make love to her in a relaxed, sleepy way that still had her tingling at the memory of it.

When she'd woken up in the morning, he'd already left to report for duty, while she'd hurried back up to the dorms to get changed for the day's session. Lieutenant Brenner had taken the entire day's classes, and though people were talking about Leigh and her, they shut up real quick whenever she got too close. Eventually, she'd forced Kayla and Nicka to tell her that the rumors claimed Leigh had been demoted from the CAFF because of her. It was exactly what she'd been afraid of, and guilt had eaten away at her all day. She'd tried to cheer herself up with the reminder that it could have been worse, he could have been sent to the ground. But that hadn't really helped.

After class, she'd made her escape and retreated back to his apartment, the only place she could think to wait for him, since she had no idea what he'd been doing all day or what his new posting might entail. Seeing him walk through the door a few moments ago had sent a definite sense of relief washing through her.

"What are you talking about?" she asked in response to his earlier question.

Leigh glared at her as he sat down. "Commander Yang just forwarded me a copy of the reports from yesterday's incident, where you and Kayla risked yourself to save Robinson. If you'd left him—"

"I know, we would have gotten out easier and you wouldn't have been injured." Mia sighed and put her own datapad aside. "But how were we supposed to know he was the traitor? We thought he was one of us. Would you have left anyone behind?"

His gaze cut away from her as he grumbled under his breath.

"What was that?" She poked him in the non-injured shoulder.

"I said no, I wouldn't have. But that's different, I have years of experience…experience that tells me trying to save morons like Steve Robinson will only get you killed, even when they don't happen to be cowardly double-crossing bastards."

"Yet you still would have rescued him. Kind of like you came to rescue me. Besides, look on the bright side. You don't have to worry about having two moles in your squadron any longer."

He reached out and trailed a finger along her jawline. "And you're going to keep reminding me of exactly who outed those traitors for the rest of our lives, aren't you."

She shrugged, schooling her expression for total innocence. "Only when I really need to."

He grinned, leaning in to kiss her, but then pulled back almost as quickly.

"Oh, Commander Yang asked me to give you this." Leigh shoved a hand into his pocket and produced a small drive to plug into her datapad. She connected it up, and chewed her thumbnail while she waited for the contents to appear. It was an information package containing—

"Oh my God!" She shot up straighter and clutched the datapad to stop it from lurching off her lap.

"What is it?" Leigh stiffened, his expression alarmed.

"Commander Yang has organized a trial training period for me in aeronautical engineering." Excitement thrummed through her and she shoved the datapad aside to throw herself against Leigh.

He caught her with a slight *oomph* and then returned

her hug her tightly.

"It's the best news, Mia. See? I told you everything would work out."

She sat back to frown at him. "But how did Commander Yang know…? Wait, did you tell him?"

He shrugged, a half grin lifting his lips as he smoothed a hand over her braid. "I may have mentioned something along those lines. I can't remember."

Mia pulled him in for a quick kiss, but then her happiness deflated almost as quickly as it had hit her. Instead, guilt burned hot and bitter. She leaned away from him to catch his gunmetal-blue gaze.

"Leigh, this is great news, but what about you? I heard you're not the CAFF anymore because of us."

He shook his head. "It's not because of *us*, exactly; it's because of my conduct. And while I may not be the CAFF any longer, I did retain a spot on the fighter squadron. It was the best-case scenario. We're lucky I didn't get busted down to the front lines. And who knows? Maybe in another few years, I can work my way back to the top."

Despite his assurance, she still felt like she'd cost him too much. "I'm sorry, Leigh—"

"Hey." He caught her chin, his gaze intent as he stared at her. "Never apologize for what you brought into my world. I wouldn't change a thing. You're my life, Mia, not some title or career trophy."

She sighed. *Well, when he put it like that…* "I love you. Sorry if you're sick of hearing that—"

"I'll *never* get sick of hearing that." He caught her up in another kiss. "And now that I'm no longer the CAFF and you're no longer a FP recruit, things are so much easier since we don't have to sneak around and have illicit liaisons in cramped fighter jets."

She sent him a mischievous grin. "I don't know, I think I'll always have a soft spot for the fighter-jet liaison."

He brought his lips closer to her ear. "I hear bay delta-eight will be empty tonight."

She slid her hands into his hair, pulling herself closer to him. "See you there."

The End

Acknowledgments

I need to say a huge thank-you to Robin Haseltine, editor extraordinaire. Without your input, without you challenging, guiding, and inspiring me in equal measure, this book would be only a shadow of its current self. Just when I think I've pushed myself and my characters as far as we need to go, you come up with ways to make sure the story is shining to its full potential. Every time we work on a project together, I am continually amazed at how we seem to be on the same wavelength and how our combined vision of what the story needs to be creates something truly incredible.

A special thanks to Jessica Snyder and Lacey Devlin for their work and suggestions in the final drafts, which made the story that much tighter. Also, thanks to the team at Entangled, everyone who had a hand in bringing this book into the world. As always, it was a team effort, and one that runs smoothly thanks to those working behind the scenes.

And to my family—every day I am grateful for every

single one of you.

To Mario, for being so tolerant of having an author for a wife, for putting up with the crazy stressed deadline moods, or when I get up in the middle of the night to make story notes, and trying your best to keep the kids entertained when I'm stuck at the computer.

To my three gorgeous girls, because you keep me grounded and I never thought I could feel the kind of love I do when I look at all of you. Because you say the most hilarious things and make life a little more awesome every day.

To my extended family, my parents, sisters, and in-laws for every time you've helped me, no matter how small the gesture, it made such a huge difference to me and even if I forget to say it, I appreciate it more than you'll ever know.